Niall MacRoslin

Alice N. York

I0611157

PROJECT
BLACK HUNGARIAN

SPY NOVEL

A CAPSCOVIL BOOK | GLONN | GERMANY

Visit CAPSCOVIL on

LINKEDIN | TWITTER | FACEBOOK | YOUTUBE | PINTEREST

www.capscovil.com

www.blackhungarian.com

ENGLISH ORIGINAL EDITION

2. Edition
Perfect Paperback
Copyright © Capscovil, 2014
ISBN Print 978-3-942358-43-9
Available as eBook

Editor: Helen Veitch
Cover design: Capscovil
Cover picture: Gerhard Tikovsky
Book adorner: Louisa Kronthaler
Pictures/sketches: Capscovil

The cover design is after an image taken on the evening of July 7th, 2013 in Zurich. The picture shows a subject of the well-known Swiss light artist Gerry Hofstetter, which was projected onto the Grossmuenster church in Zurich.

ATTENTION: ORGANIZATIONS AND CORPORATIONS

For information on special offers for exclusive editions with individual design as presents for business partners, or on bulk purchases for sales promotions, premiums or fund-raising, please write to: projects[at]capscovil.com

EXPERT OPINIONS

A modern, fresh and fast-moving thriller set in the evolving world of electric vehicle technology. Totally (and perhaps disturbingly) believable with twists and turns from beginning to end. Loved it!

Michael E. Parris JP, BSc, CEng, FIMechE, FIET – Head of Secure Car Division, SBD

Electric mobility is as complex as it gets and a closed book to many. The authors have succeeded in portraying the topic in an enjoyable and attractive way not only for enthusiasts but also for everybody new to electric vehicle technology; and in combining it with an ingenious storyline.

Neue Mobilitaet – Magazine of the German Federal association for eMobility (BEM e.V.), New Year's editioin 2015

Electric mobility has started to rock the automotive world. Recently strangers to the industry, companies like Google start to compete with the long-established players. Those are the facts. Project Black Hungarian names them all and uses them to build an intriguing spy novel.

Andreas Burkert – Chief Editor Drive and Style – Active Woman

There is only one recommendation that can be given to all who are interested in electric vehicles and espionage: Read it! Very intriguing!

OEKONEWS.AT – Austria's daily news on renewable energies and sustainability

It's a fact that not only techies get their money's worth with this spy novel. In their first co-project, the authors create a fascinating adventure by shining light on the pros and cons of emobility.

Recommended reading – Ebersberger Zeitung

THE STORY

The Board for Industrial Research and Development has been shaping major political decisions since 1929. You haven't heard of them because no-one has. They're efficient, discreet and professional. Working under the guise of a multi-faceted consultancy firm. But a new threat to their customers means all that could be about to change. After much deliberation, a decision has been made.

A new technology is to be tested in an extensive field trial, and the electric car expedition WAVE offers the perfect cover. Naturally, BIRD has no desire to see it succeed. The usual countermeasures are taken and a team is dispatched. The mission is to be low-key, no more than a routine training exercise: an opportunity for BIRD to blood the next generation of field operatives. There is, it seems, little that can go wrong.

But the new recruits are young and impulsive; quick to act when caution should be the name of the game. One bad decision leads to another, and soon the mission is spiralling out of control. What BIRD doesn't know is that there is another elite force on the scene, a crack unit sent by security agency DISECUPRO to protect the technology and its engineer.

Suddenly, all eyes are on WAVE.

ABOUT THE PROJECT

Projekt Black Hungarian is the first book of its kind. It is the unusual combination of a fictional story and facts and true events which happened during the electric vehicle rallye WAVE 2013, and characters whose role models are dyed-in-the-wool enthusiasts taken from real life that make this novel unique.

The adventure lets you share the thrill of young spies who are recruited by a ruthlessly led secret organisation, and manipulated shamelessly. At the same time the story takes you on a virtual trip to fascinating locations and beautiful landscapes that were visited during the rallye.

A special delicacy, if you will, is that through the eyes of the spy characters, you can take a clandestine peek at how today's intelligence agencies like NSA or GCHQ operate while gathering information. Suffice to say, it's a good thing there are responsible agents working against them. In addition there's some interesting facts on electric vehicles.

A very special electric car acts as role model for the „object of desire". It's not a new vehicle by Tesla Motors. Nevertheless it is real and, in October 2014, it's developers set a new world record for driving purely electric for more than 726km without charging while climbing some 5000 meters in elevation.

***

More information on the project is available here:

http://blackhungarian.com

THE ROUTE

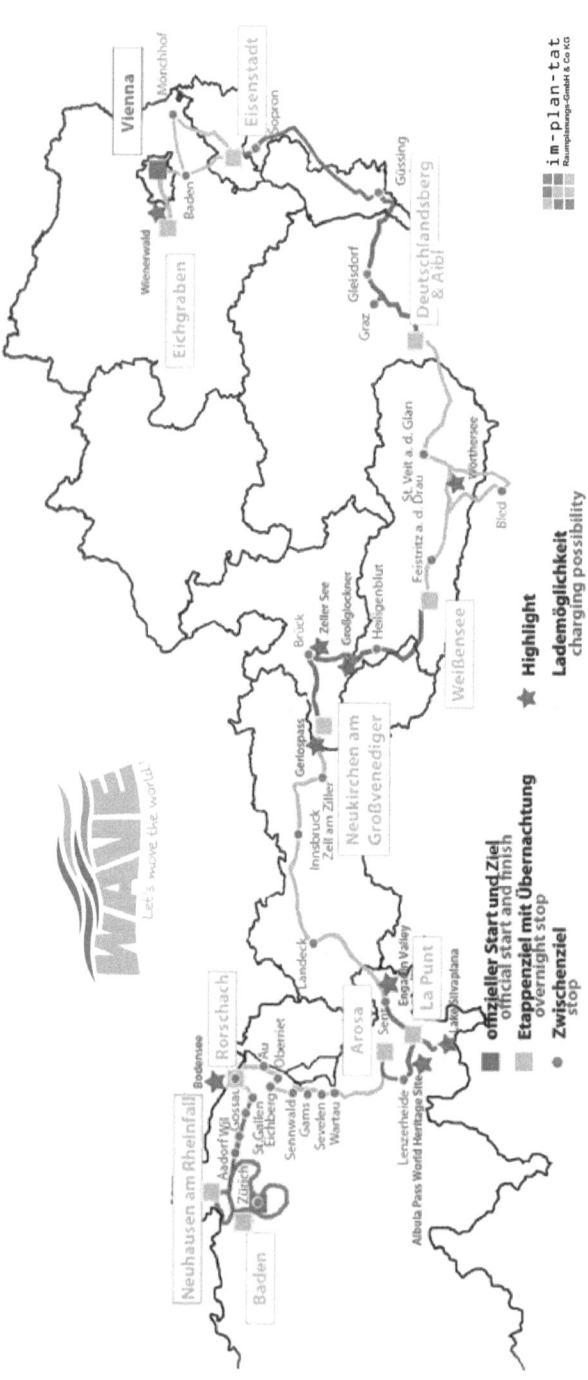

CHARACTERS

Christian Adler	CEO of Adler Reilly and BIRD
Dominik Brandt	Director Operations of BIRD
Céline Dufort	Director Finance of BIRD
Walter Mikesch	Director Intelligence of BIRD
William Steinberg	BIRD spy - Operations department
Conrad Jaeger	BIRD spy - Operations department
Nils Karrat	Rookie hired by BIRD
Hendrik Herder	Rookie hired by BIRD
Peter Prohaska	BIRD spy - Intelligence department
Marc Kudling	Ext. consultant for Evs at Adler Reilly
Uwe Macellaio	Ext. consultant for hazardous materials at Adler Reilly
Alain Blanc	Investor
Magali Zampieri	DISECUPRO agent and bodyguard
Martin Tauer	DISECUPRO agent for IT security
Frank Loden	DISECUPRO Chief of Integrity
Arina Rhomberg	Founder and president of DISECUPRO
Tom Schmidt	Entrepreneur and friend of Alain
Andrej Pečjak	Technologist and Managing Director Institut Metron
Jasna Pečjak	General Manager of Institut Metron
Stephan A. Schwarz	Club president of Swiss Tesla Owners Club
Eva Štravs	Director Tourism BLED
Janez Fajfar	Mayor of BLED
Louis Palmer	Tour director of WAVE
Tamara Hillinger	WAVE participant
Manfred Hillinger	WAVE participant/dep.president Tesla Club Austria

Marco Mila	WAVE participant
Simone Barra	WAVE participant
Jochen Breuer	WAVE participant
Andreas Wacker	WAVE participant
Angela Wacker	WAVE participant
Erich Camenisch	WAVE participant
Peter Franke	WAVE participant
Jean-Pierre Pané	WAVE participant
Monika Pané	WAVE participant
Florian Berg	Student, writing a field report about WAVE
Stephan Schwartzkopff	WAVE participant
Olaf Feldmann	WAVE participant
Rafael DeMestre	WAVE participant
Anastassyia Jurina	WAVE participant
Ernst Scheufel	WAVE participant
Hannes Hauer	WAVE participant
Gordon Feet	WAVE participant
Leora Rosner	WAVE participant
Robort Michelsen	WAVE participant
Johann Axmann	WAVE participant
Franz Sattler	WAVE participant
Martin Lanz	WAVE participant
Andre Lugger	WAVE Roadside Assistance
Thomas Rot	WAVE Roadside Assistance
Vivien Renlo	WAVE support team
Jaromir Vegr	WAVE support team
Andreas Ranftl	WAVE support team

PROLOGUE

Dominik

Spring – Vienna

"We need to meet."

"Now?"

"Now."

"OK, Dominik – but this had better be good."

It was. Though he doubted Adler would see it that way. Christian Adler, CEO of Adler Reilly, grandson of Tobias Adler: visionary, emigrant, founder. Tobias, who had come into the world with nothing and bequeathed an enduring legacy; Christian whose wealth was so great he had neglected to think of the next-in-line. Strange, Dominik Brandt thought to himself, to see a dynasty coming to an end before your own eyes.

He was sitting in the presidential suite of the five-star Hotel Sacher, one of Vienna's many gifts to the rich and famous. The Madame Butterfly Suite, as it was also known, was a vast space, comprising not only a generously proportioned bedroom and art-deco bathroom but six other rooms besides. A spectacular view of the city meant it was a far more attractive proposition than a decent-sized family home.

Everything stood ready for the CEO's arrival. The long conference table was decked out with coffee, fruit, pastries, and sparkling water, almost all of which would go to waste. At the head of the table, where the CEO insisted on being seated even if it was just the two of them, Dominik had laid a small, immaculately presented dossier containing a précis of the director of intelligence's findings. The DI could not be there in person, but along with the financial and legal directors would be taking part by video-link. There would be no rap on the door: the CEO didn't knock – especially when he had been dragged out of a meeting at the UN building. What had it been this time? Dominik couldn't remember. Only that it had been important, and official: Adler Reilly rather than BIRD.

The CEO might not knock – but he *would* expect to be greeted upon entry. When Dominik heard the footsteps – that measured, rhythmical tread which somehow managed to convey both calm and a hint of menace – he sprang to his feet and moved swiftly towards the door.

"Dominik, your timing is faultless as ever."

Always that air of sarcasm, of superiority. The pair shook hands in a perfunctory manner. The CEO was a head taller than his number two, but older as well by thirty years, his hair now grey where once it had been dark. Both men were impeccably dressed. Dominik watched as the older man helped himself to a glass of sparkling water. What was the difference between them, he wondered? The tailor-made suits, designer watches, expensive shoes, even the tan: that was all the same. But whereas Adler oozed authority, and was, at this stage of his life, a veritable *éminence grise*, he – Dominik – still had an air of schoolboy awkwardness. Their ages, yes, that had something to do with it, but did it not, when all was said and done, boil down to the simple fact of their upbringing? The CEO had that confidence, that insouciance which one associated with people from a certain kind of background: an easy, devil-may-care charm that surely came gift-wrapped with an Ivy League education and a lifetime of financial security. Dominik, on the other hand, was neither insouciant nor particularly charming, and any confidence he had gained was the result of sheer hard work. While the CEO exuded power, Dominik could call only on naked ambition. A distasteful quality, perhaps, but one that might yet come in handy if, as now seemed likely, Adler was to leave no heir.

"Shall we begin?"

"It's all there," Dominik motioned towards the dossier at the head of the table. As always, he allowed the CEO a few moments to read over the document, taking advantage of the brief lull to freshen up in the guest bathroom. From there, he heard what could only be described as a snort of derision.

"Electric cars?" Adler was shaking his head. He was old enough to remember his grandfather telling him about the first: developed in Britain by one Thomas Parker, the inventor also responsible for electrifying the London underground. "Is this some kind of joke?" he said. There it was – that calm, that hint of menace.

"No joke, sir. Deadly serious." Dominik had expected precisely this reaction. Hence the presence of the organization's other big-hitters. At the mere touch of a button, if required.

"You're telling me that the outcome of this race is somehow important? What's it called again?" Adler searched inside the document. "WAVE?"

"No, sir, the outcome has no bearing: it's an expedition, not a race." There was a note of relish in his voice. "It's the test we need to keep an eye on. The technology. If our information is correct – and we've rarely been wrong before – there is an electric car in the field with a range of one thousand kilometres. Do you know what that means?"

An impassive stare from the CEO.

"It means if it's successful, there's going to be a lot less money coming our way from oil."

No doubt Adler was thinking that they had been right before. In 2008. That was why they had adopted a holding structure; it was probably the reason the company had survived. "Where did you get this information?" the CEO asked.

"There was a text message, in London. From a pre-paid cell phone. We don't know who sent it," Dominik said.

"Get me Dufort."

Of the three that were soon to join by video-link, the financial director was the only one Adler trusted one hundred percent. He had no time for Legal, and viewed Walter Mikesch, the director of intelligence, with a suspicion that bordered on contempt. Probably this was because the latter made his living unlocking people's deepest, darkest secrets – the irony being that Adler himself had provided the key.

Dominik had often wondered just how far the CEO's influence must extend for him to avail of nigh-on unlimited access to databases from all over the world. A whole country's emails, text messages, and phone conversations could be analyzed and divided into the most miniscule categories, streamlined to focus on a single person and their immediate environment. Detailed profiles of an individual's life, containing information both the private and professional, could be drawn up at the touch of a button.

To the outside world, Christian Adler was the face of the international consultancy firm Adler Reilly, founded at the turn of the nineteenth century in the US. Nevertheless, some years ago, he had distanced himself from the day-to-day running of Adler Reilly in favour of cultivating a complex network of favours and counter-favours, which could be cashed in at any moment, anywhere around the globe. In that sense, he was merely carrying on the work of his grandfather, Tobias, who had established the Board for Industrial Research and Development, or BIRD, in 1929, after unforeseen circumstances had left his consultancy firm on the verge of ruin. BIRD, a top secret organization whose 100 members were hand-picked from Adler Reilly's own employees, was responsible for ensuring that the consultancy firm retained their dominant position in all market sectors. Though specializing in lobbying, BIRD's global representatives also dabbled in illegal surveillance, blackmail, espionage and sometimes even murder: whatever it took to keep those in power in check.

In the meantime Dominik had done the necessary, and Céline Dufort appeared before them on one of the conference room's three projector screens. Another zap on the remote control and she was joined by the remaining two members of the committee. The CEO may not have asked for them specifically – nor, in practice, was there a lot they could do at this stage – but their presence was still a requirement when important decisions were being made.

"Céline, how nice of you to join us. Your radiance is undimmed even by satellite."

She squirmed.

"Tell me if what Mr Brandt here says is true."

Céline Dufort, elegant, sophisticated, but old enough to be immune to the questionable charms of her CEO, replied: "Dominik is right as always. Though perhaps he should have mentioned that oil is only part of the story. What do the initials ICE mean to you, Mr Adler?"

A moment's pause. "Internal combustion engine."

"Precisely," she continued. "The automobile industry has invested so much in the internal combustion engine that a change now would spell disaster. Think of all that training gone to waste, not to mention the cost of new research and development. But even that's just the tip of the iceberg. Walter has more details."

The CEO turned reluctantly towards his director of intelligence. Dominik was certain that it was Adler's connections in industry and government that made him believe he had the upper hand on Walter. The DI's department received an annual budget of tens of millions of dollars, paid on standing order. Aside from Adler, only Céline Dufort knew the precise details of this arrangement.

"Thank you, Céline. The electrification of the car industry would necessitate a whole range of new measures, all of which have serious implications for our business partners. It would mean a new charging infrastructure and back end system, as well as a complete overhaul of the service industry. The automobile industry may be a massive, well-oiled machine but it is not equipped to deal with the requirements that will soon be placed upon it. Take charging stations, for instance." Walter Mikesch paused. "Drivers expect their navigation systems to tell them not just *how* to reach their destinations but *if* they have the range to do so. If the battery is running low, drivers need both the charging stations *and* the onboard technology to locate them. Then you have the fact that EVs are built differently from their traditional counterparts. They are not nearly as prone to breakdown and require less maintenance. In other words, mass-market adaption would see the service industry suffer hugely: not just the service centres themselves, but all those selling replacement and spare parts, as well as other con- sumables. To cap it all, there's a wealth of new jobs to be created, a ge- neration of developers and technologists to be trained, and as Céline has already indicated, a significant group of experienced professionals who will suddenly find themselves on the proverbial scrapheap–"

The DI was cut off mid-flow. "Meaning? In English, this time." The CEO's gaze was back on Dufort.

"Meaning that the continuing development of the electric car di- rectly affects our business interests. The core activity of our most sig- nificant Western clients stands to be damaged beyond repair. Existing structures and arrangements that were decades in the making could be torn apart in one fell swoop. As for power dynamics, I hardly need say that they'd change overnight. You could wake up tomorrow and find the industry as you know it gone forever. This is real. And the stakes are higher than they've ever been before."

"And what does my – my team of *experts* – propose?" Not even so much as a glance towards Intelligence or Legal.

That was Dominik's cue. He was getting frustrated. Hadn't Adler read the file?

"We are proposing, sir, that the technology cannot be allowed to succeed."

"You want to send people in?"

Dominik nodded. "There's still time to get them on the list. We need to make sure this product is binned before it gets anywhere near the market. WAVE is just a test."

"I thought it was an expedition," the CEO smiled to himself.

Dominik was unmoved. For all his occasional awkwardness, he

was a good actor. Don't panic, he told himself. He could see that the CEO was reluctant to cede to his wishes. People of his age were often either deeply suspicious of technology or disinclined to take it seriously. With Adler, he suspected the latter. After all, he hadn't got this far because of technology. But then again, Dominik mused, he hadn't got this far on merit either.

At last Adler spoke again, his playful side now no longer visible: "OK, but keep it low-key. Probationers only. And one more thing. I don't want to hear another word about it. Understood?"

With that, he was gone. He hadn't even waited for Dominik to respond.

Dominik switched off the video link. What to make of it? Hadn't Adler always said that the Board for Industrial Research and Development took priority? That the consultancy firm was only there for when people started asking questions? To allow BIRD to operate in the first place? What had changed? Dominik was damned if he knew. He cast his eye across the conference table and the expensive pastries that adorned it – *he* certainly wasn't going to eat them – before heading towards the window for a final glance at the newly departed CEO. He saw the old man hail down a taxi, and wave it away grumpily as soon as he realized it was an electric, one of around 150 in the Austrian capital: the latest in a series of environmental schemes designed to make the city a pollution-free zone.

The second cab he hailed – God be praised – was a more traditional model.

Dominik Brandt watched as his superior climbed in and sped away into the distance.

CHAPTER ONE

Dominik

Spring - Vienna

A day had passed since the meeting of the executive committee – the evening spent working, late – and Dominik was still in Vienna. It wasn't out of any great affection for the city, which he had always found preening and self-satisfied, too full of people like Adler, but because he had agreed to catch up with an old friend. Normally, of course, such a notion would have been anathema to Dominik.

Indeed, he doubted whether he had ever uttered the phrase "it'd be good to catch up" to a fellow human being. He certainly hadn't last night, at any rate, when he had called the Thai ambassador to the UN, Chaipura, to arrange the meeting. Meeting? There, you see. He wasn't even sure if Chaipura could be properly classed as a friend. That said, Dominik did know that it was time for him to start cultivating his own network. If he was serious about taking Adler's place, he needed powerful connections of his own. In this regard, Chaipura fitted the bill perfectly.

The pair had met at the Grand Palace in Bangkok the previous year during the opening ceremony for one of Dominik's bridges. "Bridging for a sustainable tomorrow", a project that aimed to improve road safety and farm-to-market travel links by building bridges in developing countries, had been one of BIRD's most successful enterprises to date, and not just because it vastly increased the organization's sphere of influence. It had also done wonders for the public image of Adler Reilly, in whose name the whole thing had been carried out. Moreover, it had been Dominik's brainchild, and – this was the crucial point, the one that had ultimately secured his promotion to director of operations – funded almost exclusively out of the public purse. A venture that had won people's hearts, benefitted the global power players, and barely cost a dime. What wasn't to love? Best of all for Dominik, however, had been the opportunity to shake the hands of countless presidents and prime ministers across Asia, Africa, and the Americas, with the odd king or queen thrown in for good measure.

The ceremony itself had been stunning, a truly regal event graced by His Majesty the King of Thailand, and culminating in a breathtaking fireworks display from across the Chao Phraya River. Chaipura had been one of the many local and international dignitaries present, and after he and Dominik had exchanged the necessary pleasantries, they had been surprised to discover a mutual passion for sailing. Later, Dominik had been ever more surprised to find himself suggesting that the two of them take to the water together when they were next in Europe. What was he doing? Was he really so lonely? Or had he subconsciously sensed an opportunity that he could store away for use at a later date?

Either way, there would be no sailing today in Vienna, despite the blustery spring wind. Only CEOs could play golf and go sailing on Wednesdays, as Adler was only too fond of reminding him. For now Dominik would just have to focus on work.

Despite the lingering presence in his thoughts of the London-bound Adler, there was a noticeable spring in Dominik's step as he made his way out of the hotel north along Kaertner Strasse and toward the underground at Stefansplatz. No doubt this feeling was triggered by the prospect of seeing Chaipura again: after all, the ceremony in Bangkok had been the scene of his greatest triumph, and that in a three-year period where, the initial months following the project's inception notwithstanding, he, Dominik, had grown increasingly accustomed to the trappings of success.

The Austrian capital's U1 line was, he had to admit, less glamorous than the Grand Palace – being with ordinary people is necessarily less glamorous than consorting with kings and queens – but it did nothing to dampen his spirits. As he alighted at Kaisermuehlen, he felt safe in the knowledge that this latest endeavour, a mere question of sabotaging, rather than pioneering, new technology, would run just as smoothly as the last.

All the while, a different feeling altogether was beginning to take root inside him. It was linked, he felt sure, to this sudden sense of infallibility, the knowledge that under his stewardship a potentially tricky global venture had come to be viewed as an unqualified success. Or maybe it was something to do with the imposing silhouette of the Vienna International Centre. Strange, at any rate, that the home of the world's foremost peacekeeping organization should evoke in him the desire to upset the status quo. Nothing serious. Just a little trick to highlight the inefficacy of the United Nations in-house security system.

The entrance was more akin to airport security control, and, having passed through unscathed, he alighted at visitor registration. There he decided to pay for a guided tour. After his passport had been subjected to further scrutiny, he was handed a visitor ID complete with its own number and barcode, which accorded him access to the main building. But Dominik had no desire to join the chattering mass of tourists waiting on the other side. From experience, he knew that all he had to do to go unnoticed was to act as if he belonged. There were some four thousand civil servants from one hundred different countries working in the vast concrete expanses of UNO city, as the building was colloquially known, and in his suit, shirt, and tie, Dominik could have passed for any one of them.

He made his way purposefully over towards one of the security barriers, scanned his ID and walked straight out into a restricted access café. As expected, no-one paid him the slightest bit of attention; any employees in the vicinity were all too busy dealing with the various requests of the tourist group.

He ordered a cappuccino and waited. The flags of the 144 member states fluttered in the breeze as if to applaud his actions. Dominik felt no guilt. He knew that Adler would have behaved with exactly the same sense of entitlement.

He called Chaipura to let him know where he was. He realized that here on this terrace, it was international, rather than Austrian, law that applied. Chaipura was a small, scholarly man not given to outbursts of emotion or, indeed, words of reproach. However, when he saw Dominik, he looked decidedly flustered. Possibly he was concerned that the latter's presence would in some way reflect  badly upon him. In truth, it had barely been registered.

"Dominik, it's a bit of a surprise to see you out here." Rare for him not to initiate proceedings with a more banal greeting. But then the eyes and mouth softened to form a wry smile as he regained his composure and offered a cordial hand. "It's good to see you. There was something you wanted to discuss? Come on, let's finish your guided tour."

They began to make their way to an interpreter's booth in one of the centre's fourteen conference rooms. Chaipura had mentioned that there would be more privacy there. As they waited for the elevator that would take them to the sixth floor, however, a thin film of sweat began to form on Dominik's forehead.

"Dominik, is everything OK?"

But there was no response, the object of Chaipura's gentle concern having been momentarily transported back to an incident from childhood. Dominik had been an overweight child, not drastically so, but enough to incur the teasing of his fellow classmates. Their jibes had taken on a crueller aspect following an incident on a school trip. Dominik could no longer remember the destination, only that at the train station he had chosen to take the elevator instead of the three flights of steps that led to the station exit. Somehow, he had become stuck there. There had been some sort of power failure and the shaft, unable to convey its only passenger to his destination, had been plunged into total darkness. Perhaps if he had had company, the outcome would have been very different. He would have had someone there to keep his spirits up, to tell him that these things sometimes happened, that there was nothing to be ashamed of. Unfortunately, the absence of such a calm head meant that after a mere half hour of confinement, with only a mounting sense of panic to accompany him, Dominik had lain crumpled on the floor, sobbing helplessly, for once not displaying even the slightest interest in the bag of sweets he knew was still lodged in his satchel. When he was finally found, some four hours later, his face was puffy and his eyes an almost bloody shade of red. Worse still, he had wet himself.

He never quite lived the shame down. The kids said he had taken the elevator because he was lazy – which was true – but somehow a rumour had spread that it was his excess weight which had prevented him from making good his exit before the darkness descended. Total nonsense, obviously, but reality is a slippery notion, and it wasn't long before he believed that part too. Against the charge that he had been unable to control his bladder, meanwhile, he had no defence. The children had been merciless, taunting him everywhere he went, mentioning it whenever he seemed to be on the verge of making a new friend. It had made the rest of his school life hell. A different person might have got over it, might have been able to save it under the filename "unpleasant childhood memories" and move on; Dominik had let it take over his life. In adulthood, he was ascetic, fastidious, and obsessed with being in control, but for all that, a man who had never quite forgotten the helpless little boy inside.

"Do you mind if we take the stairs?" Dominik said finally.

"No, of course not. I had forgotten how much you like to keep fit."

Once they had ascended the six flights of stairs, the small talk interspersed at regular intervals with Chaipura's heavy breathing,

Dominik was surprised to discover that the conference room into which they emerged was almost completely brown. Brown floor; brown chairs and desks; brown gallery; brown walls; brown roof panelling. Perhaps monochrome was the secret to securing lasting international peace. The pair made for one of the interpreter's booths situated in the gallery above the main stage. It was shrouded in darkness. Chaipura didn't switch on the light.

"Funny, I can't seem to shake the feeling that we're engaging in something illegal."

"In the UN?" Dominik smiled. "I don't think you have anything to worry about."

"So, what is it I can do for you?"

"A favour. Those two kids who did the security for you at the Grand Palace. Something's come up. Can you get hold of them for me?"

"I can give you their details, sure. Is it for another event?

"Something like that."

Chaipura started to reach for his wallet. "I think I might even have it here." A few moments passed while he sifted through the assortment of business cards that he kept on his person. "Bingo. They come as a team. Good luck finding this one though." He pointed to one of the names on the card. "He's more into partying than work. Could be anywhere."

For the second time during their short exchange, Dominik Brandt smiled, this time to himself. He didn't think BIRD would have any trouble locating his whereabouts.

After all, for Walter Mikesch's department, someone like Nils Karrat was only ever a click away.

21

CHAPTER TWO

Nils

Spring – Sylt – Zurich

Sylt was a place of contrasts. Although measuring less than one hundred square kilometres, Germany's northernmost island had long been established as a major party destination for the country's rich and famous.

Back in the old days, the Hamburg media had decamped here in droves in the hope of gaining exclusive access to the private lives of the nation's pop stars, actors, and playboys. Recently, however, interest had shifted from celebrities to the island itself. The western shoreline was gradually being eroded, and it was said that a single stormy weekend could result in the loss of 100,000 cubic metres of sand. The damage, which was a result of global warming, could only be partially offset by a multimillion-dollar effort to curb the erosion by flushing vast quantities of sand onto the Frisian island shore. As if a group of children were desperately heaping dry sand on their castles in the face of the inevitable tide.

For Nils Karrat, all this was of secondary importance. The island's shrinking coastline was far less diverting than its endless supply of beautiful people. Nils had spent the day admiring them from his position on the beach and, as he made his way towards the Sansibar, his thoughts turned to the evening ahead. A couple of drinks and then on to Kampen? After all, what were holidays for? He had come to Sylt to let his hair down and was prepared to go wherever the night took him. In a place like this, there was always the chance he would meet someone…

He grinned. If, to avail of the corporate speak that had somehow infiltrated even the *demi-monde* of "unofficial surveillance", he were to list his *core competencies*, his technical expertise would come a distant second. Certainly, he was good with technology, but it was his way with people that made him stand out from the crowd. People – but women in particular. At just over five foot nine, he wasn't the tallest, but he more than compensated for his lack of height with his good looks and charm. Wiry and slim, with longish, straight, dark-brown hair that he was wont to flick back when it fell in his eyes, he also had the good fortune of being both an excellent anecdotalist and a practised listener. What women really liked about Nils, however, was the fact that he obviously liked them too. There was no agenda with him. Being with women wasn't a way of impressing the boys, comparing conquests across a table of empty beer bottles and shot glasses. He simply enjoyed their company, and more often than not this interest was repaid in kind.

He found a table and sat down. Before he had a chance to order, however, he was surprised to see a waiter approaching with a bottle of 2005 Roederer Cristal Brut and two glasses. It was one of the most expensive items on Sansibar's wide-ranging drinks menu. Confused, Nils turned to the other guests on the outdoor terrace before looking over towards the single-storey, glass-panelled beach shack from where the champagne had emerged. Nothing there. How odd. He wasn't *so* good with people that they'd donate an expensive bottle of Cristal without his having been introduced to them. He sighed, knowing that he'd have to send it back. He couldn't afford a tenth of the price.

"Look, I'm sorry. I'm not quite sure what's happened here but I think there's been a mistake," he said, thinking that, whatever happened, this little incident had to be a good sign.

"There has been no mistake, I assure you. Unless, that is, you are *not* Nils Karrat." The smooth, authoritative voice hadn't come from the waiter but from a figure that had, like the champagne, apparently appeared out of nowhere. He was about the same height as Nils, tanned with close-cropped, blond hair and sunglasses, and dressed like a member of the jet-set. "May I take a seat?"

Nils, feeling more and more intrigued, motioned for him to sit down.

"Thank you. I have a proposal for you. You like champagne, don't you?"

Nils nodded, stifling a grin. It was like something out of a Bond film. He waited, curious to see how things would play out. For now, there was no harm in accepting a free glass of champagne. With a bit of luck, he thought to himself, this Bond would be more Roger Moore than Daniel Craig. Nils could cope with a casually raised eyebrow and a bad pun; he was less keen on the idea of being beaten up and left for dead.

Still, it was strange. Nils couldn't shake the feeling that he had seen this man somewhere before. He tried to jog his memory. In the meantime, it wouldn't do any harm to hear what he had to say.

"When we finish, I'm going to give you twenty-four hours to consider my offer. I won't make it a second time."

Nils spent the next few minutes listening in awe, as the man outlined not only the nature of his proposal but the rewards on offer. It soon became clear that this was about much more than a simple job. It was about developing new projects in emerging markets, taking responsibility for multimillion-dollar deals, and shaking hands with presidents and monarchs across the globe. About halfway through the monologue, with the aid of a business card that had been passed discreetly into his possession, Nils was sure of two things. First, he knew where the pair had come into contact; and second, it wasn't going to take him twenty-four hours to consider what Dominik Brandt, Senior Management Consultant New Businesses, was proposing.

The deal was simple: Dominik's company represented a client that was in the process of developing electric vehicles for the mass market. Although he omitted to say how, Dominik had learned that a potentially revolutionary piece of technology was to be tested at an EV event in central Europe. Naturally, the company was interested in finding out more. He realized what he was asking wasn't exactly kosher, but if Nils accepted, his job would be to locate the technology and submit a report of his findings. Top secret, of course. No-one was to know he was there.

As if to ward off any reservations that Nils might have, Dominik then emphasized that it was a competitive market and that this sort of thing went on the whole time. These days, there were even university courses on how to wage economic warfare. Dominik knew because he had attended one himself. It went without saying that if Nils was successful in locating the technology, there would be an even greater opportunity just around the corner. No-one at the headquarters in Zurich doubted Nils' ability to get the job done. They had been most impressed with his work in Thailand. The hidden camera was a wonderful innovation, so unobtrusive and effective. And the word was that he had designed it himself. How did it work again?

"The tie?" Nils asked. Although he knew that he had seen Dominik in Bangkok, he wasn't sure exactly what he had been doing there. Nor why it should make the slightest bit of difference what anyone in *Zurich* thought. Nils had landed the Thailand gig in Austria, not Switzerland. Still, he supposed the answers would reveal themselves in time. The way Dominik had spoken, as if socializing with the world's leading figures was the most natural thing in the world, had made quite an impression, and it was time to step up. "Well, it's quite simple, really. It's no different from any other camera, except that the lens needs to be small enough to fit inside a necktie. But the rest is pretty much the same. One-touch video recording, then USB to download the footage." He neglected to mention the fact that he had also developed a high-capacity battery pack that enabled the device to stay powered for three times as long on a single charge.

"I am impressed by your modesty, Mr Karrat. But let me assure you, if it really was that simple I would not have travelled from Hamburg especially to meet you. Nor would I be able to offer you such generous remuneration for your services." Brandt pulled out an expensive-looking pen from his breast pocket and scribbled a figure on the napkin before passing it across the table.

Nils gazed open-mouthed at the sum he had just been offered.

"There are certain conditions attached. First, if you agree to work for us you must carry out our instructions to the letter. To the *letter*, Mr Karrat. Any deviation from the role you have been assigned and you will forfeit your entire wage. That's non-negotiable. Second, on no account can you mention who you are working for or what you are doing. We have taken the liberty of providing you with a cover story. The event organizer has kindly allowed you to join the expedition under the proviso that you write a video blog and publish it on your website. Use your own name by all means."

"OK, anything else?"

"Yes: bring your friend. The one from Bangkok."

With that, Dominik was gone. Nils sat back and reflected on what had just happened. Perhaps a more cautious individual would have been taken aback by Dominik's approach. Nils, however, was flattered. Of all the people in the world, he thought to himself, Dominik had chosen him. He knew that if he could get this job right, then it wouldn't be long before he too was travelling the world in Armani. Thailand, his last overseas trip, had been fun, but he had been forced to stay in a backpacker's hostel, which had detracted from the glamour somewhat. This time it would be different. Anyone who could afford to spend that much on a bottle of champagne would make sure his employees were well looked-after. Besides, if Dominik was to be believed, this was only the beginning. Nils pictured himself in Venice, in Jakarta, in Marrakech: life would be nothing but one great big, all-expenses-paid party!

He steadied himself.

If he could just get this job right.

First things first: Hendrik. He lit a cigarette and took out his cell phone.

"Hey, dude. I wasn't expecting to hear from you so soon."

"Believe me; I'm just as surprised as you are."

"So, what gives? I thought you'd be on your second bottle of champagne by now."

Nils laughed. He was – though it was considerably cheaper than the first.

"Listen, I've just met this amazing guy."

"Nils – I don't know quite what to say…"

"Oh, give it a rest! You know what I mean. It was a business deal. I think I've just landed us a pretty sweet job."

"OK, let's hear it."

Nils related the events of the last hour, while his friend listened in silence.

"So, where do I fit in?" Hendrik asked when Nils had finished.

"How do you mean?"

"I mean what's my role in all this?"

"I guess he didn't say."

"He didn't say? So basically some guy in a bar bought you an expensive bottle of champagne and offered you a stupid amount of money to do what? Spy on a bunch of people driving electric cars? Come on, Nils, doesn't that seem a little strange to you? He didn't even tell you who he worked for, let alone how he knows about me."

"Oh relax, will you? He's connected to Bangkok in some way, that's how he knows about you. As for who he works for, it's fucking undercover surveillance, Hendrik. He's not going to come steaming in and tell us absolutely everything, is he? Though now I come to think of it, he did say that he was a management consultant, based in Switzerland."

"OK. But you still haven't answered my first question."

"About your role? Well, he asked for you specifically so he must have something in mind. Come on, Hendrik. It's a lot of money. Think of what we could do with that sort of capital. Plus, it's only ten days. What's the worst that can happen?"

A pause. "Should I make a list?"

Nils knew that was a good as a yes. In truth it had been a little unfair of him to allude to the business; the mere mention of money would have been enough. Hendrik didn't have any, and the debts left by his parents were beginning to spiral out of control.

"One more thing," Nils said. "How quickly can you get to Zurich?"

Arriving at Zurich central station two days later, Nils and Hendrik had been instructed to make their way to the Savoy, where they would be received by Dominik himself. As they entered the spacious lobby, however, they were dismayed to discover that they had been stood up. There was a large chandelier, a spiral gilt metal staircase, and a wonderful oak-panelled reception desk – but Dominik was nowhere to be seen. Although there were two members of staff behind the desk, neither of them accorded Nils and Hendrik so much as a second glance.

"How much did you have to drink the other night?"

"Not enough to dream all this up, if that's what you're thinking."

Precisely what Nils didn't need. After more or less assenting over the phone two days before, Hendrik had grown increasingly sceptical as the hour approached. On the way to the hotel he had even mentioned the proximity of Zurich's main prison to the city's financial district, as if the fact that a European capital should contain both a banking quarter and a penitentiary was somehow confirmation of the link between wealth and criminal activity. And now Dominik's no-show would give him further ammunition. Nils looked across at his friend. There it was: the quizzically raised eyebrow; the *I told you so* glance that was usually the preserve of unhappily married couples. For someone who was quite content to spy on people for money, Hendrik couldn't half come over all moralistic when the mood took him.

But then again, Nils thought to himself, that was probably what made them such a good team. Where he was friendly and outgoing, Hendrik could be shy and thoughtful, preferring to exercise caution against Nils' natural sense of adventure. In life, too, the Fates had dealt them markedly different hands. For Nils it had been a straight flush: loving parents, liberal upbringing, and a fully funded scholarship at a prestigious technical college; now he had his own company and was beginning to make his way in the world. Hendrik, on the other hand, had been on a losing streak for as long as anyone could remember. A few years back he had buried his parents and kid sister following a car accident; later he had lost a lot of money on the sale of the family home. There was no inheritance, only debts. He had needed a risk-taker like Nils to help him get back on his feet. Now the two were flatmates, business partners, and firm friends.

Just then, Dominik walked in and Nils breathed a sigh of relief. He was dressed slightly less extravagantly than on the previous occasion but still looked the part in a slim-fit suit and brown patent leather shoes.

"Gentleman, I'm terribly sorry to have kept you waiting. I had to drive my sister to the hospital at the last minute."

Nils didn't remember Dominik mentioning anything about his family on Sylt. Still, memory was unreliable – particularly after a couple of bottles of champagne.

To his surprise, it was Hendrik who spoke first.

"Nothing serious, I hope?"

"A nasty fall, but fortunately everything is fine now. Families need to look after each other, wouldn't you agree, Mr Herder? I'm Dominik Brandt, by the way," he offered his hand. "Mr Karrat, good to see you again. Now, I'll leave you two to freshen up." He gave Nils a scrap of paper containing an address. "See you at one o'clock on Bahnhofstrasse."

"Did you see that?" Hendrik asked an hour later as they made their way down Bahnhofstrasse and left towards the lake, where Brandt's company offices were situated. "The way he offered to take my second bag up himself."

Nils had also been a little surprised. This wasn't the Dominik Brandt he had met on Sylt, but rather a more caring, considerate version. No matter, he thought to himself: as long as Hendrik was back on side. When they reached the door, they found Dominik waiting this time.

"You never mentioned you worked for Adler Reilly," Nils said.

"That's because I don't. At least not directly."

As he led them through the spacious confines of the Adler Reilly compound, Dominik explained that the company he worked for was in fact a subsidiary of the consultancy firm, though it retained offices here in Zurich to save on costs. It was financially independent from its parent company and enjoyed all the flexibility of a stand-alone business, but remained more interested in developing projects than acquiring its own premises. "Recruitment is a priority too," Dominik added, with a smile.

From the open-plan offices, whose glass fronts overlooked the city below, it was through to a small private room with a table and two chairs facing a projector screen. No doubt it would soon feature the first of many PowerPoint slides. Nils wondered when the use of a PowerPoint presentation had become synonymous with quality. The idea was everywhere you looked. Business meetings, university lectures, even primary school classes. If technology was a means of protecting yourself from the harsh realities of the world, then the role of the PowerPoint presentation was to distract you from the shortcomings of its author. Somehow humans were no longer capable of directly engaging with anything other than technology; it had become the filter through which genuine experience was distilled. Nils sighed. Despite being a people-person, he knew that he was part of the problem.

No-one in his line of work relied on their wits any longer: instinct had been superseded by the presence of high resolution software.

In the far left-hand corner, diagonally behind the projector, was a desk with two contracts sitting together side-by-side. There was something strangely ceremonial about the layout. Add a vase of flowers and it would be as if Nils and Hendrik were two newlyweds signing the register upon exchanging their vows.

Nils wondered if there had been a marriage by PowerPoint yet, the order of events relayed in bullet points so that the public could share in the joy of the happy couple without ever having to look in their direction.

Dominik invited them to sit down and they were soon joined by a bearded, dark-haired man in his thirties.

"Marc Kudling is our technical expert," Dominik said. "He will provide Mr Karrat with support in Zurich while Mr Herder is out in the field. First, though, I wanted to say a few words about our motivation."

Nils was momentarily taken aback. He had to stay in Zurich while Hendrik was off gallivanting around central Europe? Not that Hendrik would be doing much of that. Still, maybe that was the point. Objectively seen, he was a much safer pair of hands than Nils: a far more reliable proposition than a party boy whose motto was *work hard, play harder*. It seemed unlikely that Brandt was unaware of Nils' fondness for a late night or two. Maybe he felt he could keep a closer eye on him in Zurich.

"So far we have been very careful not to divulge too much information." Dominik had the floor again, and Nils dismissed all other thoughts from his mind. "This is partly because we don't want people exchanging idle gossip. And partly because there are still a number of things we don't know ourselves. I wonder if either of you have heard of super-credits?"

"They're an incentive designed to encourage car manufacturers to supply ultra-low carbon vehicles."

"Very good, Mr Herder. As matters stand, certain EU measures dictate that no new passenger car should have CO_2 emissions of greater than 130 grams per kilometre. The amount had originally been set to fall further by 2020, to 95 grams per kilometre. Due to Germany's intervention this has been pushed out by one year. But these figures are just an average. According to current legislation, super-credits allow an EV with emissions of less than 50 grams per kilometre to be counted as two and a half vehicles, enabling the manufacturer to emit the equivalent extra amount of CO_2 from the rest of their fleet. The regulation can be applied to a maximum of 20,000 vehicles in total per manufacturer. What this means in practice is that two EVs with theoretical CO_2 emissions of 50 grams per kilometre allow a car manufacturer to sell *five* gas-guzzlers with emissions of 200 grams per kilometre and still come in under the target average of 130 grams per kilometre."

Nils was beginning to wish that Dominik had used a PowerPoint after all.

"Would you believe that in spite of this rather generous regulation, certain factions of the automobile industry are lobbying for delays in the reduction of the target average!"

"Unbelievable," Hendrik was shaking his head.

"So where do we fit in?" Dominik continued. "Well, as I have already intimated to Mr Karrat, we represent a client developing electric vehicles for the mass market. Some weeks ago, our client, a modest outlet with a genuine interest in promoting EVs in order to lower CO_2 levels, came to me in some despair. There had been whispers at a trade show that this year's WAVE trophy was to serve as the testing ground for a game-changing new technology. Needless to say, no-one knows who's behind it. It could be a large company, or a small company working for a large company. It might even be a subsidiary that enjoys financial independence from its parent company, rather like we do from Adler Reilly.

"The point is, anything's possible. If I were a betting man, however, I'd say there's a major player involved somewhere. The rumour goes that the technology is not being developed out of any environmental

concern, but rather as a kind of feasibility study. Should it be successful, whoever is behind it will make sure the design is kept under lock
and key until such time as it makes financial sense to unveil it. Now, to
outsiders, this might all seem like a step in the right direction.

"But the reality is that what's rumoured to be happening at
WAVE could set the electric vehicle industry back years. Our client is
absolutely convinced that this technology is being developed purely
out of the manufacturer's desire to exploit existing EU legislation and
use EVs as a means of expanding their production of gas-guzzlers. I
hardly need point out that such a manoeuvre would constitute a very
real threat to the enduring welfare of our planet."

Nils was surprised by the emotion in Brandt's voice. The man he
had met on Sylt was a far more controlled figure.

"Now," he continued, "whether that's all true or not, I cannot
say. Nevertheless, I feel a responsibility to my client to confirm at
least that this technology exists. That's where you two come in. Only
when we know what we're dealing with, can we begin to take appropriate action. Your brief is to find this technology and await further
instruction."

Dominik's final sentences were accompanied by the sound of
Hendrik making to rise from his chair. Nils put his head in his hands.
Shit. All that money; all that time spent persuading him. Only for him
to…

But wait, he was heading towards the desk. Nils could hardly
believe what he was seeing. It was more than just out of character;
it was absolutely unheard of. Without even looking at the conditions
set down within, Hendrik turned to the last page of the contract and
signed his name.

He hadn't even bothered to wait for the technical expert.

CHAPTER THREE

Hendrik

Spring – Zurich

After signing the contract, Hendrik Herder turned to find his friend nodding and smiling alongside him. Truth be told, he wasn't in the least surprised. Nils was probably still thinking of the outrageous sum of money he had been offered on Sylt.

If any further confirmation was needed, it could be found in the way Nils skimmed the details of the agreement until he reached the page that dealt with the money. The sum, apparently, was the same, and he had no hesitation in signing on the dotted line.

"Welcome on board, gentlemen," Dominik said, as he collected the two contracts. "For now, though, I leave you in the capable hands of Marc Kudling. He'll tell you everything you need to know about electric vehicles."

Dominik had scarcely departed before Hendrik and Nils were greeted by a cheery "hello". It came from the corner, where their new technical adviser had been seated throughout.

"I'm responsible for electric mobility. Please call me Marc. I don't stand on ceremony."

Hendrik and Nils were only too pleased to take him up on his offer. Although they sometimes dealt with business people who expected to be addressed more formally, both preferred to operate on a first-name basis. Besides, there was something about Marc that didn't quite fit with the image of Adler Reilly. Lightly bearded, and dressed in sneakers, jeans, and a sweater, he looked more like one of Hendrik's university friends than the employee of a multinational consultancy firm. In fact, it soon transpired that he was an extern, on secondment at Adler Reilly for the duration of the contract.

"So, let's make a start. Have either of you driven an electric vehicle before?"

To his embarrassment, Hendrik had never even been near one. Nils was different, however. Growing up, a generous allowance had ensured that he had access to all the latest toys. But surely he couldn't have tried everything. Besides, had electric vehicles even been around while they were at university?

"I drove a smart car from Car2Go in Hamburg recently. I think it was a micro-hybrid," Nils said. "That's a kind of electric vehicle, isn't it?"

Marc smiled. "I'm afraid, what you've got there is what's known as greenwashing." Hendrik's gaze went blank. "That's when you promote the perception that your car is green, even though the reality is somewhat different. That's not to say that Car2Go don't do important work. But a micro-hybrid is not an EV. Admittedly, they have started offering the purely electric version of the Smart in certain cities. But the original model is called a micro-hybrid because the engine can be switched on and off without wasting fuel. Instead of an alternator, the car comes equipped with a generator, so that the engine shuts down when you hit the brakes at a stop." Marc paused, more serious now. "Somehow I didn't think either of you would have driven a proper electric car, so that's what we're going to do today. I just have to make a quick call. Help yourselves to coffee." He gestured towards a Nespresso machine in the corner of the room.

In the train, in the hotel, and now here as well! Hendrik couldn't understand why these machines were so popular. Ten capsules, each weighing five grams, cost around five euros. That made buying 500 grams of coffee an expensive business, to say nothing of the waste they produced. People were getting lazier and lazier. It seemed as if the need to appear chic outweighed environmental concerns. Hendrik decided to help himself to a bottle of water.

In the meantime Marc had returned. "I've got a real treat in store for us. The car's waiting in a showroom just around the corner."

Hendrik wondered what manufacturer would have a dealership in the middle of Zurich's financial quarter. As far as he knew, Ferrari and Lamborghini were still to join the electric vehicle market...

"Before we go any further, I'd be interested to hear the first thing that comes to mind when you think of an EV," Marc continued.

"Scalextric?" Nils ventured.

"Well, they're certainly electric," Marc joked.

"Limited range," Hendrik said.

"What do you think? How far can your average EV go on a single charge?"

"About one hundred kilometres?" Hendrik replied. Nils nodded in agreement.

Over the course of the next few minutes, they discussed other issues such as the weight of EVs, the lack of charging stations, and the cost of production.

"Not bad for starters. They're some of the most important problems facing manufacturers. Now I suggest we get going – and have a little fun in a Scalextric of our own…"

The showroom, as Marc had called it, was just around the corner from Adler Reilly. They paused in front of a Tesla Motors shop, and Hendrik caught sight of a white sports car, whose design was unfamiliar, though vaguely reminiscent of an Aston Martin. Inside, Marc was greeted by a young woman.

"Good day, Mr Kudling. My colleague in Frankfurt called to say you were coming. You can take the white vehicle outside. It's almost full and should have a range of at least 350 kilometres. If you could just sign this liability-waiver and hand me your driver's license."

While Marc took care of the formalities, Hendrik and Nils decided to have a look round.

The shop had a white-tiled floor and was very clean, almost sterile. One of the walls was adorned with coloured swatches and various rim types. Further to the right of the room was a large screen, containing all sorts of information about the company's history. Hendrik, however, was more interested in the car they would be driving and was soon joined by Nils in the front seat of the display vehicle.

"Looks great," Hendrik said, as he turned towards Marc. The latter seemed to be finished with everything and was gazing at Hendrik through the passenger window. "The display is almost twice the size of an iPad screen," Hendrik continued, his eyes focused on the dashboard. "And you're saying it can go up to 350 kilometres?"

"That's right. It's the Tesla Model S. The company was founded about ten years ago; its headquarters are in Silicon Valley, California. The first model was the Roadster, developed in conjunction with a British engineering foundry. By 2012, around 2,200 vehicles had made it onto the market, but unfortunately production has since been discontinued." Marc gestured towards a poster that showed a red, two-person sports car parked in front of a series of wind turbines. "However, thanks to its success, Tesla raised enough capital to begin work on the Model S. In the first year alone they built and sold more than 20,000!"

"Strange that I've never seen one," Nils remarked.

"Not really, when you think that each year more than eighty million cars are manufactured worldwide. Until now, the majority of Teslas have been sold in the US. Still, all that could be about to change. Switzerland already has its own Tesla club, as do Austria and many other European countries. But enough of that. I can tell you the rest on the drive," Marc shooed the pair outside towards the vehicle stationed in front of the entrance.

"I see they have thought up some nice extras," Hendrik said, as he opened the passenger door. The touch-sensitive handles had popped out automatically.

"Pretty cool," Nils agreed from the backseat. "What does the P85+ on the hatch stand for?"

"Performance plus," Marc said. "The best there is, with an optimized chassis and 421 HP. That's about 310 kilowatts in new money. Thanks to the wider tyres, it can go from zero to one hundred in 4.4 seconds. Maximum speed 210 kilometres per hour…" Marc's enthusiasm was obvious. "There's a normal model with an 85-kilowatt-hour battery; the smaller one comes in at 65 kilowatt hours." He tapped the large screen in the middle of the dashboard, waited for a map to appear, and typed *Restoroute, Lully* into the search engine.

Hendrik saw that the 173-kilometre journey would take just under two hours.

"We're going via French Switzerland to test one of the new superchargers."

"Superchargers?" Hendrik queried.

"A kind of fast-charge station. Tesla is currently building a whole network of those across Europe and the US. We'll leave the car there and get something to eat. Then on the way back I'll let you take the wheel."

That suited Hendrik just fine. He'd had more than his share of dry lectures at university. Sometimes it was better to forgo the theory and just get a feel for the real thing. He could always ask questions later, after experiencing the EV for himself.

Once they were moving, his first feeling was astonishment. He hadn't even heard the motor start. Nor, he realized, was it making any of the noises he'd come to associate with traditional gasoline models. As they approached the motorway, the acceleration forced him back in his seat.

"How cool is that?" Nils exclaimed.

"Amazing," Hendrik agreed.

"One of the main differences between electric and gas is the instant torque," Marc explained. "It even convinces the petrol-heads."

After two hours they pulled into the motorway service area at Lully, and Marc reverse parked so that they came to rest alongside the charging station. According to the in-car system, they could have driven for another 117 kilometres.

"If what Tesla say is true, it should take less than half an hour to charge the battery fully. Superchargers have a charging capacity of 135 kilowatts. If you want to know how much that is, a normal wall socket won't go any higher than 3.7 kilowatts. A high-voltage socket, on the other hand, let's say 400 volts, will give you 11 kilowatts. The first isn't enough for a car like this, but with a high-voltage connection in the garage, you could charge in about seven hours. For a smaller car, a normal AC socket will do just fine."

Following Marc's instructions, Hendrik inserted the thick charging cable into the back of the car, near the rear lights on the driver's side. A green light signalled that a successful connection had been made. In the meantime Nils inspected what, in other cars, would have been the engine compartment, but here served as additional trunk space. The motor, as Marc later explained, was located between the rear wheels, as, even with the rotor, it was still significantly smaller than an internal combustion engine. The battery made up the underside of the aluminium bodywork, with the low centre of gravity it created increasing the vehicle's overall stability.

Little more than an hour later, the trio returned from their meal, the EV battery now fully charged and their own stomachs replenished by ample portions of Swiss raclette.

Hendrik allowed Nils to take the first half of the return leg, as he knew how much his friend had been looking forward to it. When it came to his turn, Hendrik felt reassured in having signed the contract. He knew he was making the right choice. Cars like this needed to be promoted, not used as a means of bypassing regulations. As he drove, he allowed himself to be swept along by the vehicle's smooth handling, with the result that by the time they arrived back at the Savoy in Zurich, he felt almost completely relaxed.

Just as the EV could give itself over to the joys of unbridled acceleration within the merest fraction of a second, however, so, too, could Hendrik's mood change suddenly for the worse. As he entered the lobby he saw Dominik descending the steps with a group of men. Although their gazes met for a moment, Dominik's eyes didn't betray a flicker of recognition, let alone respond to Hendrik's greeting. Instead he simply walked past, as if he had never seen him.

"That guy... I just don't get him," Hendrik said to Nils.

"Who?"

"Dominik. Totally blanked us."

"Dominik? Well, I didn't see him. But give him a break – he was probably in the middle of talking to someone," Nils responded, though it was clear that he had been momentarily distracted by the presence of an elegant blonde in a short skirt and dizzyingly high heels.

Hendrik shrugged his shoulders. Had he been mistaken? Perhaps. At any rate, the feeling persisted that something about Dominik wasn't quite right. For a start, he was completely different from how Nils had described him over the phone. He was humble and family-oriented, where Hendrik had expected selfish and brash. And that speech... In the heat of the moment, it had sounded impressive. But there was something curiously rehearsed about it. Hendrik wondered whether it was a simple case of jealousy. Did he envy Dominik the expensive suits and meetings in luxury hotels, the knowledge that he had made something of his life? Maybe that was it. After all, being confronted with success was difficult at the best of times.

The next morning, theory was on the agenda. Marc had decided to start with the basics.

"I wanted to begin with the question of why it makes sense to switch to electric in the first place. We all know that our fossil fuel reserves are not infinite. It'll be some time before they're completely exhausted, but that doesn't change the fact that they're running out. In addition, we're releasing enormous amounts of carbon monoxide into the atmosphere, causing irreparable damage to the environment in the process. Fortunately, people are slowly beginning to see sense, and a number of industries have turned to renewable energies as an alternative source of fuel. That's where electric vehicles come into play.

"The price of gas is increasing exponentially, and if we still want to be a mobile population in thirty years, then EVs need to be developed now. But let's leave the cost of oil aside for a moment... Did you know that an electric motor is almost three times more efficient than an internal combustion engine? If you put one hundred euros worth of gas into a traditional model, around seventy percent ends up as waste heat on the motorway. Naturally, a portion of that can be used to increase the temperature inside the vehicle – but an internal combustion engine can't tell the seasons apart and things can get pretty warm in summer. True, heating an EV does have an impact on range, but at least it's your choice. Besides, you can always wear a jacket!"

A loud knock on the door stopped Marc in his tracks and provided a welcome break for Hendrik and Nils. In strode a pale man dressed in a beige suit. He was slightly grey at the temples.

"Peter, I wasn't expecting you until later," Marc said. "May I introduce my colleague Peter Prohaska. He's been working in data analysis for a few years now, and is an Adler Reilly man through and through."

"I thought I'd pop in to say hello," Peter said, as he helped himself to coffee. "I heard we had a couple of new recruits." He spoke rapidly, making what he said at times difficult to understand. "So, Marc's been telling you all about electric mobility? Did he take you to the Tesla store? To see the nice young lady?" Peter grabbed a handful of biscuits from the table.

Marc grinned and shrugged his shoulders innocently.

"Anyway," Peter became more serious. "I've just heard that I'll be joining the team at WAVE. Which one of you is Hendrik Herder?"

"That's me," Hendrik said, shaking his new colleague by the hand.

"Peter. Please to meet you. I'll be taking a backseat during the operation. If you have any questions, please don't hesitate to ask. Otherwise, I'll leave you to get on with things yourself. We've all got to start somewhere, after all."

"Thanks, I appreciate it," said Hendrik. "Perhaps we could go for a beer later?"

"Sounds good," Peter looked at his watch. He seemed to be an impatient man. "Listen, I have to go. I'll see you later."

After this unscheduled break, Marc was ready to begin again. This time he focused on the main components of an EV, including the electric motor, battery, and converter.

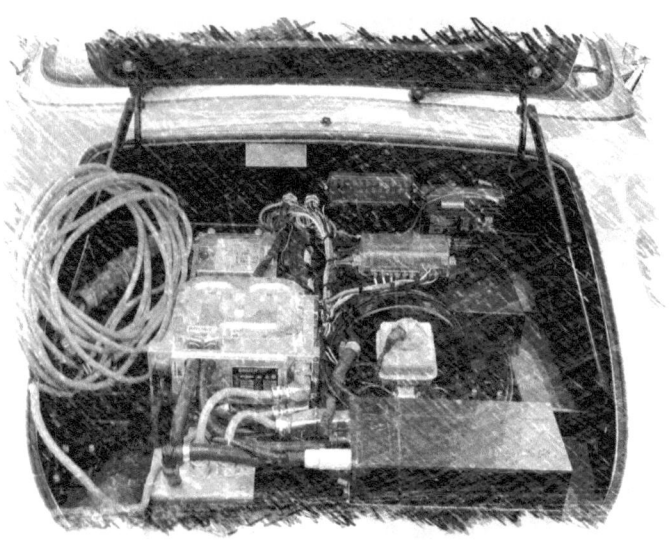

Without the converter, Marc explained, nothing would be possible. The charging station, the battery, and the motor all supplied different types of current, and it was the converter's job to ensure that everything ran as smoothly as possible. Hendrik could vaguely remember from school physics that batteries supplied DC, whereas the motor produced a three-phase, or alternating, current. Still, Marc went on, the most important thing was the electronic steering system, a kind of control centre which monitored all the various processes taking place, whether it was charging the battery or supplying the motor with enough electricity.

"I've got a list of all models that are currently, or shortly to appear, on the market," Marc said. "Make sure you have a good read through before tomorrow before we deal with the individual models in detail. This afternoon you'll be looked after by Uwe Macellaio. He's going to be talking about batteries, as well as leading a short session on hazardous materials," Marc concluded before taking his leave. It was time for lunch.

Hendrik looked across at his friend. "I'm tired just listening to that. Impressive knowledge, if a little heavy on theory."

Nils nodded. "Let's go down to the lake and get some fresh air. I think my brain needs oxygen."

"Nicotine, more like. What happened to you last night? When I left, you were still in Indochine."

"Must have lost track of time. It was only a few drinks. There was this girl... did you see her? We went to Hard One and then on to Kaufleuten."

Hendrik rolled his eyes. Typical. Nils cared less about who he was with than where they were going.

"I saw that, you know. Besides, we were only talking. I was the perfect gentleman," Nils gave Hendrik a friendly pat on the shoulder. "Now, how about a nice tuna steak at the Terrasse? My shout. We'll be able to claim it back on expenses."

Not for the first time, Hendrik realized he would never be as carefree as his friend. But what the hell. It was too nice a day to wolf down a sandwich and head back to the office. Better to prepare for the next round of theory with something a little more substantial.

"Tooth scaler?" Nils asked, after their plates had been cleared away. They were outside in the garden. The food had been superb.

Hendrik gazed at him, still uncomprehending.

"You don't know what that is?" Nils teased. "That's a real gap in your education." He turned to the waiter and ordered two glasses of Valdobbiadene to go with their coffee. "Apparently the fizz cleans your teeth," he explained, laughing.

When the Prosecco arrived, the pair clinked glasses. Nils had adjusted to their new life as if to the manner born.

The prospect of an afternoon spent discussing the intricacies of electric vehicles ensured that they stretched their lunch break out for as long as possible. Perhaps, Hendrik thought as they slowly made their return, he would have to get an espresso from one of those damn machines after all. The first hour after lunch was always the worst. Try as he might, he could never take anything in. What came next, therefore, was something of a surprise.

Marc's colleague, it seemed, also worked as a DJ, and he obviously knew a thing or two about post-prandial torpor. As Hendrik and

Nils entered the room, they were greeted by the latest Latino sounds.

"My current mix." With his curly, dark hair and dimples, their latest tutor seemed barely older than they were, although he was nearly half a head taller. "Gets things going on the dance-floor, if you know what I mean," he continued mischievously as he offered Hendrik and Nils his hand. "I'm Uwe."

Like Marc, Uwe was an extern, hired by Adler Reilly to work on specific contracts. His main area was hazardous materials, a category that included lithium-ion batteries and how they were used in electric cars.

"If you ask me," he began, "technology is both a blessing and a curse. On the one hand, these batteries enable us to keep driving without having a major impact on the environment. On the other, there are certain things you need to look out for. The electric three-wheelers used by the Swiss postal service are a good example. A few years ago, a number of them caught fire overnight. It seemed the batteries were to blame. EMPA, the Swiss Federal Laboratory for Materials Science and Technology, was asked to look into the possible causes.

"However, after various tests, which saw researchers fully charge batteries and then supply them with more energy, or, in some cases, even pierce them with iron nails, it appeared that the real cause lay elsewhere. There was no doubt that the batteries were extremely warm and producing gases that were subsequently leaking. Nevertheless, it transpired that the fire was a result of sparks emanating from the circuit boards of the battery management system. These circuit boards had been installed directly onto the battery casing. In the end all that was needed was a bit of silicon to seal the circuit boards, and the fires would be a thing of the past." Uwe showed them a few pictures. "What I'm trying to say is that it all comes down to the materials used. These differ according to battery type, even if everything falls under the heading lithium-ion."

Over the course of the next hour, Uwe provided details about the various types of battery already in use, and those currently being developed. When they broke for coffee, however, Nils seemed more interested in Uwe's SoundCloud than in the differences between lithium-iron-phosphate, lithium-polymer, and lithium-air batteries.

Hendrik preferred to maintain a discreet distance, and poured himself a glass of water.

"What's the plan, guys?" Uwe asked later in the afternoon. "Should we go for dinner in the Prime Tower? Clouds is definitely worth a look. I played a set there recently and the view from the thirty-fifth floor is sensational. The bar is pretty well stocked too. Besides, I've got a hankering for some Aberdeen Angus beefsteak."

Hendrik nudged Nils under the table before flashing a smile at the consultant. "OK, but only if you're paying. And we'll have two tooth scalers to finish." Even if he knew he could never be quite like Nils, there was still no harm in trying…

"A tooth scaler? That's for women. Real men drink an iced Siberian," Uwe responded.

Now it was Nils' turn to gaze blankly into the distance.

CHAPTER FOUR

Alain

Thursday evening, six weeks later – Eichgraben

WAVE, or the World Advanced Vehicle Expedition, to avail of its full title, was by now in its fourth year. Encompassing various beauty spots across Austria, Switzerland, and Slovenia as part of an intense, ten-day programme, the world's largest electric vehicle rally was an offshoot of the Zero Emissions Race, an event which had seen four teams travel eastwards across the globe from Geneva in order to generate popular interest in sustainable mobility and transport ahead of the 2010 UN Climate Change Conference in Cancun.

Alain Blanc knew this because the tour director Louis Palmer, also the organizer of both races and the first man to travel solo around the world using solar energy alone, had just told the room. Louis had been active in environmental circles for well over a decade, but it was his round-the-world trip that had finally secured his reputation as a sustainability pioneer upon his return in 2008. The trip in his 'solar taxi', Alain was astonished to hear, had lasted a total of eighteen months.

Right now they were in Eichgraben, a small market town that was part of Vienna's extensive commuter belt, as well as being the scene of the WAVE pre-expedition briefing. Alain gazed around the room. If, through his endeavours, Louis had aimed to awaken people's interest in sustainable themes, then he had succeeded handsomely. For instead of the quartet that had set out from Switzerland in 2010, the number of teams had increased tenfold to forty, some seventy-five participants in all, the vast majority now tightly squeezed into the small conference room, waiting to introduce themselves to their fellow EV enthusiasts. Something about the setting had made Alain think about a school reunion, and indeed a number of those taking parts had greeted their fellow participants with open arms before the briefing started. The gesture told Alain everything he needed to know: it was good to be back.

As he watched Louis trace the 1,800-kilometre route from Eich-graben to Zurich on the stage in front, Alain reflected on his own journey. Born in Montreal, he had travelled the globe extensively, taking in places such as Ecuador, Argentina, and Alaska, not to mention the small matter of an Antarctic expedition along the way.

This latest detour was the culmination of a chain of events which had been set in motion by a last-minute decision to take a mountaineering holiday in Scotland. Alain had always been a keen hill-walker, and the flexibility he enjoyed as the owner of a lucrative sportswear business allowed him to indulge his passion more or less whenever – and wherever – he pleased.

So just imagine his surprise when he ran into Tom Schmidt in Edinburgh as he made his way north to Fort William, en route to climb Ben Nevis. Schmidt was CEO of one of the several companies Alain had a share in. That was another advantage of being a successful businessman: having the financial security to invest in others. Schmidt's company had been founded a few years back and installed EV charging stations around the world, a worthy cause that Alain, as a committed environmentalist, had felt compelled to support. Schmidt had just come from a meeting with Transport Scotland, where the focus had been on a proposal to ban internal combustion engines from Scotland's roads by the year 2050. After an entertaining few hours spent sampling a wide variety of gins as part of a tasting session, Alain had persuaded Schmidt to accompany him on his trip north to scale the UK's highest peak.

The next day the pair tackled the ascent together, a climb that, under normal circumstances, would have taken somewhere between three and four hours to complete.

That it took more like four and a half was the result of a long, winding conversation that ended near the summit with Alain offering his financial backing for a project that, if successful, stood to change the face of the automobile industry as people knew it. How delightfully incongruous that the agreement was made in a place where no car – petrol, hybrid, or electric – was ever likely to venture.

The key moment had been when Schmidt, fearing that the combined effect of the wind and rain had sapped the pair of any remaining conversation, had broken with convention and decided to talk shop. Alain hadn't minded. He had spent enough of his life on expeditions to know that they passed a lot quicker if you had something to distract you from the monotony of putting one foot in front of the other. And besides, what Schmidt was saying was interesting.

He explained to Alain that one of the main barriers to the electrification of the car industry was so-called 'range anxiety': the fear than an electric vehicle might run out of battery at an inopportune moment and leave its passengers stranded by the side of the road. This was a particular problem in colder countries, he continued, where the lower temperatures placed further limitations on the distance vehicles could travel.

When you combined the relatively limited range of most available EVs with the time it took to charge them at a standard household socket, then the outcome for EVs was lose-lose. After all, a gasoline model could go twice as far, and filling up didn't mean an overnight stay.

A solid network of fast-charging stations would alter the equation in favour of the EVs, and of the several companies offering those stations, Tesla was exceptional at getting things done. Within the past two years they had been rolling out an impressive network of their superchargers in the US and Europe. These superchargers enabled Tesla drivers to operate back at fifty-percent range within twenty minutes. For those who were even more pressed for time, there was the possibility to exchange the battery. Although a much quicker process, it obliged drivers to pay for the privilege.

Tesla's concept was all very well in theory, Schmidt went on, but the truth was that the vehicles themselves were often prohibitively expensive. Moreover, right now superchargers were only partially fitted with solar modules. If the energy they required came from coal-fired power stations, CO_2 emissions would in fact be higher, meaning that EV drivers were doing more harm to the environment than in a conventional gasoline model. Schmidt's own company, he added, was careful to ensure that any energy needed for *their* charging stations was generated by either the wind or the sun.

Schmidt paused. But what if range were taken out of the equation? That was the question recently put to him by a Slovenian technologist from an independent research institute. The man, whose name was Andrej Pečjak, was not a completely unknown quantity, having previously worked for Schmidt's company on a freelance basis. He claimed to have developed an entirely new concept, one that took all the most crucial factors into consideration – battery type and lifespan, charger, electric motor, converter, intelligent steering – and would enable a four-seater electric vehicle to travel nearly 1,000 kilometres on a single charge; that is, some seven or eight times the current average.

Satisfied that Andrej was serious about his claims following an initial trial, Schmidt had agreed, after a protracted round of negotiations, to finance the road-test. The details were still top-secret but, if successful, they would produce a series. The only thing they needed was capital. Would Alain be willing to make a further investment?

"Isn't that a conflict of interests? What happens to your charging stations when they're no longer needed?"

"Well, they'll still be needed. Just not so often. Besides, this is bigger than money. We're at the vanguard here."

Alain smiled at the memory. Being a pioneer was all well and good, but it was just as important to be a role model. As Louis Palmer began to bring his opening speech to a close, Alain looked across the sparsely decorated conference room at Andrej Pečjak and his wife, Jasna.

One of the conditions of the investment had been Schmidt securing Alain a place on the expedition. Alain reasoned that he wasn't just investing in the technology but in its inventor as well, and that meant seeing how the latter operated at close quarters. He had to say that so far he was impressed. To the outside world, Andrej gave no indication that he was on the verge of achieving something truly remarkable. He went about his business calmly, shaking hands and greeting the various teams with the utmost warmth and respect. Despite the excitement he must have been feeling – an excitement shared by Alain, though for different reasons – the technologist seemed relaxed.

Finally, the tour director requested that all participants be back in the conference room in precisely one hour. "Be on time," he had said: a phrase that would become all too familiar as the event progressed. In the meantime, windows were opened, and the majority of participants took the opportunity to stretch their legs before storming the buffet. Alain followed Andrej at a distance, watching as the technologist exchanged a joke with one of the other participants, a wild-haired man whose anti-Wackersdorf campaign T-shirt led Alain to believe that he hadn't been particularly well disposed to the controversial 1980s Bavarian Minister-President Franz Josef Strauss.

Though the file on Andrej hadn't mentioned his political leanings, it had underlined his credentials as a technologist. He had recently taken part in the Rallye Monte Carlo des Énergies Nouvelles, where his car had won two separate categories: first place in both consumption and electric vehicles. No mean feat when one considered the competition, which included Mitsubishi and Tesla. Strangely, there had been nothing in the media about it. Stranger still had been the race committee's decision to ban converted electric vehicles from participating in future competitions. According to the file, Andrej hadn't protested against the decision; instead, he had been proud that his performance had ruffled a few feathers.

Alain supposed he would have to introduce himself at some point. Not yet, though. He was feeling strangely nervous and still needed a little time for his cover story to crystallize in his mind.

"Oops, sorry." His train of thought was momentarily interrupted as a young man carrying expensive-looking film equipment almost bumped into him.

"No problem," Alain smiled back. Probably someone involved in publicizing the event. Hendrik Herder, his badge said. *Official blogger.* "Nice way to spend a few days," he added.

The young man smiled slightly nervously in response before moving towards the front. There would be time for introductions after dinner.

Once the buffet had come and gone, Alain had retaken his place ready for the next round of speeches. His interest in this stage of proceedings was linked to the second condition of his investment: namely that the technologist enjoyed the protection of two trained agents for the duration of the event.

The agents he had hired came from the company DISECUPRO, which stood for Discreet Security Providers, DSP for short, and had its headquarters in Switzerland. It was a small, family-run enterprise, which specialized in providing security arrangements for a wide range of figures from public life. In an age where intelligence agencies, especially in the US and the UK, were no longer synonymous with the word trust, it had been the company's integrity that had stood out. They seemed somehow to have internalized the concept, to the extent that the head of operations, one Frank Loden, had even introduced himself as "chief of integrity". Frank had assured Alain that Andrej Pečjak would be protected around the clock. He would assign a male-female team to the operation, as that would be the easiest way of keeping their identities a secret. Frank didn't envisage that getting them in would be a problem. Although Andrej had equipped his vehicle with various security mechanisms, which could be activated at any time, the pair would also be supported on the ground by a third agent whose brief was to guard the technology at night. This third agent would also be part of the expedition support team. All further details had been withheld: the less Alain knew about the operation the better.

Still, sitting there watching the individual teams introduce themselves, it was hard not to speculate. There were people from all over the world taking part and it seemed that the vast majority were couples. Perhaps, Alain thought to himself, opposites *didn't* attract after all. How else to explain the fact that so many of the participants clearly shared the same interests as well as the same bed?

Andreas Wacker was the wild-haired man Alain had seen talking with the technologist before dinner; a romantic, it seemed, who had followed his English wife, Angela, back to the country of her birth. They were team number one, and were driving the TWIKE.

Next up, in an orange-coloured Tesla Roadster, were Manfred and Tamara Hillinger, an extremely polite and reserved couple from Austria, who had shared first place last year with a TWIKE team.

Manfred was about average height: a slight man whose studded left ear lent him the air of an eternal student. Tamara seemed shyer, a fact emphasized by her decision to leave the talking to her husband. They were the sort of people it was impossible to judge on first impressions, and would, Alain was sure, make for an effective undercover team.

Rafael de Mestre, meanwhile, was an exuberant Spaniard who had recently completed an eighty-day round-the-world-trip in a Tesla Roadster, during the course of which he had met his current travelling companion, Anastassyia from Kazakhstan. Next was the German-French duo Martin and Magali, driving the Picasso C Zero. Apparently they were on their honeymoon; their team name, at any rate, was "Just Married". Gordon and Leora were the drivers of a Peugeot iOn, but that was about the only thing Alain knew for sure. He supposed it didn't particular matter if they were a couple or not. Either way, his interest had been most piqued by the penultimate pairing: Jean-Pierre and Monika, a rather unassuming-looking couple who both hailed from Switzerland, where DSP headquarters was located. Their vehicle, an orange SAM, was one Alain had never seen before. The final couple to introduce themselves was Andrej Pečjak and his wife, Jasna. They were driving a converted Mazda 5.

All in all, a strange situation was developing. Andrej was convinced that no-one knew about the technology or what he was really doing at WAVE – though the agents, of course, were only too well aware. In truth, the only cast-iron certainty was that neither party knew about Alain, as he hadn't told Frank that he would be attending WAVE in person.

Alain allowed himself another glimpse of the Swiss. Jean-Pierre with his baseball cap, khaki shorts, T-shirt, and beginnings of a paunch hardly seemed agent material. He looked more like a supporting character in an American buddy comedy: the sort of easy-going friend who had a kind word and a smile for everyone. Monika was more convincing as a highly trained operative: smallish but strong and with hair the colour of straw. The only thing she had in common with her husband was a penchant for khaki shorts.

Could it really be them?

After his place on the expedition had been confirmed, Alain had set about doing the usual research. He wanted to get his hands on everything there was to know about WAVE and as much as could be found on Andrej. Truth be told, he sometimes even preferred this preliminary stage to the expedition itself. There was something deeply satisfying about being well prepared, about risk assessment based on research. It was an imaginative exercise as much as anything else, even if it had a tendency to gravitate towards the morbid.

There was no denying that if you imagined a sequence of events and followed it through to its logical conclusion, you would be better placed to deal with it in reality. So Alain had found, at any rate. Even then, he always tried to make room for a little spontaneity. Like the time in Ecuador he had driven all over town just to help a couple get married. There had only been one slot available at the registry office and Alain, as tour organizer, had taken it upon himself to ensure the young lovers had all the paperwork signed by the relevant authorities. He had felt like a movie star when he hailed down a taxi and instructed the driver to "step on it and hang the cost." In the end it had been some night – even if had left a sizeable dent in his wallet.

According to the file, the greatest threat to WAVE – give or take the odd accident here and there – was traffic jams. Alain had read that a few years ago, several participants had caused such a tailback on the roads that angry motorists had launched eggs, onions, and tomatoes at their vehicles, in quantities sufficient for a sizeable breakfast kedgeree. An absurd scenario perhaps, but one that would surely provoke a reaction if it were to happen again.

What if a projectile hit the vehicle of one of the more combustible participants and the incident escalated into full-scale road rage? What if, in the resulting furore, a car was damaged, or worse still, a passenger was injured? What if that car belonged to Andrej? What if Andrej himself was subsequently rendered incapable of taking any further part in the expedition? It was far-fetched, for sure. But it seemed sensible to be prepared for the worst-case scenario.

"Next we have the Bolt, a converted Mazda RX8, driven by Alain Blanc."

The voice came from the front and before he knew it, Alain was walking towards the stage as if on auto-pilot. He had barely been paying attention. The endless stream of participants had sent him into a daze. They were interesting, passionate people – but somehow the excitement he had been feeling before dinner had given way to fatigue.

Upon arrival, he cleared his throat and inhaled deeply.

"Good evening. I must confess I feel something of a fraud standing in front of you tonight," he began. Better to stay as close to the truth as possible. "We've heard some amazing stories, and so many of you have had wonderful experiences. Well, I'm just a replacement – but that doesn't mean I'm looking forward to the next week any less. Thank you for the opportunity, and here's to a successful and enriching few days."

Short and sweet, and if the reaction of the other participants was anything to go by, charm personified. If it wasn't for his business interests, who knows, maybe he could have had a successful career as a diplomat. He imagined himself at a convention in Geneva somewhere, effortlessly defusing disputes between representatives who had been at loggerheads since time immemorial…

As he took his seat once more, Alain began to wish he had mentioned his attendance to Frank. Then he might have known who the agents were. Might have. In truth, there was no guarantee Frank would have told him. After all, he could have legitimately argued that it would compromise the safety of the operation. DSP prided themselves on their discretion: the less that people knew about them, the better. That went for clients and for those they were being paid to protect.

Alain would just have to trust Frank and his team to make the right choices. If there was a problem, they'd find a solution. Experience had taught Alain to believe in other people. It was one of his greatest strengths.

As he reclaimed his seat, his thoughts were interrupted by the sudden appearance of a boy who couldn't have been much older than nine. There he was up at the front now, introducing himself to the other drivers as if it were the most natural thing in the world. He was tall for his age, with short, mousey-brown hair, a baby blue T-shirt, and a red baseball cap. Alain chuckled to himself: actually, this kid was a better public speaker than most of the people who had been on stage that evening. His name was Florian and his family was from one of the so-called Alpine Pearls, a tourist association comprising municipalities from six different Alpine countries. Florian was writing a report on electric vehicles for his school magazine and would be spending each day with a new team in order to meet as many drivers as possible. Before he left the stage he asked which team would take him first. Cheeky little rascal, Alain thought to himself, as a number of hands shot into the air.

When he finished, Alain saw Florian exchange a high-five with the official blogger offstage. He remembered now that there had been a presentation by a representative from Alpine Pearls earlier in the evening and that someone had mentioned a nephew. Which town had they been from again? Alain sighed. Another mystery that would have to remain unsolved…

Still, at least one thing was clearer now. While Florian was speaking, Alain had suddenly realized what was so odd about the whole evening. Four and a half hours of speeches and presentations and not a drop of booze in sight. Perhaps it was linked to the tour director's dislike of CO_2: a zero tolerance policy that encompassed any pollutant, whether it affected the environment or the human body.

Finally, after all the teams had introduced themselves, Louis Palmer went through the details of the route. On more than one occasion, he referred to the "Roadbook", which contained an index of all places, distances, and hotel reservations, as well as specific information about arrivals and departures each day. "Follow the Roadbook" sounded as if it would soon become the second mantra for WAVE participants.

Speeches over, Alain began to wend his way slowly but surely towards the hotel bar. He was definitely ready for a night cap: a quick glass of red wine to ease his passage into sleep ahead of the early start the next morning.

The bar itself was a drab affair, the sort that was supposed to remind its guests of home but somehow contrived to achieve exactly the opposite effect. Alain was surprised to find the technologist already ensconced there, his laptop open and his website awaiting news of the day's events. He had hoped to keep his distance for the first few days. People tended to behave more naturally when you were a fly-on-the-wall.

"Can I get you a drink?" He decided there was no point ignoring him. Somehow that always made you more conspicuous.

"Thanks, but I'd better keep it to one. My wife's just gone up. Besides, I have no desire to get on the wrong side of our tour director."

"The Abstemious One? If he gets his way he'll have the breathalyzers out in the morning."

"Quite," a mischievous smile spread across the technologist's features. "Why don't you join me so we can at least enjoy our solitary glass of wine together?"

"I'd be delighted."

"You know that you're driving one of my cars," the technologist said, once Alain had sat down.

Alain settled in and made himself comfortable. Somehow he couldn't help feeling that his evening had only just begun.

CHAPTER FIVE

Hendrik

Thursday evening – Eichgraben

Despite the lateness of the hour, it was still mild outside. The wind, which had been blowing intermittently throughout the introductions, appeared to have ceased, and had been replaced by a quiet that seemed more in line with a remote suburban library than a hotel and bar serving alcohol into the night. Hendrik Herder didn't mind. He had come to get some fresh air and take a look at the cars charging in preparation for the start tomorrow.

Most of the participants, he assumed, had gone to bed, though there had been a couple of them in the bar drinking wine. He couldn't remember their names – there were too many participants for that – only that they were similar enough to cause confusion. One of them, all receding hairline and sinewy, powerful-looking forearms, had obviously taken part in similar events before and was talking to the newcomer about a coincidence that connected the pair in some way. Looking back through the doors, he saw that both had now taken their leave.

The same went for Peter Prohaska, the agent who had been assigned to Hendrik to help him negotiate his first mission. Peter was knowledgeable but clearly a difficult man to work with, and not just because he spoke with a strong, indeed often incomprehensible, Austrian accent. He was a strange mix of pig-headed and vulnerable and even Hendrik, who wasn't particularly given to analyzing people, could sense that he had been dealt a heavy blow by the past. For all that, he was perfectly good company when the mood took him and the two had enjoyed a pleasant enough evening in Zurich following the conclusion of the technical briefing. It had been Peter who had suggested that Hendrik take advantage of the opportunity to get a closer look at some of the cars parked outside, while he himself sidled off to bed: a privilege afforded to him by dint of his status as senior partner. It didn't bother Hendrik particularly. He wouldn't have to put up with it every night. Since they weren't "official" participants – Hendrik was film crew; Peter part of vehicle support – they wouldn't always be staying in the same hotel together.

It was a short walk to the parking lot and the peace and quiet took Hendrik back to the train journey he had taken from Munich that morning. Despite his initial reservations about the project, he felt that somehow everything was going to be OK. It had been a rough few years, and the last thing he needed was another get-rich-quick scheme. But Dominik was an unusual client in that sense. The fact that he was so politically engaged had come as something of a surprise. Granted, there had been the odd moment of uncertainty, particularly at the start, but gradually this feeling had given way to an overwhelming sense of well-being. Thanks to his new colleagues, Hendrik finally felt as though he belonged somewhere. Even Nils had mentioned how much happier he seemed.

Meanwhile, the journey itself had done nothing to dissuade Hendrik from the notion that things were looking up. The highlight had been catching sight of a group of rabbits burrowing away on a lush green meadow somewhere near Wallersee, a young deer grazing lazily in the background nearby. It was the sort of picture-perfect image that must have been sold in tat shops up and down the country. Not even a corpulent gentleman who seemed to be using his newspaper as a means of deliberately encroaching upon Hendrik's seating area had been able to spoil the mood. Nor the sudden appearance, in the middle of nowhere, of a single empty chair on a hillside.

In fact, so peaceful and idyllic had the journey been that only those of a truly cynical persuasion would have allowed themselves to entertain negative thoughts of any kind along the way. Hendrik might have been naturally sceptical, but he was no cynic, and he had arrived in Eichgraben feeling refreshed and ready for the task at hand.

Suddenly a throng of voices coming from the parking lot pierced the evening air and roused Hendrik from his reverie as he made towards the cars. He came to his senses with a jolt, and realized for the first time that he was nervous. He knew that he didn't have a whole lot of experience to fall back on. If things went wrong, then… Best not to think about it. It didn't look like he would get much done tonight anyway. There must have been – what? – six or seven different people congregated by a group of EVs outside.

"Have you met Marco by the way? Simone's team partner. They're driving the Leaf."

"I have to say, I can't wait to get going. Have you seen this year's route? Some of the landscape will be staggering!"

"Electric motorbikes. Wow, cool! I've never heard of Biiista before. Can I have a go?"

"They're called Johammer now."

"Actually we don't need to charge tonight. The battery's already full."

It was difficult to understand the conversations, as they were all taking place across one another. Nevertheless, there was a real sense of camaraderie between those speaking. Hendrik had always felt envious of those who belonged, as it was something that he had had a hard time achieving. Casting that thought aside, he ventured forth into the mix. A youngish man with a crew-cut and stubble appeared to be helping someone else out. His name, according to his badge, was Vivien, one third of the expedition's technical support team.

"That should be it, Simone."

Hendrik wasn't sure what remedy had been applied, only that the solution had been quick and effective.

"Thanks, Vivien," said a figure emerging from under his vehicle.

"Ah, the official blogger, come to look at the cars in peace, have we?" The voice belonged to a middle-aged man with longish, greying hair, unassumingly dressed in dark-blue jeans and a check shirt. His fleece body-warmer seemed an unnecessary luxury given the outdoor temperature. "Stephan Schwartzkopff," he offered his hand. "If there's anything you want to know, don't hesitate to ask."

"Anything?"

"Well, within reason. I won't be divulging any trade secrets!"

He hadn't even divulged what car he was driving.

That still left the two bikers. The pair were standing next to their machines laughing with – or maybe at – one of the participants. For some reason, the butt of their joke was claiming he could walk on his hands.

"Just wait until you see this," he was saying. To judge by his accent, he was Italian. Something of a clown, obviously.

"What do you think, Franz? Should we have a bet on our Mediterranean friend?" one of the bikers said.

"Not tonight, Johann. I think I'm off to bed. Marco can wait… Do you have the key?" replied the other biker.

"Does anyone want to play football with me?"

Hendrik turned to see Florian looking up at him, wide-eyed.

"Florian? It's a bit late for you, isn't it?"

"I'm not tired. C'mon, the goal's between the Mazda and the Nissan."

The pair kicked the ball about for a few minutes before Florian decided he was tired after all. In the meantime, Marco had started talking to Johann, while Vivien from support was checking that the vehicles were all charging properly. Hendrik sighed. Perhaps it would be better to sit tight and wait for another opportunity. There was still plenty of time, after all.

In the safety of his hotel room, the wall TV flickering soundlessly in the background, Hendrik reflected on his evening's work. It hadn't been a complete write-off. He had managed to publish his first official blog, a mixture of cliché and faux insight that, in terms of its literary quality, was unlikely to stand the test of time. The film component was far stronger. Not that it mattered. Ultimately, it was more a question of keeping up appearances. The daily report, on the other hand, which he had yet to submit, was a slightly more complex affair.

He activated the encrypted connection, and logged onto the intranet. To save time, he and Nils had been registered as Adler Reilly employees. Hendrik saw that Nils was still online. Did he ever sleep? Hendrik opened the chat and sent him a message.

> HENDRIK: WORKING LATE?
>
> NILS: HARDLY, I'M IN THIS COOL BAR...
>
> HENDRIK: THOUGHT YOU MIGHT BE. SO HOW COME YOU'RE ONLINE?
>
> NILS: I NEED TO DO SOME RESEARCH FOR WALTER. SOMEONE AT THE OFFICE SHOWED ME HOW TO DOWNLOAD A SPECIAL PROGRAMMER FOR MY CELL. I THOUGHT A BEER COULDN'T HURT.
>
> HENDRIK: LUCKY YOU. CHANCE WOULD BE A FINE THING.
>
> NILS: WHAT'S GOING ON WITH YOU? ANY LEADS?

Hendrik could imagine him winking conspiratorially. He explained how the first evening had gone.

> HENDRIK: IF DOMINIK'S SUSPICIONS ARE CORRECT, THEN THE NISSAN COULD BE A CANDIDATE
>
> NILS: COULD BE... JUST LET ME CHECK THE FIGURES. I'M PRETTY SURE IT'S ONE OF THE HIGHEST-SELLING EVS.

Hendrik waited.

> NILS: OVER 100,000 VEHICLES SOLD SO FAR AND COUNTING.
>
> HENDRIK: STILL, IT'S UNLIKELY. REMEMBER THE DI'S CRASH COURSE IN BUSINESS MANAGEMENT? THE MORE ELECTRIC VEHICLES

A COMPANY SELLS, THE LOWER THE COST OF PRODUC-
TION. BY BRINGING OUT A NEW PRODUCT, THEY'D RISK
CANNIBALIZATION.

NILS: YOU MEAN THE MARKET SHARE OF THEIR EXISTING PRO-
DUCT WOULD BE NEGATIVELY AFFECTED?

HENDRIK: PRECISELY. PLUS, I THINK THEY WOULD HAVE SENT A
DIFFERENT TEAM. THIS GUY, MARCO, DOESN'T SEEM THE
TYPE TO KEEP A SECRET. THERE'S ANOTHER CAR I'D LIKE
YOU TO CHECK OUT THOUGH. A BLUE CABRIO. IT LOOKS
AS IF IT WAS BUILT FROM SCRATCH.

According to his list, the car was being driven by one of the
men who had introduced himself in the parking lot: Stephan Schwartzkopff. It looked light and fast, and capable of travelling for long
stretches at a time. In comparison, the Tesla convertibles were unlikely
suspects. The Roadsters, co-developed and built by the English design
mavens Lotus, had been discontinued in 2012.

Hendrik logged out and began to write his report. Once it was
uploaded, Nils would use it to form the basis of his research and contact Hendrik in the morning with further instructions. The same procedure was to be observed each day.

That was a lot of
legwork when you fac-
tored in Hendrik's sur-
veillance activities, not
to mention the small
matter of writing and
filming for the web-
site blog. At least one
would be useful for the
other, he thought. He

stretched back on his bed. There was bound to be a surplus of willing
scribes seeking a more reputable forum for their nightly musings on
electric mobility. After all, there had been no shortage of young men
crouched over their laptops when he had first entered the bar that
evening.

Even allowing for the kindness of blogger-cum-strangers, however, it was still unclear how Hendrik was going to get any sleep over the next few days. It was something he had never quite understood, the fallacy that people could continue to operate effectively after a lack of sleep, a point of view that was most glaringly misguided in the case of influential politicians and decision-makers. You only had to look at political leaders to see how badly they aged during their time in office. The exception was good old George Dubya – but apparently he made a point of being in bed by nine. More recently Hendrik had read that an intern in the UK had died, *died*, after pulling a straight seventy-two-hour shift. Madness what these bastards expected of you. He knew that he was going to have to find an effective way of recharging if he wanted his judgment to remain intact. What a shame he couldn't plug himself in at the same time as his battery. At least he had stocked up on enough energy drinks to get him through the next ten days.

Report filed, he switched off his laptop and started getting ready for bed. There was nothing more from Zurich: that meant tomorrow he and Peter would simply continue as before.

For now, though, it was time to call it a day. It might be his only chance of getting a decent night's sleep.

CHAPTER SIX

Magali

Friday afternoon – Baden – Eisenstadt

Magali Zampieri was sitting eating her lunch on one of the benches outside the Grand Casino Baden. She was dressed in grey cargo trousers and a loose-fitting T-shirt, an attempt to disguise her compact, powerful physique, and her mid-length, brown hair was streaked with blond. Like the rest of the participants, she and her "husband" Martin – she was still having trouble pretending they were an item – had made their way from Eichgraben via Vienna that morning, and now had the afternoon to spend at their leisure in the historic spa town.

At least after a fashion. From what she had seen of the tour director, she doubted whether he really "did" leisure. The whole expedition had been planned down to the very last detail, and today's only concession to her or to anybody else's free time was the forty-five-minute break for lunch. After that, a guided tour of the city was scheduled, followed by a grou

Next it was the casino and the expedition's first award ceremony, presided over by the city's mayor. Then the hour-long drive to Eisenstadt and another guided tour. The evening would  conclude with an additional round of political glad-handing at a local wine festival, if, that is, anyone had any energy left. It was exhausting just thinking about it – and that was without taking her official job into account.

Seeing that Martin was still chatting to the technologist and his wife, Magali sat back and admired the casino. Originally a part of the Kurhaus, it had been Austria's first all year-round casino, securing Baden's status as the country's premier spa resort, before being forced to close during the Second World War. April 1945 had seen the city badly affected by bombing and for the next ten years Baden had served as the principal Soviet outpost in Allied-administered post-war Austria. The casino itself had eventually moved to the Kongresshaus in 1968 and, after multiple renovations, was finally reopened to the public in 1995. It was set amidst acres of garden land, and given the glorious sunshine, Magali had little difficulty imagining the Habsburg Court decamping here in its entirety for long, lazy summers spent against the backdrop of the vast Italian Neo-Renaissance structure. Hardly surprisingly, the area was now one of the city's main tourist attractions.

The final cars were arriving. Thanks to Martin's work prior to the start of the expedition, Magali had managed to memorize the names of all participants. But as she watched them park on the small gravel driveway in front of the casino entrance, a normally pedestrian area that had been opened for the purpose of displaying the eco-friendly vehicles to the public, she was struck by just how many them had been accompanied by their partners. It seemed an odd decision for a couple to spend ten days of their annual leave travelling around Europe in an electric car. Maybe they had been swayed by the chance to spend time with a group of people who shared the same principles. Or perhaps the stunning Alpine landscape had been the decisive factor. At any rate, apart from the video-blogger, the only exception to the rule appeared to be a red-haired British journalist who was covering the event for some magazine or other. Even he, it was said, would be joined by his partner at a later stage.

At that moment, Magali's thoughts were interrupted by the sight of a small boy ducking and weaving between the cars, camera in hand. Apparently, Florian had sacrificed a part of his school holidays to attend WAVE, and judging by his demeanour it didn't appear to be a decision he was regretting.

Magali returned to the subject of WAVE participants and their partners. Officially, of course, she was with Martin. In fact, they were newly-weds. Magali couldn't remember whose idea it was to pose as husband and wife, and she had certainly baulked at the proposed team name of "Just Married", but actually it had proved to be something of a masterstroke. Most likely it was Frank, the pair's handler, who had come up with it. In his absence, Martin was sure to claim it. *Martin.*

The most annoying thing about Martin was that she *did* find him attractive. Yes, he could be judgmental at times, but he was also caring and intelligent and, best of all, he didn't take himself too seriously. But a relationship? Magali wasn't sure. There *had* been that one time in New York when they were working together. Back then Martin had been responsible for intelligence, while Magali had dealt with security. Just like now in fact. Somehow the moment had got the better of them.

Perhaps the successful outcome – coupled with the victory champagne – had made it inevitable? Either way, there had been nothing since. True, Martin had briefly attempted to pursue her. On one occasion, he had even presented her with an iPad complete with a playlist containing all her favourite songs. The gift had come in an elegant cherry-wood case. Obviously Martin knew what she liked best. He had had the words "New York" engraved on the underside. For a time, Magali had been unsure what to do with the gift. Eventually she had decided simply to accept it and move on. After all, a gift was a gift. There was no need to reciprocate the gesture. Sometime after that, Martin seemed to lose interest. Maybe he had simply thought better of it: mixing business with pleasure was rarely a good idea, particularly in their line of work.

Now they had been reunited and Magali was feeling nostalgic. For New York? Perhaps. But, no, it was something more general than that. She didn't know where it had come from, this feeling, only that it was somehow linked to the expedition – all that time spent driving on the open road.

That was how Magali had first come to the attention of DSP. She had been in her mid-twenties then and a fixture on the amateur motorcycle racing scene. The only female competitor, naturally. At one particular meet, she had taken a bad fall in qualifying and been obliged to start at the back of the field. She had responded with the drive of her life, fearlessly manoeuvring her bike from one side of the track to the other in order to gain whatever advantage she could over her rivals, and eventually finished in third place.

Afterwards she had been approached by an elegant businesswoman who introduced herself as Arina Rhomberg. Arina said she had been impressed by Magali's strength and determination and that she could use someone like her in her organization. She had left Magali her card. A new business venture: high-end security, based in Switzerland. Magali would need to undergo training – self-defence, martial arts – but the job was hers if she wanted it. A once-in-a-lifetime opportunity. Take a little time to think about it, she had said, then call this number. Ask for Arina. One more thing: you're not married, are you?

"Come on, time's up. The technologist is on the move. Or had you forgotten who he was already?" The teasing voice was Martin's. The guided tour was about to begin.

"I've charged your bag," she replied mischievously, knowing that he wouldn't be able to resist correcting her.

"You mean the battery."

"That's what I said. It was my pleasure, by the way." She, too, could tease with the best of them.

Secretly, she had to admit that the solar bag and the two additional panels she had attached to the car window had been well worth it. At some point, charging all their mobile devices through the car battery would have forced them to make an unwanted stop. This way – as long as it wasn't pouring with rain – she could ensure that her various devices charged on the move.

"Despite its neoclassical face and popular association with Emperor Franz I of Austria, Baden has in fact been an important spa town ever since the Roman era. Soldiers stationed at Vindobona, now Vienna, would come to Baden to bathe in its sulphuric hot springs and remind themselves of the Mediterranean culture they had left behind. We shall pass by the Römertherme, or Roman baths, later on our tour," said the lady from the tourist board, and pointed to a wooden panel that depicted a man bathing.

The group had assembled at the main square, near the town hall, and were making their way through the town's pedestrianized area. It was doubtful whether they would see a great deal, given that they were on foot and only had a grand total of forty-five minutes. Magali consulted her notes. In fact, the tour had been optional – for all those except her and Martin, anyway. Whatever Andrej and Jasna decided to do, she and Martin had no choice but to follow.

While the technologist and his wife were away from their vehicle, it was watched by Vivien, a young man from Switzerland who was travelling as part of the support team. Frank had agreed with the contractor that Andrej's vehicle would be guarded around the clock, and this promise necessitated the presence of a third agent. For her part, Magali was happy Frank had decided to send Vivien. As Magali knew from experience, Vivien was both efficient and discreet. His main role was to guard the vehicle at night and make contact with Martin and Magali only in the event of an emergency. Officially, there was no connection between the trio, and they were to pass themselves off as ordinary participants for as long as possible.

"Baden's status as the Austrian imperial family's summer residence of choice meant it was frequented by a number of celebrity guests, most notably Johann Strauss, composer of *Die Fledermaus*, whose character Frosch may or may not have been based on the town hall's resident jailer; and Ludwig van Beethoven, who I'm sure needs no introduction."

They had stopped on Rathausgasse, outside a museum dedicated to the latter, one of the many houses he had stayed in during his visits to Baden. Apart from a dark-green plaque in front of the entrance, there was nothing to suggest the great musician had ever resided within its four walls.

On the way back, Martin had managed to procure a wreath of white roses from somewhere and was now presenting them elaborately to Magali. She had no choice but to accept, giving rise to a series of "oohs and aahs" from the other participants.

"It must be love!" cried a Swiss man called Erich. He was near the front of the group.

"To look at him, you wouldn't think he was much of a romantic," Magali replied coquettishly.

"I should think that's the case for most men," Erich's German colleague, another Peter, chimed in.

A chorus of male approval.

"It's just nice to see two people so obviously in love," Jasna Pečjak added. She was a lively, exuberant presence with flame-red hair.

Magali blushed and felt suddenly uncomfortable, trapped in a role she had no desire to play out in front of strangers. All this make-believe was frustrating, if only because a tiny part of her wished it was for real.

"One person you won't find a museum to in Baden is Count Leopold of Sacher-Masoch, an Austrian writer and journalist who is famous for giving his name to the term masochism, or the enjoyment of receiving pain…"

Some thirty minutes later, the guide dropped them at the theatre, whereupon the group walked the short distance to their next appointment at the spa gardens. It was about ten past one. Just time for a quick photo. Then on towards the casino.

"Why do you have to be like that?" Magali complained.

"Oh relax, will you, it was just a bit of fun," Martin countered.

"Bit soon for you two to be arguing, isn't it! I thought you were on honeymoon," Jasna waded in.

"Everyone put their hands in the air and wave." Louis Palmer's voice soon drowned everything else out.

"Always the same. Just smile and wave," Jasna laughed.

Inside the casino was a fuse of new and old, with both modern and antique elements jostling for position: a testament to its own potted history perhaps. Certainly, it was very grand. Two curved, red-carpeted staircases led up to the entrance. The whole site was housed on a single floor of the Kongresshaus, with table games at the front, a bar in the middle and poker tables and slots located at the rear. Magali imagined how beautiful it must be at night with the chandeliers on and the people dressed in their evening finery, sipping cocktails and betting distractedly on outcomes they couldn't possibly predict. Glamorous was the word that came to mind.

Right now, though, it was anything but. Dark and nigh-on deserted, the casino's only customers were a group of casually-dressed electric-vehicle enthusiasts, most of whom were determinedly anti-gambling, awaiting the outcome of the Design Award. At least the champagne would add a certain *je ne sais quoi* to proceedings. Along with the presence of the mayor... Magali helped herself to a glass. She wasn't expecting any trouble.

"I take it I'm driving then?" Martin again. Such a wise-guy.

"First sensible thing you've said all week."

As the official business began, all conversation came to a standstill, with participants eagerly awaiting the results of the first competition. Andreas and Angela from Team TWIKE emerged victorious, along with Stephan Schwartzkopff, whose blue cabrio Magali had admired in Eichgraben the night before. The overall winner, however, was a Norwegian man named Robort. Slightly embarrassingly, he failed to attend the ceremony itself, preferring to sit among the palm trees lining the casino entrance and take advantage of the afternoon sun. Following the conclusion of the presentations, a number of participants decided he had the right idea and followed him back out into the light. Only a select few stayed to try their hand at the games on offer.

The first thing that struck Magali as she gazed around the casino were the surveillance cameras. These were built into the ceiling and partially hidden by black, semi-circular glass panels. Although she had needed to be aware of what was going on around her during her stint on the racing circuit, it was joining DSP that had truly opened her eyes. It wasn't just the martial arts training – though that, naturally, had been a help – but the sessions on surveillance and information gathering, with their focus on the tactics adopted by friend and foe alike.

She counted ten roulette tables in total, all of them equipped with an electronic board displaying the results of the previous 300 spins. Was that a help or a hindrance, she wondered. Statistics had no bearing on the outcome, as the results were tabulated *after* the wheel had spun. Roulette was a game of chance, whereas life was what you made of it. Still, it would be interesting to see how many professional gamblers adopted a fatalistic stance when it came to their own existence.

She and Martin had taken separate sides of the floor in order to keep an eye on Andrej. The latter was deep in conversation with a dark-haired British man named Gordon, whom Magali had overheard talking about an electric speedboat the previous day. Apparently he had built it and sailed it up and down the Thames. So many strange and wonderful people…

Magali moved in closer to take a better look at her charge. In order not to arouse suspicion, she and Martin would have to find a way of befriending him. Martin, she suspected, would be the best bet, as the pair clearly shared an interest in technology. If that failed, they could always try his wife, Jasna.

The technologist himself was medium height with short, dark hair and an impressive widow's peak: in his mid-fifties probably, though he could have passed for ten years younger. He was obviously still fit, with a wiry strength not dissimilar to that of Magali herself. There was a mischievous quality about him that was most apparent when he smiled. Magali noticed that he had laughter lines around his eyes. Right now he was telling Gordon about something that had happened to his father. She had missed the first part of the conversation but soon became engrossed.

"... a casino back home. My father had been commissioned to write a book on the psychology of gambling. It was right at the start of the project. He was still researching and wanted to experience things for himself. So anyway, after a couple of hours on the floor, he sees this man. He's playing blackjack, losing big. By rights he should stop, cut his losses, and call it a night. But he keeps playing. My father is fascinated at first but then just plain worried. It's as if this guy has fallen into a trance. He must know he's not going to recoup what he's already lost; still he carries on blindly.

"My father starts watching him more closely, doesn't take his eyes off him for five, maybe ten, minutes. Then he takes a few pictures. Eventually the guy turns round. You know when someone's watching you, right? You can feel it. Well, this guy must have felt something – because otherwise he would have just kept on going. He looks my father straight in the eye. He's got these piercing blue eyes, I can still remember my father saying how amazingly blue they were. And then he stops. Stands up, takes his jacket, thanks the croupier. But before my father can see what happens next, he feels these big hands on his shoulders. It takes my father a minute to work out what's going on. He can't believe it. They've taken his film and destroyed it, and now they're throwing him out of the casino. They never let him back in. The book got shelved a couple of months later."

Magali realized that she had been playing absent-mindedly with the roulette wheel. All of a sudden, Martin was there as well.

"I thought you were trying to send me some sort of coded message," he said.

"Oh give over. Surely you can't be that paranoid! It's a roulette wheel, for Christ's sake. It's not even in use!"

They emerged into the light just in time to see a Tesla speeding out of the car park, a racing start that sent gravel flying in all directions and left a number of bystanders chuntering under their breath.

"That's the sort of thing we should be worried about," Magali said. "You've seen the file, remember."

"I know, I know. I've read what happens if you don't keep the public onside. Let's hope our friend hasn't eggs-acerbated matters." A chuckle at his unexpected verbal dexterity. Followed by a more serious question. "Why do you think the blogger was filming it?"

"I'm not sure he was," Magali replied. "Officially, at least. Louis is having a word with him now."

"A beer says that doesn't end up on the expedition website."

"Then I really won't be able to drive." Magali laughed.

But the question remained.

What was so interesting about a speeding car?

Next stop, Eisenstadt. Where Baden had served as the Hapsburg summer residence, Eisenstadt was for many years the seat of the Hungarian noble family, Eszterházy, most famous for their association with the Austrian composer Joseph Hadyn, who enjoyed some three decades of patronage as the family Kapellmeister, or chapel master, and moved with them among their various palaces.

They had parked outside Schloss Ezsterházy, a mix of baroque and classical architecture that was also home to the Hadynsaal, a glorious three-storey concert hall where the great composer had written and performed many of his works for the first time.

"It's been a day for composers, alright. Maybe that's how we should communicate with each other," Martin said. "You remember the scores in the church?"

"We'd have to check new recruits could read music first," Magali said distractedly. She was more interested in keeping an eye on Andrej.

"How does that mnemonic go again? Father Charles Goes Down And Ends Battle? Or was it Battle Ends And Down Goes Charles' Father?"

"What the fuck are you talking about, Martin?"

"You're right. Best stick with roulette. All those flats and sharps. It's enough to drive you mad."

The wine festival later that evening was memorable for two incidents, only one of which had anything to do with wine. After the city tour, Magali and Martin had, like the majority of participants, driven from the castle to the parking lot of Burgenland Energie – a local company that derived its name from the region – before plugging their vehicle into its designated charging point and indulging in a rare luxury: a taxi ride to the site of the evening's entertainment.

"I have to say, I'm a little disappointed," Magali said upon arrival. "I was expecting something more like their famous *Festival of 1,000 Wines*."

"Oh, stop it would you. It's not a whine festival!" Martin replied.

The joke had been inevitable, but as it turned out Martin was right. The festival might have been smaller, but the atmosphere was no less convivial, and there had certainly been more than enough wine on offer to dull the senses of Robort, the Norwegian, who was perhaps celebrating his victory of earlier that day. What would Louis Palmer make of it all, Magali wondered, having seen how sensitive he was to the behaviour of WAVE participants in his reaction to the blogger's filming of the speeding Tesla. Fortunately, he appeared not to have noticed.

So much for the first incident. The second, however, was potentially more serious.

At just before eleven, a group of participants who were staying in Sopron had gone to retrieve their vehicles prior to undertaking the short drive across the Hungarian border. Though Andrej and Jasna were staying in the same Gasthof as Martin and Magali, they had been chatting to someone about to make the journey and decided to accompany them to the parking lot. It had been that sort of evening. Good food, good wine, good conversation: in short, the kind of night that no-one wanted to end.

The scene that greeted them at the parking lot, however, was mildly chaotic; and the atmosphere was strangely tense.

"Our Nissan hasn't charged," a voice was complaining loudly. It belonged to Simone, a member of the Italian team.

"I've spoken to Burgenland Energie," Jaromir said. "There was a blown fuse. The current must have exceeded its limit and caused a chain reaction." Magali liked the Czech's accent. Somehow she could easily imagine him surrounded by children listening enthralled as he told them one story after another.

"It could have been the Teslas," Andrej said. "They need a 32A three-phase current. The system probably wasn't ready for it."

"How come the cars didn't resume charging once the power supply was back on?" Magali asked.

"Ours did," Jasna replied. "Andrej removed the safety mechanism that comes as standard these days."

"It's totally superfluous anyway," Andrej took up the thread. "It prevents EVs from automatically resuming charging after a power cut. They brought it in because these big American companies are petrified of being sued."

"It all dates back to that case in the nineties," Martin said, as he gazed around the parking lot. "It resulted in a five-billion-dollar pay out. I don't remember which manufacturers were involved. The cause was improperly welded petrol tanks."

"All this talk of safety mechanisms… It doesn't explain why we've been *physically* disconnected from the power supply," Tamara said, visibly frustrated. "And we weren't the only ones either. TWIKE

76

and Stephan Schwartzkopff had the same problem. You know Stephan? He drives the blue cabrio."

Magali surveyed the fleet once more. It was probably just a coincidence: some parking lot attendant who had exercised a little too much caution in the wake of a momentary blackout. But then, she noticed, one of the cars affected was the Tesla she and Martin had seen Rafael driving away from the casino at breakneck speed. What the hell had happened here? Anti-EV protesters? Climate-change sceptics? She realized she needed to be on her guard. Speaking of guards, where was Vivien?

Meanwhile, Martin was doing his best to calm everyone down and soon the tension had partially dissolved. It helped that everyone travelling on to Sopron still had enough battery to make the trip. Jaromir had already called the Louis to let him know what had happened. Most of the vehicles would still have a whole night to charge.

On the walk home, the technologist was in an understandably reflective mood. No doubt he was a little concerned about what had happened. On some level, he must have known that he and  his wife were potentially at risk. A part of Magali longed to come clean and tell him they would be safe. Instead she was obliged to reprise her role, holding Martin's hand as they watched Andrej accompany his wife silently up to their room, forgoing the opportunity to have a final drink at the bar.

CHAPTER SEVEN

Hendrik

Friday evening – Eisenstadt – Sopron

Hendrik was standing in the parking lot at Burgenland Energie. Since he wasn't officially part of any team he had to hitch a lift with a new person each day.

"Are you going to Sopron too?" Alain asked. "I can take you but it might be a little tight." He offered a hand, gestured towards the profiler, and shrugged his shoulders. The gesture made Hendrik think he must have spent the odd night in less comfortable surrounds than the back of an electric car. Luckily the red Mazda was a four-seater, and had more than enough room for Hendrik's luggage and film equipment.

Sopron was twenty-five kilometres away; Alain's car could only go thirty-four before it needed to be recharged. The effect a second person would have on the range was difficult to say. The irony of the situation was not lost on Hendrik. The Bolt was one of the cars he *hadn't* tampered with.

"Not to worry, I'm sure it'll be fine," Alain said optimistically.

As they set off, Hendrik reflected on what had been another long day.

There had been a message from Nils that morning, but it had been so vague that Hendrik had been thrown into a panic. The message had read:

THE BLUE CABRIO. STEPHAN SCHWARTZKOPFF AND OLAF FELDMANN. DEFINITELY A CONTENDER. TIME TO GET CREATIVE.

He had felt suddenly out of his depth, with no prospect of

swimming to safety and shore. What the hell did "creative" mean? Was it some kind of initiative test? Why did everything have to be so damn cryptic? What was he supposed to do? Sabotage the car? During the day, he hadn't had much time to think about it. Baden had been hectic. First the guided tour, then the casino followed by the prize-giving. After that, he had taken a number of photos of the vehicles in the parking lot. The weather had been superb and he was happy with the results.

Strange only that Louis Palmer had banned him from uploading the footage of the dark-blue Tesla speeding away later in the after-noon. Hendrik had thought it was interesting. EV drivers were known for trying to conserve energy – but this guy Rafael had obviously had enough already. What did it mean? Was it because he had energy to burn? Hendrik decided to send Nils the film, though he hoped his friend's response would be more intelligible this time around. After Baden, Hendrik travelled with the two Italians to Eisenstadt. Marco was as crazy as ever, while Hendrik learned that his colleague, Simone, worked in the electric vehicle industry as a consultant. The car, Simo-ne said, was not his own, but one that had been placed at his disposal for the duration of the expedition: confirmation of the conclusion Hendrik and Nils had reached the night before. The Nissan driven by team Alpine Pearls couldn't be a contender.

As for his "creative" endeavours, Hendrik was pretty pleased with his solution. After a glass of wine at the festival and a few minu-tes spent filming the traditional brass band, he had decided to creep back towards the Eisenstadt parking lot where the vehicles were stati-oned, confident that his absence would go unnoticed. Once there, he had checked that no-one was looking before disconnecting four cars from the power supply. All the while, his heart felt as though it were about to jump out of his skin.

Although it was the cabrio's range he wanted to check, it was im-portant that people didn't assume it had been targeted specifically. To this end, the Teslas provided the perfect smokescreen: those returning from the festival would remember the incident at the casino and link it to Rafael's antics in the car park. They might even speculate that it was a message from the tour director. *Behave or your expedition will be over.* The TWIKE he had selected at random.

Hendrik had then returned to the festival to find a slightly red-faced Peter discoursing at length on a complex technical matter with other members of the support team. He was pleased that Peter had found his feet so quickly. The pair had agreed that they wouldn't spend too much time together during the day, and naturally the agreement extended to the evening as well. In truth, Hendrik had no great desire to socialize with Peter anyway, partly out of concern that he might give himself away, and partly because when he did have a moment to relax, he preferred to spend it with people who were oblivious to the real reason for his presence at WAVE.

Having given Peter a wide berth, he had eventually taken a seat at the table opposite a couple called Tamara and Manfred, quiet ty-pes with whom Hendrik felt an immediate affinity. Perhaps it was the Austrian accent, which reminded him of cozy old coffee houses. They were so likeable and down-to-earth that spending time in their company couldn't help but calm his nerves. They were also, it soon tran-spired, driving a Tesla Roadster, which for a moment made Hendrik decidedly uncomfortable. Toughen up, he told himself. They would never suspect he had anything to do with it.

As the evening went on and the brass band continued to belt out the crowd's favourite numbers, the trio were joined by a silver-haired man in his late forties who kept them entertained with a selection of amusing stories from his travels. Alain, Hendrik later discovered: a modest, personable sort with a gift for making people feel at ease. A keen photographer and nature-lover, if his photos were half as good as his stories, then he deserved to be a millionaire.

It had been such a pleasant hour or two that Hendrik had al-most completely forgotten about his actions in the parking lot, when suddenly there was a commotion on the table opposite. A couple of loud sighs followed by a round of expletives. All at once the vehicle support team had dispersed and were moving around the different areas with a message for participants.

"I'm sorry to interrupt but we're asking people to return to the car park," it was Jaromir, the oldest member of the group. "No-one's sure exactly what's happened but apparently there's been a blown fuse and some of the cars haven't charged properly. Andreas and Vivien are down there already."

A blown fuse? That, Hendrik had not been responsible for. But as he made his way back to Burgenland Energie in the company of his newfound friends, he knew that it might just work to his advantage. He realized that in the eyes of participants, whoever had disconnected the cars *could* have done so for safety reasons: an honest motive, whereas previously it would have appeared only suspicious.

"Who knows. Olaf?" Stephan Schwartzkopff had said after surveying the scene. His composure could only mean one thing. "Makes no difference, anyway. We've got more than enough to spare."

His confidence, it turned out, had been well founded. For by the time Hendrik and his Canadian chauffeur made it to Sopron, Stephan and his blue cabrio had already been there for twenty minutes. Sometimes it was the little things that carried the most significance. Peter said that the pair hadn't charged for more than twenty-four hours, which meant their vehicle had a range of at least 150 kilometres. Whether it could go any further was another matter – but Hendrik was pleased with the initial outcome of his experiment.

Their accommodation for the evening gave new meaning to the word "basic". Hendrik's room was on one side of the main house, a kind of annex that looked like a motel. It was extremely cold and when he went to brush his teeth, the tap water tasted strangely metallic. He realized there was a garden, but its green contours could barely be made out in the darkness. It was unlikely, at one in the morning, that it would be seeing any use. Overall, the atmosphere was one of indifference, if not hostility. A foreign location could always carry an air of menace, but for some reason the quiet reminded Hendrik of his childhood home after the accident: familial but no longer familiar.

With a great deal of effort, he connected his computer to a bare socket that was hanging loose from the wall. After attaching the footage of the speeding Tesla, he sent Nils a quick email to say that he'd be taking a closer look at the blue cabrio the next morning. He'd had enough excitement for one evening. Besides, the walls were thin and the rooms had no curtains. If he started snooping around now, at this hour, someone was bound to hear him.

He stretched out on the bed, hoping his fatigue would prevent him from taking an unwanted trip down memory lane. Home, or his recollection of it, was a place he had no desire to go.

The next morning in Sopron, Hendrik was awoken by the mutterings of his fellow housemates. He looked at his cell phone. Five thirty. Too early for anyone to be on the move. He turned over and returned to his dream. He was standing behind a tree, gazing at the burning wreckage of a car. Behind the closed doors, he could see hands waving at him, as if begging for help. It was raining hard, and soon his T-shirt was soaked through and clinging unpleasantly to his skin. He ran towards the next tree in the hope of escaping those beseeching hands. But it made no difference. The same scene greeted him wherever he went, whatever tree he hid behind. Suddenly he realized who the hands must have belonged to. It was their size that gave them away. They were so small. His baby sister. Her hair, he saw now, was streaked with blood and she was screaming at him, but he could no longer make out the words…

He sat up with a start, his body drenched in sweat. What did it mean? Was someone watching him? Dismissing the thought, he looked at his cell. Just after half past six. The muttering from before had ceased. The others were probably having breakfast. He had a quick shower, got dressed, and went to see what was going on. No sign. Funny, there was no reason for them to have left. A quick glance at the Roadbook told him that they weren't due at their next port of call until ten that morning. Departure from Eisenstadt was scheduled for twenty to eight.

Outside, the garden looked altogether more welcoming in the early morning light. Disproportionately large in comparison to the house, it was well tended and contained an old-fashioned picnic bench that overlooked the rest of the plot. Hendrik imagined the bench had been the scene of many a lazy lunch. It would be wonderful in the evening sun: the smell of barbecue smoke in the summer air, people drinking and talking around the table while their children played contentedly in the background, the school day no more than a distant and rapidly receding memory.

He decided to take a seat on the bench, before dialling Jaromir from vehicle support.

"Hello." The voice was unmistakeable.

"Hello, Jaromir. This is Hendrik, part of the film crew. I got a lift to Sopron with Alain last night, but it looks like everyone's left without me."

"Are you sure? Alain isn't here, anyway. Why don't you give me a call back in twenty minutes if you still can't find him."

Not exactly the response Hendrik had been hoping for, but perhaps Jaromir was still sore at having to provide a taxi-service on top of all his other duties. He had been forced to give one of the participants a ride home from the wine festival at a relatively early hour the previous evening. How would they be feeling this morning? Hendrik had always been fascinated by different people's responses to alcohol. It crippled some, but had no discernible effect on others. He thought of a school friend who seemed to be able to drink all night and still wake up with a clear head the next morning; others, he knew, were not so lucky, and would spend entire days in bed, unable to move for fear of doing themselves further damage.

In truth, here was no harm in waiting a little longer. There was always work to be done in the mornings and Nils was sure to be online. He went back inside and retrieved his laptop before reclaiming his seat on the bench. The reception was astonishingly good, and he had no difficulty in logging on to Adler Reilly's intranet. Unsurprisingly, there was indeed a green tick beside Nils' name.

HENDRIK: MORNING, IS ZURICH STILL STANDING?

NILS: MORE OR LESS...

HENDRIK: SPARE ME THE DETAILS.

NILS: SLEEPLESS NIGHT?

HENDRIK: SWEATY BUT NOT SLEEPLESS.

NILS: SOUNDS PROMISING!

HENDRIK: DEFINITELY PROMISING... HANG ON A MINUTE.

A man had appeared from nowhere. Hendrik couldn't place him. He was wearing a horizontally striped T-shirt that was slightly too tight, cropped check trousers, and slip-on shoes. His socks were pulled up above his ankles. A navy-blue baseball cap completed the ensemble.

Not the most sartorially elegant specimen Hendrik had ever seen but he still looked like a bear of a man, his broad shoulders suggestive of immense upper-body strength. He was speaking on his cell phone, pacing up and down the gravel drive. There was something guarded in the way he moved, a suspicion of his surroundings that served only to draw further attention to what he was doing. He had the air of a man who assumed he was being watched. For all that he was looking over his shoulder, however, he was yet to lay eyes on Hendrik himself.

From his position on the bench, Hendrik was seized by a fleeting recollection of an incident involving the man that had taken place earlier that day. An incident, or was it an image? He racked his brains for an answer, but none was forthcoming. Frustrated, he realized that he couldn't even use the man's car to jolt his memory. There were none in Sopron that morning. He was just about to get back to his conversation with Nils when he overheard the man say something that in almost any other circumstances would have been completely devoid of meaning. Even now, it didn't make much sense. But he was sure of it: he had heard the words "Lonely Viking".

It was as if a switch had been flicked inside his brain. Suddenly he found himself transported back to Eisenstadt and the Schloss Ezsterházy.

NILS: HENDRIK? ARE YOU STILL THERE?

HENDRIK: YEAH. WAIT A SEC...

He checked the list of team members that every WAVE participant had been issued before the start of the expedition. It contained the name, contact details, and vehicles of all those involved. Just as he had suspected: "Lonely Viking" was the name of one of the teams taking part.

Hendrik could remember the car now: it was a single-passenger, three-wheeled Corbin Sparrow painted a deep shade of red. In his mind, there was a man stretched out on the paving stones beside it; he looked like a mechanic giving the car a service. It was Gordon, the British man whom Hendrik had identified as a potential replacement blogger should his workload become unmanageable.

What was it about the Sparrow that was so interesting? Certainly, it was different. There was barely room for a sports bag, let alone a fully grown passenger.

He sent Nils another message.

HENDRIK: I'VE GOT A GUY HERE ON HIS CELL. ROBORT MICHELSEN. LONELY VIKING. LOOKS SUSPICIOUS. ANY WAY WE CAN LISTEN IN TO WHAT HE'S SAYING?

NILS: YEAH, NO PROBLEM...

HENDRIK: SO, YOU'RE A MAGICIAN AS WELL?

NILS: LONELY VIKING, YOU SAID? JUST GIVE ME HIS CELL NUMBER AND WE'LL BE UP AND RUNNING.

HENDRIK: I DON'T KNOW ABOUT THIS...

NILS: C'MON, PEOPLE HERE DO IT THE WHOLE TIME. A COUPLE OF THE GUYS FROM INTELLIGENCE ACTUALLY WROTE THE PROGRAMME. WORKS WITH MOST CELL PHONES. AND YOU CAN READ TEXTS TOO.

HENDRIK: PRETTY SCARY STUFF.

NILS: SCARY? YOU MEAN COOL... JUST WAIT A SECOND.

In fact, it didn't take that much longer, and soon Nils was providing Hendrik with a summary of what was being said.

NILS: OK, HE'S TALKING ABOUT EXECUTION, SORRY THE EXECUTING OF A STRATEGY... PRODUCT PORTFOLIOS, KEY GROWTH SEGMENTS, OPERATING SYSTEMS: GIBBERISH, BASICALLY. WHY ARE WE LISTENING TO THIS? WHAT DOES IT HAVE TO DO WITH EV TECHNOLOGY?

HENDRIK: EVERYTHING, POTENTIALLY. DOMINIK SAID IT'S A COMPANY THAT WANTS TO EXPAND THEIR PRODUCTION OF TRADITIONAL GASOLINE CARS. THAT'S THE GROWTH SEGMENT HE'S REFERRING TO. AS FOR OPERATING SYSTEMS, I'M NOT SURE. MAYBE SOMETHING TO DO WITH AN IN-CAR INFOTAINMENT SYSTEM? I READ SOMETHING ABOUT THAT IN CONNECTION WITH GOOGLE RECENTLY. WHOEVER IT IS HAS TO HAVE A STRATEGY...

NILS: BUT IT'S A SPARROW, RIGHT? YOU KNOW THEY'RE AIMED MAINLY AT COMMUTERS? AND THAT THEIR RANGE IS USUALLY AROUND 50KM? IT WOULD HAVE TO BE ONE HELL OF A REVOLUTION!

HENDRIK: HOW DO YOU KNOW SO MUCH ABOUT SPARROWS?

NILS: THEY'RE ALWAYS IN FILMS. THAT MIGHT GIVE THEM THE FINANCES BUT IT'S STILL A LONG SHOT. THE CAR WOULD NEED TO HAVE CHANGED BEYOND ALL RECOGNITION FOR IT TO BE THE ONE WE'RE AFTER. THE CAB'S STILL A FAR BETTER BET.

Hendrik logged out and sighed. He had thought – just for a moment – that he was onto something. So, Marco and Simone were out; and now it seemed Lonely Viking could be added to the list. Going on what Marc Kudling had told them, it probably wasn't a Tesla either, at least not a Roadster. After all, production had ceased in 2012. The cars he had seen were originals. They hadn't been converted and they weren't big enough to house all the components you'd need to achieve a range of 1,000 kilometres. If it had been a different model, on the other hand…

Although an independent company on the surface, a number of large companies had recently bought into Tesla. Admittedly, Daimler had just reduced their share from ten to four percent, but that figure had been safeguarded against a lurch in the market. Toyota's share was three percent, an amount that had been worth fifty million dollars a few years back, and the company had yielded a tidy profit – on paper at least. In return, Tesla supplied both companies with components and designs for eco-friendly vehicles. The powertrain of the current B Class, for instance, was based entirely on a model developed by Tesla; while the Californians were also responsible for the batteries employed in Mercedes' Smart. For their RAV4, Toyota received the powertrain that had been developed for the Roadster and Model S respectively.

Such mutual dependence opened the door for widespread speculation. The American government, Hendrik had read, had invested over 400 million dollars in developing the Model S. Whether they would be so generous with the supposedly revolutionary technology being tested at WAVE, however, was doubtful. Given the perilous financial climate, American citizens surely wouldn't allow it. Moreover, Tesla were currently concentrating on installing their supercharger network worldwide, not to say the production of the new crossover Model X.

All in all, it seemed Nils was right: for now, the blue cabrio was his best option. He could look at the other vehicles a little more closely in time. For now, he needed to stay patient.

Meanwhile, Robort had finished his call and retreated inside, still unaware of Hendrik's presence, it seemed – and certainly unaware that his conversation had just been wiretapped by a riverside office in Zurich. Hendrik looked at his watch. Almost twenty minutes had passed and still no sign of Alain. He decided to call Jaromir again. Vehicle support were there for a reason and he shouldn't feel guilty about requesting help to resolve a situation that was beyond his control.

Before he could connect, however, he realized that his own cell was ringing. Peter. He'd better pick up.

"Where the hell are you? We're supposed to be in Guessing by ten."

Good morning, Peter. No, actually I didn't sleep that well, since you ask. It was very cold last night. How was it in Eisenstadt?

"Look, sorry, I've been held up in Sopron. I'm going to need to get a lift from either Alain or Jaromir. Make your own way and I'll see you there."

"Right, see you there."

It's very kind of you to offer Peter, but really I'll be fine. There's no need for you to come all the way out here.

The silence at the end of the line was replaced by the sound of footsteps on the gravel drive. It seemed Alain had returned from whatever it was he had been doing.

"Sorry, I didn't mean to spook you. The others were all leaving early, so I took the car into Sopron to charge while you were asleep. I still haven't got the hang of this EV malarkey. And all these calculations are twice as hard in the morning," he said with a shrug. "Oh, by the way I brought you some breakfast." He threw Hendrik a couple of crescent-shaped pastries. "*Kifli,*" he said. "Hungarian yeast rolls. When in Rome and all…"

"Thanks. I'll swap you one for an energy drink." The pastries looked just like croissants. "But how far away is it? The car, I mean."

"About ten minutes maybe. So we should leave as soon as we can."

"OK, give me a minute to get my things together."

The cold, allied to the strange dream of the night before, meant Hendrik had no wish to hang around any longer than was necessary. It was time to move on. The Lonely Viking would just have to make do without company for the rest of the morning.

Sopron, which Hendrik and Alain approached on foot, was now a popular tourist destination slowly beginning to acknowledge its German-speaking culture and heritage once again. Still boasting a medieval centre, the city, formerly part of Austro-Hungarian Empire and home to one of modern-day Hungary's oldest universities, had suffered greatly at the hands of the National Socialists, and lost almost its entire Jewish population. Later it had been captured by the Soviets and become part of the People's Republic of Hungary. In 1989, the town had marked the site of the so-called Pan-European Picnic, a peace demonstration that saw the first successful border crossings of GDR citizens into the West, and helped accelerate the fall of the Berlin Wall.

If Sopron's story represented the history of twentieth century Europe, then Guessing's narrative belonged to a more modern era. Their next destination, Hendrik read online, had been one of the poorest regions in Austria in 1988. Struggling to afford its annual fossil-fuel bill, local councillors had decided that monies spent on fuel oil could remain in the local economy if the town started producing its own energy. Lacking wind, but rich in biomass thanks to the surrounding forests, residents had begun to use decomposing wood to run a small district heating system in the early nineties. By 1996, with the support of the mayor, the system had been expanded to encompass the town as a whole. In 2001, Guessing had become home to a biomass gasification plant, the first of its kind anywhere in the world.

"Today the plant produces enough energy for the entire town, while using less than half of the biomass that grows in the forests around," Hendrik read aloud.

"A number of new businesses have sprung from the development, creating not only a range of new jobs, but also annual revenues that are twice as high as the fossil fuel bill the town was once unable to afford: a tale of renewable energy success, whose model is, in turn, being re-used to make the entire district energy-self-sufficient."

"Impressive stuff," said Alain. "But I'm afraid we're going to have to give it a wide berth."

This represented a break from protocol, as theoretically their movements ought to have been dictated by the programme of the day's events. Still, rules were made to be broken. It was only a matter of time before someone chose not to "Follow the Roadbook" and in this case, they were fully justified. Besides, they needed to charge the car again.

After sending Peter a brief message to explain what was going on, Hendrik took the opportunity to get to know his chauffeur a little better. He remembered from the briefing on the first night in Eichgraben that Alain was a late replacement. For whom, he hadn't said. Given his own status, Hendrik was naturally wary of anyone who had registered late for the event. But Alain's story seemed to check out. He said he had a new clothing range coming out – sportswear, Hendrik remembered – and that they had been scheduled to do a photo shoot at Großglockner. The model had pulled out at almost exactly the same time as the person who was supposed to be driving the Bolt. When he had seen the route, Alain had decided to do the modelling himself. That, Hendrik supposed, was one of the perks of being your own boss.

Aside from learning about his business interests, Hendrik had also listened eagerly to Alain's tales of the Antarctic. The purity of the nature had made such an impression on him that he would, he said, be prepared to go back anytime. In fact, it was the time he'd spent in the South Pole that had first given him the idea for his winter clothing range. More than that, however, it had provided him with a reason to devote a part of his energies – not to say a sizeable chunk of his income – to saving the planet. That all this could be lost was senseless. It was the greatest crime humankind had ever perpetrated, and one for which only an isolated few were being brought to account.

Hendrik felt suddenly proud. One could always question the means, but for the first time he was sure that what he was doing was right. Yes, he was living a lie, and had engaged in some questionable practices, but ultimately it was only because he cared. He cared that a car manufacturer was testing the boundaries of EV development, only to lock the information away after successful testing and keep producing gasoline models. He cared that whatever progress was made would ultimately count for nothing. At some point in the future, EU legislation might outlaw this kind of industrial chicanery, but for now people like Dominik represented the only chance of doing something about it. *Only when we know what we're dealing with, can we begin to take appropriate action.* Those had been his employer's words, and Hendrik felt reassured that the process was already underway.

The drive had also established beyond any doubt that Alain's car was not the one Hendrik was looking for. True, range was not the only factor to be taken into consideration, but it seemed unlikely that an EV carrying revolutionary new technology would need to charge twice in a single morning – even if Alain freely admitted it would perform better with a different driver. However, it was precisely the Bolt's untapped potential that made Hendrik feel as though he were on an adventure.

"Forget general safety concerns. The real danger for EVs lies elsewhere," Alain said, as the latest in a series of cars honked its horn in protest at their presence on the motorway. They were travelling at fifty kilometres an hour in an effort to conserve battery power. "Angry motorists, that's your number-one problem. Some people *really* don't like being held up. I did a little research before I joined. Could be a bit of colour for your blog maybe. How's it going anyway?"

"Oh, you know. Good days and bad."

"Best to keep on an even keel. It's only a blog, after all. There are plenty more important things to be losing sleep over."

That, Hendrik knew from experience, was only too true.

"Now, isn't it about time we found somewhere to eat?"

They came off the motorway at the next turn and pulled in to a cafe that was also registered as a charging station. Unfortunately, it was out of service.

"We just drove past a Ford dealership. They've been partners with Mazda for ages. I bet they'll let us charge in their garage," Hendrik suggested.

"Good idea," Alain said, as he turned the car around.

The pair were welcomed with open arms and there was even a little surprise in store for them at the back of the dealership: an old Ford Model T, supposedly the world's first affordable automobile – and a model which, apart from a short-lived revival to mark the company's centenary in 2003, had ceased production almost eighty-five years before.

"Now *there's* a little colour for your blog!"

Strangely enough, it was true. The Ford was *red*, a far cry from the company founder's most famous quote, and had a brass radiator and headlights. It must have been an old model, as it didn't have a door for the driver. While they waited for the car to charge, Hendrik took some photos, and shot a brief film of Alain describing the chain of events that had led them to the T. Then they thanked the staff, who had also recommended a good restaurant nearby, and continued on their journey.

In the restaurant, another surprise awaited them.

"If it isn't Team SwissGermany! I'd recognize those green T-shirts anywhere," Alain greeted the unmistakeable pair. Erich, from Switzerland, was almost two heads shorter than his gangling German colleague, Peter.

"How strange," Erich replied. "C'mon, let's push these two tables together."

"What are you two doing here?" asked Peter, who had almost nothing in common with his namesake, Hendrik's colleague Peter Prohaska. "I mean, we've got an excuse. The Ampera's range is only sixty kilometres and we needed to charge."

"Actually we had a really nice morning," said Erich, a bubbly character who was going prematurely grey. "We stopped to charge in a small village somewhere between Eisenstadt and Guessing. While we were looking for some breakfast, we drove past the local fire brigade. There had been a party the night before, and the last of the stragglers were just about to leave. It was six in the morning."

"One of them was pretty loaded," grinned Peter. He really was nothing like the Peter Hendrik knew.

"But they were so helpful," Erich continued, "and really looked after us. While the car was charging, we trooped across the road to a bakery. Turned out that most of the local farmers were there – so we got to know them too. It was pretty great actually."

"And yesterday we drove past one of Austria's leading automobile associations. They didn't realize they had a charging station until we told them. Amazing, isn't it?" Peter said.

"Weird," Erich agreed. "Oh, by the way, did you know that my son was invited for a test drive with Tesla's European CEO yesterday? It was his birthday," he added with some pride.

Hendrik could have chatted to the pair for hours, but lunch had come and gone in a flash, and he and Alain needed to get back on the road to Gleisdorf. Next stop was the racing circuit. They were going to have to drive fast to make it on time – and ensure that Hendrik didn't experience the full force of his colleague's tongue.

Things were already in full swing when they reached the circuit. Nominally, it belonged to a driving school but today it would be home to the expedition's Slalom Trophy. There was a palpable sense of expectation amongst the participants as they carried out their final preparations. They didn't have long to get things right: the cars set off at two-minute intervals, beginning with the first team named on the official programme. Hendrik wasn't sure how many had already finished their lap, so he excused himself – Alain, it seemed, had missed his opportunity – and made towards Peter Prohaska, who was watching eagerly from the sidelines.

"Good of you to have joined us," Peter began, a remark that did little to set his colleague at ease.

"Sorry, we were having a few problems with the car."

"A few problems digesting your lunch, more like." The retort carried none of the venom Hendrik had been expecting. In fact, Peter was smiling. "Don't worry. Sometimes you need a little time-out. As long as you're here when it matters."

Hendrik was momentarily taken aback by this unexpected display of empathy and struggled to find the correct response.

"Thanks," he said eventually. "What can you tell me so far?"

"I think we have a good opportunity to narrow our search here." Peter was serious again, almost scholarly. He had always struck Hendrik as more theorist than field agent, and his manner suggested a love of books rather than people. "If we assume the car we're looking for is one that can go long distances, then its driver won't want to charge any more than is strictly necessary. There'd be no point in the test otherwise. If EVs are to hit the mass-market, then it's a question of reliability and endurance, not speed."

"Meaning?"

"Meaning, whoever is behind the wheel will want to replicate normal driving conditions…"

"… and not a scene from the French Connection. So, they won't take part?"

"Unlikely: they won't want to draw any attention to themselves. Far better to assume that they're taking part but not at full tilt. That they're conserving their energies, so to speak."

"So, who can we rule out?" Hendrik asked.

Peter consulted his notes. "The Chargelocator. Rafael de Mestre and Anastassyia. They're well placed to win."

"Good. That's a Tesla Roadster anyway." Hendrik was keen to show Peter that he hadn't just been eating his lunch.

"The Stromos did well."

"What about him?" Hendrik gestured towards the man who had been drinking with Alain a couple of nights before. The pair were shaking hands. The man with the receding hairline was wearing a broad grin.

"Andrej Pečjak? He's an interesting guy, actually. I was speaking to him the other night: runs courses for young mechanics back home in Slovenia – in mechatronics. It's not him, though. His company *converts* normal vehicles into EVs. It doesn't build them from scratch. His file says he barely makes any money from it. Anyway, he was definitely trying to win!"

"OK, I'll put him down as unlikely," Hendrik said.

Hendrik wondered what Andrej's connection to Alain was. Alain might have been a good ten years younger, but both clearly enjoyed a glass of wine. Was there any more to it than that? It was hard to say. While he was thinking, another car had finished, a white Peugeot iOn, covered in sponsors' stickers. Gordon and Leora, according to Hendrik's list. A good time: they had certainly been trying.

"What about the blue cabrio?" Hendrik asked.

"They were right at the start, while you were still digesting. The car's a peacock but it finished well down the list. There'll be time to check it out tonight." Then with a wry grin: "you know, considering you're the official blogger you're awfully good at keeping a low profile. How do you get away with it?"

Hendrik wasn't sure if Peter was referring to the previous night. He was just about to attempt an answer when he saw Florian bounding towards him with an expectant look in his eyes.

"Sorry. Duty calls," Hendrik said, as he took the baseball cap from Florian's head and ruffled the nine-year-old's hair. "We can play football tonight in Deutschlandsberg."

Florian didn't seem to mind and went off in search of a new playmate.

"There are a few teams we can almost certainly rule out," Peter continued. By now, Florian was playing football with a guy called

Ernst. Though more than ten years apart, the pair could easily have passed for brothers. "TWIKE and the orange SAM might be pretty low on this list," Peter said, referring to their finishing times, "but they're too unusual to have mass appeal."

"I'm not sure we can just rule them out like that. The fact that they're so unusual might work in their favour. Especially if the majority think they're some kind of side-show," Hendrik protested.

"The TWIKE can only go at eighty-five kilometres an hour. That's not enough for the mass market. As for the SAM, have a look at it. It's not big enough. How's it supposed to have room for all these new components?"

Hendrik sighed. It wasn't always easy being the junior partner. Granted, both vehicles were unlikely candidates, but he didn't want to be too hasty. He knew that the TWIKE had a range of more than 500 kilometres, and surely its top speed wasn't set in stone. The SAM, meanwhile, was built with only ten percent of the components used in a traditional vehicle. Could Peter be sure that there were no additional battery cells contained within its fibreglass body? No, was the short answer – but Hendrik had no desire to enter into an argument with his colleague at this early stage.

"How about team Just Married?" Hendrik changed the subject.

"They didn't take part."

"Funny. Martin doesn't seem the type to miss out on all this fun," Hendrik said.

"Maybe his wife's pregnant?"

"In that case, don't you think they'd have watched from the sidelines?"

"You're probably right. Whatever they were doing, I don't think we should rule them out just yet."

"And support?" Hendrik realized that would also be a good disguise. After all, if it was good enough for Peter.

"Leave them to me. I'm working on it."

At this point the pair were interrupted by Louis Palmer. The tour director announced that it was time to make for Deutschlandsberg.

There was a school event there and the children would be disappointed if participants didn't arrive on time.

Despite the name, Deutschlandsberg turned out to be a small Austrian town on the Slovenian border. By the time Hendrik arrived, there were so many children running around he could barely get out of the car. The event had been scheduled to coincide with a local school sports day. Later, the children would have the chance to take a closer look at some of the EVs, with demonstrations to increase their awareness of environmental issues and create enthusiasm for the topic of sustainable transport. As official blogger, Hendrik knew that a lot would be expected of him here. It wasn't just a question of filming and gathering material; he would also need to package it the right way.

In the event, the kids made it easy for him. They were just so thrilled to be a part of everything that their excitement was contagious. Hendrik shot a variety of scenes from the afternoon, as well as conducting an interview with Florian about his thoughts on WAVE so far. The finished product was bound to get a few hits on the expedition website and, in the hands of the right people, it would make a powerful propaganda tool.

Dinner that evening was in a series of marquees that had been constructed specially for the occasion. There were so many people around that space was at a premium. After wolfing down a steak, Hendrik was glad of the opportunity to stretch his legs while the others were still finishing their meals. Taking his rucksack and camera, he made for  the cars parked at the opposite end of the field. The blue cabrio was sandwiched between two vans and thus obscured to the naked eye.

It was the perfect chance to lift the hood and take a closer look at the battery inside. He fished a screwdriver out of his rucksack and set to work, glad that the field around him was deserted. He estimated that he had about ten minutes before participants would start filtering out of the marquees. Would it be enough time? His heart started to beat a little faster and he paused to wipe the sweat from his brow. Another glance over his shoulder. A deep breath. It was now or never.

Then, suddenly, there was a sound. Someone was nearby. Hendrik heard light breathing and the occasional footstep. He kept the hood open, anticipating that whoever it was would retrace their steps and head back towards the buffet.

But the sound persisted, the footsteps drew nearer – soft, measured, only audible in the evening quiet – and the sweat started to glisten on Hendrik's brow. For some reason, he thought of his dream that morning and felt a shiver go down his spine.

He closed the hood as quietly as he could, but his hands were sweaty and he lost hold of the screwdriver. No time to retrieve it now. He got down on his knees, as if searching for something: his glasses, perhaps, or his wallet.

"What are you doing crawling around in the dirt?"

"Jesus fucking Christ, you scared the shit out of me. What are you doing out here?" It was Peter Prohaska.

"I came to warn you. Dinner's about to finish. They'll be out in a minute. First cars are already leaving for Aibl and we're due to go with them."

"OK, we'll have to do this another time."

Peter dropped Hendrik off at the hotel in Eibiswald so that the blogger could check in and file his report before heading to Aibl. Hendrik was almost done when the shrill sound of his cell pierced the air.

"Hello?"

"Hendrik, it's Nils. What the hell's been going on down there? I've just had Dominik in the Zurich office. He was going spare, talking about how the whole event would be cancelled. Apparently, he's been listening in to Louis Palmer's phone conversations."

"What are you talking about? Can we rewind a couple of steps?

What do you mean, the event being cancelled?"

"You'd better check your inbox."

Hendrik reached for his laptop and logged into his account. He clicked on the link, took one look at the webpage and vomited all over the floor. The image of his dying sister flashed through his mind.

"Hendrik?"

"I should have trusted my instincts," Hendrik said finally, after he had gathered himself. "I knew from the start this was too good to be true."

"It's just a stupid coincidence, Hendrik. Don't worry. After he calmed down, Dominik made a few calls. Said he knew how to ensure the event wasn't cancelled. We'll still get our money."

"Our money? Are you serious? That's all you can say?"

"Relax, dude, it's not like you were responsible…"

Hendrik put the phone down before Nils could finish his sentence.

He felt sick again.

All he could think about was the screwdriver.

He couldn't stay here, not tonight.

CHAPTER EIGHT

Magali

Sunday morning – Eibiswald

The next morning Magali was sitting at the hotel breakfast table with Martin, playing happy couples. The capacity of the human body to remain in one place while the mind was somewhere completely different had never ceased to amaze her. First Eisenstadt, and now Deutschlandsberg. Magali reflected that a lot had happened already.

But she also knew that she had a role to play: one that Martin seemed to be relishing more and more each day. Just then Andrej and Jasna emerged and Martin invited them to join their table. Anyone passing outside would have assumed they were two happily married couples enjoying a holiday together.

"Coffee, I need coffee!" exclaimed Jasna, trying but failing to stifle a yawn. Even when she was tired, she seemed to have more energy than most people. "I can never get used to these early starts."

Her husband passed her a cup and poured the milk.

"It'll be nice to get a few things from home later." Jasna turned to Magali. "Are you two lovebirds coming to Bled?"

"I'm sure we'd be delighted," Martin answered. "It sounds very romantic. I've heard you can take a gondola out to the island."

"Don't forget about the Kremšnita," said Andrej.

"Kremšnita?" Martin smiled pleasantly.

"It's a Bled specialty: vanilla and custard cream cake. You *absolutely* have to try it." Jasna said. A sip of coffee and she was back to her quirky self. "You won't get it anywhere else."

"Kremšnita," Martin confirmed. "Lovely. Magali has something of a sweet tooth, don't you, dear?"

Magali hated how much he was enjoying this, how good he was at talking for her.

"Darling? You're not still thinking about last night, are you?" he said with mock concern.

Before Magali could answer, the technologist took up the thread.

"I'm sure everything's fine. There's no way Louis would have allowed the expedition to continue if there was a real problem," he said reassuringly.

But Magali knew that something wasn't quite right. And so did Martin – even if he was doing his best to hide it.

It had all started the previous evening. Some of the participants were staying in Deutschlandsberg overnight and had already left for the hotel. Andrej and Jasna, on the other hand, were about to set off for Aibl, where another event was scheduled.

Mindful that they were almost always on their tail, Martin had suggested that for once they depart *before* the technologist and his wife. After all, it wasn't as if they didn't know where they were going. Somewhat reluctantly, Magali had agreed. It was only a short drive to Aibl and they could just as easily provide protection from in front as from behind.

Within ten minutes, Magali was regretting her decision.

"Oh relax, will you? They're grown-ups. They probably just got held up at a red light." As usual, Martin had failed to acknowledge the gravity of the situation.

Andrej and Jasna were nowhere to be seen.

"Easy for you to say, Martin. You're not the one who's actually supposed to be protecting them. Oh, why did I bother listening to you in the first place?" Magali snapped.

"So now you're seeing red! And there was me thinking you were colour-blind!"

"Cut it out with your stupid wordplays. The light was amber.

Let's focus on how we're going to find them."

"Simple. We get to Aibl and then we wait."

But after almost half an hour there was still no sign.

"What do we do now?" Magali asked. By now, they had been joined by the others attending the event. It was just before nine.

"We sit tight."

"What if they had an accident? That drunken guy we saw, on foot, swaying uncontrollably by the side of the road. We almost ran him over."

"The one who looked like Hendrik?"

Just then Martin was interrupted by the sound of his cell. A text from Louis. Addressed to all participants.

WE HAVE A SITUATION THAT NEEDS TO BE RESOLVED. PLEASE WAIT FOR CONFIRMATION BEFORE DEPARTING TOMORROW.

"What does it say?" Magali asked.

"There's a situation."

"That needs to be resolved. I've just got it too."

"What the hell?"

"What is it, Martin?"

"I've just had a look online. There's an article. Breaking news. Some sort of fire in Deutschlandsberg. An electric car. Two injured."

"Shit. What else does it say?"

Martin read from his cell: "*Another nail has been driven into the coffin of the electric car industry tonight as stunned onlookers at a school charity event watched a vehicle go up in flames in Deutschlandsberg. Though details are still emerging at this point, the incident is believed to have been caused by a malfunctioning battery pack...*" A pause while he waded through more text. "The *second incident of its kind in recent months... Concerns about the general safety of electric vehicles growing by the day...* Nothing from Louis yet. Though apparently it's *inconceivable* that WAVE should continue." Martin raised his eyebrows quizzically: never a good sign. "And there's a little footnote: *a further catastrophe was only narrowly avoided when a fire engine arriving on the scene collided with a nine-year-old girl.* Fortunately she escaped with a broken leg. Bystanders say it was a minor miracle she survived."

"Passenger and driver?"

"Hospital for further tests."

"It doesn't say who?"

"Doesn't say who or which car."

"I'm calling Frank."

"OK. Hospital?"

"The hotel's closer. Maybe they checked in first."

There was no point going to the hospital until they had names. The hotel was in Eibiswald, about a mile and a half from Aibl. Magali felt her heart beating quicker and quicker as they drove. She was not normally given to panic but right now she couldn't help feeling rattled. First the incident with the cables in Eisenstadt. Now this. How often did lightning strike twice?

She called Frank and told him what happened. He said he would use his contacts in the local police to see what he could find out. He didn't sound amused. They should never have let Andrej out of their sight in the first place.

When they reached the hotel, the car park was deserted. Magali thumped the steering wheel in frustration. Once. Twice. Three times. Then came another surge of panic. Enough to make her feel as though her heart would jump out from under her skin.

"Fucking do something!" she rounded on Martin. Her compa nion was frantically leafing through the Roadbook, searching for Magali didn't know what.

"There's another hotel," he said at last. "Gasthof Hasewend. It must be just opposite."

Magali had already jumped out of the car and was sprinting towards the courtyard on the other side of the road. Martin followed. The technologist's car was there and the door on the driver's side was open; it looked like Andrej had just popped into the hotel for a minute. Jasna was sitting in the passenger seat.

"Why don't you go and see what's happening?" Magali said, taking a step back. "You're Intelligence, after all." Her sense of humour was showing signs of recovery. "And whatever you do, don't look relieved to see them."

She watched Martin move towards the car as the technologist emerged from the building. The latter put his hands through his hair, as if disturbed by whatever he had just seen, before remembering himself and offering Martin a perfunctory hello. At this point a taxi came to a halt in front of the hotel, deposited a frustrated-looking Peter Prohaska outside the entrance and disappeared into the night.

By now Martin and Andrej had been speaking for several minutes. Martin was all nods and smiles, while Andrej was more serious, bordering on withdrawn. Their exchange came to an abrupt end when the technologist gave an exaggerated shrug of the shoulders. Perhaps they had become aware of the third party lurking in the shadows. For whatever reason, Peter had chosen to remain outside.

"He didn't look too pleased," Magali said, as they returned to their car.

"Talk about sticking your nose into other people's business," Martin said with more than a hint of annoyance. Peter had only just gone into the hotel.

"Don't worry about him. So, what did Andrej say?"

"It *was* the video blogger. Hendrik…" Martin had managed to compose himself. "They found him wandering around by the side of the road. Andrej's just taken him up to his room. Says he doesn't know what's wrong. Couldn't get much sense out of him."

"He probably just needs a good night's sleep," Magali ventured. "Things always look better in the morning. Most things, anyway," she grinned mischievously at Martin. "What did you tell them?"

"I said we thought we'd seen Hendrik too and decided to check. They're staying in the same hotel as us tonight."

"OK, we'll let them check in and then follow them to Aibl. If it's all the same to you, I think we'll stay behind them this time."

"You know that we have to leave the car in Aibl overnight to charge?" Martin said, before putting on his sad face. "Perhaps we'll have to spend the night apart…"

"Are you offering to stay in the car park? Actually, that doesn't sound too bad. But seriously, no. We're newlyweds. Team Just Married. We can't sleep apart. Besides, we have to stay with Andrej. Frank's asked Vivien from support to keep an eye on the car."

"What do you know about him? This Vivien?" Was there a trace of jealously in Martin's voice?

"He's a good man. I've worked with him before. Very conscientious."

There was no harm in letting know Martin she was a fan of the young Swiss.

"We're only to make contact with him in the event of an emergency," she added. "Frank made that very clear."

"So what's this?"

"As far as Frank knows, it's still an unhappy coincidence."

Back at the breakfast table the next morning, Martin was still in full husband mode. Had he really just called her "sugar-pie"?

Then, Manfred and Tamara also entered the hotel dining room.

"Good morning. Did you sleep OK?" Jasna asked. "Why don't you pull up a couple of chairs?" She turned to Magali. "Their hotel room was taken when they arrived last night."

"Andrej and Jasna were kind enough to let us sleep on their sofa," Manfred said. "Luckily, the room was big enough for all four of us."

Magali gazed across at Martin. He looked just as surprised as she did. Granted, it hadn't been Andrej's car that had gone up in flames. But could they really be sure that last night was a coincidence? And now this?

Two participants slipping into Andrej and Jasna's room unnoticed?

"Is everything OK, darling?" Martin asked solicitously. "I think it's wonderful that we're all getting on so well."

Magali nodded. She had understood. For all his quips Martin was a good agent: the sort of man who came through in a tight spot. Despite his initial surprise, he clearly wasn't worried about Manfred and Tamara.

Magali looked at her watch. Frank was due to call any minute now with details about last night. The waiting game. Always the same. Part of you longed for some action; the rest dreaded the call to arms.

One way or another she would soon know.

She looked across at Martin. He was talking to Jasna about Thailand. The Slovenians, it seemed, had recently spent time there climbing: a useful piece of information, to be stored away for future reference. Anything to help them cultivate a relationship with the pair.

Meanwhile, the plates were cleared. Manfred and Tamara began to disperse. Suddenly the clock on the wall provided the only sound. Tick. Tock. Tick. Tock.

Then, at last, the phone.

"My mother," she said, as she excused herself from the remainder of the group.

"Make sure you say hello!" Martin called behind her.

"Frank. Any news?" There was an edge to Magali's voice. She felt a surge of adrenaline pass through her body.

"I've spoken to the local police," Frank said calmly, deliberately. As though there were a third option after fight and flight. Stay cool. Stand your ground. Think.

"And?"

"The report is inconclusive; but the drivers have been most helpful."

"The drivers? I thought they were in hospital?"

"Yes, as a precaution. They made statements to the police beforehand. Olaf and Stephan are doing fine."

"So it *was* the blue cabrio?"

"Yes, though it wasn't mentioned in the article."

"Something's not quite right here, Frank."

"Funny, that's just what I've been thinking. You see, the police are certain that the accident was caused by a sharp object on the road. But the drivers deny it. They say they didn't hit anything. They say that somewhere between the event and the hotel, the car simply caught fire. The pair were breathalyzed at the scene: neither of them had been drinking; and both were in full control of their faculties. It seems they exited the vehicle and then calmly alerted the fire brigade before calling the tour director."

"But an EV doesn't just catch fire. The cabrio couldn't have been overheated and it certainly wasn't fully charged. They must have hit a sharp object."

"Well, the police didn't find anything on the scene. More importantly, the base of the vehicle was intact."

"Meaning?"

"Meaning the drivers are almost certainly telling the truth. Whatever caused the fire was already *inside* the car."

"So what was it?"

"I'm afraid there is a limit to police goodwill. They weren't prepared to release all details just yet. Even to a security agency such as ourselves."

By now Martin had joined her, leaving Andrej and Jasna to finish their coffee. He was trying to say something.

"For Christ's sake, what is it?"

"The article. Ask him about the article."

Magali returned to her previous conversation.

"There was an article online within forty-five minutes. OK, you expect a rush job with a local paper, but the story was picked up pretty quickly by a major corporation. Doesn't that seem strange to you? Wouldn't an international paper normally check they had their facts straight before going on the offensive?"

"Not necessarily. The major corporations all have contacts in the police. Maybe someone had an axe to grind. Electric vehicles are a pretty emotive topic."

"OK. So, where do we go from here?"

Frank took his time to respond. Magali imagined him weighing the different options in his mind: a tightrope walker performing a delicate balancing act. One false move and he would slip and fall.

"Louis Palmer may be satisfied that last night was an accident. But I'm not. There's still no logical explanation for what happened. Supposing it was sabotage? Then there's someone out there who's after the technology."

"And we can count ourselves lucky they picked the wrong car."

"Right."

Magali knew what was coming: the call to arms.

"I want you to stay on high alert," Frank confirmed. "At least until we know more. I'll keep working on the police. I've got a few friends there. Maybe they'll be able to tell us more." A pause. A crackle down the line. "Whatever happens, make sure the technologist is safe. And tell Martin it's time he did a little sniffing around."

Magali smiled. Anything to prevent him from playing the dutiful husband.

CHAPTER NINE

Alain

Sunday morning – Eibiswald – Bled

As Alain exited the hotel and headed for the bus stop on the other side of the road, he remarked on how fresh the participants waiting there looked. Three sets of couples – there really were a lot of them at WAVE – as well as Hendrik, who, on closer inspection, didn't appear quite so bushy-eyed. He had probably had a rough night, sitting up waiting to hear exactly what had happened so that he didn't get into any trouble with his blog.

Alain had tried to do a little digging of his own at first but ran into a brick wall when he called the tour director. For whatever reason, Louis was determined not to release any information, even though most of the story had appeared online within an hour. Alain hadn't actually read it – the internet on his mobile had stopped working – but enough details had emerged over the course of the evening to convince him that Andrej was not in any immediate danger.

That said, emotions had definitely been running high. The vast majority of the group were incensed by what they perceived to be an orchestrated media campaign aimed at discrediting the electric vehicle industry; and several people had commented on the fact that if the car *hadn't* been an EV, there would almost certainly have been a fatality.

"Not that they'd have reported *that*," someone else had said. "It's only news if an EV goes up in flames."

By that stage, a certain amount of wine had been consumed and more than one team had morosely predicted the end of the expedition. They had been wrong, of course. A second text that morning had confirmed it. Whether this latest missive had been met with joy unconfined was a moot point. Most probably felt like Alain: glad that the expedition would continue – naturally – but still temporarily blunted by the night before.

"Did you get lost on the way to bed?" Andrej asked as Alain took his seat beside him at the bus stop. They were waiting for a taxi but had taken temporary shelter from the drizzle.

"What time did you leave?" Alain asked.

"Before you obviously," Martin joked.

"People were saying the end was nigh," Alain said dramatically.

"Did you hear about the girl? A lucky escape by all accounts," Jasna said. "Apparently the drivers are fine too. Though still a little shocked I'd wager."

"Luckily, I've got the perfect antidote to last night. How would you like to come and see my institute in Bled?" Andrej asked.

Alain thought about it for a moment. You could tell a lot about a person by where they worked. A company took after its founder in the same way a dog came to resemble its owner. Alain was interested to see Andrej's operation at close quarters. He nodded his assent. "Does the offer extend to our blogging friend?" he asked. "He looks even worse than me." Then to Hendrik: "And there was me thinking I'd had a late night…"

Before he could finish, however, Andrej shot him a look. Stop, it said. Now's not the time. Alain knew better than to kick a man when he was down.

"Why doesn't he come with us?" he whispered to the technologist. "I can take him." Then even quieter: "Try and see what the matter is."

"Hear that, Hendrik?" Andrej patted the blogger's thigh. "Fancy a trip to Bled?"

The response was muted, but there was enough to indicate consent.

"Well, that's settled then. I'll see if anyone else wants to come once we get to Aibl."

At Aibl, Alain was greeted by the sight of one of the support crew folding away a camp bed. Had the young man really spent the whole night guarding the cars? If so, it could only be one of Frank's agents. Or had Louis hired someone following the incident in Eisenstadt?

Alain glanced quickly at the list of participants to see if he could find a name.

"Now *that* is dedication to the job," he said eventually. "Thanks, Vivien."

"My pleasure," the latter responded, raising his hand in acknowledgement. Alain couldn't quite place the accent. He sounded like Frank.

"Dedication to the job?" another male voice. Martin this time. "I don't know. It looks quite *romantic* to me. The great outdoors, with only the stars – and each other – for company." He looked over at his wife.

Was that a roll of the eyes? Alain couldn't be sure. He guessed there were better ways to spend your honeymoon.

As they waited in the parking lot, the news quickly spread that Stephan and Olaf were OK, but would be taking no further part in the expedition.

There followed a quick group photo to commemorate the expedition's thousandth Facebook 'like' and then they were ready to go.

The participants were splitting again, with the majority making their way to St Veit, where they would attend an energy exhibition and undertake a guided tour. Only a select band would visit Andrej's hometown of Bled. Referring to the team list, Alain made a mental note of those in the second, smaller category. Aside from Jaromir, the support, there was Andrej and Jasna, Martin and Magali, Manfred and Tamara, as well as a young blond-haired man whom Alain hadn't met before: a shy geologist who had introduced himself as Jochen. Alain and Hendrik would make up the final car.

The presence of the same two couples from the bus stop was interesting. Clearly Jean-Pierre and Monika, the Swiss pairing Alain had seen on the first evening, weren't the agents he had hired – otherwise they would be making the journey too. Alain breathed a rather uncharitable sigh of relief before resolving to keep an eye on Manfred and Tamara and the newlyweds. Unless Frank had been misleading him, it had to be one of them.

Soon after departing for Bled in convoy, however, Alain realized that he would have his work cut out. How could he keep an eye on those in the other cars, when his *own* passenger was behaving so strangely? This was not the chatty, relaxed young man of the day before. Yesterday, Hendrik had been asking questions: about Alain's business, about his expeditions, about the car he was driving. Today, he hadn't even bothered to get in the passenger seat, hadn't even made the effort to pretend he was interested. Instead he was curled up in the back, sleeping off whatever demons had visited him in the night. He hadn't even acknowledged Florian when he had tried to say goodbye.

Every now and then, Alain would check on Hendrik in the mirror. All the colour of the previous day seemed to have drained from his face. Even in rest he looked pallid, exhausted. Alain wondered what on earth could have happened to induce this change. He was still none the wiser when the cars pulled up, soundlessly, at a cemetery. They had crossed into Slovenia via the Seebergsattel, an Alpine pass that offered a glorious panoramic view of the

Kamnik mountain range, and driven down into the Jezersko valley. The landscape had been breath-taking, with a smattering of grey clouds on hand to obscure the vertiginous peaks and lend the scene an air of menace. Real beauty always brought with it a sense of foreboding; for a second Alain wondered what terrible secrets the valley contained. Then he gazed once more at Hendrik, his expensive equipment sleeping peacefully alongside him.

The cemetery would scarcely have improved his mood. Set in the valley and enclosed on all sides by the mountain range that towered above it, it was a wonderful, peaceful spot, populated by the stones of those to whom eternal rest had already been granted. There was a solemnity to the participants as they ventured forth to pay their respects; a sense that whatever had transpired in Deutschlandsberg could easily have led to this, or a scene just like it.

Upon returning to the car, Alain was pleased to discover that Hendrik's own rest had been temporary in nature. He was sitting up now, yawning and stretching, rubbing the sleep from his eyes.

"Feeling better?"

But once again the answer was so quiet as to be almost inaudible.

Not even the technologist's institute could bring Hendrik out of his shell. Alain had to admit it wasn't quite what he had expected either. He had been joined by Manfred and Tamara, while Martin and Magali remained outside.

"What are those?" Manfred asked, pointing to a set of battery modules that Andrej was in the process of fitting to one of the vehicles on display. Elsewhere, spare parts were strewn across a table surface; while the trophies Andrej had won in Monte Carlo were displayed in the corner.

"They're special high-density cells," Andrej replied. "I get them from a company in South Korea, a family business. We've worked together for a long time. Actually they sponsored me in Monte Carlo. Are you interested in batteries?"

"It was one of the focal points of my master's degree," Manfred said. "But the subject didn't really grab me until I started driving EVs."

"And now he wants to know everything about them," Tamara added, as she took a photo of the pair.

Alain wondered whether an agent would take such an obvious interest in their client. Wouldn't they choose to remain in the background, like Martin and Magali? In truth, either was possible; for the time being it wasn't worth worrying about.

In the meantime, he had worked out what it was about the institute that was different. It was the light. This was no dingy garage filled with the smell of oil and cigarette smoke, but something altogether more pristine. The walls were painted white, and the light was reflecting off the hood of one of the vehicles on display: a converted Beetle cabrio that could easily have been as old as Alain himself.

"Jasna will take the Beetle down to the lake when we're finished here," Andrej said. He must have noticed that Alain was admiring it. "Our daughter needs it to get home later. We'll park it by the shore – the tourists will love it!"

The tour continued. In the adjoining room there was a mini-lecture hall for students of mechatronics, which had obviously been developed by Andrej himself. Here, Alain had discovered, aspiring technologists were taught the rudiments of electric vehicle conversion. Given the amount of CO_2 produced in manufacturing traditional gasoline models, it made no sense to simply destroy them when they were no longer deemed to be of use. Better to convert them: to use what was already available instead of starting again from scratch.

Upon closer inspection, Alain realized that the institute was directly attached to the technologist's house. In one corner, he spied a flight of stairs that led up to the rest of the property, the very same route, indeed, that Jasna had taken moments before. And so, little by little, a picture was emerging. Andrej ran a modest, homely enterprise with an eye for the unorthodox and an ear pricked towards the future. The conflation of work and living space, meanwhile, told Alain how dear the cause was to his heart. EVs were part of him, an extension of his personality, just as the institute was an extension of his home.

Manfred and Tamara were clearly just as thrilled by what they had seen.

In fact, the only sore point was Hendrik. He hadn't shown the slightest bit of interest in the tour, preferring instead to mope from room to room like an overgrown child. Not even the items in Andrej's workshop, with which, thanks to his camera lens, he could have communed at a point of remove,  had stirred him from his apathy. Alain sighed. He was beginning to lose patience with the boy. But what could he do? He had no desire to subject him to a public dressing down. That was bound to make matters worse. Perhaps a word in private would help?In the end, he decided it was best to wait and see whether the blogger's mood would improve over the course of the afternoon. Perhaps the astonishing natural beauty of Bled, the "image of paradise", as the great Slovene Romantic poet France Prešeren had once described it, would reinvigorate him and force him out of his shell.

As they arrived at the esplanade, Alain realized just how smoothly everything had run up until now. The old Czech guy from support was already in place and had soon connected the vehicles to the distribution board so that they could charge. He was a seasoned campaigner, Jaromir, but he clearly took his job seriously. His battered little white Peugeot was almost bursting under the weight of all the different equipment it was obliged to carry. He was currently helping Jochen charge his orange Think, hoping no doubt to avoid a repeat of the incident in Eisenstadt, when a system malfunction had left a number of cars unable to draw on the energy supply.

Alain glanced at the Roadbook. It was some 150 kilometres from Aibl, where the cars had last charged, to Bled, and a decent portion of it had been uphill. He might have been a novice when it came to EVs, but he knew that they could only recuperate energy when travelling downhill. If they were to make it as far as Weissensee, their final port of call that day, it was essential – with the exception of Andrej – that they charged here.

After briefly stretching their legs, the group had been welcomed by a party that included a representative from the local tourist board, as well as the town mayor. The latter, a bespectacled middle-aged man named Janez Fajfar, had excused himself from lunch as he had an important meeting to attend. In addition to his official duties, he was also a patron of the Moro Foundation, which helped provide financial relief for foreign nationals studying in Slovenia.

A few minutes later, everyone was safely ensconced on the terrace at the Park Hotel, a popular local destination that had gained renown thanks to the work of its celebrated pastry chefs. Eva Štravs, the tourist rep, was speaking. Her hair had been rendered a wonderful shade of auburn by the afternoon sun. It had turned into a glorious day.

"In some ways, the last fifty or sixty years have seen life in Bled change beyond all recognition. Even those of us who are too young to remember its break-up," a glance at Hendrik, by some distance the youngest member of the group, "will have some concept of the former Yugoslavia, a multi-national state formed in the aftermath of the Second World War, which comprised six Socialist Republics and two Autonomous Socialist Provinces and was thus home to an immensely diverse population."

Alain gazed around the table. Of the dozen or so who had made the trip, only Jaromir seemed to be momentarily uninterested. But then, having grown up in the former Czechoslovakia, it was safe to assume he was no stranger to Soviet satellite states. Eva was unperturbed: "Divisions occurred along national, religious, and linguistic lines, and each of Yugoslavia's various members – Slovenia, of course, included – had its own constitution, as well as its own parliament and political leaders.

"Overseeing everything was Yugoslav President for Life Josip Broz Tito, whose summer residence, just opposite Bled Island, is now one of the region's most popular luxury tourist hotels." The group looked across the lake to the island, and from there tried to work out exactly where the former leader's mansion was situated. "Yugoslav communism was a brand apart from that practised in the Soviet bloc under Stalin; in fact, having adopted a neutral policy during the Cold War, Yugoslavia became the first communist country to open all its borders to foreign visitors in the late 1960s. But don't be fooled. Tourists have always visited Slovenia, and Bled in particular: a phenomenon that pre-dates the formation of the Socialist Federal Republic of Yugoslavia by a century or more."

As if to emphasize what Eva had just been saying, Alain suddenly became aware of a horse and cart in the background, a curiously old-fashioned addition to a scene that also contained the latest in electric vehicle technology.

A waitress approached their table, a student probably, earning a little money to fund some great adventure later in the summer. Perhaps she had benefited from the Moro Foundation. Alain couldn't tell where she was from. At any rate, she looked slightly apprehensive at the prospect of remembering so many different orders.

"Why don't we make things easy for the young lady," Andrej took over. "Is there anyone who does *not* want to try the regional specialty?"

The group remained silent. They had clearly been looking forward to a much-needed sugar hit. Driving all day was a tiring business.

"So, Kremšnitas all round?"

"Minus one."

Alain turned to see where the voice had come, even though he already knew.

"Hendrik, are you sure? You might not get another chance."

117

"Sorry, I'm not hungry."

It was the most he had said all morning. Alain checked to see if there had been any discernible change in the blogger's colour. He was still very pale. At least he seemed willing to make a basic social effort, Alain thought to himself. Better he was sitting amongst people than sleeping in the car. Perhaps the arrival of the vanilla cream cake would reawaken his somnolent appetite.

While he waited, Alain took the opportunity to reflect once more on his staggeringly beautiful surroundings. It was not hard to see why Bled had become such an attractive tourist destination. Quite apart from the mild year-round climate, there was also the small matter of Bled's stunning geographical location. Situated alongside a glacial lake, which appeared almost impossibly blue in the early-afternoon sunlight and was itself overlooked by a medieval castle on the north shore, the town was also home to Slovenia's only natural island: the site of a pilgrimage church whose bell tower visitors would ring for luck once they had successfully ascended the ninety-nine stone steps leading up to it.

"So, you can take a boat out there?" The question, from Martin, was utterly superfluous. There was someone on the water right now.

"What kind of boat is it? I haven't seen one of them before." Tamara asked.

"We call it a *pletna*. It's a flat-bottomed boat, a bit like a gondola." Eva responded.

"Only this is better than Venice. Much more romantic," Manfred squeezed his partner's hand.

"Maybe we should renew our vows, darling," Martin said. For the second time that day, Alain sensed there was a little tension between the newlyweds.

"Renew them? But we've only just got married!" Magali exclaimed.

"You'll have to be quick," Eva chipped in good-naturedly. "It's tradition for the groom to carry the bride up the stairs."

"And *that*," even Jochen, who had thus far been a silent presence, was getting involved, "is never going to happen. Have you seen what we're about to eat?"

The picture of the vanilla cream cake did not suggest it was part of a sportsman's diet.

While they waited for their order to arrive, they were re-joined by the mayor, who had returned early from his meeting.

"Of course there is more to Bled than vanilla cream cake," he said, perhaps sensing that the group would soon be all too focused on eating. "

"How many inhabitants does Bled have?" Jochen asked.

"Around 8,000. Though many people come to visit, especially to hike in the Triglav National Park."

"That's true. Jasna and I go ice-climbing there in the winter."

"Most Slovenian organizations abroad are named either after Bled or Triglav," Janez Fajfar continued. "But despite its fairy-tale appearance, Bled has not always been blessed with good fortune. The suicide rate here is some thirty times the murder rate. Why that should be the case, I'm afraid I cannot say. Perhaps there are historical reasons. For my part, I have always felt tremendously lucky. Back when I was a student, Tito's policies ensured that a Yugoslav passport was a highly desirable commodity. It meant we were granted access to the West. That was almost unheard of in the communist era."

At this point, the mayor was interrupted by the appearance of the waitress. She had enlisted the help of a colleague to help bring the cakes over to the table. Alain had to admit that they looked superb. There was something wonderful about food that had been so lovingly prepared: the vanilla cream painstakingly measured so that it came to exactly double that of the whipped cream on top, both elements then sandwiched between crusts that had been oven-baked to perfection. There was even a mathematical precision to the sprinkling of the icing sugar. And the taste… heaven in a mouthful. Alain was immediately overcome by a sensation of pure, innocent pleasure. Nor was he alone in this.

"Ten million sales!" Jaromir exclaimed. Some of the mixture had become lodged in his moustache.

"And who's to say there won't be ten million more?", Jochen said.

Magali, meanwhile, was in raptures. "I think that might be better than sex," she said, looking pointedly over at her new husband.

Manfred and Tamara started to giggle. Martin, Alain noted with some surprise, was not in the least upset. In fact, he was laughing along with the others.

"Do you mind if I have the keys to the car?" Hendrik asked suddenly. Having not ordered a cake, he had found himself excluded from the conversation.

"Sure," Alain replied, slightly taken aback by the request. Hendrik still didn't look the picture of health.

"What do you need them for anyway?"

"My camera. I thought I might have a little wander round. Maybe take some photos for the blog."

Alain was in no position to refuse him. After glancing over towards Andrej to make sure he had taken in the latest development, he tossed Hendrik the keys.

"Thanks," Hendrik said, predictably fumbling the catch.

"Forgive me if I don't join you." Alain motioned towards his stomach. "It's just that I might need to stay here for a while…"

It didn't look as though the other members of the group would be ready to move for some time either.

"This is like a spa break," said Tamara eventually.

"A spa break with cake. Now, who wants to share another Kremšnita?" The chances of Martin renewing his wedding vows had just gone from slim to none.

Alain wasn't sure when he had first become aware that Hendrik had been away rather longer than expected. They were such a large group – and his companion such a quiet presence – that he had barely noticed his failure to return. To add to the confusion, several other people had come and gone in the meantime. The mayor had returned to his office; while Jochen had gone with Jaromir to check on the progress of his EV, which, along with the others, was charging in the car park below.

"Where's Hendrik?" Alain asked once the remainder of the group had retired to the car park for a group photo. "Did you see him?"

Jaromir shook his head; Jochen hadn't seen anything either.

"He's been so quiet all day," Tamara said.

"He's got my car keys. Wait, I'll give him a call," Alain removed his cell from his trouser pocket. There was no response.

"Something's not right," Andrej said. "We should go and look for him."

"Wait a minute. He might call back."

Alain had no reason to suppose that Murphy's law didn't apply in Slovenia. He didn't want to send out a search party, only to discover that Hendrik had been in the gents' all along.

After a few minutes, Alain tried him again. There was still no response.

"We need to do something, Alain," Andrej said. "Let's make use of the Beetle and divide our resources."

Alain was beginning to feel ever so slightly nervous.

"He went to get his camera. Where are the best photo spots around here?"

"Take your pick. Still, probably the castle. But..." the technologist's voice trailed off.

"But what?"

Alain found himself wondering what had happened the night before. Did Andrej know something he wasn't willing to share?

"But what, Andrej?"

"You heard what the mayor said."

It took a moment for the information to sink in.

"You don't mean?" The notion was so absurd Alain almost emitted a nervous laugh. But then he was forced to admit that he barely knew Hendrik. More to the point, he had no idea why anyone would want to take their own live. Was it the result of a string of setbacks: the drip, drip effect of life's failures, culminating in a desperate act of defiance? Or something more spontaneous: a split-second decision, taken in ignorance of its consequences?

Clearly Andrej didn't know either, and it was the first time Alain had seen anything remotely like panic spread across his normally relaxed features.

In fact, the whole group was tense.

"I'll call the castle and make sure they let you in," Eva said.

Then she disappeared with Jochen to search the area around the lake. Manfred and Tamara said they'd concentrate on the esplanade. Meanwhile, Jasna would join Martin and look in the town itself. Magali offered to remain in the car park in case Hendrik turned up there; while Jaromir took the spa gardens.

Alain and Andrej jumped into the Beetle, before heading up towards the castle. It was a short ride and the journey passed in silence.

Upon arrival, Alain was dismayed to discover that the structure was spread across two floors. A series of attractions had made it a popular tourist destination. There was a printing press, a wine cellar, even a forge. Hendrik could have been anywhere.

"You take the lower courtyard," Alain said, as he made his way up the stairs to the terrace overlooking the lake.

On the upper floor, a crowd of people were admiring the glorious view. Alain could see Bled Island and Tito's villa; further in the distance he could just make out the Julian Alps. But there was no time for that now. He ducked and weaved his way through the masses: members of tour parties, backpackers, families on holiday. Everyone had a camera; and all Alain could hear was the clicking of lenses, the various entreaties to smile. But Hendrik was still nowhere to be seen.

Upon reaching the edge of the terrace, Alain inhaled deeply. It was a good drop down to the lake and the jagged rock face would ensure that no-one survived the fall. He glanced down at the lake below. No sign of anything untoward. He breathed a sigh of relief. If anything had happened, the castle would have been closed by now, the tourists long since ejected.

That meant Hendrik had to be somewhere else. Perhaps he had already emerged at the car park down by the restaurant, having lost track of time, oblivious to the panic his disappearance had created. Perhaps, Alain thought, he was finally tucking into a vanilla cream cake, having regained his appetite along with the colour in his cheeks.

Then all of a sudden, he saw it. No more than a shape at first, nestled in amongst the castle foliage. Drawing closer, its form was unmistakeable, but even as he held it in his hands Alain was struggling to comprehend what it meant. There was no question that it was Hendrik's camera: Alain recognized it from the car. But what was it doing here?

Alain took a moment to think things through. He needed to find Andrej. To compare notes. Maybe the technologist had been more successful.

He checked his cell phone. No word from anyone in the town below.

Just then Andrej emerged at the top of the stairs and, seeing Alain, gave a shrug of the shoulders.

"No sign?"

Before the technologist could reply, however, Alain realized his mistake. In amongst all the commotion, he had somehow missed the chapel. It was in the upper courtyard, right in front of his eyes; and there was nothing to suggest it wasn't open to the public. He motioned for Andrej to follow.

The chapel was the most precariously placed of all the preserved buildings: east-facing and perched on the very edge of the castle rock. Inside, it was poorly lit and Alain's eyes took some time to adjust. There was an altar, overlooked by frescoes on either side depicting a king and queen. A group of people appeared to be crowded around something.

Or was it someone? Suddenly, Alain was reminded of a scene from his own childhood when, walking in the local Botanical Gardens, he had become separated from his parents and, after a frantic initial search, decided that there was nothing to do but sit down and cry. Eventually he had been found. His parents had been alerted by a group of concerned onlookers who had encircled Alain as he wept quietly to himself. The only difference was that Alain had been no more than three or four at the time, whereas the figure hunched in on himself, hands covering his face and emitting the occasional cry of anguish, was clearly some two decades older.

"Hendrik, there you are. What on earth's the matter?" Andrej had forced his way through the crowd.

The response was instantaneous and Alain couldn't help feel emotional as he watched the scene being played out in front of him. The younger man had risen unsteadily to his feet and almost fallen into the arms of the technologist, a distressed son finding comfort in the embrace of his father. For a time nothing was said between the pair, and the silence was punctuated only by the sound of Hendrik's convulsive sobbing. In the meantime the crowd had dispersed, either because they wanted to give the scene's main actors some privacy, or, more likely, because they found the sight of a grown man weeping on his friend's shoulder distasteful in some way.

A few minutes later, Alain and the technologist had managed to lead Hendrik back out into the upper courtyard. Andrej, a word of comfort giving way to the occasional gentle question, was doing his best to get to the heart of the matter. In between the sobs, Hendrik was making little or no sense.

"I don't understand what you're saying, Hendrik," said the technologist. His voice was gentle but Alain could detect the first hints of exasperation. "It was a freak accident. There's no way that you or any of the other participants are responsible for the fire in Deutschlandsberg."

"But I shouldn't have been looking at it so closely." A heave. "Someone could have died."

"But they didn't. A girl broke her leg. Hendrik, you're not making any sense," Andrej continued.

The technologist signalled for Alain to join him for a moment in private. They left Hendrik perched on a wall, alone with his thoughts.

"Does any of this mean anything to you?" Andrej asked.

"He's a sensitive boy. The only thing I can think of is that he's been shaken by the girl. She's the same age as Florian," Alain replied. "As for the fire, he was on his way to Aibl when it happened. He's not thinking straight."

"So, what do we do? Are we agreed that he's in no fit state to carry on?"

"Let's just concentrate on getting him back down to the parking lot for now. We can decide the rest later."

Confab over, the pair returned to the younger man. Alain was glad to see that he had calmed down somewhat, but in principle he agreed with the technologist: there was no way Hendrik should be allowed to continue.

CHAPTER TEN

Magali

Sunday afternoon – Bled

"Look, all I'm saying is he was drunk last night and disappeared while we were having lunch today," Magali had taken up position on a hill overlooking the vehicles. She was talking to Frank.

"And there's no sign?" Frank said.

"Not from our end, no," Magali responded.

"How long has he been gone?"

"More than two hours. We were supposed to leave at three."

"What about the technologist?"

"He went up to castle to look for him with the guy driving the red Mazda." Then, as if she had anticipated her superior's objection: "I've got the technology covered here. Martin's with Jasna."

"You're supposed to be watching the technologist as well. Without him, there'll be no technology."

Magali sensed that Frank, for once, had got out on the wrong side of bed.

"I did the best I could under the circumstances. If I'd gone after him, there'd have been no-one to watch the car," she defended her decision even though she knew that Frank was right. Agents were paid to make decisions under pressure. She should have gone with Andrej; and Martin should have stayed with the car. But everything had happened so quickly...

"So, you want some information?" Frank continued. "On Hendrik?"

"Anything you can find. We know almost nothing about him."

"OK, I'll call you back," Frank promised.

In the meantime, all Magali could do was wait. She didn't imagine for a moment that Alain would harm the technologist, but she ought to have been there to make sure. In the distance she could see Manfred and Tamara waving at her. There was still no sign of Hendrik.

Half an hour later, Martin wheeled back into view on the esplanade. He jumped out of his car and started running towards her. He must have found something. Just then, Magali's cell phone beeped. It was a message from Alain. Hendrik had been found and would be down from the castle shortly. There was no further information about his condition.

Magali took a deep breath and composed herself before pressing redial.

"Frank. We've found him."

"A split-second is all it takes for an operation to go wrong. You should have gone with him. What if it had been a trap?"

Magali fell silent. If it had been a trap, then she and Martin would no longer be in a job.

"It was a calculated risk," she said eventually. Frank was right. She didn't know Alain – even if she somehow felt that she could trust him.

"Well, then it's lucky you're good at maths. Hendrik's family was killed in a car accident six years ago. Three fatalities, including a younger sister. It's just possible yesterday's events triggered some sort of reaction."

"I'll ask Andrej where the nearest hospital is."

"No. At least, not yet. There's something not quite right here. I made a few calls, checked a few records. Hendrik was a long-term resident in the Zurich Savoy before joining up with the expedition."

"So? His parents died. He probably came into some money."

"Perhaps. Only, he didn't pay for it. He didn't pay for anything during his stay. Food, drink, accommodation. You name it. He got it for free."

"What are you saying, Frank?"

"I'm saying, what was he doing there? Louis Palmer isn't working for any major companies. He's doing this alone. Sure, he wants to increase the profile of EVs and he needs help to publicize things. But there's no way he'd pay for a blogger to do anything *before* the expedition."

"You mean that Hendrik has a benefactor?"

"Seems that way. I've got two agents on the ground in Bled. People we've worked with for a few years now. They'll take him somewhere safe and question him, maybe get him a doctor if he needs one. The official line is he needs medical treatment."

"OK. How will we know who the agents are?"

"Don't worry about that," said Frank.

Magali walked over towards Martin and embraced him, taking the opportunity to update him on the situation.

"Looks like someone was missed," Jochen grinned. He and Eva had just returned from the lake.

"I always worry when Martin's away," Magali said. "A friend of mine lost her husband and two kids in a car accident. They'd only popped down to the shops. Whenever she hears about something like that now, she just freaks out." Suddenly an idea formed in her mind. "Maybe something similar happened to Hendrik?"

Magali hoped her little lie would set the others thinking, while they waited for Andrej and Alain to return.

Just then someone's cell rang and Magali looked across to see Eva take a call. She knew enough about DISECUPRO to work out what it meant. So, Eva was an agent as well. Somehow Magali wasn't surprised. At the very least, a tourist rep would have a good idea of who was entering and leaving the country. She watched Eva coolly take in whatever instructions she had been given and slide her cell back into her jeans pocket.

As she did so, Magali couldn't help but feel a little jealous. It was as if she had just witnessed her work being outsourced to a more capable consultant: someone who could deliver results that were twice as good in only half the time. And even though Magali knew that they'd need another person to deal with Hendrik if she and Martin were going on with the group, it was hard not to feel slighted. Stupid, but then human nature, she concluded, had a lot to answer for.

By now, the whole group had reassembled and were waiting for the Beetle to return. It had been an emotional twenty-four hours, what with the fire and Hendrik's disappearance. Everyone was eager to ensure that the blogger was OK.

As Alain helped Hendrik out of the car, Eva stepped forward to suggest that the boy be checked out by a doctor. You couldn't be too careful with this sort of thing. Since she wasn't part of the expedition, perhaps it was best if she looked after things from here. If Andrej would just let her borrow the Beetle…

Magali detected more than a hint of reluctance to the technologist's assent. Perhaps he was wondering why Eva had assumed there was anything wrong – the pair had given no information about Hendrik's state of mind – or perhaps he  had wanted to drive Hendrik to the hospital himself. Maybe, just maybe, *he* was a little jealous, too. All Magali could say with any certainty was that Alain seemed equally nonplussed. Both he and the technologist looked on in frustration as Hendrik and Eva exited the scene.

Martin sprang to her aid. "Did he say if he'd been involved in an accident or anything like that in the past?" he asked Andrej. "It could explain his reaction."

Andrej considered the question briefly. "That's an interesting theory."

"It was Magali that came up with it."

"It would make sense," Andrej said. "He's a sensitive boy. He cares about the people around him."

"He said he was responsible for last night," Alain had joined the group.

Magali signalled to Martin that he should go and keep the others out of range while the trio continued their discussion.

129

"But maybe he meant a different accident?" Magali said.

"It's possible," Andrej said. "He was pretty confused when we found him."

"The main thing is he's on his way to get treatment. He's in good hands with Eva, I'm sure. But it looks like the expedition's going to need a new blogger. What should we tell Louis?" Magali asked. The seed had been well and truly planted.

"I don't think it's right to bring mental health into it. Especially when we're still not sure. Can't we just say he was taken ill?" Andrej asked.

"Agreed. There's no need to be any more specific," Alain said. "He's ill, and he's been taken to hospital. End of story."

Only it wasn't. Not for Magali. As the group departed for Weissensee, she let Frank know what Hendrik had said. Even allowing for the confusion created by his parents' accident, Hendrik had admitted responsibility for the fire.

And that, she knew, could scarcely be ignored.

CHAPTER ELEVEN

Hendrik

Sunday afternoon - Bled

Ever since he had received the news about the fire the previous evening, Hendrik had felt strangely detached from what was going on around him. It was as if he had witnessed it all – the drinking, the drive to Bled, the afternoon at the castle – from afar, and despite knowing what must come next, been incapable of exerting any control over his actions. Perhaps that was why he didn't feel any sense of shame, at least not about the way he had reacted.

What did make him ashamed – because it had been within his control – was accepting this job in the first place. He had allowed himself to be convinced by a man whose credentials he hadn't thought to check: to be influenced by an idealistic turn of phrase when he should have demanded an argument of substance. Though he didn't doubt that Dominik was genuine, that the motives behind the mission were sound, he *had* begun to doubt whether the ends justified the means. Exploiting regulations to line your own pockets was cynical and underhand but was it any worse than endangering the lives of innocent people to prevent it?

Even if it had been an accident…

All he had wanted to do was take a closer look at the blue cabrio, and then Peter had scared him. On any other day, the screwdriver would not even have left his hand.

"So, are you going to tell us what happened?" It was a woman's voice, and at least the second time she had asked.

Where was he? The last thing he could remember was being driven down from the castle by Andrej and Alain. Had he fallen asleep in the meantime? He sat upright with a jolt and tried to take in his surroundings.

Amazingly, he appeared to be in a treehouse: a stylish two-storey structure with what looked like sleeping quarters on the top floor and a terrace that doubled as an entrance to one side. The building work must have been recently completed because the wood still smelled brand new. He saw that he was next to a window. He stood up and looked out.

There was no doubt about it. He was in the middle of a wood, and there were other treehouses, all connected to each other by a series of wooden bridges. In the distance he could faintly hear the murmur of a stream.

Where the hell was he? He was no longer in Bled; that was for sure. At least not in the town itself. He craned his neck and saw that there were a number of tents below. Further in the distance, they became much larger – did one of them have a Jacuzzi? Hendrik pinched himself to make sure he hadn't slipped into an alternate reality. But no, his eyes were not deceiving him.

The whole site had the air of an adventure play park, the sort he had visited with his parents as a child. It could only be some sort of upmarket campsite, though as yet devoid of holiday-makers.

"Where am I?" he asked, still somewhat disorientated.

"In what will be Bled's first eco-friendly tourist resort." A different voice this time, that of a man. "A place for people to step back and rediscover the beauty of nature." Hendrik looked up towards the viewing gallery but there was no sign of anyone there.

The woman stepped forward. Hendrik recognized her from the meal earlier that day. Her hair seemed darker out of the sunlight. What was she called again?

"Hendrik, my name is Eva. Perhaps you can still remember. Tell us what happened in Deutschlandsberg," she said softly, before adding: "We know about your parents."

"My parents? What do they have to do with anything? They're both dead." Hendrik was surprised by the aggression in his voice. Obviously he was still shaken by the events of the night before. It wasn't just that he had put people's lives at risk. It was that he had done so out of self-interest. Whatever the environmental implications, deep down he knew that the primary motivation had been financial.

He also knew that the incident had stirred up some much older feelings. Feelings that had been left to fester, like an open wound. Yesterday evening the wound had become infected and he had acted like a delirious patient. He needed to take a hold of himself, to regain control, to breathe.

"Who are you anyway?"

"We represent the interests of a private client," the man said. He had been on the upper floor all along. This time Hendrik managed to get a good look at him.

"You're the mayor of Bled," he said. It was somewhere between a question and a statement.

"That's right. My name is Janez Fajfar."

"We won't hurt you," Eva said. "All we want to know is who you're working for. Then we can take you to see a doctor."

"A doctor? But I'm not ill," Hendrik protested.

"Excessive drinking, erratic behaviour, uncontrollable displays of emotion. I'm no expert, but it doesn't sound like you're the picture of health." There was no hint of accusation in her voice. If anything she appeared sympathetic. "You said you were responsible for last night's fire. So, who are you working for?"

"Last night's fire? How did you know…" Hendrik's voice trailed away.

"That's not your concern," the mayor said, before softening somewhat. "Nor is it the concern of the tour director. We have no desire to damage your reputation, only to establish the facts."

The facts. For the first time since he had started working this job, Hendrik wondered what they were. He had no idea what Dominik was intending to do beyond confirming the existence of the technology. Was that what had been bothering him? That the surveillance mission could only ever be phase one; and that sooner or later he was going to be called upon to justify his fee?

"There's only so much I can say. I'm under contract. I don't want to get myself into any more trouble."

"What about the fire? You said it's got nothing to do with your parents. Does that mean you were responsible after all?" Janez asked.

Hendrik had to weigh up his next move very carefully. There was no way of telling whether these people operated inside or outside the law. Either way, he doubted they would let him go – was he being held captive, by the mayor of Bled? – until he told them what they needed to know.

"Best stick to the truth," Eva said.

"Because you've got no idea what we already know," Janez added.

There was a long pause. Hendrik had never been much of a gambler and now was hardly the time to start. Why hadn't Dominik sent Nils? He was better at bluffing, far more assured when it came to playing the game. For a moment he considered making use of the traumatic death of his sister, but he realized there was every chance these people knew who he was anyway.

"OK," he sighed. "My best friend and I were hired to do a surveillance job. There's supposed to be a car."

A good opening. Vague but to the point.

"You mean an EV?" the mayor said.

"Right, an EV. A game-changer apparently. Different from all the others on the market. It's being tested at WAVE, and we're supposed to find it."

"So, what is this? Some kind of industrial espionage? You're working for another car company?" Eva asked.

"No, nothing like that." What could Hendrik do? He couldn't tell them he was working for Dominik Brandt. The link between Dominik's company and Adler Reilly wasn't clear either. "We were told that the car was being developed to facilitate the ongoing manufacture of vehicles with dangerously high CO_2 emissions. You've heard of super-credits, right?"

"Yeah, it's a sort of *quid pro quo* system. You apply an average to a car manufacturer's fleet. Low CO_2 emissions balance out the less environmentally friendly vehicles," the mayor said.

"You're an eco-terrorist, then?" Eva furrowed her brow.

"Who said anything about eco-terrorism?" Hendrik was becoming exasperated. "We were hired to confirm the car exists. Nothing more." At least not yet.

Another pause.

"Do you believe him?" Janez said to his partner, deliberately avoiding eye contact with Hendrik. An old trick, no doubt, designed to make him squirm, to embarrass him into providing more information. Only, there wasn't a great deal more he could say.

"Sure, I believe him. He doesn't look like a liar to me." Eva turned towards Hendrik and changed tack. "You must be hungry. When was the last time you ate something?"

"Yesterday evening," Hendrik said. He was surprised by the new line of questioning.

"Then you'll need your strength. I'll go and see if there's any food going spare from the restaurant."

Why were they offering him food? What they were planning to do with him?

"Let's have a little chat while we wait for Eva to return," Janez said. "Tell me, how do you explain the fire?"

"I was following a lead."

"What are you, a private detective?"

"Is that what *you* are?" Hendrik asked defiantly.

"I'm the mayor of Bled. And you're wasting our time."

Suddenly Hendrik understood. Eva was softening him up, while the mayor turned the screws.

"To confirm the existence of the technology, I need to check the cars," Hendrik said.

"Check them? How?"

"Monitor their range, track their performance," Hendrik paused. If they knew it was him, he might as well say it: "examine their batteries."

"With the hope of finding one that's different from the rest?"

Hendrik nodded.

"And your friend? What's his role in this? Where is he?"

"In Zurich. He helps with the analysis. Checks the serial numbers of the parts, which company makes them, that sort of thing. Some of the stuff he can do is pretty advanced." Hendrik wondered if he had already said too much.

"So, what happened to the blue cabrio?"

"It was a screwdriver. I dropped it, and then it must have pierced the battery somehow."

"It was an accident?"

Hendrik nodded again. He had felt a crackle of emotion in his voice and needed to compose himself. A nod was as good as a "yes".

"So," the mayor began, "what happens if you find it? The car, that is?"

"I don't know."

"You don't know?"

"If it's there, I file a report and wait for further instructions," he stammered. He no longer felt in control of the situation. "But since no-one knows if the car exists…"

There was a long pause. "It exists alright," Janez finally said. "And as far as we know, it doesn't have anything to do with super-credits."

Hendrik was struggling to comprehend what was going on. He hadn't been harmed. And he didn't appear to be in any immediate danger. But did that mean Janez and Eva were telling the truth? His head was spinning.

"You're in luck." Just then, Eva had returned with a plate containing a mountain of grilled fish. "There's an actor visiting the site tomorrow. He's thinking of shooting a film here. Anyway, the chef's been in to prepare a meal. I hope he doesn't mind. It looks as though it's been freshly caught."

The food looked mouth-wateringly good.

"Can we talk outside for a moment?" Janez turned to his colleague.

The pair descended from the treehouse and headed towards a shingle beach. Hendrik waited until they were gone and then crept out onto the terrace to see if he could listen in to what they were saying.

But it was no good. All he could make out was the odd phrase.

In the meantime, the mayor had taken his cell phone out of his pocket and was making a call.

"I don't think so… it's difficult to say…"

What he was saying might have been about Hendrik – but then again it could just have easily been official business.

He saw that they were making their way back to the treehouse, and quickly returned to his food.

When the door opened, Hendrik was confronted by a pair of serious faces.

"When was the last time you contacted your friend in Zurich?" Eva asked.

"He called me yesterday evening, after the fire," Hendrik replied.

"And you haven't spoken since?" The mayor this time.

"No."

"But there must be a procedure you need to follow?" Janez pressed.

"A procedure?"

"You know, so your employers know where you are?" Eva said.

"A procedure. Right. I'm supposed to provide a daily update."

"Well then, you'd better call him," Janez said. "Let him know you're OK. That everything's as it should be. And whatever you do, don't mention us."

As Hendrik took out his cell, he realized his hands were shaking. He had never been too good at poker. Whatever he said, Nils was bound to see through the lie...

CHAPTER TWELVE

Dominik

Sunday evening – Zurich

"So much for low-key. You're all over the news."

It was early evening, the day after the fire, and Dominik Brandt was in an emergency meeting with Christian Adler. Of the other members of the executive committee, only Walter Mikesch was present. Financial and Legal weren't needed on this occasion.

The CEO slammed the paper down on the desk.

"At least," he said, for the most part still managing to contain his anger, "the story will create some negative publicity. Make people think about the wisdom of investing in an electric car – *more* people, I should say."

Adler grimaced before continuing: "But now it's time to get them out. Before we draw any more attention to ourselves."

"We can't, sir," Dominik said. "I had our contact draft that article myself," he motioned towards the paper. The story it contained was a rehash of the previous evening's edition. "The tour director took the bait. He wants to prove the doubters wrong and show that EVs are safe after all. WAVE continued as normal this morning."

"I don't think you understand. I said, get them out."

"With respect, I don't think *you* understand, sir. You remember what we said before the mission began? That this technology could change the face of the automotive industry. Well, WAVE still represents our best chance of finding it. We could spend years looking once it's finished. Once all these cars have returned to wherever it is they came from." Dominik allowed what he had said to sink in.

"What about the boy? Peter Prohaska hasn't heard from him all day," Walter said all of a sudden.

Dominik hadn't anticipated the question. He knew that Hendrik's report was overdue but there were all sorts of reasons for that. According to Nils, Hendrik and Peter had gone their separate ways that morning. There was no reason for them to have been in contact. Why had Walter chosen this precise moment to raise the issue?

"So what? We agreed that Peter would take a backseat," he shot back. "Hendrik's supposed to be cutting his teeth on this."

"Am I hearing this right? You've lost contact with an operative?" Adler thundered. His hands were positively shaking with rage.

Dominik watched him move towards the drinks cabinet and pour himself a Scotch: an expensive brand, the name of which gave new meaning to the word "unpronounceable". After a long sip, he looked ready to continue.

Just then Dominik's cell rang. Perfect timing. He held up a hand to say that the CEO should wait, before exiting the room.

"Nils. What have you got for me?"

"A missed call. From Bled."

"Bled? But they should be in Weissensee by now. Wait a minute. Did you say a *missed* call?"

"That's right."

Dominik was not amused. "We're not paying you to ignore the phone."

"I was doing some analysis with Marc. I didn't want to take a break – we were nearly finished."

"Was it Hendrik?"

"Yeah, he left a message, said he'd call back."

"I'm beginning to have my doubts about him. Are you sure he's up to the job?"

"Yes. One hundred percent. Whatever happened yesterday, there must have been a good reason. Hendrik's thorough. He probably just wanted to confirm something before filing his report."

"Find out what the hell is going on! And do it now!"

Dominik ended the call and returned to Adler and Walter. He needed to mind his step. The CEO was at breaking point, and

Dominik had no desire to tip him over the edge.

"Hendrik's still in Bled. He must have broken off from the expedition."

"I'll talk to Peter," Walter said, wresting the initiative from Dominik and the CEO. He moved to a corner of the room.

"Peter, it's Walter," he said. "Can you shed any light on Hendrik's activities since the fire?"

The CEO had taken another sip of his drink, but was now visibly struggling to control his temper. Dominik had seen him like this before. The pacing, the biting of the fist; all the tell-tale signs were there.

"OK, I understand. Thanks, Peter."

Walter summarized what he had just heard. "Peter was with Hendrik until the early evening. After Deutschlandsberg, he dropped him off at their hotel. Says everything was fine. But then Hendrik didn't show that night, wouldn't pick up his phone. Eventually Peter found him back at the hotel, being looked after by two participants. Drunk, apparently. So drunk, in fact, that he had to be helped up to his room."

"I WANT THIS THING SHUT DOWN," Adler erupted. His voice was so loud his glass almost shattered.

"Don't worry, I'll take care of it," Dominik said.

"And make sure that idiot Prohaska is transferred to the arse-end of nowhere for a very long time."

"With respect, sir, Peter's my man," Walter said. "And he's just given us a valuable insight into what's actually going on down there."

"I don't care! He's had his chance." Though he was speaking to Walter, Adler was right up in Dominik's face, wagging his finger. "You'd better make damn sure this mess is *cleaned* up. Have I made myself clear?" he said, slamming the door shut behind him and stomping off down the corridor. When the mood took him, he could be breathtakingly ruthless.

"Don't you think we're being a little hasty?" Walter said after he'd made sure the CEO was no longer in earshot. "We don't even know who caused the fire."

"We know enough. I put Hendrik on this to see if he was good enough to make the grade. But clearly he can't hold it together. If he's drinking, who knows what he's said. We can't afford to take the risk."

"What about his friend?"

"Nils? Don't worry about him. I've got him worked out. Money, fame, ego; that's what makes him tick. People like him are easy to control."

"And Hendrik's out of the picture, just like that?"

"Can't you see how risky it would be to let him continue? I've had my doubts about him from the start."

"You planned this?"

"We have to think about the next generation. A certain amount of collateral was inevitable. Adler might be losing his nerve, but he's right about Hendrik."

Walter gave Dominik a puzzled look.

"And Peter?"

In truth, Dominik had been trying to get rid of Peter Prohaska for some time. Sending him back into the field had been too good an opportunity to miss. Especially with a rookie. The slightest bit of trouble and Prohaska was bound to be shown up. The man was a fool.

"When things die down, Peter's to be *replaced*, not transferred. Adler doesn't understand the markets. That means he can no longer judge which operations are important. But I'll tell you something now: this technology could ruin everything for us and we need to make sure it doesn't see the light of day. So, once Hendrik's been removed from the scene, I'll have a new man slip into Peter's role and continue the mission."

"That's not what Adler wants," Walter said.

"Come on, Walter, you know as well as I do it's time for a change. The old man's finished. Even Jaeger admits it," Dominik lied.

"Jaeger? For Christ's sake, Dominik. You're not sending Jaeger?"

Dominik half expected the director of intelligence to issue a more sustained objection, but he just shook his head as he closed the door behind him, his question left hanging in the air.

Alone again, Dominik took a deep breath and made two calls.

The first was in line with the CEO's wishes.

The second was in direct contradiction to them.

CHAPTER THIRTEEN

Nils

Sunday evening – Zurich

Nils Karrat had always thought he was a good judge of character – but now he wasn't so sure. Maybe it was pressure of the situation. Or maybe it was because he had never been tested like this before. All he could say was that in the past twenty-four hours, he had seen two people react in a way he would never have predicted.

First, Dominik. So cool, so in control when they had first met; he had seemed genuinely put out by the fire the previous evening and had allowed his temper to get the better of him. OK, he had seemed a little calmer just now – WAVE, after all, was back in full flow – but his voice had still carried an undercurrent of menace.

And Hendrik? What was there to say about him? He had always been a little vulnerable perhaps, a little short on self-confidence, but for all that he was without question the most reliable person Nils had ever known. Going off radar was completely out of character. Nils realized that the only time he had felt any less than one hundred percent confident in his friend was when he had been required to vouch for him just now.

Still, as long as he had managed to convince Dominik, it didn't matter if he had yet to convince himself.

Suddenly, Nils' thoughts were interrupted by a knock on the door. He looked up to see Walter Mikesch. From everything Nils had heard, the director of intelligence was a good man who disagreed with a number of modern surveillance practices. He was also Peter Prohaska's immediate superior.

"We need to talk," Walter said.

"Sure. How can I help?" Nils asked.

"Not here. Meet me outside in ten minutes."

First Dominik, then Hendrik, now Walter. Nils knew that bad luck was supposed to come in threes but what did this particular chain mean? He tried to call Hendrik one last time before venturing outside.

It was a warm summer's evening, the sort that made you want to forget about work and head straight to the nearest bar. Nils and Walter didn't quite have that luxury, though at least the change of scene would enable them to speak freely.

They decamped to Old Fashion, a bar within easy walking distance of the office and, a good place for an early evening cocktail. The bar laid claim to being Zurich's oldest drinking establishment and the interior was, accordingly, in keeping with tradition. It certainly did a good trade. Indeed, it seemed as if half of Zurich was currently housed among its leather seats and fire-red antique wood-lined walls. The result was that upon ordering their drinks, Walter and Nils had no choice but to make their way out into the courtyard, which was quieter than inside, though in truth still no place for a private conversation.

"Shame about the name," Nils said. They hadn't been able to find a seat.

"What do you mean?"

"It's *old-fashioned*, not *old fashion*," Nils said.

"Well, they've always had a modern attitude towards grammar. Ever since it was established in 1886," Walter joked.

"So, what did you want to talk to me about?" Nils said. Although the crowd of drinkers made things more public, it meant the pair were less likely to be overheard by anyone who mattered.

"It's your friend," Walter said.

"Hendrik? What about him?" Suddenly Nils was more alert.

"Is there anyone who can help him? If something were to go wrong, I mean." Walter was looking him straight in the eye.

"Well, there's Peter – but you know that already."

"Peter's not a man for a crisis," Walter said matter-of-factly.

"Besides, he won't be there much longer. I mean someone else,

145

someone from the outside."

"Peter's going to be replaced?" Nils said.

When he realized that Walter wouldn't be drawn further on the matter, he decided to change tack.

"C'mon, Walter, this is all a little cloak and daggers for me. I'm guessing you know about the fire and that Hendrik went AWOL afterwards. Hell, maybe he even caused it. At least that would explain the way he reacted. The point is, he's back with us now." He lit a cigarette, the pair's outdoor location providing him with a rare opportunity to smoke. "I just spoke to Dominik. Nothing's changed. Our mission's the same as before. Whatever happened last night, Hendrik still has a chance to find the technology and put it right."

"That might be the impression Dominik gave you, but I was there after your conversation ended."

"And what did Dominik say?" Nils was confused.

"Enough to give me cause for concern. I've been in this game too long to see a young person's life destroyed. After I finished with Dominik, I called our financial director. She's just opened a large fund for an external operation, beginning tonight."

Which young person's life was being destroyed? Hendrik's? Nils felt a shiver go down his spine. "I'm sorry, Walter, but I'm not quite following you. What are you getting at?" he asked, trying to conceal his discomfort.

"There's a plane scheduled to land in Lesce later this evening. That's ten minutes from Bled. A rental car's been booked. Wherever your friend is, he'll be a lot safer among people. He needs to get back to WAVE as soon as possible. Jaeger won't dare touch him there."

Walter finished his drink and made to leave. Then he stopped himself. There must have been a look in Nils' eyes – bewilderment perhaps – that caused him to issue one final set of instructions. "Look, there's a pay phone in the bar. It's so old no-one will have bothered to put a tap on it. No-one will connect it to you. Call your friend, tell him to get back to WAVE, but don't say anything more. If you act quickly, he might still get out of this alive."

"Walter?"

"You can explain everything later. Right now, I need to take care of your cell phones. It should only take half an hour."

"I thought our lines were secure?" Nils furrowed his brow.

"Usually, they are – but Dominik likes to keep an eye on the rookies."

With that Walter was gone.

Nils downed his drink, stubbed out his cigarette and went inside. His mind was racing, and his hands had started to shake. Could Hendrik's life really be in danger? According to Walter, it was. Suddenly Nils thought about all the different surveillance tools he had used since the mission began. He remembered how easy it had been to listen in to the Lonely Viking's conversation in Hungary; how Dominik had been one step ahead of Louis Palmer after the fire.

Still, up until a few moments ago, it had all seemed like a harmless game. He never imagined that someone was listening in to *his* calls, the same way he had listened in to Robort's in Sopron. He stopped, tried to think clearly. It could be some sort of loyalty test. A kind of initiation for new recruits.

But could he afford to take that chance? His instinct told him Walter was telling the truth – and that meant Hendrik was living on borrowed time.

Nils spied the phone mounted on the wall to the right side of the bar counter and made towards it. There was a good chance it would be a secure line. Modern-day hacking relied on the internet, on access to databases, and on exploiting mobile communication; more than that, it relied on surreptitiously installing hardware connected to internal memory, microphones, loudspeakers, or GPS modules.

That was how Nils had known Hendrik was still in Bled: someone, somewhere would have fitted a component to his cell, which revealed his data and location at all times, and enabled his conversations to be recorded. This component would have been installed before purchase, by intercepting the phone en route to the retailer, and once it was installed, the owner would have little chance of protecting their data. After all, a piece of hardware, whatever it was, could only be encrypted against a *known* threat. If you didn't know that threat existed in the first place, what chance did you have?

The people in Walter's department could simply activate the microphone, and listen in to your conversations. If necessary, they could even control other functions remotely. Encrypted data was rarely a problem either. All it took was for a certain amount of money – call it a few million – to change hands between the manufacturer and the organization in question and a loophole would be built into the encryption algorithm. Truly, nothing was safe from these people.

Nils was staring at the old phone. Time to get moving. He knew that when he was done, he would need to remove all traces of the call having taken place, as anyone sampling the voice would be able to link it back to him.

He inserted a coin and dialled. The alcohol had made his breathing heavier. He waited for the connection. Finally, there was a ring, then another, and another. A bead of sweat had formed on Nils' forehead. He realized there was no guarantee Hendrik would accept the call. Not from a number he didn't recognize.

Strange, how time slows down when your heart is racing. Nils could only have been standing there half a minute at most, but already it felt like an age. There were people staring at him; he could sense a pair of eyes trained on him now. Just pick up. He couldn't wait much longer. Soon he'd have to replace the phone and return to his seat. If he reacted out of frustration, if he slammed the receiver back into its place on the wall, he'd only draw attention to himself. The seconds ticked by, each one elongated by the knowledge that Hendrik was in trouble. And that Nils could do nothing to help.

After a minute Nils took a deep breath, replaced the receiver, and tried to fix his gaze on his would-be tormentors, on those who had been mocking him as he stood waiting by the phone. To his surprise, however, all he could see was the publican and a man sitting quietly reading the paper. The latter was smartly dressed with a closely shaved head and thick, horn-rimmed glasses. In his mid-thirties perhaps.

Nils thought he recognized him from somewhere but couldn't say for sure. If he was a spook, then he wasn't taking the slightest bit of interest in what Nils was doing.

So where had it come from then? This feeling of being watched?

Panic, perhaps. Yes, Nils thought, that was it. Panic had rendered him incapable of processing his immediate surroundings.

Just as he was about to make the walk back to his seat, Nils' cell vibrated. He groped helplessly for it in his pocket. Even the simplest of tasks seemed suddenly way beyond him.

One step at a time, he told himself. First find it, then make sure it's answered.

"Hendrik. Where the fuck have you been?" his voice was a mixture of anger and relief, drawing glances from several onlookers at the next table, of whom Nils was all of a sudden blissfully unaware.

"Sorry, I had to go to the doctor. I was sick last night, remember?"

"OK, Hendrik, listen to me," there was something in his friend's voice that rang false, the same sense of panic that Nils was feeling himself perhaps. "My battery is about to die. I'll call you back. Just make sure you pick up this time."

Nils returned to the telephone on the wall and dialled.

Hendrik picked up after the first ring.

"You need to get back to WAVE," Nils hissed into the receiver. "Is there someone who can drive you to Weissensee?" The question was redundant. Nils had checked the GPS data of the other teams and seen that they had left Bled long ago.

"No, everyone's left. It looked like I was going to have to go to the hospital. They couldn't afford to wait."

"OK, that makes things more difficult. But listen to me, you just need to get back."

"What's going on?" Hendrik sounded unsettled.

"I'll tell you later. Just concentrate on finding someone who can drive you to Weissensee. I'll call you back in half an hour."

After ending the call, Nils went back outside for another cigarette. What the hell was he supposed to do with thirty minutes? He thought of all the moments in his life he had waited, just hoping for time to pass. As a child he had counted sheep before bed; in adulthood a sleepless night had meant working his way back from five hundred. What had he done in school? Doodled, perhaps? Or passed notes around the class? He hadn't smoked, at any rate, and he realized that without thinking he had taken a second cigarette from the packet. Keep the mind active, he thought. Smoke, drink if necessary, but make sure you keep a clear head.

Having finished his cigarette, he returned to the bar. Time passed quicker when you took a drink. His second of the night. Twenty-two minutes to go.

What did it all mean? Only last night, things had been moving along just fine. Now Hendrik and Peter were on their way out, and it seemed reasonable to assume that he, Nils, would soon follow. But why? He didn't understand. There had been a minor incident and Hendrik had disappeared for a few hours. So what? Was he really supposed to believe that that had been enough to sign his friend's death warrant. Because that's what Walter had said: "if you act quickly, he might still get out of this alive." Nils shook his head. He knew that what they were doing was against the law but the way Dominik had put it, they were also doing the world a favour. OK, so the coverage of the fire hadn't helped the cause. But did they know for sure that Hendrik was responsible? Were they worried he might talk? The more Nils thought about it, the more plausible it seemed that Hendrik's contract could be terminated – but his life? That was another matter.

Fifteen minutes. What about Walter? Surely he was too experienced to have misinterpreted the signs, too knowledgeable to have seen something that simply wasn't there? Nils realized with a start that if Walter *could* interpret the signs, then there had to be a precedent. Someone who had been dealt with in the same way.

Twelve minutes. There were a lot of things that didn't add up. Dominik's company was small, politically engaged, and represented a client producing EVs for the mass market. But somehow it was also connected to Adler Reilly and had access to their offices, employees, technical resources, and much more besides. In other words, the best of both worlds.

They could obviously afford to dabble in industrial espionage, but this, what Walter had said was going to happen, was altogether more drastic. Silencing an employee for fear that they might speak out of turn was murder. If it ever got out, no-one would care about the cause. *If it ever got out*, Nils thought. Could he go to the press? If he did, he'd be compromised, that was for sure. Phone-tapping, illegal acquisition of information; in the wake of last year, they'd throw the book at him. He could kiss goodbye to his career and say hello to a lengthy jail term.

Seven minutes. Nils began to root around in his pocket for some change. In among the coinage, a mix of Swiss francs and euros, he felt something small and rectangular, a tattered business card or a scrap of paper perhaps. He had no recollection of having put it there himself. Upon extracting it, he was amazed to discover that it was a note from Walter. He must have slipped it to Nils as he left. There was a number messily scrawled on it. Finally, a message Nils could understand. He might not be able to go to the press but he could always speak to Walter. Going on tonight's performance, the director of intelligence was more than willing to put his neck on the line.

Three minutes. Time to concentrate. Forget about any pieces that didn't fit and make sure Hendrik was safe. The man with the paper had been replaced by a woman, though their reading material remained the same. The barman was currently engaged in wiping the surfaces.

Nils' cell phone beeped to reveal a message from Walter:

GOOD TO TALK. WE'LL DISCUSS YOUR PROGRESS AT A LATER DATE.

"Good to talk" meant the coast was clear. Nils called Hendrik again.

"I don't care what happened with the blue cabrio yesterday or what you've been doing since," he said urgently. "But you need to listen to me now. There's something strange happening. I'm going to try and get to the bottom of it, but right now I need to know where you are."

"I'm still in Bled. I'm sitting in a garden restaurant by a beach, surrounded by trees on all sides, the only sound the burble of a passing stream. There's a pool to my left. The water looks amazing: clean, refreshing, and just perfect for a late night swim—"

"Hendrik, I don't have time for this."

"That's your problem, Nils. You never listen, but you expect others to listen to you. I've just told you where I am."

"OK, sorry. It just wasn't the answer I was expecting."

"You told me I needed to get back to WAVE, so that's what I'm doing. I've met a couple of people heading that way, they run this eco-resort that's just about to open. We're leaving in five minutes."

"They're going to take you to Weissensee?"

"To the east shore. We're taking the back roads."

"Wow, you've lucked out," Nils was happy, for the moment, to go along with Hendrik's story. Even if he didn't believe a word his friend was saying. "You must have improved your powers of persuasion."

"More luck than judgment," Hendrik said. "The guy's dad lived in Bled. Turns out he helped smuggle a couple of East German hitch-hikers into Austria back in the late sixties. They had escaped from some sort of state-sponsored holiday. Guess which route they took?"

152

"Across the Triglav national park in the Alps, then over the Austrian border just before you get to Italy?" Nils guessed.

"Bingo."

"So why's the son doing it now?" Nils was genuinely curious.

"Don't know. I guess it's a way of remembering his father. It was pretty amazing, what he did. If he'd been caught, he'd almost certainly have gone to jail."

"What about when you get there? To the east shore, I mean."

"I'll call Alain en route. Hopefully he can pick me up and take me to Techendorf."

Hendrik seemed remarkably, suspiciously, calm. It had to be an act. He hadn't even asked why he needed to go back. Perhaps he didn't want to know.

"Just be careful. When you get back to WAVE, continue as if nothing's happened. Don't say a word to Peter about this. And make sure you keep your cell phone charged. Do you understand?"

"Loud and clear."

"Hendrik, this is serious."

"I thought you only cared about the money," it was the first time Hendrik's voice had betrayed any hint of emotion. Whatever story he had spun Nils, it couldn't have been true. There was more to his disappearance than sickness; and more to tonight than a couple of environmentalists taking a trip down memory lane.

"Forget the money," Nils said.

But Hendrik had hung up.

Nils returned his cell phone to his pocket, shot a glance at the barman, and returned to finish his drink. Sooner or later he knew he would have to provide Hendrik with more information. But for now it was all about the game.

For some reason, Nils was still in, even if Hendrik had already been forced to fold.

CHAPTER FOURTEEN

Alain

Sunday evening – Weissensee

It hadn't been an easy decision to leave Hendrik behind in Bled, but Alain was sure it had been the right one. The boy was in good hands with Eva Štravs and, as it turned out, Alain couldn't have afforded to wait anyway. He needed to keep to his own schedule.

En route to Weissensee, he had been obliged to make two phone calls. The first was to arrange a photo shoot for his new clothing range at Grossglockner the next day. Officially, of course, that was the reason he was at WAVE. In among all the confusion, he had to ensure he didn't forget his own cover story: that for the purposes of this trip, he was a businessman taking advantage of a happy coincidence, rather than an investor with an interest in EV technology.

The second call was made harder by the first because it demanded that he remembered the exact opposite: namely, that he *was* an investor, and that the happy coincidence was entirely manufactured. He had promised to give Tom Schmidt, who had first brought the new EV technology to his attention in Scotland, an update on the situation. He realized that if he had called Schmidt earlier that afternoon, he might not have known what to say. Since then, however, things had turned out far better than anyone could have predicted: Hendrik had been located, safe if not sound, and was receiving the treatment he required; while Andrej had dealt with a difficult situation in a calm, dignified, and above all human, manner. If the technology was even half as accomplished as the man behind it, Alain had told Schmidt, he was making a very sound investment indeed.

Upon arrival in Weissensee, he parked the Bolt and connected it to the charging point. He entered a large hall to find the participants, about seventy-five in total, seated at a series of long tables, each one seating up to fifteen people. Despite the fact that it was a group event, it was the first time since the pre-expedition briefing in Eichgraben that everyone had been in the same room together. Alain sat down in the nearest chair and found himself next to Jean-Pierre and Monika, with two of the bikers also alongside. A little further up the table was Florian, who, like everyone else, had already helped himself to a plate of food from the buffet.

"Welcome to all those late-comers," Louis Palmer was saying.

Alain looked up toward the stage to see Louis standing in front of a projector screen. To the right was a guest speaker, about to make a presentation. Alain felt mildly embarrassed at having been singled out but, looking round, he was forced to acknowledge that he was indeed the last of the Bled contingent to have found their way there.

"What's your excuse?" Monika asked with a grin.

"Martin and Magali broke down and they still managed to get here before you!" her husband, Jean-Pierre, added.

"They broke down?"

"Some sort of software error appa-rently," Jean-Pierre continued. "Martin had to get a tow up with the local fire bri-gade," he giggled.

"How did I miss that?" Alain asked – though he knew it must have happened when he had stopped to make one of his calls.

"Same way you missed this, I suppose," the first biker said good-humouredly, pointing to a bandage adorning his arm. "Because there are so many damn people, it's difficult to keep track…"

Dressed all in black with a permanent three-day beard, he see-med the rough-and-ready type, though no less friendly for that.

"I *told* Johann he was taking the curves too fast," said his colleague. Alain thought his name was Franz, but he couldn't remember.

"But you still haven't answered my question," Monika pressed.

"Oh, there was a problem with Hendrik. He had to go to the hospital."

"Hendrik's in hospital? But he's OK, isn't he?" Florian asked. He must have overheard what the adults had been saying.

"Yes, he'll be fine. It's just routine. Nothing to worry about." The last person Alain wanted to upset was Florian.

He turned back towards the stage.

"…of *PlanetSolar*." Louis had just finished introducing the theme of tonight's presentation, and the lights in the hall had been dimmed in preparation.

PlanetSolar, Alain soon learned, was the name of the first ship to sail around the world powered exclusively by solar energy: a remarkable dream that had been realized through a combination of hard work and no little enterprise. Having overseen the building of the vessel, the speaker, Rafaël Domjan, had spent 587 days at sea with his crew, visiting the seven continents of the globe. The hardest part, he said, had been the sixty-day crossing of the Pacific Ocean, which had tested each of those on board to the very limit. They had been surrounded by nothing but water, unsure whether the light from the sun would be enough to keep their battery charged and the catamaran afloat.

There had been lighter moments too, however. The highlights for Alain were the pictures of Rafaël's voyage, the most striking of which showed a group of baby seals dozing peacefully on the vessel's skids as they soaked up the afternoon sun. At that point a great deal of cooing ensued from the audience. Alain noted that Florian, by some distance the youngest member of

156

the expedition, seemed particularly thrilled.

Unfortunately, the presentation was deprived of the ending its narrative deserved, when the projector suddenly stopped working. A hush descended on the audience, as they waited to see whether the fault could be mended. When it became clear that there was nothing to be done, the room filled once more with chatter. A number of people went to check on their vehicles, while some switched tables in order to discuss the presentation. Florian said he was tired and politely excused himself before going to bed. Shortly afterwards, Jean-Pierre and Monika did likewise.

Alain himself was in no rush to call it a night. Instead he tried make sense of what had happened earlier that afternoon. He was forced to admit that he had no idea what was wrong with Hendrik. What had he meant when he said he was responsible for the accident in Deutschlandsberg? It didn't make any sense. How could he possibly have caused it? Perhaps Andrej and Jasna would know more. He was just about to go in search of them when Jochen, the shy geologist from Bled, sat down beside him.

The sound of a nearby cell phone prevented the pair from entering into conversation. Its ring was deafening and must have been at full volume. It took some time, and a few dirty looks, for Alain to realize that it was his own device. He thought he had switched it off an hour ago. Strange, how the mind played tricks. Still, it wasn't half as strange as the sight of the name on the display. After fishing the cell from his pocket, Alain practically fell from his chair in disbelief.

"Hendrik? You're the last person I expected to hear from tonight!"

Jochen gazed at him expectantly.

"You're what?" Alain said, obviously concerned. "No, it's just a bit of a surprise, that's all. Gastritis? Well, yes. I suppose that makes sense."

Alain turned to Jochen. "Hendrik's been discharged from hospital. Apparently he's about an hour from the east shore. He's asked to be collected from there." The look on Alain's face was one of disbelief.

Jochen looked equally perplexed. "OK," he replied with a shrug. "Are you going to drive?"

"I guess," Alain said, "though it's a bit of a pain. It would mean recharging again tomorrow."

"Well then, you could always…" Jochen stopped short of finishing his sentence. "You could always…"

There was a glint in Alain's eye. "Take a boat? Well, it's a beautiful summer's evening, after all. You in? It might be easier with two. I'm not sure I want to row all that way alone."

There was a blanket ban on motor boats in Weissensee, save for public transport.

Jochen smiled and nodded.

Hendrik was still waiting patiently on the line.

"OK," Alain said. "Jochen and I will be there to meet you. But you'll have to bear with us. We might be a while," he rang off.

The pair slipped silently out of the hall. There were a number of boats dotted along the shore. You could plan things as much as you liked, Alain thought to himself, but the best decisions were the ones made spontaneously.

"How about that one?" Alain pointed to the vessel closest to them. "Remember, it's only stealing if we don't bring it back."

"Too small," came the response. The voice was familiar but it didn't belong to Jochen.

"Manfred? What are you doing out here?" Alain hadn't been aware of anyone listening in to their conversation.

"You'll need something a lot bigger – you're bringing an extra man back, baggage in tow."

"He's got enough baggage to fill three boats," Alain joked. It was a flippant, off-hand remark, designed to mask his confusion at Manfred's unexpected appearance. What was he doing outside? Manfred was quiet and undemonstrative, a man who clearly cared about the well-being of others. But there was no reason for him to be out here at this moment in time.

Suddenly a switch flicked inside Alain's head. Of course. He realized he had almost completely forgotten about the agents. Before Bled, he had managed to narrow it down to two couples. Now Manfred appeared to have given himself away. There was something about the way he had emerged from the hall; about the way he had reacted to Alain's choice of boat.

A civilian would have tried to dissuade him from taking it; an agent would make sure he selected the right one…

After leaving Manfred behind on the shore and making good initial progress, Alain took a break from rowing to run his fingers through the water. It was surprisingly warm. Surely, he thought, a glacial lake in the middle of the Alps ought to have been cooler. The name was interesting, too. It translated as the "White Lake", a moniker that alluded to the colour of the water, caused by banks of chalk located along the shore.

It was a fair distance from Techendorf, where the participants were staying, and the further east they went, the more uninhabited the area became. To a greater or lesser extent, this state of affairs mirrored the interaction between Alain and his rowing partner. Having conversed at the outset, they had now settled into a comfortable silence, with both allowing their thoughts to drift peaceably along the lake until neither, it seemed, had recourse to think at all.

Alain looked at his watch. It was getting late. Soon darkness would descend upon the lake and it would become difficult to navigate. Right now, though, the sun was winning its battle against the moon and of all the nights to have to wait alone, with only the sky and the hills for company, Hendrik had chosen the best one.

"Is that him?" Jochen asked, as they approached the shore. It was the first thing he had said for some time.

Alain's gaze honed in on a lone figure sitting and waiting by the bank, a small backpack lying unattended to the right of the rock on which he was perched.

"That's him," Alain said. He wasn't absolutely sure, but the chances of it being anyone else were slim. It would be one hell of a coincidence if another man was waiting to be picked up in that precise spot.

They eased their pace slightly as they rowed into the shore. There were more people around than Alain had expected. There was a campsite, which housed a diving school, and a Gasthof of some kind by the southeast bank. It would have been a good place to leave the distractions of urban life behind.

Alain had to admit that Hendrik's condition didn't seem to have improved since the afternoon. Despite the fine summer weather, his face remained pale and he appeared desperately short of sleep. In contrast, his handshake was exaggeratedly firm. In the absence of words, it communicated two messages: first, that he was better; and second, that there should be no mention of what had gone before.

Alain considered for a moment before making his decision. Whatever the handshake had *tried* to say, Hendrik still didn't look well.

"It's good to have you back, Hendrik. You had us pretty worried there," Alain began, once they were underway. "Did the doctor say anything about what might have caused it?"

"The gastritis? Oh, the usual. Stress, worry…"

Stress? But surely covering WAVE was his dream job? He was surrounded by interesting people and being paid to film some of the most spectacular landscape Europe had to offer. Perhaps, Alain thought, Magali had been right: someone close to him had died in an accident, and whatever happened in Deutschlandsberg had simply been too much for him to bear. If that was true, then Alain was about to take a big risk by broaching the subject of the fire. But he felt Hendrik had a right to know.

"I thought I should tell you that Stephan and Olaf are OK. They're upset that they won't be taking any further part in the expedition. But they're OK. The little girl, too. It was an accident, Hendrik. An unhappy coincidence. Call it what you will. Something got lodged in the battery. A sharp object that pierced the casing. Anyway, it created enough of a hole for air to get through and cause a short circuit. That's what triggered the fire. It's an open-and-shut case. Me, Jochen, the tour director: everyone's satisfied there was no foul play. It's time to draw a line under it once and for all."

Alain looked across to Jochen for support. After what seemed like an age, the latter obliged.

"These things happen," he said. "Today, for instance, after you left, at Feistritz an der Drau, there was some problem with Martin and Magali's car. They couldn't make it up the final hill," he smiled as he rowed. He was on the same side as Alain; both were facing the blogger. "Anyway, the upshot was they had to get the emergency services involved. Magali had to complete the journey on an e-bike, while Martin stayed in the car and got a tow to Weissensee. From the fire brigade!"

Alain was laughing now, too. It had been a rather unusual sight, Jochen went on, not least because the EV was almost the same size as the fire engine.

"The point is," Alain took over, "that machines sometimes malfunction, and we don't always know why. You just have to accept it and move on."

He waited to see whether his words would have any effect on Hendrik. But the blogger seemed more preoccupied with the contents of his backpack. Alain interpreted this as a good sign. It was atmospheric out here on the lake, now that the chalk deposits were providing a second source of light. Alain wondered if Hendrik was preparing to shoot a short film, to be uploaded later on his blog: a sure-fire statement that he was ready to put the events of the last twenty-four hours behind him.

A few seconds later, his real motive became clear. He had become distracted by a car that had emerged on the road at Neusach. Alain remembered hearing that there were two newcomers joining WAVE, though whether later that night or tomorrow morning he couldn't say. One of them was said to be an EV enthusiast who had read about the fire in Deutschlandsberg and, in the wake of what he perceived to be an attack upon the industry, had decided to join the expedition to lend his support.

Too late, Alain realized that Hendrik was now taking photos of the car. Indeed, he appeared to have the lens trained on the driver. His hands, Alain saw, were shaking.

"Hendrik, are you OK?"

There was no response, but Alain could see how tense Hendrik was. The car was a traditional model and, strangely, it appeared to be slowing down. It was so dark, it was impossible to say whether the driver would be able to make them out from the shore. What was he doing? Could it be the owner of the boat, Alain wondered? But no, it was probably just someone who had got lost. A third possibility was that the driver had become spooked by the sight of three grown men rowing on the lake in the middle of the night. That would be enough to make anyone slow down. Particularly if one of the men was filming the whole thing. Shit, he was probably just about to call the police…

"Do you recognize him, Hendrik?" Alain asked finally.

"He's looking at me," Hendrik replied.

"He's looking at you? What do you mean, he's looking at you? He can't see you: you've got a camera in front of your face."

"Nils was right. They're coming for me."

"Who's Nils?" Alain asked. When no response was forthcoming, he grew firmer. "Hendrik, I said who's Nils?"

But Hendrik had fallen silent once more. At this point Jochen, who had been impassive throughout, gently urged him to lower the device and they continued on their way.

Alain couldn't make head or tail of it. Why had Hendrik been discharged from the hospital? He was still withdrawn and, moreover, appeared to have added acute paranoia to a growing list of medical complaints. Alain sensed that something wasn't quite right. OK, so the driver was real. But he was no demon; more likely it was someone on their way home from work. Alain looked towards the shore again and saw that the car was no longer in view.

"Do you have somewhere you can sleep tonight?" Alain asked. "There's room with me if you don't."

It had been phrased as a question, but by the time they had arrived and returned the boat to its original spot, Alain knew he wasn't presenting Hendrik with a choice.

Happily, the evening passed without further event and the scene that greeted the pair the next morning was a glorious one: the sky cloudless, the hills green, and the lake a deep shade of blue. Maybe that was the reason Hendrik showed no sign of the distress that had gripped him only six or seven hours before. Indeed, he seemed much more like his normal self as he took leave of Alain's room and stepped out into the cool morning air.

Alain followed closely by his side. A number of the participants were already up and about, enjoying a moment's repose before they recommenced their journey north and west towards Heiligenblut. There was a photo scheduled at nine on the bridge between Techendorf and Weissensee, after which the EVs would depart in convoy. Louis Palmer, for one, was delighted to see Hendrik, as he hadn't been able to organize a replacement film crew.

As they walked, the pair came across Martin and Magali, who, after their travails the previous evening, were still charging their vehicle in preparation for departure.

"Hendrik!" Magali said. She seemed genuinely pleased to see him. "There was a rumour you were back. Everything OK?"

"A touch of gastritis, that's all."

Initial pleasantries exchanged, Magali left the blogger to chat with Martin before approaching Alain.

"How does he seem?" she asked.

"I don't know. He's better this morning. But he was pretty spooked last–"

"You look tired," Magali hadn't allowed Alain to finish his sentence. "Why don't you let us look after him today? We'll be charging for another couple of hours at least."

She motioned towards their car. "Hendrik can get his filming done, then come and relax with us for a bit. Ease his way back in a little."

Alain thought it over for a moment. A little bit of peace and quiet was bound to do Hendrik good.

"OK. But call me if you need anything," he said, before heading back through the parade of cars towards the Bolt.

Perhaps, he thought, a change of scene was just what Hendrik needed.

CHAPTER FIFTEEN

Magali

Monday morning – Weissensee – Grossglockner

Hendrik's return had put Magali in a difficult position. Having spoken to Frank and heard what Eva and Janez had discovered, she felt duty-bound to ensure that Hendrik was monitored at all times. However, his presence also complicated the task that she and Martin had been assigned: namely, to protect Andrej and the technology. If monitoring Hendrik and protecting Andrej amounted to the same thing, then great. But until she knew for certain, she would have to find a way of keeping an eye on them both.

That was where Martin came in. During the course of the expedition, he had regularly driven Magali up the wall. Jokes about sex, jokes about marriage, jokes about the unlikelihood of a pair of newly-weds honeymooning around Europe in an electric car. It was as if he were making preparations for life after DSP, when his stand-up routine would take the comedy world by storm. But however annoying they were, Magali was forced to admit that Martin's quips had made him a popular figure among participants.

Aside from the technologist and Jasna, one of the friendships Martin had struck up was with a certain Andre Lugger, a German in his mid-thirties who was travelling with an Austrian man named Thomas Rot. The pair were driving a converted Volkswagen T5 and, over the course of the expedition, had provided a number of different teams with roadside assistance. They had all sorts of tools and adapters in the back of their van, not to mention space for two e-bikes, one of which Magali had used the previous day when their car was having difficulties. But Andre's real pride and joy was a small, battery-operated espresso machine.

As luck would have it, the T5 was stationed alongside Martin and Magali's EV that morning. Knowing the importance of keeping all the principal actors in one place, Martin had managed to persuade him that Hendrik's return provided the perfect excuse to showcase his latest acquisition. An impromptu reunion was scheduled for after the group photo. Magali had suggested that Andrej and Jasna join them, as she knew the pair would be delighted to see Hendrik.

So far, so good. Assembling everyone in one place had proved far easier than Magali had anticipated. In the meantime, she took the opportunity to relocate to a small meadow to one side of the town hall. She needed to speak to Frank in private. Earlier, Martin had explained what he thought had happened to their car the previous evening. As his field of expertise was IT and information security, he had taken it upon himself to do a little detective work in the wake of the incident. He had soon established that the cause couldn't have been a hardware failure. Since then he had been closely examining the log data and command sequence. A few minutes ago, it appeared he had found the confirmation he was looking for.

"Frank, Magali here."

"What is it?"

"As you know, we had a few issues with our car last night. Our motor kept packing in. Martin was able to rule out a hardware failure."

"Then it must have been something to do with the software."

"Precisely. Martin's just told me that someone manipulated the battery management system."

"Any idea who it could have been?"

"No, not really." Magali racked her brains, hoping to remember something unusual: a throwaway remark, anything that didn't quite fit. "It must have happened after Bled. Louis said last night that there were two new people joining. One of them is an unscheduled arrival: a guy who wants to show his support after the negative press coverage in Deutschlandsberg. Still, there's nothing unusual in that. There's been a fair bit of coming and going since the start. A lot of the participants are small business owners. They can take a few days off here and there but if something comes up, they need to be back at home to deal with it." Magali interrupted her speech to chastise herself. "But what am I saying? It can't be the newcomers. They arrived after Feistritz an der Drau."

All this time Frank had remained silent, waiting for Magali to find a solution of her own accord.

"Feistritz. Wait, there was something," she continued. "We were a little late arriving after Bled, but not so late we couldn't make a brief stop. I went to get us a drink while Martin stayed behind to keep an eye on Andrej. I had to climb a few stairs  and when I got to the top, I had a bird's eye view of all the cars. I saw someone sitting on the bonnet of our EV. He was doing something with his laptop. I didn't think anything of it at the time because it was one of the support team. Peter, his name is. Peter Prohaska. It looked like he was sending an email or maybe writing a blog. I wouldn't have had him down for a professional."

The word stung Frank into action.

"Well, there's no doubt it's professionals we're dealing with." Magali waited for him to explain. "Do you remember what I told you last night? What Eva and Janez said about Hendrik? That he didn't start the fire deliberately."

"You also said he was working for someone."

"That's right. He's been hired to look for the technology. He said that he has a friend in Zurich who's helping him."

"OK, so Hendrik's working for someone. That doesn't change the fact that he was in Bled when our car was tampered with."

"Or that he's callow and inexperienced. The point is he's working for a professional organization that is trying to find the technology you've been hired to protect." Frank paused to allow the information to sink in. "There have now been two incidents. Only one of them can be put down to Hendrik. From this, we can deduce that either he is part of a larger team, or that there are two *separate* organizations."

"We've persuaded him to join us for the day. The guy who picked him up from the east shore said he was behaving strangely last night. Like he had seen a ghost or something."

"Maybe he had. His friend told him to get back to WAVE as soon as possible. That there was someone on his tail. We know that he's disillusioned with his employer and worried about his safety. See if you can get any more information out of him. But go a little easy on him. We don't want a repeat of yesterday. I'll concentrate on Peter Prohaska."

With that, he had rung off. Magali looked at her watch. Only half an hour to go until the photo. People were already starting to make their way over toward the bridge. Not for the first time, Magali was taken aback by the scale of the expedition: forty separate teams, three dedicated vehicle-support units, a professional video blogger; and somewhere in among all these people, representatives of an organization searching for the knowledge that she and Martin already possessed. Did Hendrik know about DSP's presence at WAVE? Presumably not. That was why Frank had used a different pair of agents in Bled.

Magali began to walk towards the bridge. The rest of the field was now doing likewise. She noted that Hendrik had his filming equipment in tow. At least, she thought to herself, whatever footage he took that day would be in their hands.

 She looked across at her colleague. He wasn't making the trip empty-handed either. In fact, he had brought along one of his favourite toys: a small drone that enabled him to gather intelligence from the air.

Between Hendrik's footage, the bird's eye surveillance, and Magali's observations with the naked eye, they would surely have the measure of anyone acting suspiciously.

A thought struck Magali. If the person they were looking for didn't know she and Martin were agents, then their car couldn't have been targeted as a warning, or a message saying they were getting too close. Instead, it had been a test designed to see whether their vehicle contained the technology. Someone was going around manipulating EVs to see how they responded to the changes made. Presumably Martin and Magali's had been chosen because of its size. Either way, there were bound to be other incidents; and whoever was behind them would be well served by the prospect of a group photo.

When she arrived, most of the participants were cleaning their bonnets or polishing their windscreens. Others were talking animatedly to their neighbours. Everything seemed to be as normal. Suddenly Magali saw Andrej on the other side of the bridge climbing a lamppost. Had he seen something? Annoyed, Magali brushed the thought to one side. Andrej didn't even know anyone was looking for the technology. He must have just been taking one final picture of all the cars before they began to depart.

In the event, there was little to suggest foul play. The photo was taken, the cars departed on time, and Martin and Magali drove back to the small parking lot to resume charging and take a look at the battery-powered espresso machine. Thomas Rot was operating it, while his companion, Andre, swam in the lake. Jasna helped herself to a cup and took her place in the sun. Andrej, meanwhile, was going over the day's route for a final time, calculating the elevation between stops.

While they were sitting drinking coffee, Magali asked Hendrik to show them the footage he had taken. Seeing nothing strange in the request, he obliged. The film didn't reveal anything unusual, just a convoy of EVs slowly making their way towards their next destination.

Reunion over, Martin seemed eager to make a move. "I guess we should be heading. The battery might not be full but the first ten kilometres are downhill. We'll be able to recuperate some energy."

"Good idea. We're already behind schedule," Magali said.

Once they were in the car, Magali took the opportunity to enquire cautiously about Hendrik's welfare. The blogger hadn't questioned the decision to be switched to a different team. Perhaps he understood that Alain needed a break.

"Alain said you had quite an adventure last night," she said, hoping to induce a reaction. "I think I'd have been petrified in that darkness."

"Actually, it wasn't just the darkness – or the water," Hendrik replied. "It was a car that appeared out of nowhere."

"I hope you got a good look at the driver!" Martin joked.

"As a matter of fact, I did. I had my camera with me. The guy was in his early fifties, I'd say. Short hair. I couldn't tell what colour. But he looked tall and strong. At one point, I could have sworn he was looking me straight in the eye." Hendrik's whole body shivered. He was obviously concerned about his own welfare. Magali wondered whether his unexpected openness was some sort of cry for help.

"Probably one of the newbies," Martin said. "Nothing to worry about."

They had agreed to go easy on Hendrik for the time being.

Their first port of call that morning was Heiligenblut, a small municipality on the border between Carinthia and East Tyrol, which was located at the foot of the Grossglockner, Austria's highest mountain, and served as the southern starting point for the High Alpine Road. In the context of the day, it was an important stop. The altitude difference between Heiligenblut and Kaiser-Franz-Josefs-Hoehe, where participants would be able to look upon the world-famous Pasterze glacier, was upwards of 1,000 metres; and that meant charging was a pre-requisite. The distance might have only been twenty kilometres, but the steady seven percent incline ensured that cars expended twice as much energy as they would on a flat surface. No-one wanted to get halfway up and then have to turn back around.

Martin parked the car next to Vivien from support. Though he had informed them that the journey from Weissensee had passed without incident, Magali felt far from reassured. Today was just about the hardest day of the expedition, and this fact presented whoever was looking for the technology with a golden opportunity. Any vehicle that had been manipulated but still managed to get through the day would have to go down as a serious contender.

Magali took a deep breath. There were so many cars in the parking lot it was impossible to see what was going on. Lots of people had their laptops out and were typing away. Magali realized that any one of them could be trying to hack into a vehicle. As long as an EV had been equipped with an onboard wireless module – or alternatively if a hacker had managed to connect a wireless adapter to the diagnostic plug – then it really wasn't all that difficult. You could even use your cell phone. Not many people knew that a car radio contained a little computer that was connected to the vehicle control unit. To hack into an EV, all you needed was a Bluetooth connection.

Magali signalled to Martin that it was time to get to work. She would keep an eye on Andrej and the technology while he conducted a data traffic analysis on his computer.

At that moment, her cell phone rang. She moved to the other side of the road where she could speak in private.

"Frank. What have you got for me?"

"It's Peter. He was in Zurich at the same time as Hendrik."

"Could it be a coincidence?"

"Same time, same hotel, same evening, same bar."

"OK, that's good. That means they're working for the same organization. So what do we do?" Magali asked.

"Get Martin to take him to one side. Tell him you know he manipulated your car. Then see how he reacts. Make sure Andrej's out of the picture. If you're too tight on him, Peter will work out what's going on and draw his own conclusions."

"We'll do it at Grossglockner if we can. There's another group photo, so we should be able to get a minute alone with him. If not, we'll have to wait until tonight."

"OK, but be careful," Frank warned. "People do all kinds of things when you back them into a corner."

Magali wasn't too worried about Peter. She knew his type. For all his bravado, he was bound to fold when challenged. Still, that didn't mean she and Martin could afford to get complacent. They would have to wait for the right moment to question him. Magali checked the Roadbook. No-one from the support team was on official duty at Grossglockner: presumably something to do with the group photo. Peter would be there, though, and perhaps the moment would present itself before the group left for Neukirchen.

When they arrived at Kaiser-Franz-Josefs-Hoehe, the majority of the vehicles were already on their way down from the glacier. The photo, it seemed, had been put forward by fifteen minutes.

Martin was disappointed. He had spent a long time in Heiligenblut calculating exactly how long they would need to charge in order to arrive promptly at three o'clock. He had even managed to delay Andrej's departure by engaging the Slovenian in conversation about artificial intelligence. Now neither of them would be part of the photo.

Fortunately, however, Peter Prohaska was still there, as he had been obliged to help a late arrival find an adapter cable for their car.

Magali went with Andrej, Jasna, and Hendrik to take a closer look at the glacier. The technologist's disappointment at missing the group photo was soon put into perspective by the sight confronting them at the viewing platform.

The glacier was simply stunning. Its mountain ice, rugged, elemental, ever-changing in shape and form, was perfectly offset by the cerulean blue of the cloudless afternoon sky. Nevertheless, for all its beauty, there was sadness here, too.

The glacier's volume had diminished by half since it was first measured nearly two centuries ago, and was receding in length with every passing year.

"What's going on over there?" Jasna asked suddenly.

"It must be Alain," said Hendrik, who had indicated his desire to take a look at the visitor centre once they were finished. He had heard you could see marmots there.

"Yeah, but what's he doing?"

"It's a photo shoot for his clothing range. That's what he told me anyway," Hendrik said, and the statement was soon confirmed by the appearance of a photographer instructing Alain to take up a number of different outdoor poses.

In the meantime, Martin had reported a problem with the car and lured Peter over to have a look at it. Magali saw that the two were talking animatedly. She wondered what Peter was saying. She looked over towards Andrej and his wife. The pair had taken a seat on a nearby bench and were enjoying the sun. How, she mused, was his test going? Had the technology been successful? If not, how much further would he still have to drive?

Just then her thoughts were interrupted by the appearance of a man who had made his way alongside her. He was in his late-thirties with a full head of dark-brown hair and a neat reddish-brown beard.

"You must be Magali," he said. "Allow me to introduce myself. I'm William Steinberg."

He kissed Magali on the hand. She played along, pretending to be flattered.

"I'm one of the new arrivals. After all that negative press coverage in Deutschlandsberg, I called Louis Palmer and asked him if I could sign up. I wanted to show my support."

Handsome, charming, and environmentally engaged, Magali thought to herself. But was he too good to be true?

Just then Hendrik emerged, pleased as punch. "I've just seen some marmots!" he said, pointing to his camera.

"Here's another for your collection," William said self-deprecatingly. He must have been referring to his colouring. Or his size. He was a small man.

"Hendrik," the blogger offered William his hand.

"William. Pleased to meet you. Do you know, it's a shame you guys arrived so late. You missed quite a scene. One of the cars had a bit of a meltdown and had to be towed up the hill."

Magali felt a horrible sense of déjà vu.

"The amazing thing was," William continued, "it was another

EV that did the towing. Can you imagine that? All this talk in the press about their inadequacies, and here we have cast-iron proof that an EV can not only deal with the rigours of one of Europe's steepest roads, but actually make the trip with *another vehicle in tow*."

"Cast-iron proof?" Magali was confused. She thought back to the bridge that morning. She was certain they hadn't overlooked anything.

"I've got it on my phone. That's one of the reasons I wanted to introduce myself. When I called Louis, he said you were travelling with the official expedition blogger. I thought the footage could be useful."

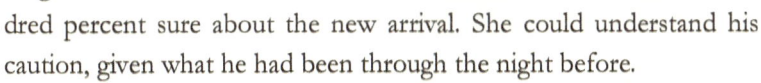

"Great," Hendrik said. But Magali could see he wasn't one hundred percent sure about the new arrival. She could understand his caution, given what he had been through the night before.

"OK, let's get together later then."

"What was the other reason? You mentioned there was more than one?" Magali asked.

"Please don't make me blush!" William said.

He smiled and fixed his gaze on Magali. She held it for a moment before allowing him to continue.

"The *third* reason," William said very deliberately. "Well, I hoped there was something you could do for me. I don't suppose you have a spare cable? In my haste I managed to forget a few things."

"I guess that's one of the pitfalls of making spontaneous decisions," Magali said. "I don't have one, but Peter might. He's just talking to my husband…"

Was there a hint of disappointment in the newcomer's eyes? Magali brushed the thought aside. Out of the corner of her eye, she saw that a number of things were happening at the same time. Andrej and Jasna were making for their vehicle, and the rest of the field would

175

soon follow suit. She signalled to Martin, who broke off his conversation with Peter and, likewise, began to ready himself for departure. Hendrik had already taken his place in the backseat.

Then she watched as William approached Peter to enquire about the cable. Strange, there was no handshake between the two, no introduction. Peter didn't seem the least bit interested in providing assistance.

Instead he had taken one look at the man standing before him and turned a deathly shade of pale.

CHAPTER SIXTEEN

Steinberg

Monday afternoon – Grossglockner – Neukirchen

William Steinberg's body language was open and friendly while he waited for the other participants to exit the scene.

"I hope you enjoyed seeing the results of your handiwork. Still, as they say, all good things must come to an end."

"What are you doing here?" Peter was barely able to conceal the terror in his voice.

"Didn't they tell you? No, I don't suppose they would have…"

"Tell me what?" Peter stumbled backwards, lost his footing, scrambled clumsily to his feet.

"Why don't we take a walk?" Steinberg said, and directed Peter towards the steps that led down towards the glacier snout. It was late in the afternoon and the parking lot was almost empty. Soon the cafes and souvenir shops would be closing, while the photographer on the slopes was long gone.

"What are you doing here?" Peter asked for the second time, as he continued to make his way down.

Steinberg had never been able to stand that whiney voice. He turned to check no-one was watching, grabbed his colleague by the upper arm, and led him in the direction of the lake that had been formed by the melt-water.

"Zurich have called the professionals in. That stunt just now could be your curtain call. What a place for it all to end!" Steinberg paused for a moment to take in the scene around him. All was quiet save for the faint murmur of a breeze. "Shame the audience is no longer here to pay tribute, to *witness* your final bow."

"What are you talking about? What am I supposed to have done?"

Steinberg was all too familiar with the sound of Peter protesting his innocence.

"Two incidents in two days. Oh yeah, I know about the first one, too. You thought it'd be a good idea to repeat the dose? Not smart."

"The first one was me. I admit it," Peter said. "It was too good an opportunity to miss. But I had nothing to do with what happened today."

"Humour me," Steinberg said. Why was Peter trying to negotiate? The time for that had long since passed. "If it wasn't you, then who was it?"

"It wasn't anyone. Just a problem with the car. The hall sensors. You know about hall sensors?"

"Enlighten me."

"In EVs, they're used to measure the position of the magnet in relation to the rotor. Normally they're glued together. It's just possible that they came apart."

Steinberg was growing impatient. He hadn't signed up to a lecture on EV technology.

"Get to the point."

"You asked me for an explanation. And that's what I'm trying to give you." The despair was evident in Peter's voice. "If the hall sensors can no longer accurately measure the location of the magnet, then you have a problem. You might still be able to drive straight or downhill, but go uphill and..." Steinberg could sense Peter was trying to wriggle free of his iron-like grip. "The cause was heat. The engine must have become too hot during the climb and the hall sensors came loose as a result."

But Steinberg was no longer interested in the technical explanation. In fact he wasn't interested in an explanation of any kind. They were standing by the edge of the glacier lake. The water had made the ground underfoot dangerously slippy. It would be all too easy to lose one's footing and fall into one of the crevices whose path the water followed down to the reservoir below.

Again, Steinberg checked that no-one was watching. The sun had disappeared behind Grossglockner and the clouds were slowly descending. Even if there was someone on the viewing platform, they wouldn't be able to see what was going on. All of a sudden, Steinberg let go of Peter's arm. The manoeuvre caught his colleague off guard and Steinberg took advantage of the momentary confusion to administer the first of three blows. The first caught Peter in the solar plexus and constricted his air supply. The second landed on his face, breaking his jawbone and shattering his teeth. The third blow was reserved for the area below Peter's left ear, damaging his cervical nerves and killing him instantly.

He rolled the lifeless body into one of the crevices and listened to Peter's bones shattering one by one as his body hurtled down toward the ground. There was a dull thud and a splash of water. It would be some time before he was found.

Satisfied, Steinberg returned to the viewing platform. There was one more thing he needed to take care of. Peter's car was still in the parking lot. He removed the number plates and replaced them with a new set. After he had checked there was nothing in the car to connect it to Peter or the expedition, he made his way to Neukirchen.

He called Dominik Brandt from the car.

"It's done," Steinberg said, when his employer finally picked up. "Peter's just had a shattering experience."

"Spare me the details. From now on, the technology is your number one priority. We need to find it before WAVE reaches Zurich. It's going to be chaos there. There's a world record attempt happening. According to my sources, they're expecting several hundred cars. Besides, Zurich's too close to home. I don't want anything that can be traced back to us. Is that clear?"

"Crystal."

"Good. I'll have someone call Louis Palmer and tell him Peter's had to return home urgently. A family emergency."

"OK. But listen, I'm worried about Jaeger. He's the CEO's man.

What if he lets on I'm here?

"Forget about Jaeger. He's not the type to question decisions made by a higher power. That's why he's so good."

It's also why he's never climbed the ranks, Steinberg thought. Too rigid in his thought processes; too much respect for hierarchy. Not like him or Dominik.

"But do we really need him?" Steinberg persisted. "He can't do anything now that Hendrik's back."

"All the more reason for him to listen to you. If he has to stay away from WAVE, then he'll need your help to find Hendrik. Who knows, maybe you'll need him somewhere down the line too," Dominik said. "It's Walter I'm most concerned about. He doesn't know you're here. No-one does. If he finds out, I'll tell him that Hendrik's return has complicated matters. That you and Jaeger are working together on this one."

"He'll buy it?"

"He will if it's the truth. When we sent for Jaeger, Hendrik was still in Bled. Now that he's gone back to the expedition, Jaeger needs a second pair of eyes. Walter knows we can't have Jaeger anywhere near WAVE."

"I understand."

"I'll make sure Jaeger knows he's reporting to you." Dominik said. "Just concentrate on finding the technology. Then I can start making good on my promise."

The purr at the end of the line told Steinberg their conversation was over. Not for the first time since he had agreed to go against the CEO's wishes, Steinberg felt certain he had backed the right horse. The world was changing and Christian Adler would soon be left behind. If they sat back and did nothing to prevent the electrification of the automotive industry, Adler Reilly stood to lose both revenue and political clout. As soon as there was a genuine, affordable alternative to fuel – that is, to traditional gasoline cars – party leaders would no longer be so easily kept in check by the demands and occasional donations of an organization like Adler's. BIRD's work was pointless if

Adler Reilly was no longer respected by the people who mattered. Dominik understood this, and after a period spent waiting in the wings, he had no desire to see his superior squander all that hard-won influence by refusing to move with the times. Both men were arrogant, but Dominik, at least, acknowledged the importance of modernization. He knew that, in this instance, overhauling the organization was the only way to preserve the status quo. He also knew that as Adler's number two, he was only one successful operation away from assuming pole position.

And Steinberg? Well, he was interested in any coup that would see him move up the food chain. Dominik had outlined the risks, but he had also stressed the rewards. Adler would not be best pleased if he knew the operation was still in progress; but if they were successful, he would have no choice but to step aside.

As for Jaeger, Dominik was right. He probably hadn't even thought to question whether the operation had Adler's approval. He would just assume it did. If it had come from Dominik, then it must have come from the CEO. Jaeger was dangerous, no doubt about it. But he was also fundamentally incapable of thinking for himself. More like a giant Labrador that had been trained to kill than an agent who survived on the strength of his wits.

Steinberg looked at the programme of events for the evening ahead. He would need to make good time to put his plan into action. One final phone call and then he could concentrate on the drive.

"Jaeger, it's Steinberg. Where are you?"

"Just beyond Heiligenblut."

"Well, take your time. Enjoy the High Alpine Road. I don't think there's much chance of our boy coming out to play tonight."

"Who's he with?" Jaeger asked.

"It's not who he's with. It's the schedule. Photo shoot, dinner, briefing. He'll be surrounded by people all night. I suggest we hold off until tomorrow. Looks like the group will be more fragmented then. Zell am Ziller, Innsbruck, Landeck, Sent – take your pick. There are any number of stops before La Punt."

181

"Anything else?"

"Yeah, get onto the experts from data analysis. I want a full background check on all participants," Steinberg emphasized the word "full". "Don't skimp on the details. From now on, I want all their phone conversations, text messages, and emails scanned and cross-checked for key words."

"Such as?"

"Jesus Christ, Jaeger. Do I have to spell it out? EV, technology, new, investment, test, range…"

"OK. Is that it?" Jaeger said.

"One more thing," Steinberg paused. "I've just spoken to Dominik. He says that Walter's been behaving strangely. For whatever reason, he doesn't seem one hundred percent behind the boss."

"So, what I can do about it?"

"Nothing, I just thought you should know," Steinberg said.

The idea had occurred to Steinberg on the spur of the moment. If Jaeger got it into his head that Walter was being disloyal to the CEO, he wouldn't give him the time of day.

"OK," Jaeger said.

"I'll call again tomorrow."

The initial stretch of road after Kaiser-Franz-Josefs-Hoehe had been a challenging one. Damn EVs. Steinberg had fully charged the battery but forgotten it could recuperate energy on the road downhill. Now the battery was so hot he could have fried an egg on it. He couldn't afford to miss the evening briefing, but there was no choice. Annoyed, he veered from the road and drove towards a mound of snow in a meadow nearby.

The battery had been installed on the underside of the car, so perhaps the cold would help stabilize the battery temperature.

It worked like a charm. After a few minutes, he was ready to go. As a precaution, he drove back up the hill for a minute or two in order to burn as much energy as he could, before continuing on his way.

After Zeller See, it was Brueck, a pretty mountain town that had been populated since the Bronze Age. Steinberg breathed it all in as he drove. He was surrounded by such beauty, and yet already he could perceive the stench of ambition, the whiff of deceit.

Alighting in Neukirchen, he was intrigued to discover that although late, he was far from the last to arrive. Clearly, he had missed the official welcome and the photo shoot, though dinner and the briefing were still to come. There was an air of discontent among the participants in the hotel that night, as if Steinberg's appearance had somehow poisoned the mood. A number of teams were complaining that there was too little time to get to know one another: just a constant diet of driving, charging, and, for some at least, uploading pictures onto blogs.

Steinberg nodded here and there in sympathy but knew deep down that it was a simple case of mid-expedition blues. It was a long eight or nine days with an, at times, punishing schedule. People were bound to be tired by the mid-point, especially if they were denied the opportunity to relax in the evenings. That wasn't the fault of the tour director, just a by-product of always being surrounded by new people. There were so many faces that you could only ever get used to one or two. This, Steinberg mused, ought to work in his favour. Yet something told him that Hendrik, if he were to disappear, would be missed more than most.

In fact, the blogger had only emerged five minutes ago, in the company of the bickering newlyweds, Martin and Magali. Martin was complaining loudly about how their navigation system had given them such bad directions they had almost ended up on the wrong side of the road. His wife looked exhausted and disappointed that they would have so little time to eat.

The briefing, which followed on from the meal, was clearly shorter than many had anticipated. A motion was passed whereby participants agreed for a member of the support team to take responsibility for the vehicles charging overnight. This was in the hope of preventing a recurrence of events from the previous week, where a number of EVs had had their cables disconnected. Steinberg chuckled: BIRD's crack team of operatives, no doubt. At least in their previous incarnation.

After that, Louis moved onto the programme for the next day. Tomorrow morning, they would travel over the Gerlos Road to Innsbruck and then on into Switzerland. Their accommodation for the evening would be an old Swiss army bunker.

"Now, arrivals and departures," Louis Palmer continued. "In addition to William Steinberg, we are also joined by Timo Schneeweiss from Konstanz. I hope you give them both a warm welcome. And some sad news. Peter Prohaska, who has done sterling work as part of our support team, has had to return home on account of a family emergency. Our thoughts are with him at this difficult time."

A brief murmur, then peace was restored.

"Peter's news does, however, leave us with a minor problem regarding the make-up of our support unit…"

"I suppose I could fill the breach," Steinberg volunteered. Things were turning out exactly the way he had planned. "Though I might need a little support myself!"

The joke met with the desired response, though when Steinberg looked closer he noted that Hendrik was pulling an odd face. Did the blogger suspect that something was amiss?

"That would be most helpful, thank you," Louis Palmer said. "Who knows, perhaps Peter will soon be able to re-join us. For now, I bid you tonight. And remember that we have an early start tomorrow. If in doubt, *follow the Roadbook*."

With that, give or take the odd final question from participants, the briefing was over. Steinberg watched as several teams filed into the hotel bar next door for a nightcap. Well, the Roadbook didn't say anything about what time they had to be in bed…

Steinberg followed them in, surveying the bar and crosschecking the faces with those that appeared in his file. Thomas Rot was there, as was Andre Lugger, along with Hendrik and several others. The talk was of how nice it was to be able, finally, to spend some time together as a group, without the twin distractions of car and computer. Steinberg kept himself at a distance from the rest. He had made enough of an impression for one day and felt it would be unwise to draw any further attention to himself.

Out of the corner of his eye, however, he noticed that Hendrik was constantly flitting between the tables, chatting with their various occupants. Never alone, always surrounded by people. Was he, despite everything that had happened, still in the process of gathering information? What had he really been doing that lost afternoon in Bled? And how the hell had he managed to get back to WAVE so quickly in the first place?

Steinberg left the bar, mulling these questions over in his mind. Perhaps the cool night air would provide him with some answers.

CHAPTER SEVENTEEN

Magali

Tuesday morning – Neukirchen – La Punt

The morning began, as it so often did, with a phone call. Magali was trying to persuade Frank that Hendrik could be a valuable asset for DSP. They might have been successful in protecting the technology up until now, but who knew whether the threat had truly passed? What was the likelihood of an organization sending two people to do a job and then giving up at the first hint of trouble? All in all, they could use another pair of eyes to help them on the ground.

"But is Hendrik reliable?" Frank was saying. "You both witnessed the fall-out from Deutschlandsberg. Can we trust him not to go AWOL if something similar happens again?"

"I'll tell you why he went AWOL," Magali countered. "He was involved in something he wasn't one hundred percent sure about. Accepting all that money meant he came into the event with a guilty conscience. Then, when it all went wrong, he blamed himself for what happened. That seems pretty natural to me. After all, he might not have done it deliberately, but people could still have died. Throw in the fact that he lost his own family in a car crash, and you've got a pretty toxic mix."

"What are you saying?"

"I'm saying he knew he was doing something that was wrong. And that's why he reacted the way he did. If we can convince him that he's working for the right side, for the good of others, rather than for his own personal gain, then... What I mean is: if I'm reading him right, it won't be nearly so easy to knock him off his stride when he believes in what he's doing."

"What does Martin think?"

"He agrees with me. Besides, we never finished questioning Peter. Now that he's gone, Hendrik's the only one who can help us find out what the hell is going on."

"Wait a minute. Peter's gone?"

"Yesterday afternoon. Family emergency, apparently."

"I don't believe that for a minute. If Peter *was* working with Hendrik then he's either been relieved of his duties or perhaps even killed. Hendrik indicated to Eva and Janez that he was in danger in Bled. That's why he wanted to go back to WAVE. And now it looks as though he was telling the truth."

"Either way, it looks like we're dealing with more than a simple case of industrial espionage."

"Find out what you can from Hendrik. But tread carefully. It's just possible he's being watched."

"Roger that. Thanks, Frank. You've made the right call."

Magali returned her cell to her pocket and signalled to Martin that their request had been approved. On the radio earlier that morning, the announcer had reported that heavy overnight rain had caused a landslide on the Gerlos Road, rendering it temporarily inaccessible.

It meant the longest day of the expedition – participants would have to drive a full 270 kilometres in order to reach La Punt that evening – was about to get even longer.

"At least it'll give us a little extra time with Hendrik," Magali said. "Where is he, anyway?"

"Packing his things."

"We need to keep an eye on him from now on."

"As if we didn't have enough to do already…"

"What side of bed did you get

187

out of this morning? As long as Hendrik remains with us, then we can kill two birds with one stone."

"You're right. I'm just worried that these people will stop at nothing. That it could get dangerous for you."

Magali had to admit that she was starting to get a little worried as well. Granted, she was trained in self-defence and knew how to handle a weapon, but she had never been in a situation like this before. Before she took the job, Frank had explained there might be a few anti-EV protesters, a few tomatoes or eggs thrown in anger, or perhaps even a little violence from time to time. He hadn't said anything about industrial espionage – and he certainly hadn't said anything about murder.

"Finally," Martin said. He had been listening to the radio. "They've opened the road again."

"Good, I'll go and find Hendrik. Andrej and Jasna are getting ready to leave. Make sure they don't go anywhere."

"OK. So how are we going to play this? With Hendrik, I mean."

"Simple. We tell him his boss has been feeding him a pack of lies from the start."

"Except for the technology…"

Magali smiled. "Except for the technology."

A short time later, the trio was ready to depart. They drove past the Krimml waterfalls and on through the section of road where the landslide had occurred. Even though the debris had been cleared, Martin still made a point of driving carefully. After all, today was the day of the efficiency test, and this was the stretch of road on which vehicles' performances were being measured. Magali wondered what Andrej's plan was. How was he going to ensure no-one noticed his car's superior performance? She stopped herself. The technologist was bound to have taken all that into consideration long ago.

Having negotiated the morning drive, they paused briefly in Zell am Ziller to charge before continuing towards Innsbruck.

"Never a good sign when it's the sponsor that wins the event," Hendrik said wryly. He had managed to find out the results of the test.

"They're definitely pushing their luck," Martin said.

"Pushing their EV more like…" Hendrik replied.

Martin's company seemed to be doing him good. After the trials and tribulations of the past few days, it was important that Hendrik felt as though he were among friends.

"Seriously, I'm sure you can appeal it," Hendrik continued.

Magali smiled. The comment had given her the perfect pretext to broach a more important subject.

"Do you prefer things to be transparent?" she asked.

"Doesn't everyone?" Hendrik replied.

Magali looked at him in the rear-view mirror. She had taken on the driving duties in Zell am Ziller.

"No," she said. "Some people lie on a daily basis. Some people lie so often it's impossible to know when they're telling the truth."

She saw Hendrik squirm in the backseat.

"Exactly what are you getting at?" he said.

It was time. Magali stopped on a dirt road and got out of the car. Martin did likewise and motioned for Hendrik to join them.

"We need to talk in private," he said. "It's better if we do it outside. Leave everything in the car. Your cell phone too."

Hendrik stuffed his phone into his camera bag and followed Martin and Magali for a few metres along the dirt road.

"I'm going to tell you a secret," Magali said. "Because I trust you. We both do."

Hendrik didn't appear to be comfortable with what was going on.

"We're not who you think we are," she continued.

There was no reaction from Hendrik. Obviously he was waiting to see what would come next.

"We're not married for a start," Martin said. "And we know you weren't in hospital in Bled."

All of a sudden, Hendrik was wide-eyed.

"We know because we work for the same organization as Eva and Janez," Magali took up the thread. "They were good to you, weren't they? They drove you back to WAVE when you asked."

Hendrik wasn't sure how to react.

"Did you feel threatened in their presence?"

"No," Hendrik said. "Not really."

"A good thing too," Martin said. "Because we're not the ones who pose the greatest threat. We might have been economical with the truth but–"

"The truth? Tell me, what is the truth?" Hendrik was warming to the task.

"The truth," Magali sighed, "is that we need your help."

"My help? Why? Besides, how do I know I can trust you?" Hendrik asked eventually, still understandably doubtful.

"Funny, that would've been a good thing to ask your employer."

"Martin…" Magali said calmly. Why had he decided to go on the attack all of a sudden?

"What? It's true! Rushing blindly into something like this," Martin continued. "What did they tell you? C'mon, let's hear it."

"That there was…" Hendrik mumbled.

"I can't hear you!" Martin said.

"That there was a piece of technology…" Hendrik paused mid-sentence to compose himself. "That there are *rumours* that a piece of technology was being developed by a major car manufacturer in order to circumvent EU legislation concerning CO_2 emissions. You know, the whole thing with super-credits. Manufacturers reduce the CO_2 emissions of a selection of cars in their fleet in order to continue producing gas-guzzlers."

"That's rubbish," Magali said.

"Total bullshit," Martin scoffed. "On two counts."

"Hendrik," Magali said, her voice softer than that of her colleague, full of sympathy. "Your employer must have believed the technology was genuine. They wanted you to find out who developed it. As for the bit about the EU, I'm afraid that's simply not true."

"How do you know?" Hendrik asked. Apparently, he still wasn't convinced.

"If we tell you, do you promise to cooperate?" Magali bartered.

Hendrik glanced down at his shoes and took a deep breath; then he squared his shoulders to face Magali. "I promise I'll try."

"Prove that we can trust you," Magali said.

"What do you want to know?" Hendrik replied without any further ado.

"Let's start with something easy: why. Why did you agree to it in the first place?" Martin asked.

Hendrik sighed. "I don't know. I guess the way it was sold to me. I thought I'd be helping."

"What do you mean?" Martin pressed.

"The super-credits. I really thought someone was using them to exploit the rules. You know, some major corporation that didn't give a damn about the environment. David and Goliath stuff. I thought I was going to help bring them down."

"So, what changed?" Magali this time.

"It just never quite added up. It wasn't me who was recruited initially, anyway. It was Nils."

"Your friend in Zurich?" Martin asked.

"Right. Only, he doesn't give a shit about the environment – or whether big businesses play by the rules." Hendrik looked sad. Magali wondered if the pair had fallen out over it.

"So he was attracted by something else?" she asked.

"Money, I guess. Or maybe he liked the idea of undercover surveillance. He's pretty vain. Thinks he's going to be the next James Bond. All that secret service stuff."

"Secret service stuff?" Magali was intrigued.

"These people are pretty well connected," Hendrik said. "And they've got some amazing technical equipment. Nils loves it there. In Sopron, for example, I had him listen in on one of the participants' cell phone conversations. We thought it could have been him. Whose car had the technology, I mean."

"Wait a minute. Are you saying you can listen in to our cell phones," Magali said. There was a trace of panic in her voice.

"Unlikely," Martin reassured her. "Frank gave us the latest

crypto-phones. With their 256-bit AES encryption, not even hard-core hackers stand a chance." He turned to Hendrik. "Is your cell phone still on?"

"Yes. In case they try to get in touch. Officially I'm still working for them."

"OK," Martin said. "It's a good thing it's in the car. In future, whenever we have something to discuss, turn it off. Take the battery out and wrap it in something. A scarf or a shawl. Then put it in a bag."

"Why? Nils told me it was a secure line!" Hendrik countered.

"Just do it," came the response. "Once we've finished talking, you can turn it back on."

"And if they try to reach me when it's off?"

"Then too bad," Martin said. "Tell them you were in a dead zone. They still exist." Martin's face took on a more serious expression. "Now tell us: Who hired you in the first place?"

"That's another thing. At least in retrospect. It was never clear. They had some connection to Adler Reilly."

"You mean the consultancy firm?" Magali asked.

"That's the one. Their head office is in Zurich," Hendrik confirmed.

"Any names?" Martin again.

"Dominik. Dominik Brandt."

"We'll get him checked out," Magali said. She nodded towards Martin.

"Hendrik," Martin said suddenly. "Why did you come back to WAVE? It's been pretty clear since Bled that you want nothing more to do with your employer."

"Because Nils said it'd be safer."

"Why?" Martin pressed.

"I don't know."

"C'mon Hendrik. Why?" Martin wouldn't let go.

"I don't know!"

"Because someone's been sent for you," Magali said. "That's why you were so spooked the other night. You saw them, saw their car."

Hendrik swallowed hard. Magali could see the fear in his eyes. She looked across to Martin, who gave a quick nod of the head.

"OK, you've proved we can trust you," she began softly. "So now we're going to tell you something confidential."

Hendrik still looked distinctly uncomfortable. Nevertheless, Magali remained convinced he'd pull through.

"Your employers. You asked how we knew they lied to you. Well, it's simple." She paused. "This technology you're so desperate to find… Martin and I were hired to protect it. Whatever your employer said, I can tell you now that it's a small company behind it. All they want is to make a difference to the environment. And they will if the technology is successfully tested this week. It will revolutionize the market."

Despite the revelation, there was almost no reaction from Hendrik. Magali had half-expected his jaw to drop and his pupils to dilate in surprise. After all, he couldn't have known there was another organization out there, just as Martin and Magali had been unaware they themselves would be called into action. Instead of surprise, however, there was only resignation. Magali realized that what she said to Frank had been true. Hendrik knew he had made the wrong choice, and he was resigned to facing the consequences.

"OK, soon we'll be in Innsbruck." Martin said, as they made their way back towards the car. "Don't say a word about this to anyone. The best thing you can possibly do right now is put on your best poker-face and concentrate on your blog. After all, that's why you're here."

Hendrik nodded but he still hadn't said a word.

As it turned out, there was almost nothing in Innsbruck to film. The town itself was beautifully situated and ought to have been something of a highlight in the participants' busy schedule. For some reason, however, the teams were greeted with little fanfare. Part of the problem, of course, was that only half of them were there. Weight restrictions limited the number of vehicles allowed on the Landhausplatz at any one given time. Thankfully, no-one was about to let it spoil their mood. The weather was glorious and once the factor thirty had been suitably applied, all those present took the opportunity to enjoy an extended break in the afternoon sun.

For the first half of the journey to La Punt, meanwhile, they were back on the motorway. Magali saw how one of the participants was hanging behind trucks in order to make use of the slipstream. The decreased wind resistance would enable them to reduce their energy consumption. Nevertheless, it was a risky business. Magali knew from the files that truck drivers were naturally suspicious of anyone on their tail for too long. Probably they were worried it was the police, or customs perhaps. Moreover, they became really angry if cars slowed them down. She concentrated on following Andrej, who was proceeding briskly in the middle lane. He didn't need to conserve any energy.

"And then there's Peter," Magali said, taking up the conversation from before Innsbruck. "Where does he fit into all of this? Can you confirm you two were working together?"

"Yes. He was my partner. It was my first mission. He was supposed to be–"

"When Louis made the announcement yesterday evening," Martin interrupted. "He said Peter had to head home. Some sort of family emergency. You didn't believe him. I saw it in your eyes."

"He doesn't have a family," Hendrik said quietly. "At least, he isn't married. I didn't spend a great deal of time with him. But I had the impression he was lonely."

"So, let's recap," Magali said. "You're still in Slovenia when you get a tip-off from your friend saying you'll be safer at WAVE. He doesn't tell you much more. But you trust him, so you go. You take the back road to Weissensee with Eva and Janez; and then a boat across to Techendorf."

"In the middle of the lake, you see a car," Martin picked up the thread. "What's it doing there? Why's the driver looking you up and down? Suddenly, you realize what your friend means. Someone's been sent to keep you quiet, maybe even take over from you. But they can't touch you as long as you're surrounded by people."

"This person, whoever he is, deals with Peter, then calls Louis. He needs to cover his tracks. But really, it's a message for you. It says: 'you're next'." Magali paused. "William. It has to be William. He was alone with Peter in the car park at Grossglockner, and now he has *literally* taken his place."

"Right. It's a double bluff. No-one would be so brazen as to have Peter's replacement actually physically replace him. It's way too obvious."

"You're forgetting something," Hendrik said. "These people aren't trying to outfox you. They don't even know you're here. Besides, it's not William."

"It doesn't have anything to do with us. Whoever it is, they need to protect their identity. Everything about William fits," Magali protested. "The time he arrived, the fact that he was the last person to see Peter."

"But he's not the guy I saw in the car," Hendrik said. "He's at least ten years younger. And I'd wager a good deal shorter. The man in the car had long legs. His head was almost touching the roof." The mention of the man in the car seemed to drain all of the colour out of Hendrik's face.

"Did you guys meet up last night?" Magali changed tack. "Wasn't William supposed to be showing you some footage on his cell?"

"Yes. But no, he went to bed before I could talk to him. I spoke to a lot of people last night. I mean, I still need to make it look as if I'm doing my job."

"Which job?" Martin asked.

"Both! Listen, the point is, it's not him. Nor is it the other guy who joined recently, Timo. He's absolutely mad about the environment. He won't even buy a bottle of water because he thinks it's wasteful," Hendrik said.

"So," Magali summarized. "It has to be someone hanging back: someone who's not part of the expedition."

"If that's true," Martin said, "then how are they going to get at the technology?"

195

"Who said anything about that? They hired me to confirm it exists. Nothing more." Even Hendrik didn't sound particularly convinced by this line of argument.

"C'mon, Hendrik," Martin chided. "You don't still believe that? They've lied to you from the get-go. They know it's here. What do you think they're going to do when they find it?"

Hendrik didn't respond.

"Let's stick to what *we* know, shall we?" Magali admonished. "We know there's someone out there who wants Hendrik out of the picture. But there's nothing to suggest this person is a participant. The likelihood is he wasn't expecting you to come back to WAVE. So what's he doing? He's biding his time. While he's waiting, he takes care of Peter. Exactly how, we don't know. It's possible Peter's been reassigned to another operation." Magali made another zig-zagging manoeuvre. "Hendrik," she continued, "we can get you out of this but we're going to need your help. We need to find out who we're dealing with here. It could be dangerous. From now on, if you see anything suspicious you come to us. Do you understand? We need you to be our second pair of eyes."

Hendrik swallowed again.

"We have to find these people."

She knew she was asking a lot but she didn't see that Hendrik had any other choice. Who else was going to help him out of this mess? Her thoughts turned briefly to William Steinberg. Whatever Hendrik said, she still hadn't ruled him out of the equation. There was something about the way he had introduced himself. He was charming, for sure, but somehow calculating at the same time. As if he wanted desperately to be liked. But then, she thought to herself, who didn't?

Certainly Hendrik was no different.

Their eyes met in the rear-view mirror.

"I'll do it," the blogger said.

Magali left the motorway, always following Andrej, and took the B-road towards La Punt. For more than half an hour nobody breathed a single word. Magali knew that she would have to call Frank to give him a status update. Perhaps he could check to see if any corpses had turned up near Grossglockner. Whatever had happened to Peter, she knew they would have to keep a close eye on Hendrik. He was too naïve, too inexperienced to look after himself.

That said, he had already provided a lot of useful information, and crucially he had given them a name. Magali had made sure to write it down.

Dominik.

Dominik Brandt.

CHAPTER EIGHTEEN

Steinberg

Tuesday afternoon – Innsbruck – La Punt

Getting rid of Peter had been easy, but William Steinberg knew that time was running short. He had three, maybe four, days to find the technology: three or four days in which to deliver a result. Despite the need for urgency, however, he was also experienced enough to know that speed alone wouldn't solve his problems.

A different operative, Steinberg suspected, would have used the body of evidence collected by Hendrik and Peter to inform their next move. But in order to recruit Hendrik, Dominik had deliberately withheld information from him. That meant whatever the blogger turned up was likely to be unreliable, no more than a basic, error-strewn guide. As for Peter, well, Steinberg had never trusted him anyway. He had no choice but to go back to square one.

That was why he had asked Jaeger to conduct a full background check on all expedition participants. He wanted to know everything about these people. What did they do? How much did they earn? Did they have a police record?

Away from their professional lives, Steinberg also wanted to know where they went to eat, what music they listened to, what books they read, what films they watched, which websites they visited, which friends they chatted to most often online, whether they were members of clubs or associations, if they took part in demonstrations, and, lastly, if there were any major events in their lives that had brought about a change in their habits. In addition, he had asked that any attempts they made to communicate during WAVE, whether by cell phone, text message, or email, were scanned for key words.

Although the communication angle hadn't turned anything up yet, the profiles were ready, and the results had come in earlier that morning. Right now, Steinberg was sitting drinking coffee near the main square in Innsbruck, looking through the files and watching his new colleagues as they tried in vain to engage the interest of the town's citizens. Jaeger had done a good job. There were a number of different leads, of which by far the most intriguing was Jaromir Vegr, a member of the support team Steinberg had joined the night before.

Given that Steinberg's predecessor had been working as part of the same unit, it seemed strange that Jaromir had been overlooked until now. If BIRD had concluded that technical support was sufficient cover for Peter, their own operative, then surely the same applied to whoever was testing the technology. Members of the support team were often the first to arrive at, or the last to leave, a particular destination. That left  plenty of scope for any business that needed to be carried out discreetly, away from the prying eyes of the masses. It also provided a good excuse not to take part in the numerous competitions – speed, efficiency, design – that were running parallel to the expedition itself.

Still, that wasn't the only thing that made Jaromir a credible suspect. Indeed, Jaeger's digging had revealed a number of interesting details about his life. Born in the former Czechoslovakia, Jaromir had been one of the signatories of Charter 77, a 1977 manifesto which had criticized the-then Communist government of failing to respect the human rights of its citizens. The majority of signatories were arrested, interrogated, and fired from their jobs. Some forfeited their citizenship; others were exiled to the West.

Jaromir Vegr, it seemed, had suffered none of these fates, but been allowed, instead, to freely indulge his greatest passion. Whether or not he had collaborated with, or acted on behalf of, the state secret police was unclear, but it was safe to assume he was practised in the art of deceit. Why was that relevant? Because it stood to reason that whoever was testing the technology was doing so in secret. If they weren't simply lying outright, then, at the very least, they would need to be pretty economical with the truth. Experience would be a great help; and Jaromir, nearing sixty, had thirty years of it. During his decade-long association with electric vehicles, he had been a tireless promoter of the EV cause in his native land. He had organized events, written articles, and supervised meetings, even completing a stint as chairman of the Czech Republic's Electric Vehicle Association. His presence on the support team, meanwhile, indicated that he had the knowledge to deal with a variety of unanticipated technical problems.

In short, if ever a man could have both designed and then concealed a game-changing new technology, then Jaromir Vegr was it. He had a mysterious past, a lifelong passion for EVs, and, thanks to his role at WAVE, the chance to go about his work in peace.

Satisfied, Steinberg checked his file for a final time to confirm what he already knew. The group was staying in La Punt that evening in a former Swiss army bunker. If he could make good progress past Landeck and over the Austrian border, then he still had a chance of being among the first to arrive. That would allow him to do a little reconnaissance work: to see whether the bunker was fit for purpose. A plan was forming in his mind. Yes, it would take discretion and no little good fortune, but already he was convinced that Jaromir would surrender his secret before the night was out.

Jaeger's research had also revealed some interesting information about Jaromir's personal life. As he began the long drive to La Punt, Steinberg turned his thoughts to how he could make use of it. It wasn't analytical work, but it did require a basic understanding of the human condition. This was a role to which Steinberg felt particularly well-suited. Ever since he was a small boy, he had known how to manipulate people to his advantage. It was a discovery he had made in elementary school, when, having struck a classmate in anger, he had successfully persuaded the teacher that he had been the victim of an unprovoked attack. Indeed, so adamant had he been that it was his classmate who had been in the wrong that the latter had eventually broken down and confessed to everything. To this day Steinberg still hadn't forgotten the value of a choice phrase or two, even if he acknowledged that violence was often the most expedient solution. With Jaromir, he would use a combination. Violence to soften him up; blackmail to extract what he needed to know.

Steinberg felt a tingle down his spine. Peter had been dealt with quickly, efficiently: a professional job that had brought little pleasure, only the satisfaction that came with completion. This was different. There was more risk involved, more that could go wrong. But there was also a great deal more to savour. The driving, the waiting, the checking that everything was in place. There was something ritualistic about it, almost romantic, in fact. A feeling of nervousness that would, if all went well, soon be transformed into elation.

Steinberg glanced up at the sky through the windscreen. After a morning of brilliant sunshine, the clouds had begun to stretch themselves lazily across the horizon. It had become darker, and Steinberg couldn't help but feel that someone, somewhere, was aware of what was about to happen.

He smiled. He realized he was being ridiculous. The weather had nothing to do with his or anybody else's state of mind. Nor, in truth, was it the job that was making him nervous. Rather, it was the aftermath, the prospect of change at the top. When Steinberg thought about it, Jaeger was the only one whose position at BIRD would remain unchanged.

Strange that in all the years they had worked together, Steinberg had never known Jaeger to display any sort of ambition. Despite this, he knew his colleague had once been an important member of the organization: a favourite of the CEO, tipped for great things. What had happened since was a bit of a mystery. Jaeger was a successful operative, known for his discretion and his ability to get the job done. But for whatever reason he had never been promoted beyond his current station. Some people, Steinberg supposed, had no desire to lead, but were content simply to follow. The fact that Jaeger was tailing Hendrik at a distance of thirty kilometres, while Steinberg actively pursued the technology, seemed symptomatic of the choices both had made.

Steinberg hadn't told Jaeger about his plans that evening. Even if Steinberg agreed with Dominik – agreed, that is, that Jaeger was unlikely to pose a threat to the new operation – he still felt it prudent to keep a trained killer at arm's length. For his part, Jaeger would never guess what Steinberg had in mind. He wasn't curious enough to ask questions about the background check. Besides, he was only interested in Hendrik. As long as Steinberg kept Jaeger informed about the blogger's movements, there was little chance of him making an unexpected appearance at WAVE.

In the meantime, Landeck had come and gone. Steinberg looked at the battery meter. It would be tight without charging, but he didn't want to make another stop before La Punt. In case of an emergency, he thought to himself, he could always call support. Just now, he was passing through the Lower Engadin valley. To the right were the Dolomites, rugged, forested, and unremittingly steep.

The left-hand side, meanwhile, was flatter, gentler, and housed a number of small villages. The area's main town, Scuol, had once been a major spa resort, but its awe-inspiringly grand hotel – among the first addresses in the Swiss Alps – had been destroyed by fire in the late eighties and transformed into a park. Steinberg could still perceive what remained of the hotel's iron columns, but where the rest had been there was now only grass.

Another forty-five minutes and he would be in La Punt. According to the Roadbook, Vivien, the youngest of the team, was on duty that night. That was good. It meant that whatever happened, Jaromir was unlikely to be missed. The bunker, as Steinberg discovered on arrival, was both impressive and impressively bland. Having passed through an enormous sound-proof steel door, a left turn took him into the first dormitory: row upon row of bunk-beds, their dirty orange mattresses complementing a parquet floor in the same dull shade.

It would be hell sleeping here, hell having to spend any time inside these four walls. Steinberg breathed in.

The stale stench of a lost generation's sweat still hung in the air. He retraced his steps to the entrance, this time turning to the right. A much smaller door led through to an area that must once have been a storeroom.  There was a single table and chair, while a thick layer of dust covered the floor. It didn't look as if anyone had used the room for years.

Although it was the perfect location, Steinberg knew he would have to act fast. He would lure Jaromir over on a pretext, get him in the bunker, and bolt the door. From there, he wouldn't need much time. Five or ten minutes would be more than enough to get what he wanted.

Slowly but surely, the participants were beginning to arrive. After a day spent on the road, with only the prospect of a long, hot summer evening to keep them going, the cool, wet weather had come as something of a disappointment. The decision to cancel the scheduled barbecue had already been taken, its replacement a vast indoor buffet cooked and prepared by the local women's association. The sight of it was enough to put a smile on even the most disgruntled of faces. Mountains of food piled high on a table that was struggling to support the weight of all the dishes it contained.

Steinberg was happy, too, albeit for different reasons. He knew that having the participants inside would make things a lot easier. He also knew that the inclement weather provided the perfect opportunity to put his plan into action.

And so, half an hour later – when the majority of the teams had arrived, parked their cars, and settled down to their evening meals, and the late arrivals, like those who had come before, had been temporarily blinded by the bewildering array of food on offer – Steinberg sidled over to Jaromir and told him he was concerned by the rain.

"The rain?" the latter said.

"Well, it's the junction boxes really. If they get too wet, the EVs might not charge."

"And what do you expect me to do about it?" Jaromir, Steinberg saw, had a full plate in front of him.

"I thought it would be a nice gesture if we made sure they were dry together. Vivien's had a long day, too. The sooner we get this sorted, the sooner we can all relax and enjoy the buffet."

"Come on then," Jaromir said reluctantly. "Let's get this over with."

The pair headed out into the rain and began to wrap the junction boxes in plastic foil.

"Sorry I was short with you," the Czech said after they had completed the job. "You were quite right, you know."

"Don't worry," Steinberg said. "By the way, have you seen where we're sleeping tonight? Talk about a confined space!"

Jaromir smiled and started in the direction of the bunker, as if to commiserate on the pair's unhappy fate.

"I haven't been in yet actually. I was about to but then it started to rain."

"Well, why don't I help you with your things?"

Steinberg knew this was his moment. The parking lot was completely deserted, and as they approached the bunker, he saw that all the lights were off inside. Everyone was still gorging themselves on the buffet.

Steinberg followed Jaromir at a distance as he descended the stairs leading down to the entrance, and then, when they had both stepped inside, he forced an elbow into the Czech's spine. The surprise of the blow was enough to knock him off balance and he lurched wildly to the right-hand side. A firm push followed by a trip and Jaromir was soon on the hard floor of the storeroom, still too dazed, Steinberg suspected, to be aware of his assailant quietly locking the door behind him. A quick kick to the ribs, then it was time for the opening gambit.

"If you've got any sense at all, you'll know why I'm here."

Jaromir was writhing on the floor, but he wasn't about to give up his secret.

"What are you talking about, you madman?"

"That's your first warning," Steinberg said, before sitting him up and striking his ribs for the second time.

"What do you want?" Jaromir had just about managed to get to his feet and take his place on the room's lone chair.

"You fit the bill, don't you? All that experience, that know-how. And that battered old Peugeot gives you the perfect disguise."

Steinberg waited for a response but none was forthcoming. He punched Jaromir in the stomach, hoping to stun his victim into speech. The Czech let out a howl of pain but still gave nothing away.

"The perfect disguise for what?" he said eventually. Steinberg had clearly winded him. "I'm just a member of support. The same as last year."

Steinberg raised his hand once more, ready to strike. What was the old man playing at? He hit him in the stomach again before essaying a kick just below the kneecap. Maybe now he would talk?

"Just a member of support! I suppose you were just a member of the Czech Secret Service as well. Enough! You're here because your EV can do something that no other model can." Steinberg decided to show he was serious. This time he struck Jaromir Vegr in the face.

"Wait," came the response, full of anguish now.

"I'm listening." Steinberg saw that there were tears in the old man's eyes.

"The thing you're looking for, it's special, right? It's something that has to be kept secret?" Jaromir's voice was cracked.

Steinberg fixed the Czech with an icy stare. Was he improvising?

Or did he really have no idea what was going on?

"Keep going."

"Look at me. I'm old. I'm old and I'm alone. I've no back-up, no support. No nothing. Why in God's name would I be entrusted with whatever it is you're trying to find? If it was that special, don't you think there'd be more than one person looking after it?" With some difficulty, Jaromir was reaching for something inside his trouser pocket. The keys to his Peugeot. "Believe me, I don't have any secrets. If I did, I'd have handed them over by now."

Steinberg hadn't taken his eyes off his victim. It was just possible that what he was saying was true. Why else would he offer Steinberg the keys to his car?

Strange, how the goalposts could shift in an instant. Steinberg had hoped Jaromir would talk, but now it was all he could do to buy his silence. He prepared to play his trump card.

"You'd have handed them over. I hope for your sake that's true. Because next time, I might just have a chat with someone who's a lot more fragile than you are. Shall I give you a clue? His name begins with F."

"You leave Florian out of this!" From somewhere, Jaromir, swollen eyed, puffy cheeked and clutching his chest, had found the energy to stand up and look Steinberg in the eye.

The latter took a step back and said calmly. "That's in your hands. For now I'm choosing to believe your story. But breathe a word of what happened here and who knows what will become of the boy. Do we understand each other, Pops?" Steinberg patted him, gently this time, on the cheek.

"You bastard," Jaromir said defiantly. "Get out of my sight."

As he unlocked the door and headed back out into the evening air, Steinberg allowed himself a smile. Whatever he knew before, Jaromir Vegr had a big secret now; and it was one he'd have no choice but to keep.

Outside, there was still the odd team arriving. Steinberg casually greeted the newcomers and returned to the buffet via the parking lot.

Although he might not have been aware of it, Jaromir had just given him a big lead.

Steinberg knew he had been wrong to suspect anyone from the support team. So, the technologist was travelling with a companion. It made sense. The presence of a second person would provide both camouflage and protection. This person would have to be someone the technologist trusted, most likely someone from his immediate circle of friends. In the past, Steinberg had taken part in operations where he had pretended to be someone's husband. But what if the technologist and his companion were together in real life?

By now, the buffet was in full swing. Groups of people had gathered to exchange stories from the road, while a town local explained why EVs had traditionally been so hard to steal. Steinberg took a seat and poured himself a glass of wine, before going over the names of participants in his head. He realized he was surrounded by couples.

Team TWIKE were unlikely candidates. There was nothing revolutionary about a three-wheeled car. The two driving the Tesla Roadster were more promising: the husband, Steinberg remembered, had a Masters in electric mobility.

Then there was Gordon and his Texan companion Leora. The former was smoking an e-cigarette and wearing a pair of colourful shades. Not exactly a master of disguise – but then being indiscreet was sometimes the best way of avoiding attention. At any rate, he was a company owner, specializing in electric boats. Steinberg continued to gaze around the room.

That still left the newlyweds and the couple from Slovenia. Steinberg quickly ruled out the latter. Where was a guy who barely kept his head above water financially going to find the money to develop a revolutionary piece of technology? His resources could barely stretch to a new phone.

If it was a couple, it had to be either the Austrians driving the Tesla or the newlyweds from France. At a pinch, it could have been Gordon and Leora.

Still, there was one thing that was bothering Steinberg. If the technology was so damn important, why was no-one watching it right now? Was the technologist so confident his car wouldn't be discovered? Or had he enlisted the services of a third party? Of someone who could provide it with twenty-four hour protection?

CHAPTER NINETEEN

Hendrik

Wednesday morning – La Punt – Arosa

Although the rain of the previous evening had abated, the morning sky was still full of clouds, and the temperature distinctly cooler than twenty-four hours before. From the height of summer, it felt as if participants had been plunged, if not into the depths of winter, then at least into the midst of a chill spring day. For anyone other than Hendrik Herder, the timing was far from perfect.

Almost a week into an expedition characterized by long days and ever-shorter nights, this Wednesday morning had been deliberately set aside as a time for rest. Teams had the opportunity to explore the Engadin Valley and, in particular, the Silvaplana Lake, a remote but nevertheless popular summer haunt for water-sports enthusiasts. But what was a lake without the sun on your back? The water would look tired and unappealing; and the surrounding landscape would be shrouded in grey. Here, as in other neighbouring parts of the country, morning fog was a feature of day-to-day life. Usually, in time, it lifted, but sometimes it was stubborn, refusing to give an inch until what lay beneath became a distant memory.

After everything that had happened, Hendrik was beginning to feel decidedly ill at ease. The truth was he was petrified. Peter had disappeared and now it seemed that Hendrik had confirmation that there had been someone tailing him since Bled. As for the latest development, the one that had seen him recruited by a concern acting against the interests of his original employer, Hendrik was still unsure. Was it really so easy to just switch sides? The problem was that the more he thought about it, the less certain he felt. He had got it wrong in

Zurich before all of this started. Who was to say he would get it right now? But did he, he wondered, have any choice? After all, it wasn't just about him anymore.

There was Nils to think about, still stuck in Zurich, surrounded by people who wanted his best friend out of the picture. Nils was a good actor but he'd need to be careful. Whatever game he was playing, it was dangerous and Hendrik feared there was only one possible ending. The pair had arranged to speak that morning, before the group set off in convoy towards the Albula Pass. Nils had indicated that new information had come to light.

Hendrik felt nervous, fidgety. It was a good thing he had lots to do. There was the small matter of the daily report – a farce, now, since he had switched sides and, it seemed, Dominik no longer trusted him. After that, the blog needed updating. This was no less important as, whoever he was working for, he still had to cover the expedition for the website. He uploaded a blog containing an interview he had filmed earlier with Manfred and Tamara. Since the wine festival in Eisten-stadt, the trio had become firm friends.

Finally, there was just time to glance at the latest news stories. In the past few days, Hendrik had read about flash floods; quarrels taking place in the EU; and, in a story that had rumbled on for over a year now, about an American citizen who had divulged state security secrets and was subsequently seeking asylum in a number of different countries. Whatever the story, Hendrik found that reading the news provided a much-needed distraction from the internal maelstrom: a veritable whirlpool of emotion that still, even three days after his return to WAVE, threatened to overcome him at any time.

He looked at his watch. It would soon be time. He made his way over toward the parking lot, surprised to see that, although the clouds had not yet parted, a number of people had indeed taken the chance to explore. That was good. Right now, he needed a little privacy. He took his cell phone out of his pocket and stared at it for a moment. It was terrifying to think that one tiny piece of software could reveal everything it had ever been used for. Luckily, Nils had assured him last time that the software had been removed and that their exchanges could thus no longer be recorded.

Nils' cell rang three times before he picked up.

"Hendrik, I'm glad you called. Just give me a moment."

Hendrik heard Nils close a door behind him softly, and imagined his friend venturing out into the morning air with a cigarette dangling from his lips. The pair were in the same country again, for the first time in days, but for some reason Hendrik felt like a wedge had been driven between them. This contract ought to have brought them closer together, but the way things had turned out, it was threatening to destroy them. Would they be able to resume their friendship once it was all over? Hendrik was forced to admit that he didn't know.

"OK."

"Is it safe to talk?" Hendrik asked.

"Yeah, we're good to go."

"You said you had something for me?" In the background, Hendrik could hear a tram announcing its next stop.

"To be honest I don't know quite what to say, Hendrik. Remember I told you in Bled that there was a fund for an external operation? Well, my contact says the budget just increased. That can only mean there's another man on the ground. He could be at WAVE already."

"At WAVE? What about the first guy?" Hendrik asked.

"That's what I'm calling about. This morning, Dominik asked me into his office to talk about making a change to my contract. He wants to give me more responsibility. He mentioned something about taking the lead on a big overseas project. Just think about it. I'd have my own team, money, the chance to travel the world…"

"I can't believe I'm hearing this."

"Relax, Hendrik. He also wanted to let me know that he thought you were doing a good job. That he was happy with your work so far. It set me thinking. Maybe I got it wrong. I was pretty het up after Bled, you know. You're my friend, after all, and I was worried about you."

"Nils, what are you trying to say? I don't have much time."

"What if whoever I thought was on your tail was there to get

Peter? To pick him up and transfer him to another mission? That would mean you're no longer in danger."

"Peter's gone."

"Precisely, Peter's gone. Dominik wasn't happy with him, so he had him replaced. That's phase one. For phase two, it's as you were. The replacement's been sent to help you find the technology."

"I don't buy it, Nils. I've had a pretty strange few days here. Dominik's been lying to us from the start. All that environmental bullshit. Can't you see none of this makes sense? I mean, if I'm supposed to be working with this new guy, why the hell don't I know who he is? And as for this project of yours, well, it's patently obvious what's going on."

Silence at the other end of the line.

"Oh? And what's that?" Nils said eventually. He sounded annoyed.

"You really can't see?" There was frustration in Hendrik's voice now. All the tension of the previous few days was beginning to spill out. "He's playing to your ego," Hendrik was shouting now, stressing the final word as though he were talking to an immensely slow child. "Dangling the prospect of a world tour so that he can keep you on-side. He's got you pretty well sussed. But think about it. Just stop and think about it for a moment. You called to say there might be someone else at WAVE. Yet neither of us has the faintest idea who it is. Why's that?" Hendrik didn't wait for his friend to respond. "I'll tell you why. Because Dominik is rotten to the core. Whatever he might say to you in private, he doesn't trust either one of us. Otherwise we'd know exactly what was going on."

While he waited for the information to sink in, Hendrik thought of all the lies he had told Nils since the start of the expedition, and felt suddenly ashamed. Despite the lecture, he realized he hadn't placed any trust in his own best friend. He hadn't told him the truth about what had happened in Bled or how he had really got back to WAVE.

"Nils, are you still there?"

"Yeah, still here." There was a weariness in his voice; a flatness that suggested defeat.

"You need to do one more thing for me. This new guy, find out who he is. I've got two names for you: Timo Schneeweiss and William Steinberg. If this guy is already at WAVE, then it has to be one of them. Can you do that for me?"

A long pause. "What have we got ourselves mixed up in?" Nils said finally, his tone as despondent as Hendrik had ever known.

"I don't know. But I'm doing my best to get us out. I can't tell you any more than that. Now, I need that name. Hack the system if you have to, do whatever you can. And, Nils, be careful. Dominik's dangerous. If he finds out you've gone behind his back like this, he won't think twice about making you pay."

Hendrik rung off just as the first cars were beginning to emerge and take their place at the start point. Hendrik waved to Alain, then to Andrej and Jasna. Next he waited for Martin and Magali to join the line. If anything, he felt worse than before. The rain that was forecast would make filming nigh-on impossible and he was starting to seriously worry about Nils.

"Any news?" Magali asked.

"There could be someone else here at WAVE. A second spy. My friend's going to confirm the name."

"OK," Martin said. "That still leaves your friend following us in the car. Here's what we do. We drive up to the Albula Pass with the rest of the group. Then at the top we, that's you and I," he gestured to Hendrik, "use the drone to see if we're being trailed. Magali, you continue down the road, make sure you stay close to the technology. We'll catch you up at Lenzerheide."

"We'll catch her up?" Hendrik was disbelieving. "Without a car?"

"We'll cycle." Hendrik noticed that Martin had attached a couple of e-bikes to the back of the car. He must have borrowed them from Andre Lugger. "Albula has an altitude of 2,315 metres. Lenzerheide is almost 1,000 metres lower. We'll make up the time, don't you worry about that. In the winter, they close the section of the road between Preda and Berguen. You travel up to Preda with the railway and sledge all the way back down."

Magali, Hendrik noticed, was gazing at Martin quizzically. "You've done your homework," she said.

"Actually, no," came the response. "I had a life before we were married, you know."

"You guys aren't married," Hendrik said. "You told me that yesterday."

Martin shrugged his shoulders. "Well, you know what I mean."

A few minutes later, they had begun the ascent, over the railway crossing and up towards the pass summit. The road snaked round and round up through the Engadin Valley. Progress was slow, even though the distance was negligible. On the way up, Hendrik caught sight of a lone cow, staring at the convoy as it passed. What was it someone had said about cows in a field? That they were content – because they had no ability to recall the past? Whoever it was, they had been wrong. This one looked positively malcontent. As if it were taken aback by the sight of all these machines travelling along the road in silence; or, rather, by the *memory* that vehicles ought to make a noise.

"Nietzsche," Hendrik blurted out, his mind still racing.

"Lost his mind because of a horse," Martin retorted.

"Said that cows were happy…" his voice trailed away. He felt he no longer understood the meaning of the word.

Soon, the summit was in view: a plateau overlooking a small lake, which housed a dwelling of some sort. A gift shop perhaps, or a restaurant and café. The grey skyline was dominated by Piz Üertsch, an imposing mountain whose peak, though barely visible, was still covered in snow. The group descended from their vehicles. Some emerged with cameras, while others scrambled up rocks to get a better view of the surrounding landscape. On a day like today – cloudy, windy, and cold – there was little for the naked eye to see.

After another group photo, participants were ready to get back on the road. Hendrik and Martin accompanied Magali to their vehicle, untied the bikes and waited until the way was clear once more.

While Martin set up the drone, Hendrik tried to reach Nils. He used his cell to send him a message. Nils had found a chat tool that enabled them to send each other encrypted messages. The phone line might have been secure, but it paid to take precautions.

HENDRIK: ANY WORD?

NILS: SOMEONE ORDERED A DETAILED PROFILE ON ALL WAVE PARTICIPANTS. WITH THE EXCEPTION OF TWO, THAT IS.

HENDRIK: SCHNEEWEISS AND STEINBERG?

NILS: NO. SCHNEEWEISS HAS A PROFILE. YOU AND STEINBERG ARE THE TWO EXCEPTIONS.

HENDRIK: WHAT DOES STEINBERG LOOK LIKE?

The description Nils gave fitted perfectly: five-foot-nine, brown hair, reddish beard. Hendrik felt a chill go down his spine.

HENDRIK: WHAT ELSE DOES IT SAY?

NILS: IT SAYS HE WORKS FOR WALTER. AND THAT HE'S EXPERIENCED.

HENDRIK: SO, HE'S INTELLIGENCE? OK, THANKS, NILS. I'LL BE IN TOUCH LATER.

The question was, could Hendrik trust what the file told him? He wouldn't have put it past Dominik to alter Steinberg's profile to make him seem less dangerous.

By now, Martin had got the drone up and running. There was a camera built into it. On a clear day, from its current vantage point, it

215

would be able to scan up to thirty kilometres of terrain.

"Fucking clouds," Martin cursed. "Still, better than nothing."

"It's Steinberg," Hendrik said. "My friend's just confirmed it. He says he's intelligence. Dangerous, but not trained to kill."

"OK," Martin said, thinking quickly. "We'll have to check the footage later. Right now, we'd better get back to Magali. Here, take this."

Martin had produced a helmet camera, Hendrik wasn't sure where from.

"In case you miss anything on the way down…"

But as he began the descent, the last thing on Hendrik's mind was filming. He needed to concentrate on the road. For a time it followed the line of the Rhaetian Railway, a mind-boggling feat of architectural engineering comprising tunnels, viaducts, and a track that crossed over itself on multiple occasions, all in order to overcome a significant difference in altitude between two neighbouring stations.

Hendrik and Martin ducked and weaved in amongst the EVs making their way down the pass, two insignificant specks of motion combating the stillness of the landscape all around. It was an exhilarating experience and Hendrik was amazed at how easily the pair covered the fifty-one kilometre distance. Thanks to the e-bike's four electrical gears, Hendrik found himself propelled forward by a force that had little to do with the speed he was pedaling. Even the occasional uphill stretch was a piece of cake.

Magali had managed to position herself near the front of the convoy and was one of the first to arrive in Lenzerheide. Just before the cyclists reached her, they wheeled past Jaromir, inscrutable as ever, and wearing a pair of dark glasses, despite the fact there had been no sun all day. Of Steinberg, however, there was no sign.

"Well, if he's doing his job properly," Magali said, after the pair had returned the bikes to their rightful owner in Lenzerheide, "he was probably up ahead the whole time."

"The first support car was due here at midday," Martin added, after consulting the Roadbook. "That's around the time we left La Punt."

"I suppose he wouldn't have had much chance to check out the cars on that last stretch of road."

"Not if they were in convoy. You need an e-bike for that," Martin said facetiously.

"So, what have we got to look forward to today?" Magali asked.

"The usual. Competition, award ceremony. Oh, and we're supposed to be testing e-bikes," Martin said.

"So the EVs will all be together in one place?"

"Seems that way."

"I just spoke to Jaromir. Have either of you seen him today? Those sunglasses can't hide the fact that he's been beaten black and blue. Says he tripped, of course, but hell, it must have been some landing," Magali said, before turning to Martin. "I've also been in contact with our boss. We've agreed that we need to observe Steinberg around the clock, even film him if possible. I want something that confirms he's up to no good, evidence we can use to get the police involved. At the moment, we can't tie Steinberg to anything, and the police aren't going to arrest anyone based on speculation. We don't know what happened to Peter and as long as Jaromir insists on his story, we don't have anywhere else to go."

"You're right," Martin said. "We need something concrete."

"What about the first man?" Magali had turned to face Hendrik. "Anything show up on the drone?"

"Let's see, what have we got?" Martin inspected the footage from before. "Visibility was pretty poor. But there's nothing. Unless you count someone pissing in the snow to one side..."

"So, where is he?" Hendrik said. "Is he still following us? My friend seemed to think he might have got it wrong. He thinks the first guy was sent to transfer Peter to another mission."

"But you don't believe him?" Magali said.

"I don't know what to believe. I know that *my friend* doesn't have any protection. And that I just promised to get him out. You said you could help both of us didn't you?"

"And we will. Your friend's in Zurich, right?" Magali asked. "That's still three days away. That leaves us plenty of time to come up with a plan."

CHAPTER TWENTY

Dominik

Wednesday evening – Zurich

"He what?" Dominik Brandt said in disbelief. This operation was beginning to be more trouble than it was worth.

"He threatened to go to the CEO. Blow the whistle on us."

"When did this happen?"

"A few hours ago. I got a little heavy-handed last night. Beat this guy up pretty bad. Somehow Jaeger must have got wind of it. I don't know, maybe this guy, Jaromir Vegr his name was, went for a drive after it happened. Found himself in the same spot as Jaeger."

"How would Jaeger know who he was?"

"From the file. I asked him to run a full background check on all participants. He must have seen a photo. So, anyway, Jaeger rang me up this morning. He was pretty sour. Said if the CEO knew what we were doing, he wouldn't approve. That I should stop drawing attention to myself. That I was going about things the wrong way."

"Sanctimonious twat. What did you say to him?"

"That it was my operation and I'd go about things however the hell I wanted, so long as I got a result. And that's when he said it. That he'd go over our heads. To be honest, I didn't think he had it in him."

Dominik sighed. "They go back a long way, those two. He's the closest thing Adler's got to a son. Even if he treats him more like a dog. Still, dogs are faithful to their masters, I suppose."

"What do you want me to do?"

"If this gets out, we're both finished. And we can't allow that to happen." He paused, waiting for a response from Steinberg. When none came, he continued: "I'll leave you to extrapolate the rest."

Another silence. "You're saying a dead man can't talk."

"I'm saying do whatever it is you need to do."

With that, the line went dead. Dominik sat back in his chair and reflected on the events of the past few days. Things were getting messy. That, he supposed, had always been the way. A new order arose out of chaos, not peace and tranquility. Peter was gone. Soon Jaeger would join him. Of those two, he would be sorry to lose the latter. Surveillance practices had changed beyond all recognition in the last decade, but an experienced head would still have come in handy.

The new generation might have known about bits and bytes, but did they know what it meant to get their hands dirty? Perhaps Jaeger wasn't the right man to teach them. He had too many ties with the old regime. He would be a reminder of Adler, of the way things used to be. By his very presence, he would undermine what Dominik was trying to achieve. No, it was better like this. With Jaeger out of the picture, Dominik could concentrate on assembling a new team.

That still left a few loose ends. Walter, for one. Dominik didn't trust him, but then again neither had Adler. With the systems Walter and his team had at their disposal, they could lay their hands on any and all individual or company data; hell, they could do the same for a city, even a whole country – and everything at the mere touch of a button. These days everyone had a digital fingerprint.

As long as he was in charge of all these resources, Walter was a dangerous customer. He could literally find out anything he wanted about anyone in the world. So how was it that Dominik knew next to nothing about him? At least, he thought to himself, Walter was unlikely to create any difficulties in the event of a coup. He had been in the game too long not to have got used to its luxuries. He would have no choice but to hang in there when Dominik took over, counting down the days until he could decamp to the Caribbean and live out his retirement on a yacht.

Hendrik, on the other hand, would be denied a place in the new regime. Dominik had known that right from the start. Steinberg could take care of him when the time came. When he died, Dominik would have to show his best friend how much he cared. There would be no expense spared at the funeral.

On the subject of Nils, Dominik still wasn't quite sure. He was impressionable, susceptible to the trappings that money and fame could bring. But Dominik wondered if he hadn't underestimated him, if there wasn't greater depth to his character after all. He had begun to put out a few feelers with the mention of a new project. The finer details were still to be determined. But soon Nils would have to choose between travelling the world and the drudgery of day-to-day life; between the lure of money and the safety of his best friend.

For now, however, all Dominik could do was wait. He stood up and walked to the window. He hated not being in control. Steinberg would have to act fast. Dealing with Jaeger might have assumed temporary priority but, after that, there wouldn't be much time. It was vital that things were wrapped up before Zurich. If there was a stink there, everyone would come under scrutiny. Dominik couldn't afford that.

He realized he needed an exit strategy. If things went wrong, he had to make sure someone else took the blame. Steinberg was the obvious choice. Dominik might have promised him the world, but when push came to shove, he knew the world wasn't his to give...

The call came much later that night, and Dominik expected it to be good news.

"Steinberg, what have you got for me?"

"I'm afraid there's been a complication. I managed to get Jaeger out here. Said I wanted to apologize. There's a wood at the back of the hotel, behind the garden."

The hotel, Dominik knew, was normally closed to guests at this time of year.

"I had it all worked out. We'd shake hands, head for a drink, then I'd spike the contents of his glass. Be as discreet as possible."

"I don't need a blow-by-blow account. What the hell happened?" Dominik seethed.

"He didn't accept it. Started arguing. Said people like me only apologized when there was something in it for them. What did I want?

221

Then this light goes on. In the sauna at the back of the hotel. Jaeger knows he can't be seen, he's still a professional, says we'll finish this later, and goes back through the woods to where he's parked his car."

"Who turned on the light?"

"Some broad. Leora's her name. I thought I'd better check she hadn't seen anything. Then I realize she's one of the names on my list. So, I invite her for a drink, talk about the importance of reforesting the world, that's her thing, you see, she wants to save the planet by planting new trees everywhere.

"Then I think to myself, if she's the one, I can put *her* out of action, get a good look at her car. I give her a roofie, then spill the contents of her glass. She gets a bit drowsy, but then once we're out of the bar, she just collapses, starts fucking frothing at the mouth. Must have been an allergic reaction."

"For Christ's sake." Dominik rubbed his eyes.

"There were a couple of people in the bar who saw us together. I called an ambulance and went to wake her teammate. They're both on their way to the hospital now. They want to keep her in overnight. And you know the worst thing?"

"It's not their car."

"Right. It's not their car," Steinberg confirmed.

Dominik was livid but he managed to bite his tongue.

"OK," he said eventually. "You did the right thing, calling the ambulance. It would have been much worse to stand by and do nothing. Whatever you do, keep a low profile tomorrow. If anyone asks you what happened, don't play the hero, just brush it off, say it's what anyone would have done."

"Will do."

"Which hospital was it?" Dominik asked. "In case we need to adjust the results of her tests."

"The ambulance was from the psychiatric unit in Chur," Stein-berg replied. "If we alter the files, we might be able to make sure she stays put for as long as we need her there."

"Leave that to me. You need to redouble your efforts. I don't want any more excuses. We need to find the technology before it's too late."

Dominik Brandt placed the phone down calmly, rose from his desk, and slammed his fist against the nearest wall.

CHAPTER TWENTY-ONE

Alain

Thursday morning – Arosa

As he made his way down to breakfast the next morning, Alain felt a little worse for wear. This time, however, it had nothing to do with his red wine consumption. In fact, as he knew very well, lack of sleep was the cause of his current predicament. He was already tired from the photo shoot in Grossglockner. Now, to add insult to injury, he had been roused in the night by a commotion at the back of the hotel, the flashing blue lights and siren wail of an ambulance putting paid to any hope of getting a good night's sleep.

 At first, Alain had been too groggy to react; and the ambulance had sped away in the direction of the nearest hospital before he had time to acknowledge the gravity of the situation. Then, with a start, he had sprung into action. Ignoring the lateness of the hour, he had put a call through to reception and asked to be connected to room thirty-four, one floor above his own.

Once the connection had been made, the telephone in room thirty-four rang three or four times before, finally, there was a muffled response at the other end of the line.

"Hello?" Alain could almost hear the sleep in the respondent's voice. "Hello, who is this?" the voice said again, more alert this time.

Alain gave a sigh of relief and replaced the receiver. He hoped Andrej would be able to forgive him in the morning. For his part, he had some serious thinking to do. He rose from the bed and opened the mini-bar, eventually selecting a bottle of sparkling water which he proceeded to open and pour. Next he pulled up a chair and sat at the small desk, its longest edge running perpendicular to the bed. There he found a notepad alongside a complimentary pen embossed with the hotel logo.

On the first page, he made a list of everything untoward, or unexplained, which had happened since the start of the expedition. Quite a roll call of misfortune: the cars that had been disconnected in Eisenstadt; the incident with Stephan and Olaf; Hendrik's behaviour in Bled; two teams experiencing the same problem in the Austrian Alps; Peter's unforeseen exit... the list went on and on. To it, he could now add Jaromir, who had emerged from La Punt with a range of injuries that scarcely tallied with his rather feeble explanation, not to mention the midnight ambulance run this evening.

The cause of at least some of these incidents, Alain knew from experience, would be perfectly innocent, as no expedition could expect to run smoothly at all times. Nevertheless, there was something that grated here, if only because, at least with regard to the latest episode, Alain had been bedevilled by a sense of foreboding that had persisted throughout the whole afternoon.

There had been something in the air as the group had left Lenzerheide and driven on for the final half hour or so toward their evening destination.

Alain had fond memories of Arosa, having spent a season working there after university. It had been something of a party destination then, and indeed it was still a popular spot for holidaying celebrities, who

valued above all the opportunity to regain the anonymity they had sacrificed to the twin deities of fame and fortune. Alain had surveyed the familiar trees and lakes and felt suddenly old, as if he had awoken one morning to find his hair transformed to grey. He had changed in the intervening twenty-five years; not, he hoped, beyond all recognition, but enough to make him question the wisdom of revisiting scenes from his youth.

This sense of melancholy hadn't been helped by the weather. The fog which had been present in La Punt that morning had spread north and west towards Arosa and covered the mid-summer landscape in a colourless grey; while the Alpine peaks loomed threateningly in the background, as if sitting in judgment on what passed below. As afternoon became evening, there was still no improvement, and the scheduled sightseeing tour was cancelled as a result.

In the meantime, the teams had trooped inside to the hotel, where they were welcomed with a champagne reception and, later on, a three-course dinner. Although the atmosphere was convivial and all those inside had chatted freely with one another, Alain had the curious sense of an opportunity lost. The expedition was nearly over, and he still hadn't managed to meet, let alone speak with, a number of the participants. That, he supposed, was natural. The bigger the event, the more disjointed it would feel. Cliques had formed over the course of the past week and they would not, now, be disbanded. If the expedition were to continue to grow next year, and there was every indication it would, then this feeling would only be exacerbated. Perhaps, Alain thought, that was the trick with all movements, with all causes. It was about fashioning a coherent narrative in the face of the differences that might otherwise derail it. After all, everyone here believed in the future of the electric car – even if it sometimes felt like the only thing they had in common.

There had been a presentation after the dinner, given by the owner of the hotel. He had explained that the participants had just dined on the site of the Swiss hotel with the largest photo-voltaic plant. The solar panels, tightly fastened onto the roof in an effort to combat high winds, were enormous and had been almost impossible to deliver on account of the town's narrow roads. But now, using energy from the sun, they facilitated the production of fourteen percent of the hotel's annual energy supply, not to mention around fifty percent of the hot-water supply, an annual saving of some 150,000 litres of oil.

To close, Louis Palmer had shown a video of the 1987 Tour de Sol, the first rally for solar-powered vehicles, itself a kind of precursor to WAVE, which that particular year had finished in Arosa. It was an enviable environmental record, but Alain found himself wondering to what extent circumstance had played its part. The roads were so narrow that coaches were banned from making the journey up to Arosa, with the result that winter hotel guests were still often collected from the station in a horse and cart.

Allied to all this was the irony that among all this talk of sunshine and solar energy, the clouds had now opened and were emitting a steady drizzle that showed no sign of abating.

He had woken with his notepad still open and the glass of water lying untouched by his side. In between the arrival of the ambulance and the appearance of the dawn, he had managed perhaps two hours of sleep. The last thing he had written was "CALL FRANK".

In the confusion of the early morning hours, Alain must have concluded that the incidents he had recorded could not be put down to coincidence alone. But was it really a good idea to call Frank? That would mean revealing he had been at WAVE all along...

The atmosphere at the breakfast table that morning was muted. Possibly it was a result of the early start, with participants still rubbing the sleep from their eyes as they tried desperately to refuel their ailing systems with a combination of coffee, juice, and pastries. Alain caught sight of the technologist, breakfasting alongside his wife. In contrast to the majority, both appeared to be well-rested: ironic, given that Alain knew that they had also endured an interrupted night's sleep.

But perhaps it wasn't lack of sleep that was responsible for the collective fatigue. Today was the so-called School Day, where teams would be joined by a number of local school pupils as they made their way north to Rorschach. Though a logistical nightmare, the idea was simple enough: by including children in the expedition, they were helping to educate the next generation about important environmental issues.

Alain had decided to tell them about his expedition to the South Pole, in order to show them just how drastic the situation had become. Alongside the burning of fossil fuels by industrial and power plants, CO_2 emissions from traditional fuel-based cars had contributed to global warming to such an extent that the ice in Antarctica was slowly beginning to melt. In fact, only fifteen percent of the Earth's original ice cap remained. Few people realized just how important ice was for the cooling of the planet. It provided a sort of air-conditioning effect. Alain often compared the situation to driving in a car that had become overheated. Without air-conditioning, you soon fried. That was easy enough for the kids to understand.

Thinking about the situation in the South Pole made his blood boil. It wasn't enough that profit-hungry corporations were destroying the surrounding nature and the lives of locals with their incessant drilling for oil; even the neighbouring countries were involved now, too. Russia and Norway had recently gone as far as to create their own arctic combat troops, both countries apparently prepared to wage an icy war in the name of something that had never belonged to them in the first place.

In the meantime, two Italians had taken their places at Manfred and Tamara's table. Alain seemed to remember that they were driving a Nissan Leaf. He was close enough to listen in to their conversation.

"Did you hear what happened last night?" the taller of the pair said.

"Hi Simone," Manfred replied. "Yes, apparently Leora was taken ill."

"One too many Pina Coladas maybe," the smaller of the Italians said. "Or could it be whatever she puts in her e-cigarettes?"

"C'mon Marco," Simone interrupted. "That's not funny."

Alain sidled over to them.

"Does anyone know what actually happened?" he asked.

"Not exactly," Tamara replied. "Some sort of circulation problem. Maybe she hadn't drunk enough water during the day. Or perhaps she's on medication that she shouldn't have been mixing with alcohol."

"There's the guy who found her anyway," Manfred gestured towards William Steinberg, who had entered via the side door. "If it hadn't been for him... well, who knows?"

"Was she alone?" Alain asked.

"That's the thing. She was with this Steinberg guy, that's the rumour, anyway."

"I thought you said he found her?"

"Found her, was drinking with her... what's the difference? At the end of the day, he's probably the one who saved her life."

Out of the corner of his eye, Alain saw the newlyweds scrutinizing William Steinberg closely as he took his place at a table alongside members of the group whom he, Alain, didn't recognize. Something here stank; Alain was ready to reveal everything to Frank.

Over the course of the past week, he had, through a process of elimination, concluded that the pair of agents he'd hired were the couple from Austria, Manfred and Tamara. As evidence, there had been Manfred's sudden appearance in Weissensee; and the fact that both had been present in Eibiswald and Bled. Now, however, Alain wasn't quite so sure. The two genuinely seemed to have little idea what had happened to Leora. Or was that just part of their act? He wondered if they had taken any measures upon receiving news of Leora's hospitalization.

He realized that now was hardly the right time to ask. It was time to take a risk.

"Alain?" Frank said. "This is a surprise! What can I do for you?"

"You can start by telling me what the hell I'm paying you for!" Alain said down the line. He was not given to displays of aggression, but something about all this had really hit a nerve.

"You asked for a service to be carried out discreetly. I can assure you that every effort has been made to facilitate your request."

"Spare me the corporate bullshit, Frank. I've got reason to suspect my investment is in danger and I want to know what's being done about it. Last night there was an incident at the hotel involving one of the participants."

"An incident has been logged and will be used to inform our continuing strategy."

"Jesus, Frank. You know part of me thinks I probably shouldn't be doing this," Alain took a moment to consider his options. "But to hell with it! I've been at WAVE from the start and I have good reason to suspect that the team you have assigned to this mission is not up to scratch."

"Impossible." Frank's answer was impressively final, supremely confident. That Alain was in fact part of the expedition didn't seem to have perturbed him in the slightest. "They're the best I've got. Whoever you think it is, I'm afraid you're mistaken."

A long pause, while Alain tried to take in what had just been said. There was, he realized, every chance that Manfred and Tamara were just ordinary citizens.

"OK, I'm prepared to take you at your word. But I've done a few sums and I'm pretty sure there's something going on. The numbers don't add up. Now, I'm the contractor. I understand that these things need to be handled with discretion, but could you at least tell me what the state of play is? I'm concerned about Andrej and the technology; this is a huge investment I'm making here."

"Not over the phone, Alain," Frank replied. "We need to be very careful. I'll send you the link to an app. Download it and then we can continue."

About ten seconds later, Alain's cell beeped. He clicked on the link and installed the software.

He realized that Frank was already writing something.

FRANK: LISTEN, ALAIN, SINCE YOU'RE ON THE GROUND, I'M GOING TO LEVEL WITH YOU. THERE HAVE BEEN SIGNS THAT ALL HAS NOT BEEN WELL FOR SOME TIME. AS THE CONTRACTOR, YOU WOULD BE WELL WITHIN YOUR RIGHTS TO ABORT THIS MISSION ON ANY NUMBER OF GROUNDS.

NEVERTHELESS, FOR THE TIME BEING, I WOULD URGE YOU TO HOLD FAST. AS FAR AS I'M AWARE, THE TECHNOLOGY IS VERY CLOSE TO BEING PROVEN. MY AGENTS ARE WORKING AROUND THE CLOCK TO ENSURE THAT THE RISK OF FURTHER INCIDENTS IS KEPT TO A MINIMUM.

ALAIN: HOW DO YOU KNOW THAT THE TECHNOLOGY IS NEARLY PROVEN?

FRANK: I'VE BEEN IN CONTACT WITH TOM SCHMIDT. HE WAS SPEAKING TO ANDREJ YESTERDAY.

ALAIN: WHAT ABOUT THE AGENTS? FOR A WHILE I THOUGHT IT WAS THE AUSTRIAN COUPLE, MANFRED AND TAMARA. BUT NOW I'M SURE IT'S MARTIN AND MAGALI. I'VE JUST SEEN THEM AND THEY LOOK FAR FROM PLEASED. SO JUST TELL ME WHAT THE HELL IS GOING ON.

FRANK: VERY WELL, SINCE YOU ALREADY KNOW THE IDENTITY OF MY TEAM... AS I SAID, THERE HAVE BEEN SIGNS THAT ALL HAS NOT BEEN WELL FOR SOME TIME. WE NOW KNOW THAT SEVERAL SPIES HAVE INFILTRATED THE EXPEDITION. THERE WERE TWO THERE AT THE START, ONE OF WHOM HAS SINCE BEEN REPLACED. TWO MORE JOINED IN BLED OR JUST AFTER. ALTHOUGH WE ARE YET TO DISCOVER THE NAME OF THE ORGANIZATION WHICH SENT THEM, WE ARE CERTAIN THAT THEY ARE TRYING TO FIND THE TECHNOLOGY. WE KNOW THIS BECAUSE ONE OF THEIR OPERATIVES, A YOUNG MAN POSING AS A VIDEO BLOGGER WHO HAS BEEN PART OF WAVE SINCE EICHGRABEN, WAS RECENTLY TURNED BY OUR AGENTS.

ALAIN: HENDRIK?

FRANK: THE VERY SAME. YOU WILL BE PLEASED TO LEARN THAT THE YOUNG MAN HAS COME TO HIS SENSES AND IS HELPING MY TEAM WITH THEIR ENQUIRIES. THUS FAR, HIS WORK HAS PROVED INVALUABLE.

ALAIN: I DON'T UNDERSTAND. HENDRIK?

FRANK: THE GRAVITY OF THE SITUATION HAS ONLY RECENTLY BEEN MADE CLEAR TO US. AT FIRST WE ASSUMED THAT WHAT WAS GOING ON WAS A SIMPLE CASE OF INDUSTRIAL ESPIONAGE. HOWEVER, A SERIES OF INCIDENTS HAVE CAUSED US TO REASSESS. I HAVE NO DOUBT THAT IT WAS THE SAME CHAIN OF EVENTS WHICH COMPELLED YOU TO GET IN TOUCH THIS MORNING.

ALAIN: YOU MEAN WHAT HAPPENED TO PETER, JAROMIR, AND LEORA?

FRANK: YES. AS I SAY, A SERIES OF INCIDENTS HAS FORCED US TO ACKNOWLEDGE THE NATURE OF THE THREAT POSED BY THESE MEN.

ALAIN: OK. BUT HELP ME OUT HERE. IF YOU WERE AWARE THAT THEY WERE DANGEROUS THEN WHY DIDN'T YOU MOVE TO CANCEL THE EXPEDITION? I MEAN, IT'S NOT AS IF IT'S JUST ANDREJ'S SAFETY THAT HAS BEEN COMPROMISED.

FRANK: YOU ARE QUITE RIGHT, OF COURSE. PETER FOR ONE HAS NOT BEEN SEEN SINCE HIS DISAPPEARANCE, AND WE ARE BEGINNING TO FEAR THE WORST. HOWEVER, WE HAVE BEEN UNABLE TO MAKE USE OF OFFICIAL CHANNELS WITHOUT FIRST ACQUIRING CONCRETE PROOF THAT HARM HAS BEEN DELIBERATELY VISITED ON ANY OF THE VICTIMS.

ALAIN: BUT YOU HAVE THAT NOW?

FRANK: YES. AS OF LAST NIGHT, WE HAVE SOME RATHER COMPELLING EVIDENCE. WE HAVE ONE OF THE SPIES ON FILM, SLIPPING BENZODIAZEPINE INTO LEORA'S DRINK. MARTIN WAS ABLE TO FILM IT ALL USING A TIE CAMERA, PROVIDED ON THIS OCCASION BY HENDRIK. THE STAFF AT THE HOSPITAL WHERE LEORA WAS TREATED HAS SINCE INTIMATED THAT THEY WERE ONLY ABLE TO GET A RESULT ON HER BLOOD TEST THANKS TO THE SPEED AT WHICH SHE WAS TRANSFERRED. RATHER IRONIC, GIVEN THAT OUR INFORMATION ALSO SUGGESTS IT WAS THE PERPETRATOR WHO CALLED THE EMERGENCY SERVICES IN THE FIRST PLACE.

ALAIN: STEINBERG! SO WHAT NOW?

FRANK: THE LOCAL POLICE HAVE BEEN INFORMED AND THEY WILL MAKE AN ARREST AS SOON AS THIS WILLIAM STEINBERG LEAVES AROSA. THE MAYOR, YOU SEE, HAS DISCREETLY REQUESTED THAT THE GOOD NAME OF THE TOWN BE LEFT UNSULLIED BY THIS RATHER UNSAVOURY INCIDENT. HE FEARS IT COULD HAVE AN IMPACT ON THE AREA'S STATUS AS A PRIME TOURIST LOCATION. WE HAVE RESPECTFULLY ACCEDED TO HIS REQUEST.

ALAIN: SO THAT'S ONE SPY DEALT WITH. WHAT ABOUT THE SECOND? YOU SAID THERE WERE TWO.

FRANK: THE SECOND MAN HAS PROVED RATHER MORE DIFFICULT TO IDENTIFY. WE HAVE NO CONFIRMED SIGHTINGS, A FACT THAT SUGGESTS HE IS MAINTAINING A SAFE DISTANCE FROM THE EXPEDITION. HOWEVER, REST ASSURED THAT MY TEAM IS WORKING AT FULL TILT TO ENSURE THAT HE

With that, the conversation was over. Alain, his anger having gradually subsided, returned to the breakfast table with much to ponder.

By the time breakfast had finished and he was back on the road, Alain felt more like his old self again. It had been the right decision to make the call, even if his own detective work had been exposed in the process. He had, it was true, felt slightly embarrassed when Frank had told him he was wrong about the agents. But, still, he could live with that, particularly if the net result was that he was better informed about what was actually going on. The only piece of information that had really stung him was the news about Hendrik. Never in a million years would Alain have thought he was capable of spying.

For now, though, a day of anxious waiting lay ahead. William Steinberg's arrest appeared to be little more than a formality. As for the second man, Alain found himself thinking back to the boat ride in Weissensee. Hendrik had been gripped by fear, and now Alain knew why. At the time, he had simply written it off as paranoia. Hendrik had been through a difficult few days and his troubles had begun to manifest themselves in the form of a persecution complex. It had seemed plausible at the time. Alain also remembered that despite his fear, Hendrik had somehow had the wherewithal to try and film the driver. Had he managed? Or had Jochen prevented him from doing so? In all likelihood it would have been too dark anyway.

Continuing his drive, Alain reflected that of all the days to be kept waiting, he had probably chosen the best one. Once he reached Wartau, after all, he would scarcely have a moment to himself. Today's School Day included a popularity contest and there would be any number of children at each of the six stops en route to Rorschach. Alain hoped they would be receptive to what the drivers had to say about their cars. After these had been introduced, it would be left to the children to decide which one they liked best.

As the day went on, a number of different candidates emerged. Martin's drone had proved popular, as, perhaps unexpectedly, had the

Lonely Viking: the Norwegian one-seater driven by Robort. In the case of the latter, Alain wondered whether it was the combination of big man and little car that had won the children over. In the end, however, the hands-down winner had been the Tesla Roadster, which had the considerable advantage of being remote-control operated. Convincing children that EVs were trendy was the easiest thing in the world if you had one that took its lead from an iPhone...

There were already one or two images that Alain felt sure would live with him for a long time. The first was of a group of schoolchildren in Gams, no more than eleven or twelve years old, advancing arms outstretched towards the gentle giant Robort as he completed a circuit of the local playground in his tiny Corbin Sparrow. For all his solitude, the Lonely Viking had company at last. The second was not so much an image as a sensation; or rather, a sensation brought on by a series of images. The sun was out and the children were in high spirits. They were laughing and joking, fascinated by the EVs being paraded before them. Some were wide-eyed, almost in awe before them. There were so many different kinds of vehicles, and not one of them made a single sound! The other children were doing whatever they could to lay their hands on a passing car. In short, their curiosity was infectious and soon Alain, too, felt both elated and optimistic about the future. He knew it was his investment that was paving the way. If Andrej's technology was successful, today's scenes would be replayed the world over; and WAVE's ripple effect would be felt for generations to come.

Back in the car on his way to his final port of call, he was prized away from his thoughts by the vibration of his cell. There was a message on his display.

The navigation system told him to bear right, and with that he had reached the final school of the day. He parked the car a few metres from the main entrance and looked across at Andrej and Jasna standing next to their car, talking to a group of children huddled in rapt attention on a grassy bank.

The sight warmed his heart and he cherished the sense of hope that the team was creating. Then he took out his cell phone and his elation vanished into thin air.

It was a message from Frank.

CHAPTER TWENTY-TWO

Steinberg

Thursday morning – Arosa – Rorschach

Halfway through the morning and just out of Arosa, William Steinberg was still trying to justify his decision of the night before. That whole business with Leora… had it really been necessary? She didn't appear to have seen anything, but then who could say, really, how the human mind worked?

Perhaps she would have remembered something later that evening, the outline of a face glimpsed fleetingly in the half-light. Perhaps, come morning, she'd have wondered what on earth Steinberg had been doing alone on the edge of a wood at that hour. Better not to take that chance. Her reaction had been, well, unfortunate, but how the hell was Steinberg supposed to know she'd been taking meds?

It had made keeping a low profile a damn sight more difficult; that was for sure. He had felt it earlier that morning as he came down for breakfast. Conversations had seemed to end abruptly, as numerous pairs of eyes alighted on the hero of the hour. Some had even congratulated him on acting so quickly, and with such a level head. Remembering Dominik's instructions, he had modestly shrugged well-wishers aside and proceeded to take his place at the table.

Only later did he realize that not everyone wished him well. Magali, for one, whom Steinberg had met at Grossglockner, seemed more interested in what he did for a living; in how he was adjusting to the demands of the expedition. She hadn't seen him the day before at Lenzerheide, she said, as the group had trekked down the Albula Pass; she hoped the schedule wasn't proving too much.

What could he say to that? He had smiled, confirmed everything was alright, and emphasized how much he was looking forward to the day ahead. A great chance for the kids to get to grips with some of today's burning issues etc. etc. Eventually, perhaps tiring of his platitudes, the majority of which, Steinberg felt sure, had been doing the rounds all morning, she had taken her leave and returned to her husband.

Back on the road, Steinberg hadn't known what to make of it. This state of affairs was soon exacerbated by the flashing LED light on his cell. A missed call from Dominik. What did he want? An update on Jaeger? An apology for what had happened the night before?

Steinberg sighed, before returning the call.

"Just in the nick of time," Dominik said as he picked up.

"What's going on?"

"It seems that you are about to be arrested and taken in for questioning. I don't know yet on what grounds. In a few minutes, you'll be asked to pull over by police. Don't panic. Just make sure you cooperate. I've called in a couple of favours. Unless you do anything stupid, there's no chance you'll be going anywhere near a police station." Dominik's tone was ice-cold. "You owe me big-time for this."

Steinberg was confused. Just this morning he had been feted as a hero. What, he wondered, had changed in the meantime? He put the thought to one side.

For just as Dominik had said, a police car hove into view and asked Steinberg to pull his vehicle over to the side of the road. There were two officers, both imposing men. They had obviously been led to believe that Steinberg was, if not armed, then at the very least dangerous. The senior officer approached, a tall figure, fit and clean-shaven.

"Are you William Steinberg?"

"Yes, I am. Is there a problem?" Steinberg said politely.

"If you would step out of the vehicle and hand over the keys please, sir."

Again, there was something in the body language of the man that suggested he was expecting resistance.

"Certainly," came the reply, the suspect still charm personified.

"William Steinberg, I am arresting you on suspicion of the possession of illegal narcotics. You do not have to say anything but it may harm your defence if you choose…"

"Sir," the second police officer interrupted. He had been standing by the car all along. Steinberg had just seen him taking a call on his cell phone. "Can I speak to you for a minute?"

"Stay here."

Steinberg knew what was coming. He wondered what Dominik had fed them this time. That he was working in the interests of Swiss national security perhaps. In truth, it didn't matter. Anything would do, as long as it allowed Steinberg to continue his operation.

"Please accept our apologies, sir," the senior man had returned. "There appears to have been some sort of misunderstanding. You may return to your vehicle. Have a good day."

Steinberg said that it was no trouble and continued on his way. But he realized why Dominik had been so frustrated. He slammed his fists against the steering wheel. The information must have come from someone at WAVE – and that meant Steinberg could no longer return there. Unless… It was time for Plan B.

He called Jaeger.

"Well, well, well, if it isn't Switzerland's most wanted." There was a note of sarcasm in Jaeger's voice. It only aggravated Steinberg further.

"You owe me an apology," he said curtly.

"For what? For last night? Forget it. Now what's this about?" Jaeger said.

"I have to go under. I need you to take care of my car."

"What am I, your nanny?"

"Just do as I say," Steinberg was becoming more and more frustrated. "How quickly can you get to Buchs?"

"Where the hell is that?" Jaeger asked.

"On the road to Rorschach. A little off the beaten track. Take the A13 northbound. There's a service area just before. Pick me up in an hour. And, Jaeger?"

"What?"

"You'd better make damn sure you're on time."

In fact, there were service areas on both sides of the motorway. Steinberg's plan was to park on the south side and quickly change his appearance before meeting Jaeger on the north side. Jaeger would ensure that the car was no longer registered in Steinberg's name. If the police discovered it, records would show it belonged to some foreigner or other – whatever Walter's team had decided.

From the car, Steinberg kept only a small case, his files, and his tablet. He needed to travel light, unencumbered by possessions. Having purchased hair dye, shaving cream, and two packs of razors, he made towards the disabled toilet. He locked the door and reflected on the events that had led to this sudden change of plan.

The police warrant itself hadn't been the issue. Sure, it was inconvenient, but Steinberg had always known that the authorities would let him go. BIRD had contacts everywhere. Even if he *had* been obliged to make the trip down to the station, sooner or later Dominik would have managed to bust him out.

The problem was who had *alerted* the authorities. It couldn't have been Jaeger, even if the two had fought the previous evening. He would have gone to Adler, not the police. That meant it could only be someone at WAVE. Who had seen him in the bar with Leora? The barkeeper, obviously. Still, he had his back turned most of the evening. There had been a couple of participants, but no-one so close that they could have seen exactly what he was doing. And there certainly hadn't been any CCTV.

The solution came to him as he was shaving his beard. It had materialized so suddenly that he completely broke off from what he was doing, as if in disbelief that the solution could have proved so simple. Of course! It was the one person who had refrained from congratulating him. The only member of the expedition who had viewed him with suspicion that morning. Magali Zampieri! Now, what did *she* do for a living?

According to the files, Magali Zampieri was a personal trainer with a studio specializing in martial arts. Her husband, meanwhile, worked as a freelancer in IT security. Relatively innocent on the surface, perhaps, and easy for an inexperienced operative such as Hendrik Herder to overlook – but Peter... He ought to have known better. What had Jaromir Vegr said that night in the bunker in La Punt? That he was "old and alone, with no back up or support"... Well, here was the back-up. For IT and personal trainer, read intelligence and security. What's more, if they were monitoring the technology around the clock, then there would have to be a third team member. Maybe Jaromir did know something after all? But wait, who was it that had been out late in Arosa, just before Steinberg had spoken to Jaeger out back? A young guy. He couldn't quite put a name to the face. He checked his files again: Vivien Renlo. According to the Roadbook, Vivien hadn't been on duty every night. Did that matter? Steinberg began to dye his hair. The important thing was that the technology was being protected, most likely by Magali and her husband.

In order to make sure, Steinberg rang a colleague in Zurich. After all, there was no need to go through Dominik every time. His colleague checked to see who Vivien and Magali had been talking to during WAVE. The results confirmed Steinberg's suspicions. Over the course of the expedition Vivien had fielded any number of calls asking for technical assistance, but none of Magali's conversations could be retrieved.

Obviously they had been encrypted. That made things a whole

lot easier. As if that wasn't enough, they had also struck lucky with another participant.

Earlier that morning, a certain Alain Blanc had used a number of key words in conversation with an unknown caller, whose identity they had tried – and failed – to trace. Alain had even mentioned a name, before the anony-mous party had pleaded with him to be more cautious.

As Steinberg finished shaving and waited for the dye to take effect, he de-cided to have a look through Hendrik's daily reports. Next he watched the films the blogger had uploaded onto the expedition website. If Martin and Magali were protecting the technology, then they would have to be near the vehicle in question at all times. When you looked at it like that, there was only one possible candidate. With each film, it became clearer that the name Alain Blanc had mentioned must be that of the technologist.

Of course, those two idiots Hendrik and Peter had ruled him out right at the start, on what grounds Steinberg couldn't be sure. Something to do with the car's performance at the slalom a few days previously; or the fact that its designer was an independent researcher. They had assumed, no doubt with Dominik's backing, that a major player was involved; not a virtual unknown with a small, privately run institute just over the Slovenian border: a man who barely scraped a living teaching students the intricacies of electric vehicle conversion.

The man's file confirmed that he had met with a major London investor at an exclusive Kensington location only weeks before the ex-pedition began. That was how Dominik had got wind something was up in the first place. Steinberg didn't know what Brandt had told the new recruits. But he did know that it was a text message from an ad-dress in southwest London that had provided the initial trigger. Well, going on what he had just learned, the investor could only be Alain.

241

Steinberg would have to take a closer look at Alain to see what else he could find out.

 Steinberg paused. He realized that he hadn't taken Andrej Pečjak seriously enough either. The man just didn't look the part. There wasn't an ounce of arrogance in him. Instead, he seemed like a modest, humble man who was struggling to make ends meet. According to his file, he had owned a scrapyard for years. Where was he supposed to have obtained the necessary expertise to bring about a revolution? For a man like Andrej Pečjak, technical innovation meant taking the motor from the turret of a disused tank and building it into an EV. What they were looking for at WAVE seemed way out of his league. Steinberg shook his head in frustration. The guy couldn't even afford to buy a new phone!

But what was this? Steinberg saw that Hendrik Herder had actually been to Andrej's home; he had visited his institute. Unbelievable! They could have had this tied up days ago. He stopped himself. The reality was they hadn't. The past was no longer his concern. He needed to concentrate on how to make things right.

He smiled grimly. How ironic that it had been the Slovenian's investor who had given him away. As for Andrej's protectors, they had done a good job. But as soon as their cover was blown, what chance did they have? They couldn't stop shadowing the man they had been paid to protect. The films suggested that Andrej didn't even realize he was being monitored. That would have been someone else's decision, most likely Alain's, or perhaps a team of financiers, who had decided the technologist's safety was paramount. Ultimately, their insistence on providing him with a safe passage had led him headlong into danger. Would Steinberg have been able to find the technology if Alain had left Andrej unguarded? The way things had turned out, the answer was almost certainly no.

By the time he exited the disabled toilet, Steinberg looked like a completely different man. Granted, he was still the same height. But without the beard he looked ten years younger, while his hair was now darker and parted at the side. For good measure, he had donned a pair of reading glasses, which he had found in the side pocket of his case. Jaeger had barely recognized him and almost prevented him from getting into the car.

"You look like a real mummy's boy."

"Just drive."

Disguised or not, they needed to get off the road. According to the Roadbook, participants were staying in Romanshorn that night. Before that, however, they would need to charge their vehicles in Rorschach. There were no facilities at the youth hostel where they were staying. It was Thursday night, and Steinberg was sure the majority would take advantage of the opportunity to have a couple of drinks. Andrej, a popular figure who enjoyed a glass of wine, would almost certainly be among them. That would leave Steinberg time to do a little snooping around. Still, he would have to be careful. At some point, news that the police had not detained him was bound to filter through.

"Jesus fucking Christ, can't you drive a little faster?" The pair had become caught behind a car moving at a pitiful speed, but Jaeger didn't seem inclined to overtake. "It's no wonder *your* cover hasn't been blown. Are you sure you've been thirty kilometres away all this time? It feels more like three hundred," Steinberg continued. Who was the mummy's boy now?

The pair were approaching Rorschach from the east. A sign indicated that there was a marina some five hundred metres in the distance.

"Stop there," Steinberg said, pointing towards the sign. "We need to lose the car."

"Lose the car? We've already got rid of one…"

"Who's in charge here?" Steinberg snapped. He was getting sick of this. "I haven't told Dominik yet, but I'm pretty sure whoever informed the police knows about you too. They might not have a positive ID, but they'll have worked out I have an accomplice. They'll be looking for a car. They *won't* be looking for a boat. Rorschach's on Lake Constance. If we want to get an idea of what's going on, the best place to do it is from the water."

"So we'll head down to the front."

"For Christ's sake, Jaeger, will you listen to me? There's not enough time. Anyway, it's too close to the train line. There'll be too many people coming and going. Here's better. Take what you need from the car and we'll go and find a boat."

It wasn't difficult to locate an unmanned boat by a deserted marina. Steinberg pretended to make a call, while Jaeger logged into the system for a second time. When he had finished altering the car records, he joined Steinberg as the latter was getting ready to board and cast off.

"I know who it is," Steinberg began to outline his plan once they were on the water. "Andrej Pečjak. We do this one thing together and then we can go home."

"What about Hendrik? Adler said..."

"I don't care what Adler said." Steinberg needed to stay calm. He couldn't do this without Jaeger. "Dominik says he might have some use for him after all," he lied, before continuing: "When the time comes, we split up. The group are staying in Romanshorn, but their cars will be charging in Rorschach overnight. We wait here until the evening. Once they've left for Romanshorn, I'll take care of Andrej's car. You take the boat on to the youth hostel where they're staying, find Andrej, and separate him from the group."

"How do I do that?"

"I don't know," Steinberg snapped. "Use your brain. Take him for a drink or something."

"I don't like it. What about his wife?"

"His wife?" Steinberg was incredulous. "Who cares about his wife, for fuck's sake? Get rid of her. She's collateral. You know how these things work."

"That's not a sanctioned operation," Jaeger protested. "I'm here to pull in an operative, not create a bloodbath."

"What does it matter? What do you think's going to happen to the technologist when we're finished with him?" Steinberg allowed Jaeger a moment to think. "Believe me, once the dust settles and he realizes Dominik made the right call, Adler will be the first to congratulate you on a job well done."

"Adler?" Jaeger said. "Shall we see what Adler makes of all this?"

Jaeger turned his back on him and reached for his pocket. The bastard. The stupid bastard.

"You know, there's a story about an old dog whose master dies," Steinberg hissed. "Do you know what the dog does? It goes and waits by his graveside." Jaeger's back was still turned but he had paused, cell phone in his right hand. Steinberg continued. "Let's turn the tables shall we? What do you think Adler would do if you died today?" Still there was no response. "I'll tell you, he wouldn't give a fucking shit. He certainly wouldn't come and visit your grave; I bet he'd barely even be willing to pay for a plot of land."

Jaeger completed a half-circle, placed his cell down methodically, and went for him. But Steinberg was ready. He kicked Jaeger in the right knee, hard, so that the big man lost his balance and toppled to the floor. Now Steinberg was sitting on him, using his hands to throttle him. Jaeger kicked out with his feet, tried in vain to escape Steinberg's grasp. But he had no chance now. His movements became slower and a hand came to rest on the deck alongside. Still, Steinberg wouldn't let go. Then all of a sudden he felt a searing pain in his left side. A knife? Where the hell had Jaeger got a knife from? Why couldn't the bastard just die? Seeing the blade lodged in his flesh, Steinberg cried out in pain, before taking hold of Jaeger's head and jerking it to one side. The sound of his neck breaking pierced the early evening air. And finally all was quiet. That would be the last time Jaeger questioned Steinberg's orders…

Nevertheless, Steinberg knew the job wasn't done. He shut his eyes and tried to overcome the pain. The left side of his body felt like it had been broken into tiny pieces. He lifted his shirt to reveal a flesh wound. At some point, it would need stitches but for now it was all he could do to control the bleeding. Cursing, he stood up and surveyed his immediate surroundings. There were no other boats for miles around.

Whatever else happened, he needed to get rid of Jaeger. Dispose of the form that lay lifeless alongside him.

He checked Jaeger's pulse to confirm he was dead and, with his last ounce of strength, threw him overboard. Already he knew there was no hope of executing his plan tonight. With Jaeger gone, he was outnumbered by at least three to one. More than that, he was cold and tired, shaken by what had just happened. The best thing he could do now was take the boat to Rorschach, observe what was going on, and then, if he still had the energy, navigate on to Romanshorn and reassess the situation. Dominik, he could leave for the time being. Steinberg knew that he wouldn't take kindly to the timing of Jaeger's death; not now that he had located the technology.

Despite the cold, Steinberg realized that he was sweating profusely, his breathing laboured and heavy. There was still no-one around. The discovery of Jaeger's body, wherever it washed up, was bound to keep the police busy for a while. Lake Constance bordered on three different countries and the resulting bureaucracy was bound to be a nightmare. The left side of his body still aching, Steinberg lay down for a moment to rest but soon the lapping of the water carried him into sleep.

He awoke with a start, unsure for a moment where he was. Then it came flooding back. He was opposite Rorschach but from his position on the water he could no longer see the technologist's car. The only thing for it was to take the boat on to Romanshorn.

He navigated towards the small harbour near the train station to consider his next move. The youth hostel where the participants were staying was within easy walking distance. But there was no way he could head to the shore for the time being. He couldn't risk being seen. Besides, he was still hurting after his fatal confrontation with Jaeger and he had no idea, now, where the technologist's car was stationed.

Taking out his camera, he saw that a number of participants were currently taking advantage of both the fine weather and the pop-up beach bar by the edge of the lake. The town looked a picture in the early evening sunlight. Located on the southern side of Lake Constance, its harbour serving both Swiss and German towns in the vicinity, there was a glorious purple hue to the sky, which, when seen upon the surface of the water, imbued the surrounding landscape with an air of infinite mystery.

The technologist, Steinberg saw, was among those toasting the group's safe arrival, alongside the pair Steinberg had recently identified as his protectors. These two looked suddenly older, more careworn, a symptom of their concern, no doubt, that their prime suspect had not only shaken off his police tail but subsequently been absent for much of the day. Would they, he wondered, have revealed their true identity to Andrej, or informed the other teams of the threat posed by Steinberg? Doubtful. They would have to unravel a web of lies first, exposing themselves to a whole series of counter-accusations in the process.

Now that he saw them all altogether, Steinberg wondered how it had taken so long for him to work out what was going on. If you knew what to look for, you could tell an operative from a hundred paces. It was something in their posture, the impossibility of feigning relaxation when in fact they were on high alert. Andrej Pečjak, on the other hand, *did* appear to be relaxed, and that could only mean he still had no idea that he was in danger.

For the moment, there wasn't a great deal more Steinberg could do except watch. It was, he realized, going to be nigh-on impossible to get at the technology without the aid of a second man. He cursed

Jaeger for giving him no choice but to take matters into his own hands.

Then out of the corner of his eye, just as he was preparing to move, he saw something that gave him a glimmer of hope.

It didn't look like much, but the sight of a nine-year-old boy playing alone by the waterfront cheered Steinberg up no end.

CHAPTER TWENTY-THREE

Dominik

Thursday evening – Zurich

Ever since Dominik Brandt had called Steinberg that morning, he had been waiting for the phone to ring. Now, as the clock ticked slowly past midnight, he was beginning to wonder if he shouldn't make the first move.

The office was completely empty. He turned the lights off and took the stairs down to the exit. Outside, it was still warm, and groups of people were beginning to spill out onto the streets. Dominik ignored them and proceeded towards the church. After crossing the Muensterbruecke, he turned right onto the Limmatquai before disappearing behind the opera house into one of the small side streets on the left-hand side. He never took the same route up to his apartment, which was situated on top of a hill near the Dolder Grand Hotel.

Anyone else would have chosen the apartment for its view over the lake and the sparkling lights of the inner city. For Dominik, however, it was the presence of the luxury five star resort that had sealed the deal. Perched  gloriously on top of the Swiss capital, it served as a reminder of everything he one day hoped to achieve.

Back at home, there was still no news. Dominik was annoyed. He couldn't afford for things to come to a standstill.

For the first time since the decision had been made, he questioned the wisdom of getting Steinberg involved. What if he failed to find the technology? Worse, what if he failed to find the technology but succeeded in removing Jaeger from the scene? That combination would make Dominik's position untenable. Not only would he have gone against Adler's wishes, he would have been responsible for the death of one of his most loyal henchmen.

The thing was he had never intended to destroy the technology. It was far too valuable for that. If he kept it, he could use it as leverage. The big wigs of industry and politics would have no choice but to listen to him if they knew he had something that could change the face of the automotive industry. And if they chose not to, well then he could always cash in. Sell the design, live off the profits...

He went to the fridge and took out a bottle of water. His thoughts drifted back towards Steinberg. Whatever he had said to him that morning, it hadn't been the whole truth. Yes, the file on him was closed. But only temporarily. One false move, and Dominik could have Steinberg's arrest made a nationwide priority. In that respect, perhaps Jaeger's death would be no bad thing. Dominik could pass Steinberg's presence at WAVE off as a rogue mission, undertaken without his permission, and no-one would be able to contradict him. Walter and Nils, after all, were still unaware that Steinberg had been sent in the first place.

Nevertheless, it was a situation Dominik hoped to avoid. Adler might believe him, might even be willing to accept that Steinberg was a law unto himself, but he wouldn't step aside; and that meant Dominik would have to wait another year, maybe more. Who knew what might happen in the meantime? Dominik was Adler's number two, but there was nothing to stop the CEO anointing a different successor.

No, for all that he had messed up, right now Steinberg was still his best bet, the one man who could ensure Dominik's path to the top remained clear.

He went to the window, tried to take his mind off the call that refused to come. Still, it was no use: in this game, no news was rarely good. He realized he couldn't ask Nils to give him an update on Steinberg's location. On Jaeger's then? No, if Jaeger was already dead, there was no sense in making it public knowledge until the morning.

He sat back down, began to rap his fingers on the mahogany wood. Where was the harm in setting his mind at rest?

He took his cell phone out and opened his address book. In the far distance, he saw a firework illuminate the night sky. Probably a trial ahead of tomorrow's Zuri Faescht.

He realized that Steinberg had answered, and was now waiting for Dominik to say something down the line.

"Sorry, go again," Dominik said. His mind had been somewhere else entirely.

"I know who it is," Steinberg said. "Andrej Pečjak. He has an institute in Bled. The only problem is he's got protection. There are two agents permanently shadowing him, they've been there right from the start."

"OK, then hold off on Jaeger, it sounds like you could use an extra pair of hands."

"Too late." Steinberg paused, as if to catch his breath. "Jaeger's gone."

"Gone?"

"Dead," Steinberg confirmed. "Probably washed ashore somewhere by now."

Dominik felt a surge of rage. He couldn't believe what he was hearing. "Hang on. You're telling me that you discovered the identity of the technologist, found out he was being protected by two agents, and *then* decided to take Jaeger out? A bit premature, don't you think?"

"You told me to do whatever I had to."

"I also said you might need Jaeger somewhere down the line. Well, that somewhere is upon us. And you…"

"I had no choice," Steinberg said. "He was about to call Adler. He practically beat me to death."

"For fuck's sake," Dominik spat. Then he took a deep breath.

"OK, it's not all bad. I can see that. I can send someone over to Slovenia, have them ransack this Andrej's office. See what we find. But that doesn't change the fact that we need his car. I hope to God you've got a plan; and that it's a damn sight better than the one you've just put into action."

"Don't worry. I'm on it. Though I'm pretty sure Adler would disapprove..."

"Leave Adler to me. The next time I hear from you, I want this thing done. Otherwise, you'll be heading straight back into Swiss custody. Do I make myself clear?"

"Clear as day," Steinberg said. "Now, if you'll excuse me."

With that, he was gone and Dominik was alone once more. After he had sent a team to Slovenia and ensured that Jaeger's death would be reported as a tragic accident, he thought long and hard about how to proceed.

Ten minutes later, his mind was made up. The events of the past two days had made it clear that Steinberg was a liability. When all this was finally over, Dominik would no longer hesitate in cutting him adrift.

CHAPTER TWENTY-FOUR

Magali

Friday morning – Romanshorn – St Gallen

Magali Zampieri was standing next to the car with her head heavy on her shoulders. She had just spoken with Frank and still couldn't understand how the police search for Steinberg had been called off so quickly.

OK, they couldn't use the conversation Martin had overheard at the back of the hotel, but Martin had filmed Steinberg spiking Leora's drink. More than that, they had a statement from the hospital confirming  that a mixture of drugs had been found in Leora's bloodstream. Forget Peter's mysterious disappearance and Jaromir's alleged fall in La Punt. Both incidents might have been useful pieces of circumstantial evidence – to complete the picture, as it were – but DSP ought to have been able to manage without them.

Magali paused. What kind of people were they dealing with here? To think, they had initially written it off as industrial espionage. That was serious enough in its way, of course, but nothing compared with the picture that had since emerged. One thing was for certain. Whoever was behind it was a significant player, in possession of far-reaching political clout. Getting wind of the police search was one thing; being able to call it off quite another.

So, who the hell were they?

 It seemed Frank had no idea. The name Hendrik had given them – Dominik Brandt – hadn't helped much either. Yes, Brandt worked for a company in Zurich, but his chief claim to fame was as chairman of a charitable foundation, which aimed to improve road safety in developing countries. What possible interest could he have in electric vehicle technology? A thought crossed Magali's mind. Perhaps it had been an impostor who had recruited Hendrik, a man with a grudge against Brandt who had thought to drag his name through the mud. After all, she reflected with a rueful smile, no-one was who they said they were anymore. Alain, king of sportswear, was merely the latest in a long line. It turned out that he was a multi-millionaire with more than a passing interest in sustainability. He had investments in a number of technology companies that dealt with the issues closest to his heart. Companies like Andrej's. Magali had to give it to him. To look at Alain, you would never think he was rich. He was polite and courteous to everyone. Everyone, it seemed, except Frank Loden.

Yesterday morning Alain had revealed to Frank that he had been at WAVE all along. He had wanted to stay in the background, he said, but the incident with Leora had been simply too much to ignore. He wanted to know why more wasn't being done to protect his investment. Frank had done his best to calm him down but had nevertheless been forced to reveal the identity of his agents. Now that it was all out in the open, Magali still couldn't say whether it was a good thing or not. Up until that point, the participants had taken it as read that Martin and Magali were husband and wife. Why would they lie about a thing like that? But things had just become far more complicated. What if Alain said something that exposed them? What would happen then? A careless word or gesture was all it took…

And now came the news on the radio. A body had been found in the lake overnight and police were treating the death as unexplained. No chance of keeping this one under wraps, as most of the participants had already known long before the news was announced. It had been one of their number who had discovered the body. Andre Lugger, whose battery-powered espresso machine had been the source of so much wonder in Weissensee, had left the group the previous evening in Rorschach. He had taken his e-boat, which had been moored at the harbour, across to Konstanz on the German side of the lake to pick up his wife, who would be joining the expedition for the world-record parade in Zurich on Saturday. On their way back early that morning, they had stumbled across a dead body that must have floated up to the surface overnight. Andre and his wife were both still with the police, but somehow the information had filtered through to various teams on the expedition. No doubt Andre had told his teammate, Thomas Rot, why they would be unable to make the start that morning, and the whole thing had spiralled from there.

Nevertheless, it was the description of the deceased that had really made Magali nervous. The radio announcer had said he was tall and in his mid-fifties. Didn't that sound like the driver Hendrik had seen in Weissensee? His friend in Zurich had told him that the first man, the man who had originally been on Hendrik's tail, had been sent to take care of Peter. The second man, they knew, was Steinberg. If the two had been working together, did that mean Steinberg was responsible for his death? They had known he was dangerous – but this had come like a bolt from the blue.

In the meantime, Martin had appeared alongside her.

"Darling, is everything OK?" he asked. Now was not the time for his games.

"We need to get him out of here," Magali said quietly. "It's not safe any longer."

"Agreed. Hendrik's been talking to his contact in Zurich. Nothing official yet, but it looks like an operative has been killed in action. That body: it has to be the man who was sent to deal with Peter Prohaska."

"That's precisely what's worrying me."

"How d'you mean?"

"C'mon Martin, think it through. Let's assume for a minute they were colleagues and that they were both looking for the technology. Now one of them is dead. Why?"

"I don't know. Could be a disagreement that got out of control?" Martin ventured.

"You really think that?" Magali said. "They're professionals."

"It's just a theory," Martin replied, slightly defensively.

"I don't buy it. Surely they're stronger as a team. I mean, why would you get rid of your back-up?"

"I have a suspicion you're about to tell me."

"Well, again, it's just a theory," Magali began, "but supposing Steinberg's not meant to be here at all? The organization all these people work, or worked, for – Hendrik, Steinberg, Peter – it's in flux somehow. There's a power struggle, I don't know, what does it matter? The point is, if Steinberg's a rogue operative, then there's no way of predicting what he's going to do next."

"So, what? He killed this guy because they suddenly found themselves on different sides?"

"Like I said, it's just a theory. The truth is we may never find out. Either way, we can't afford to sit tight until something else happens. Right now, Steinberg has all the aces. We can't say for sure he knows it's Andrej; but he *does* have a copy of the Roadbook. That means he can predict our movements, say where we're going to be any time, day or night. The trouble is," Magali exhaled deeply, "we can't do the same for him."

"What are you saying? That we need to play him at his own game?"

"Precisely," Magali confirmed. "We need to get Andrej away from WAVE. If we do that, then the ball will be in Steinberg's court."

"OK, so what's the plan?"

"My guess is that Steinberg only comes out at night. That means the sooner we act the better. But first of all we're going to have to tell Andrej who we really are. I've just spoken to Frank and he agrees it's the right thing to do."

Despite the initial shock of discovering that his technological breakthrough had been the subject of such intrigue – obviously he had no idea he was being protected – Andrej had reacted to Magali's revelation in exactly the way she had expected: calmly, and with great dignity. There had been no recriminations upon receiving the news: only gratitude that Martin and Magali had carried out their task in such a discreet and professional manner.

Needless to say, however, Andrej remained deeply concerned that his presence at WAVE might cause other people harm, and together the pair had managed to hatch a plan. Astonishingly, it had been Andrej who had provided the germ of the idea. The first stop that morning was at EMPA in St Gallen, a research centre that was part of the Swiss Federal Institutes of Technology Domain. The participants were due to receive a guided tour where they would learn about the latest developments in materials science.

What the Road-book didn't say – but what Andrej knew on account of having worked there in the past – was that the company had a second site, a little further west in Duebendorf, which focused on electric mo-bility and, in particular, battery testing. If Martin and Magali could manage to get Andrej and Jasna to the second site without being seen, then two of their problems would be solved. First, Andrej and Jasna would no longer be part of the expedition, thereby ensuring their safety. Second, the location of Andrej's hiding place would enable him to test the impact of his technology – and confirm his initial claims that it had been a success.

How Steinberg would react to Andrej's disappearance was another matter. By removing Andrej and Jasna from the scene, wouldn't they effectively be revealing which car had the technology? But then maybe Steinberg knew already. Whatever the case, he would be forced to make a move, and that would at least flush him out into the open.

"That still leaves us one problem," Martin said. He had beckoned Magali to one side in order to speak with her in private. "If we go, we expose Hendrik. Can we afford to take that chance?"

"No. That's why *we're* not going. To the majority, we're still ordinary participants. Besides, we've agreed to help Hendrik's contact. In Zurich, remember?"

"So we'll need another mode of transport?" Martin said.

"Yes. And I know just the person to provide it."

It wasn't far from Romanshorn to St Gallen, but the situation made for a tense drive. Martin and Magali both had their eyes on the road, on Andrej and Jasna in front, and it was left to Hendrik, by now a permanent feature in the backseat, to break the silence. They had decided to let him in on the plan.

"So, it's Andrej. Does he know about me? About what I was doing before?"

"No," said Martin. "We didn't think he needed to."

"The way he was with me in Bled. Given everything that was going on, I don't think I deserved that." Hendrik sighed. "If there's anything I can do..."

"There might be something," Magali said. "We need someone to keep an eye out for Steinberg while we may make sure everything's in place. The question is, are you up to the task?"

Hendrik shuddered. But he was nodding his head.

"OK, so let's run through it one final time," Magali continued. "We stop at a side street behind the institute, where Frank will be waiting with his truck, tailgate open. Vivien will be there to assist. Andrej arrives and drives his car straight into the back of the truck. Frank and Vivien lock up, and get everything ready for departure. It's an industrial area so the sight of a car being loaded won't raise any eyebrows. But as a precaution, Frank will make sure he's parked out of sight. We'll keep an eye on everything else in the meantime."

"Once the coast is clear," Martin picked up the thread, "we'll park our car and walk over to EMPA. There's an official welcome, then breakfast. After that there's a guided tour. Andrej's contact at EMPA, Marcel, will confirm that things are ready in Duebendorf. That's our cue to let Frank know they can leave."

"Vivien works for you? And Frank? Who's Frank?" Hendrik asked.

"He's our mission control," Martin replied. "And yes, Vivien's one of us. Who did you think was watching the car at night?"

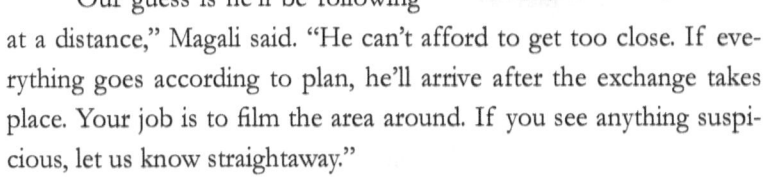

"If anyone asks where Andrej is, we tell them that he needs to check something with his car," Magali said. "Once he's in Duebendorf, he can call Louis Palmer and say he's had to pull out of the expedition. Louis will be annoyed, especially after losing Steinberg and Vivien from support. But one day he'll understand."

"What *about* Steinberg?" Hendrik asked. "What if he's there?"

"Our guess is he'll be following at a distance," Magali said. "He can't afford to get too close. If everything goes according to plan, he'll arrive after the exchange takes place. Your job is to film the area around. If you see anything suspicious, let us know straightaway."

They arrived to find Frank waiting with Vivien. The former looked younger than Magali remembered. Perhaps it was the freckles, brought out by an extended period of summer sun. The rear door to the E-FORCE truck stood open and within a minute Andrej had disappeared inside. Although the whole thing was over in a flash, it had felt like an age. With relief, Magali realized that there didn't seem to be anyone else around. Hendrik gave her a nod to confirm this.

"This must be the greenest rescue operation there's ever been," Martin said. Magali was glad to see he hadn't lost his sense of humour. "An EV, being transported to safety by an electric truck. It's a good thing Frank has so many contacts he can rely on. But surely he could have brought us a case of Feldschloesschen as well."

"Let's get going," Magali said, ignoring Martin's reference to the beer logo on the side of the truck. "Marcel could be waiting for us already."

The EMPA building loomed large in the background. Stretching high into the clouds above and towering over everything in its immediate vicinity, it looked like a vision from the future; the creation of a dystopian fiction writer, rather than that of a respected and highly decorated Swiss architect. No-one seemed to have noticed that Andrej and Jasna had gone. In part this was due to the commotion caused by the reappearance of Andre Lugger and his wife. A small group had formed around them and they were obviously divulging the details of their gruesome discovery earlier that morning.

Magali went inside to meet with Andrej's contact. A slim, dark-haired man was drinking coffee and chatting to a much older man in the far corner by a window. Magali recognized the younger man from the photo Frank had sent them. She knew from Andrej that Marcel was a tireless promoter of EVs, as well as a walking dictionary on all related topics, particularly battery technology. Coming from Andrej, that was some compliment.

Magali stood listening to the pair's conversation.

"Since I've retired," the old man was saying, "I've finally been able to devote more time to the World Resources Forum…"

Magali moved towards a table containing hot drinks and pastries. After helping herself to coffee and a croissant, she waited for the agreed sign.

"Merde!" said Marcel all of a sudden, looking across at Magali. The old man was startled, but soon realized that Marcel had spilled coffee on his trousers.

"Here," Magali approached, offering Marcel a serviette from the pastry table. When Marcel accepted, she knew that everything was in place.

"Is this your guardian angel?" the older man said. "We could have done with you around when I was CEO…"

Magali shrugged her shoulders and smiled. On another day she might have stayed to chat, but right now she had more important things to consider.

"We're good to go," Magali informed Frank, as she made her way back outside.

She was pleased with her morning's work. With Andrej safely transported, it appeared that the mission had been an unqualified success.

"Anything?" Magali asked, as Hendrik and Martin emerged from their various duties.

"Nothing," they said in unison.

Magali breathed a sigh of relief. Out of the corner of her eye, she noticed Alain coming towards them.

"Well done. It looks like you got him out just in time."

"Let's not start celebrating yet," Magali cautioned. "We've done the hard work but we still don't know how Steinberg will react."

"The ball's in his court now," Martin added. "We've got him exactly where we want him."

"So, what now?" Alain asked. He had pointedly neglected to acknowledge Hendrik's presence.

"Now?" Magali said. "All we can do is wait."

CHAPTER TWENTY-FIVE

Nils

Friday afternoon – Zurich

Over the course of the past forty-eight hours, Nils Karrat had been thinking about poker. Was it a game of skill or a game of chance? That you had no influence over the cards you were dealt suggested the latter, but then the key was not in the deal. Rather, it was in how you *reacted* to it. An inexperienced poker player revealed their hand in an instant; a seasoned veteran gave no indication of whether it was good or bad.

Well, Nils' hand was bad. He could say that much for certain now. He had tried to deny it, perhaps more out of guilt than anything else. It was his fault that Hendrik had been dragged into this mess. His fault that their lives were both in danger. That was the truth. There was no getting around it. He had been deceived, blinded by the riches on offer, and lured into taking on a job that could only ever end in disaster.

For poker players who wanted out of the game, there were two options. The first was to take the financial hit and fold. If the loss was too great, and you happened to be mixing with the wrong crowd, it meant a lifetime looking over your shoulder. Nils could get out, but how could he be sure Dominik wouldn't collect on his debt? That left the second option. Prepare your exit – but convince the people that matter you're in it for the long haul. Put on your poker face and wait for the others around you to fall.

The first casualty had been the night before in Rorschach. Nils had spent the morning trying to confirm the victim's identity. Thanks to Walter, he had access to a whole range of information on the system. It included high-level clearance for the reports on existing projects. Naturally, Nils could have accessed some of it on his own – Hendrik's updates, the films – but beyond a certain point, people of his rank were informed of developments only on a need-to-know basis. Well, this was something Nils clearly didn't need to know...

Still, once he was sure, he wasted no time in contacting Hendrik. He used the same chat tool as before. According to the software provider, not even intelligence agencies could trace it.

NILS: DECEASED CONFIRMED AS CONRAD JAEGER, 51. THERE'S SOMETHING NOT RIGHT ABOUT IT. LOCATION OF DEATH ORIGINALLY GIVEN AS RORSCHACH. IT'S SINCE BEEN CHANGED TO "UNKNOWN".

HENDRIK: COVER UP?

NILS: THAT WAS MY FIRST THOUGHT AS WELL. WILL KEEP DIGGING.

HENDRIK: GOOD. WE NEED TO TALK. THERE HAVE BEEN DEVELOPMENTS. I THINK WE CAN GET YOU OUT.

NILS: CALL ME IN FIVE. I CAN'T TALK HERE.

Nils checked no-one was following him and made his way out into the rain towards Spruengli. The good thing about his new job was that his colleagues didn't work regular hours. No-one batted an eyelid if he left the office suddenly on a Friday afternoon. Still, even that knowledge did nothing to calm his nerves. He knew that what he was doing was highly dangerous. His hands were sweating and he could barely even light the cigarette he was holding. The drizzle looked as if it was setting in for the day. Strange, the effect of rain on the buildings around. They seemed taller somehow, more imposing. For a moment Nils wondered whether they might not be listening to what he was about to say.

He walked on past Spruengli, in the direction of the Paradeplatz, hoping that the trams would make it impossible for any passers-by to eavesdrop on his conversation.

A drop of rain landed on his cell phone. He waited patiently for it to continue its journey down to the ground.

Then when the call came, he answered.

"Hendrik, what have you got for me?" he said urgently. His nerves were getting to him.

"Good news. The technology's safe." The relief in Hendrik's voice was palpable.

"The technology? How d'you mean? I didn't think anyone knew who had it."

"There's something I have to tell you." Hendrik sounded strange. "You might not like it."

"You leave me to decide that," Nils said. "Now, what is it?"

"I haven't been entirely honest with you. Ever since I got back to WAVE, I've been under the protection of two agents. They were hired to ensure the technology survived the race intact."

"And they told you which car it was?" Nils was confused. "That doesn't make any sense."

"No, I only found that out this morning. I've been working with them, you see."

Nils didn't see, but he continued anyway. "And they trust you?" he stammered. "I mean, you trust them?"

"I didn't have a choice. Initially, anyway." Hendrik paused. "But they trust me because I've been able to give them vital information."

"Which came from me?" Nils asked.

"Right," Hendrik confirmed. "So they trust you too."

"Where are you?"

"We're en route to Baden, about thirty kilometres from Zurich. Haven't you got anything else to say?"

"Only that I'm sorry," Nils said. He was feeling downcast. "I should never have dragged you into this."

"Don't worry about that now. Let's concentrate on how we're going to get you out."

Since when was Hendrik so in charge of the situation? After a morning spent looking after his shoulder, Nils felt like a nervous wreck.

"OK, I'm listening," he said, after a pause.

"There's a world-record parade tomorrow in Zurich. EVs, people everywhere. If you can get here before it starts, then we'll be able to make sure you're safe. That gives you the rest of the day to tie up any loose ends. I'll call this evening to confirm we're on." Hendrik stopped talking. Clearly, he had something on his mind. "This guy who's been helping you. Is he reliable? That is, can you trust him?"

"He's the one who saved your life. I don't know about you, but that's good enough for me."

When Hendrik had told him to use the afternoon to "tie up any loose ends", Nils wondered whether his friend had any concept of what that might entail. Nils had seen the systems Dominik had in place, witnessed first-hand the ease with which people could be tracked down. And now he was supposed to – what? Erase all traces of his and Hendrik ever having worked for Dominik's company? See to it that they could spend the rest of their lives in peace?

Fortunately, help was at hand. Nils reached into his pocket and scrabbled around for the note Walter had left him a few nights ago in the bar. The number it contained was an outside line. Not for the first time, Nils found himself wondering if Walter had helped other people out of similar predicaments in the past.

"Walter? I need to see you."

"Nils, I've been expecting your call. Meet me at Old Fashion in half an hour."

Outside, the drizzle persisted, and Nils was glad of the temporary shelter provided by the bar. It was quieter than it had been on the previous occasion, with only a few afternoon drinkers sipping beer and passing the time. A sign warned patrons that the premises were monitored by CCTV. Nils shuddered. Although he was sure no-one had followed him, he wouldn't, if the question was asked, be able to deny that a meeting had taken place.

"I think I know what this about," Walter said. Nils had been unaware of his presence. He had emerged from a corner, with a glass of sparkling water in his hand. "And if you're worried about being caught on camera, don't be. I've had it disabled."

"You said you couldn't bear to see a young person's life destroyed. Does that go for me as well as for Hendrik?"

"You want out?" the DI said.

"I can't be a part of this any longer. I thought all we were doing was a little industrial espionage. Nothing too heavy… But now this? I know Dominik's linked to Adler Reilly somehow, but I just don't understand what the hell is going on."

"I can tell you only that you were recruited at an inopportune time. The whole business stinks. There are two stories here. One is about the technology; the other about the dawn of a new era. Dominik's making a play for power and woe betide anyone who gets in his way."

"Is that what happened? In Rorschach? Someone got in the way? What about Peter?" Nils was speaking so softly he was worried Walter wouldn't understand what he was saying.

"Rorschach? I was given to understand that the location of *that* death was still unknown," Walter said. He gave Nils a look that suggested he was only too aware of the change to the file. Perhaps, Nils thought, he had been responsible for it himself. "No matter. The point is, I can guarantee your safety. You don't get to be director of intelligence without stumbling upon a few secrets."

"You can erase our files?" There was no way of knowing just how much information Adler Reilly had on them already.

"I can make sure that Dominik has no interest in pursuing the matter once you and your friend have disappeared. Allow me, by the way, to introduce Stephan Schwarz, my escrow holder."

Walter beckoned towards a man sitting in the corner of the bar. Upon Walter's signal, he approached.

"Your what?" Nils said.

"Let's call him the keeper of my secrets."

Nils turned to greet the bald-headed man with thick-framed glasses. He realized it was the same man he had seen on his previous visit, nearly a week before. Again, Nils felt a sense of unease. What had Schwarz being doing here last time? And why the hell was Walter so damn calm?

"Stephan is an architect and a good man to know in the event of an emergency," Walter continued matter-of-factly. He must have seen some terrible things. How else to explain that he could take all this in his stride? Unless he was bluffing too… "He is also, coincidentally, the president of the Swiss Tesla Owners Club."

"Pleased to meet you," Nils said.

"Likewise," said Stephan. "If you need anything – and I mean *anything* – don't hesitate to call me on this number." Stephan slipped Nils his business card.

"Thanks. You don't know how much I appreciate this."

"Think nothing of it," Stephan said kindly, before taking his leave.

"Walter, what's going on here?" Nils asked, turning to the DI.

"You said you could get me out."

"And I can. Nevertheless, I think it would be prudent to wait until you are free from any immediate danger before cutting all ties. As you know, there is still an operative at work. A man with a death on his conscience."

"And Stephan?" Nils said.

"Will help you in the event that I cannot. All I'm saying is: don't play your hand until you are certain of your opponent's intentions. I take it you have a plan?"

"Tomorrow morning," Nils confirmed. "There's a parade. I have people to help me go under."

"Very well. Perhaps it is better if I am not in full possession of the details. When you leave the hotel tomorrow morning, give every indication that you will be returning later in the day. Once you are clear of danger – and only then – call me on the same number you used today. I will take care of everything from there. Until I receive your call, however, I will assume that you are still working on behalf of the Zurich office. Is that understood?"

"Understood. But what will you do? If things turn nasty?" Nils liked Walter. He was a good man. Nils wondered how he had ended up here, doing all this dirty work. Perhaps, he concluded, Walter had simply been in the wrong place at the wrong time.

"That is not in anyone's interests. Least of all Dominik's," the DI concluded. "There's been far too much heat already. Sooner or later someone's going to have to take a step back and allow things to cool down."

With that, Walter was gone, and Nils was standing outside in the rain once more. He wondered what Walter had meant by that final remark. Perhaps only that unnecessary bloodshed was always bad for business. A cliché no doubt – but then more often than not, clichés were grounded in reality: simple truths that, by dint of their legitimacy, had come, in time, to be universally acknowledged.

Whatever. If things went according to plan, Nils would soon be able to go home. Walter would take care of the room, as well as negotiate any difficulties caused by Nils' disappearance. That still left a few things to be taken care of. No matter who they worked for, no-one could travel without money and a passport. Irrespective of what happened tomorrow – and Walter had just advised him to keep his options open – Nils would need to stash some items overnight in a locker. The train station was the obvious place. A small amount of cash and a change of clothes. Nothing too valuable. His passport he could keep in his back pocket.

After that, it would be a question of waiting. For Hendrik to confirm the details, and then for events to take their course.

The best way to pass the time would be to carry on as if nothing had happened. The most successful card players were blessed with the ability to give nothing away. No matter what was going on in their heads, they refused to engage with the world outside. Tonight, Nils would do likewise. He would go back to the office, work late, and wait for Hendrik's call.

It was vital that no-one looked behind the mask: that no-one saw beyond his poker face.

CHAPTER TWENTY-SIX

Magali

Friday late-afternoon – Baden bei Zurich

Ever since the group had departed from St Gallen earlier in the day, there had been an end-of-term feel to proceedings. The participants were relaxed and friendly with one another, basking in the glory of having all but achieved their combined aim. Of course things had always run smoothly enough between them, but up until today the possibility of failure had lingered like an unwanted guest at a dinner party.

Now, teams knew there was only a weekend left to negotiate; and that the distance between locations was negligible. On top of that, there was genuine excitement at the prospect of being part of a world-record attempt. Some 400 electric vehicles were expected for the parade in Zurich the next day and the event would coincide with the triennial Zueri Faescht, a three-day festival that saw revellers descend on the capital from all parts of the country.

Try as she might, however, Magali Zampieri could not get herself in the party mood. It was true that she had every right to be satisfied with her day's work. Andrej, Jasna, and the technology were now safe. The E-Force truck had provided that extra bit of protection. After all, who would have thought that an electric HGV belonging to a local Swiss brewery could contain anything other than the refreshing drink it advertised?

In addition, from what Magali had heard, there was every indication that the test drive itself had been successful. Truly, it seemed, a revolution was just around the corner. Needless to say, Alain had been delighted at the news and was already planning a meeting with Andrej to discuss the next steps. His companion for the day, Magali had noted, was Florian. In the past few days, the nine-year-old had travelled with any number of different teams, and his desire to tell anyone who would listen about his experiences was infectious. But not even his excitement at co-piloting the Bolt for the first time was enough to dispel the notion that there was still work to be done.

The problem, in a nutshell, was Hendrik. Until Magali had more details concerning the nature of his erstwhile employer, relaxation of any kind remained a distant dream. Ever since the discovery of the dead body, she had been certain that Hendrik was in serious danger. He had gone white as a sheet in St Gallen when Andre Lugger and his wife had shown him photos of the deceased. It was, he confirmed, the same man he had seen in Weissensee on the night of his return to WAVE. In that moment – Magali could see it in his face – he had realized how lucky he was to be alive.

When they arrived in Baden later that afternoon, the whole group was received by the local sponsors at the Brown-Boveri-Platz. At least being surrounded by so many people would provide Hendrik with a modicum of protection if Steinberg were to come looking for him here. In the meantime, the sponsors had laid on quite an event: a small street party with a number of stands offering freshly cooked produce for the participants to enjoy, while their vehicles remained stationed in the square alongside.

After eating, participants trooped into one of the neighbouring offices to listen to a presentation from ABB. The company, it tran-spired, was a global leader in energy and automation technologies, and the office in Switzerland significant enough to employ 7,000 staff. Over the course of the presentation, Magali learned that they had developed an infrastructure for electric vehicle charging that applied nationwide in countries such as Japan, Denmark, and Estonia. The premise was simple: all charging stations enabled vehicles to operate at one-hundred-percent capacity within half an hour.

After the presentation it was time for the city tour. Participants had been divided into separate groups and invited to test a range of electric bikes as they took in Baden's sights. Away from the safety of the office building, however, Magali realized just how exposed Hendrik was. Steinberg was still on the loose and Hendrik was sure to be an easy target pedalling alone on his bike. But they couldn't say no to the tour, at least not without seriously offending their hosts. Magali had briefly considered forbidding Hendrik to take part – but it would have caused quite a stir.

In the end, she and Martin did their best to keep the blogger in the middle of their group. If Steinberg turned up, they'd just have to improvise. The problem was that in the Friday afternoon traffic it was almost impossible to stick together, and there was every chance Hendrik would be left exposed.

Whether it was her nerves or the warm summer afternoon, Magali couldn't say, but soon after departing she was absolutely drenched in sweat. Her T-shirt was clinging to her back and her hands were so clammy that she could barely grip the handlebars. Every now and then, she would look across at Hendrik. He was sweating profusely, too, gazing frantically all around him. It was obvious he wasn't taking in any of the sights, and his eyes betrayed a genuine sense of fear. Magali wondered whether it was his own safety he was concerned about, or that of his friend. How she longed to tell him that everything would be OK. But she knew she couldn't. Steinberg might appear at any moment and there was no predicting what he would do next.

The minutes seemed to stretch out for hours at a time, and Magali could scarcely believe they'd only been cycling for forty-five minutes when they finally turned back into the square where they had left the EVs earlier that afternoon.

At least the youth hostel, where the participants were staying that night, seemed more secure. The building was located at the end of a cul-de-sac on the river Limmat, and was overlooked on the other side by a steep, wooded hill that no person in their right mind would attempt to descend in the moonlight. There was a large parking lot in front of the building and, unlike on the bike tour, it would be easy enough to keep an eye on the surrounding area.

Soon the other participants had arrived and were engaging in an impromptu game of football. Jochen was there, as were Manfred and Tamara.

But the star of the show was Florian. After the best part of a week spent cooped up in an EV, he was revelling in the new-found space at his disposal, and currently running rings around his opponents.

Just then, Magali's thoughts were interrupted by Martin.

"Apparently, there's a good little pub near the youth hostel. It overlooks the river. We can have a drink there while we talk about the plan for tomorrow," he said.

Although there was a lot to discuss, the trio made their way to the pub in silence. Whatever else they were thinking, their introspection was linked by a common theme. It was only a matter of time before Steinberg realized that Andrej's vehicle was no longer part of the expedition. There was no way of knowing of how he would react. Would he come for Hendrik? The blogger's face suggested he thought he might. Or would he concentrate, initially at least, on locating the technology? For her part, Magali assumed it would be the latter. Whatever he did, there was only the smallest of windows in which to ensure that Hendrik and Nils were brought to safety.

Magali looked around her. She hadn't realized the pub's situation would be quite so open. There was, she was amazed to discover, no roof. Nevertheless, as long as it was light, they would be safe here. No-one could come and go unnoticed, and any boat that appeared on the Limmat would be in clear view the whole time.

"Thank God it's not raining," Martin said finally, to break the silence. "Otherwise we might actually find ourselves washed out to sea."

No doubt he was referring to the name: Flotsam and Jetsam. Still,

Magali couldn't pass up the opportunity. "You know that Switzerland's landlocked, don't you?"

"Figure of speech," Martin waved her aside. "Now, who's having what?"

By the time he returned with the drinks, the moment of levity had passed.

"What have you told Nils?" Magali asked.

"That I'd contact him once we'd finalized our plans. He won't be short of things to do. But essentially I said he needs to be there at the start of the parade."

"That's not going to work," Martin said. "It's a world-record attempt."

Magali looked at him quizzically.

"Meaning," he continued, "that events have to be filmed from four different angles. If Nils is there at the start, he'll be on camera with us. In order to make a clean getaway, it's vital we don't leave any traces. If his employer knows about us, it won't take long for them to put two and two together. We need a head-start. And we're not going to get one like this."

"OK, so what do we do?" This from Hendrik. "I've been looking at the route. It's a horse-shoe. The start and finish points are the same."

"We have to make sure we're at the front," said Magali. "That way we'll be among the first to complete the circuit. Then we pick Nils up – let's say at eleven – from somewhere where there are no cameras: somewhere that's not part of the route."

"It starts at the Utoquai. According to the Roadbook, downtown Zurich will be closed to traffic. It says to go via Kreuzplatz. That's in the southeast of the city. We could meet Nils there?" Martin said.

"And then?" Hendrik asked.

"Then we drive you both to the nearest safe-house and wait to see how things pan out. You'll need new identities," Magali said.

"New identities?" It seemed Hendrik had only just realized the gravity of the situation.

"How else did you think you were going to get through this?" Magali said.

"I don't know... I just..."

"Hendrik," Magali's voice was softer now. "No-one knows who we're dealing with here. It'll be safer for everyone this way. Now, go and make that call. Make sure everything's ready for tomorrow."

She watched Hendrik rise and move ten or twelve paces away from the table. She could understand his reluctance to give up his name. With his parents gone and no surviving siblings, the Herder line would soon be at an end.

"He'll be OK," Martin said. "He's tougher than he looks."

Magali wasn't sure, but she was heartened by Hendrik's appearance on his return.

"And?" she said.

"It looks like everything's under control. Apparently Nils has just seen Dominik. He wants to discuss something with Nils first thing on Monday morning."

"So he doesn't suspect anything?"

"Seems that way. Apparently he said he's not even sure the technology was at WAVE in the first place. I'm to finish filming for the official blog and then go to the Zurich office on Wednesday."

"Dominik's obviously lying," Magali said.

"Nils sounded confident. He also has someone he can call in case of an emergency. It could be a useful contact: he's the chairman of the Swiss Tesla Owners Club. They'll be represented tomorrow."

"And your own files?" Martin asked.

"Nils says that's all been taken care of."

"OK, good," Magali said. "We've got a long day ahead of us

tomorrow. I suggest we all get an early night. It's going to be busy downtown, and if we want to get to the front of the parade we'll have to leave before seven."

Martin and Hendrik nodded their assent, and the trio trooped off in the direction of the youth hostel in the hope of getting a good night's sleep.

The traffic the next morning was worse than they had anticipated. A combination of the parade and the Zueri Faescht, allied to the closure of the city centre, had contrived to ensure that the going was slow. So slow, in fact, that Martin was moved to question whether the parade hadn't in fact started some way outside of Zurich.

Finally, however, they turned into Feldeggstrasse, following the road towards Bellerivestrasse, which became the Utoquai as they approached the city centre. The WAVE archway marked the start and finish of the world-record attempt and soon they had taken up position two or three cars from the front of the line, behind a group of vehicles belonging to the event sponsor, which would lead the way.

The weather was sunny and warm, and along the quayside, a number of marketeers were setting up their stalls for the day to come. The people of Zurich were already out in force, whether as a result of their curiosity at the EVs, or in anticipation of the second day of the city's seventy-two-hour party, Magali couldn't say. In different circumstances, she might have found the mood infectious and become swept up in the moment. Instead, all she could feel was a mounting sense of panic, a sentiment that was hardly allayed by the presence of her two co-passengers, both of whom appeared, for reasons Magali couldn't fathom, as though they hadn't slept for days.

Hendrik's face had taken on the pale sickly colour which Magali had come to associate with the aftermath of Bled; while Martin had dark circles under his eyes, and seemed both distant and distracted. Perhaps he was thinking about what Louis Palmer would have to say about the loss of both the expedition's official blogger and team Just Married, neither of whom would be undertaking the "Tour of Open Doors" through the canton of Zurich with the rest of the participants.

Meanwhile, slowly but surely, the other vehicles were beginning to join the line.

There were all sorts of converted EVs and teams of bikers, from all over the world. Magali had never seen such a range of different vehicles. There were small and large, converted and custom-made, and the vast majority were draped in the flags of the countries they represented. As well as the flags, a dash of colour was added by the various sponsors' stickers adorning the bodywork of each car. In addition to a fleet of smart cars, Magali also caught sight of a Rimac, the world's most expensive electric vehicle. Further back, there was a group of around fifty Tesla Roadsters. Magali assumed they were from the club.

Their reassuring presence aside, Magali was beginning to feel increasingly uneasy. There were so many people on the streets, so many faces she didn't recognize. It would be all too easy for Steinberg to have slipped in unnoticed among them. Next she looked across at Hendrik. The tension was writ large across his face. How could it not be? He had endured one of the most traumatic weeks of his life, and he still wasn't safe from harm. At least for the time being, he had returned to the car, having spent the previous few minutes with Magali filming the various EVs for the expedition website. All the while Martin had supplemented Hendrik's camera work by filming the scene from on high with his drone.

The tour director, Louis Palmer, wasn't helping matters either. He was pacing up and down with his phone to his ear, bemoaning the presence of the marketing stalls along the route. Magali could imagine what he was thinking. The world-record attempt had to be completed within a certain period of time, as the streets in this part of Zurich could only remain closed for so long.

As the clock neared ten, and the drivers were beginning to ready themselves for departure, Magali saw Tamara approaching from a few vehicles back. She was poking her head into each of the cars as she passed. Some sort of message from Louis perhaps?

"Is something the matter?" Magali asked when Tamara was within earshot.

"It's probably nothing," she called back. "But Florian's not with Erich. He was supposed to be taking him today. Florian wanted to be in the Ampera. As hybrids, they're bringing up the rear of the parade. If the Guinness Book of Records only recognizes vehicles that are purely electric, then it's easier if the ones people are unsure about are stationed at the back. For Florian, that would have meant getting a good look at all the other cars as they passed on the bridge. But," Tamara paused, "he's not answering his phone."

"OK, is there anything I can do? Maybe I can go and have a look near the front?" Magali signalled to Martin that he should keep an eye on Hendrik. "We can use the drone too," she said to her, "see if Florian's wandering around somewhere. He seems like a sensible boy. If the worst comes to the worst, I'm sure he'll manage to find his way back to the start and wait there. Once the parade starts, we're not going to be able to get out and look."

Magali raced towards the bridge, slicing through the hordes of curious spectators who had congregated along the route. Right now, a missing boy was the last thing she needed. She looked right and left, but still there was no sign of Florian. Gazing for a moment up at the skies, she realized what had been bothering her for the best part of an hour since her arrival. It was the noise of the propeller airliners, depositing parachutists onto the pontoons floating on the sea below. Mystery solved, Magali continued to look for Florian, tearing across the bridge to the other side of the road. Eventually, however, she was forced to admit defeat.

Neither Martin nor Hendrik had heard from the boy either, and after a quick phone call, it was decided that Magali should remain on the bridge for the duration of the parade. The horse-shoe route meant it was the best position from which to check individual cars as they passed. Martin and Hendrik would take the EV and pick her up as they drove back across the bridge on their return to the start point.

A gun shot sounded in the air. The parade had begun.

It soon became clear that despite being on the bridge, Magali would have little chance of checking each car before Martin and Hendrik returned. For all the hours of organization Louis must have invested in the parade, it soon descended into chaos. Somewhere along the line there had been a serious breakdown in communication. Magali watched in disbelief as the EVs making up the convoy slowly became separated from one another. The first hint that there was a major

problem came when Magali realized the convoy was sharing its route with the Zurich trams.

Perhaps it wouldn't have been so much of an issue if these had appeared on the half hour. But they came with astonishing frequency – at intervals of around ninety seconds – and, as they had right of way, drivers had no choice but to wait until they had passed. While they waited, vehicles that were not part of the parade were able to join the line, so that instead of a convoy of 400 EVs, observers – and, Magali assumed, those entrusted with deciding whether a world record had been achieved – would be confronted with a procession of five or six EVs interrupted not just by traditional gasoline models but also by the presence of the trams in the lane alongside…

As if that wasn't enough, part of the route was taken up by a large construction site, and the various stall holders setting up their wares had begun to encroach on the area that had been specifically marked out for the convoy. The sight of Louis angrily remonstrating with these, and, in some instances, forcibly removing them from the route, was the stuff of high farce: more reminiscent of Basil Fawlty at his most comically ineffective than a skilled and practised event organizer in control of all he surveyed.

The sun rose higher in the sky and her neck was starting to burn. Half an hour had passed and half of the cars still hadn't crossed the start line. A second wave of parachutists landed, to the applause of the crowd. For some reason, their presence was making Magali nervous, too. Manfred and Tamara crawled past the bridge and shook their heads. Where could Florian be? Magali paced up and down, hoping she hadn't missed anything. Her skin was beginning to tingle from the sun. Car upon car passed soundlessly, none of them, it seemed, containing a nine-year-old boy.

By the time Martin and Hendrik returned to the bridge half an hour later, it was clear that it would still be some time before the parade was over. In the distance, she could see the Ampera and the police smart car that made up the rear of the parade. Magali sighed. There was nothing she could do about Florian now. For the moment she would have to focus on Hendrik and Nils.

"Biggest parade of EVs," Martin scoffed. "More like longest traffic jam… Did you have any luck with Florian?"

"What do you think?" Magali said eventually. "There are 400 cars here, interspersed with trams and vehicles that have nothing to do with the parade. To tell the truth, I could barely even tell which drivers were part of WAVE."

"Should we be worried?" Hendrik asked.

"No," Magali said. It was important not to unsettle the blogger. "Let's stay calm. Florian travels with someone different each day. There's probably just been a mix-up. Maybe he switched cars without telling someone. Anyway, there's no point worrying until the parade's officially over. There's nothing we can do before then. Right now, we just have to concentrate on our original plan. Is Nils there?"

"He's waiting in a café. I'll tell him we're on our way."

Just then, Magali's cell rang. An unrecognized number.

"It seems that Zurich is quite the place to be," the voice said. "Only there's one person missing out on all the fun. Where's Andrej Pečjak?"

"Who is this?" Magali said.

"Do I really need to say? To think, I was under the impression you were *good* at your job."

"Well, I must be better than you."

"Do you think?" the voice said. "Well then, perhaps we could help each other out a little. You've got something I want…"

"I've got nothing to say to you," Magali replied impatiently.

"Please allow me to finish. You've got something I want. And I dare say that soon you'll want something I have."

"Cut the crap, Steinberg. What I *want* is for you to stop talking in riddles."

"Oh, there's no riddle here. He's got brown hair, likes playing football. I'd guess about nine years old…"

"OK, you have my attention," Magali stopped the car and snapped her fingers frantically in Hendrik's direction. The blogger was in the middle of making a call.

"So, we're in agreement?" Steinberg said. "Good, then I'll proceed. I will be in Neuhausen am Rheinfall at nine o'clock this evening.

On the same side as Castle Worth. Bring the technologist and the car, and the boy will be yours."

With that, the line went dead.

"Shit!" Magali thrashed wildly against the dashboard. "Hendrik, tell Nils there's been a change of plan. I'm calling Frank."

She dialled and waited for him to answer.

"Frank, we have a serious problem. Steinberg's got Florian. He's demanding an exchange. Florian for Andrej and the technology."

"How the hell did this happen?"

Magali sighed. "We're not sure. But I don't see that we have a choice here. He's nine years old for Christ's sake."

"We can't afford to mess around," Martin chimed in. "You've seen what he did to Jaromir…"

Magali took up the thread before Martin could finish his sentence. She knew what he was going to say.

"OK, let's think this through. We need to give him Andrej. We need to give him the car. But is there some way we can avoid giving him the technology?" In the meantime, Magali had put Frank on loudspeaker.

"Andrej could modify it," Martin said. "But it'd be a big risk."

"Will you be quiet," Magali snapped. "I can't hold two conversations at once. We don't even know for sure that he has Florian. Frank?"

"It'd be tight. But it might be our only option. I'll talk to Andrej and get back to you."

In the meantime, Hendrik had finished speaking to Nils. The blogger looked distressed.

"Hendrik, what's the matter?" Magali asked.

"He's gone back to Dominik," came the response. "Reckons he can be of more use to us there. Said he'd phone his contact, get these Tesla drivers to scour the road to Neuhausen."

"No, not yet. Call him back. See if he can pick up a signal on Florian's cell phone. If not, focus on Steinberg. We have to assume he's been in Zurich. But where's he going next? What's his plan? I want as detailed an outline of his movements as possible. Then we can use Nils' contact to better effect." Magali leaned over towards Hendrik. Not for the first time, the blogger's face was buried deep in his hands. "He's doing the right thing," she said, by way of comfort. "Nils, I mean. You know that, don't you?" Hendrik nodded in response. "Call him, then we'll wait and see what Frank has to say."

All of a sudden, time seemed to stand still. Magali became acutely aware of her co-passengers' movements. Martin was staring into space, while Hendrik manoeuvred his phone into position as if in slow motion. Outside the car window two women embraced: long-lost friends, perhaps, who had stumbled upon each other unexpectedly in the street. A man emerged from the bakery carrying a cup of coffee and a bag of pastries. Out of the corner of her eye, Magali spied a group of young people heading back into town for a second day of partying. She felt envious; and wondered whether the life she had chosen had been the right one after all.

Before she could reach a conclusion, however, the familiar sound of her cell pierced the morning air.

"Aren't you going to answer?" Martin said.

Magali shook herself awake. The ringing had come from a world away: an alarm call that had muscled its way into her dreams.

"Hi Frank."

"Andrej says he'll do it. We'll just have time to modify the car. It'll still look the same on the outside. What are our instructions?"

"Steinberg said he'd be there at nine," Magali replied. "I assume he'll tell us more when the time comes."

"Perhaps he doesn't have it all worked out yet," Frank said. "That could be good or bad. I suggest we keep our distance in case he does anything rash."

"Send Andrej in alone?" Magali was disbelieving.

"Not alone. *Ahead.* I'll take up position on the Swiss side by Laufen Castle. There's a viewing platform there. You and Martin remain in the vicinity. We let the exchange take place. No bystanders, no pressure. We'll meet at seven thirty at the military airport in Duebendorf."

"And Florian?" Magali asked.

"My guess is Steinberg's mainly interested in the technology," Frank said. "That his plan is to hand Florian over to Andrej and take the car on somewhere for testing. What about the boy's parents?"

"On holiday apparently. Officially Florian's still part of the expedition. We just don't know who he's travelling with."

"Good. Keep it that way. Tell Louis Palmer that Florian's been picked up by a relative who also happened to be at the parade. There's no need to involve anyone else for the time being." Frank changed tack. "You said you weren't sure if Steinberg even had Florian in the first place."

"We're looking into that," Magali confirmed. "Seeing if we can establish a trace."

"OK, then I suggest someone stays behind in Zurich to ensure that all our bases are covered. Much as I hate to say it," Frank said, pausing before articulating his thoughts, "we need to plan for the worst."

"Agreed. If we're not going to be there in person, then we need a way of contacting Andrej."

"That's all under control," Frank said. "In addition to the control unit with its artificial intelligence, the guys at EMPA are fitting Andrej's car with an extra radio module. Once the radio module's been connected to the control unit, we'll add a piece of software to facilitate communication with a smart watch. It might look like an ordinary sports watch but it's modified and provides a reverse communication. Andrej has it now. If he enters a certain number combination, we'll know he's received our message. If he doesn't confirm within three minutes, the vehicle's horn will sound twice. You should be able to hear it as long as you're within 500 metres."

"What do we do if that happens?" Magali asked.

"Then we'll have to improvise," Martin said. Magali could see that he didn't want to make Hendrik feel any more nervous than he was already.

"As soon as we're finished with the programming, I'll send Martin the information he needs to access the app in the car," Frank confirmed.

"Understood. See you at seven thirty." Magali brought the call to an end. She was glad Frank would be providing support. After nine days on the road, she was beginning to feel decidedly fatigued. This mission had sapped more energy from her than she cared to admit. She felt like she had been running on adrenaline alone for the previous forty-eight hours. Finally, someone else was there to lighten the emotional load.

"Hendrik?" she said. But she hadn't realized the blogger himself was still engaged in conversation.

"No, that could be very helpful," he was saying. "Thanks Nils. Fingers crossed we can get you out sooner rather than later."

"Good news?" Martin asked.

"Interesting, at any rate," Hendrik said. "Last trace of Florian is about half an hour before the start of the parade."

"And Steinberg?"

"In Neuhausen already, it seems. He's been caught on camera in a cafe there. The car he used was reported stolen from Zurich shortly after the parade began. It seems he drove straight to Neuhausen," Hendrik's voice trailed away.

"Which means Florian's with him. He didn't stop anywhere along the way?" Magali asked.

"Well that's the thing. There aren't many cameras on the B-roads but he must have taken a pretty strange route out of Zurich. The car was seen near the main train station. That's not the quickest way to leave the city. But what I really don't understand is how no-one saw him. It's almost as if he fell from the sky."

The parachutes, Magali thought. He must have arrived by parachute.

"Steinberg's not from here," Martin said. "And besides, you've seen. It's total chaos."

"I'm not saying it's anything conclusive," Hendrik said. "But the route he took is an avenue we ought to pursue. I'm going to stay here and meet with this Stephan Schwarz. The Tesla Club guy. See if we can't put together a more detailed picture of Steinberg's movements this morning."

"Sounds good," Magali said. And then, turning to Martin, "careful, he'll be out for your job next."

"Make sure you call Alain," Martin said. "Hendrik's going to need some help out there."

CHAPTER TWENTY-SEVEN

Steinberg

Saturday late-morning – Zurich – Neuhausen

In the end, it hadn't been a difficult decision. Jaeger was gone, and Steinberg was still carrying an injury from their deadly confrontation. This was the only way he could still achieve his aim. The last chance to ensure he didn't return empty-handed. The problem was what Dominik would make of it.

In all likelihood, nothing. After all, Florian was only a single phone call away from safety.

After his pa-
rachute landing
– an idea that had
come to him while
researching the
Zueri Faescht pro-
gramme – Stein-
berg had approa-
ched from the lake
and, in the shade
of the trees lining

the waterfront, managed to go completely unnoticed. Florian, he had discovered through BIRD's system the night before, would be travelling with one of the Amperas. Steinberg hadn't used excessive force on the boy or frightened him unduly. All he had done was offer him a ride during the world-record parade.

To his credit, Florian hadn't been sure. In fact, he had done his parents proud. Instead of blindly accepting the invitation, as, Steinberg supposed, many nine-year-olds would have done in his position, he had stepped back because of Steinberg's change of appearance, before asking where he had been. He hadn't seen him for several days. No response. Then, seconds later, when Steinberg had tried to change the subject and begun to talk about his car, Florian commented that it was no longer the same one as before. Smart kid.

But Steinberg persisted. Like most nine-year-old boys, Florian had a weakness, and it went by the name of fast cars. When Steinberg mentioned that he would be driving a Rimac, a Concept One for the world-record parade, and reeled off the Rimac's impressive features as if he was quoting from the manufacturer's brochure, the boy was ready to do anything for him. As a gesture of goodwill, Steinberg even let Florian bring his football along.

The only hairy moment was when, a few minutes later, Florian had asked why they were going in the opposite direction from the parade. Well, what could Steinberg do? He had to say something.

"Because you're my wild card."

And it was true. At that point, Steinberg still hadn't been sure how best to deploy Florian. He knew the last thing Dominik wanted was another death on his hands. But he also knew that taking the boy was his only means of ensuring Andrej emerged from wherever it was he was hiding.

Next there was the question of the meeting point. As a location, Neuhausen wasn't ideal. At this time of year, it would be swarming with tourists: countless groups of holiday-makers all eager to catch a glimpse of the spectacular Rhine Falls. Someone might see him, or witness something untoward. But then again, perhaps the crowds would ensure his safety. Whatever the case, Neuhausen was close to Germany, and that's where Steinberg was headed. The car needed to be dismantled, so that Dominik's team of experts could ascertain what secrets were contained within. After that, who could say? It would be up to Dominik to keep to his end of the bargain: use Steinberg's success to depose Adler and install himself as BIRD's commander-in-chief. Then all he had to do was wait for everything else to fall into place.

Reflecting on the chain of events some hours later as he stood admiring the water cascading down into the river below, Steinberg couldn't have said exactly when the idea had come to him. Call it luck. Call it inspiration. In truth, it didn't matter. The main thing was he had come up with a plan, the final stages of which he was about to set into motion.

He reached for his phone. It was the second time he had called Magali that day.

"Tick tock. Tick tock. The clock is ticking. I trust you have made your decision."

"Andrej'll be there. Along with the car."

"Then listen carefully. Tell him to park the car by Worth Castle and approach the river on foot. I'll be waiting underneath the restaurant by the shore."

"What about Florian?"

"Ah, yes. My favourite nine-year-old companion. I had quite forgotten about him."

"Cut it out Steinberg. Is he still with you? Put him on the line."

Steinberg pressed a button on his cell phone and allowed the pre-recorded message to play.

"I can barely hear him."

"What did you expect? You have been here before, haven't you?" As if on cue, a rush of water thundered into the Rhine, deafening all those around and causing several onlookers to emit a shriek of delight as they became soaked by the spray.

"If anything should happen to—"

"See you at nine."

Perhaps Steinberg ought to have waited to hear what Magali had to say. But he had no desire to listen to another empty threat.

If anything should happen to Florian, I'll make sure your life's not worth living.

The only way anything would happen was if Magali and her crack squad of operatives were stupid enough to make a mistake. And if they were, well then they didn't deserve to find the boy alive in the first place.

Steinberg took one final look at Europe's largest plain waterfall. There was something fitting about things coming to a head here. It would be a tumultuous spectacle. A grown man, betrayed and despondent, attempting in vain to make himself heard above the reverberating waves; alongside him a second figure, calmly issuing an ultimatum to which his opponent would have no choice but to accede.

 And now, Steinberg thought to himself, for the final flourish. Right at the base of the waterfall, he had noticed a spot where all sorts of items had been floating for hours. Steinberg took Florian's football and tossed it, along with boy's cap, into the water below. The gesture was graceful, theatrical, and for a moment Steinberg bestowed upon the items the audience which he himself had lacked. He watched them crash against the surface of the river, then

seconds later come to attention, bobbing up and down on the water as if in thrall to the rhythm of the waves. All the while he imagined the horror which their appearance would create, and – because he couldn't help himself – allowed the corners of his mouth to curl up, just for a moment, into a smile.

Then he looked at his watch. Andrej would soon be here. And the cavalry wouldn't be far behind.

Although he had been aware of the technologist's identity for some days now, as he stood next to him Steinberg suddenly felt as though he were looking at Andrej Pečjak for the first time. The technologist was not particularly tall – in fact, the pair were of a similar height – but he obviously kept himself fit. There was a wiry elasticity to his frame, as befitted a man who spent much of his spare time climbing. He was, Steinberg guessed, around the same age as Jaeger. Andrej did not seem interested in Steinberg's new look.

"Are you alone?" Steinberg asked.

The technologist glanced around about him, as if to say "do you see anyone else?" There was something vaguely aggressive about the gesture, a hint of real anger that took Steinberg by surprise. Probably something to do with the boy. Human beings were capable of being enormously complex, but throw a nine-year-old child into the mix and the atavistic urge always surfaced.

"God help you…"

"If I've done anything with the boy? Yes, funny. You're not the first to express that sentiment."

"Then where is he? I thought this was all agreed."

"I don't recall mentioning any specifics. I'm afraid you've been misled. Now if you'll care to excuse me I have to make a call."

Andrej was rooted to the spot.

"Magali. Yes, he's arrived. Thank you for being such a good sport. Now, the boy." Steinberg made a point of catching the technologist's eye. "I'm afraid he's still rather in the thick of the action, as it were." He checked to see whether Andrej would follow his gaze, then looked up towards a large rock situated in the midst of the waterfall, before continuing his conversation with Magali.

 "Best not to *push* these things, don't you think? After all, we don't want anything untoward to happen. Nature can be such a cruel beast." Next he focused on the surface of the water, where the football and the cap were still sway-ing wildly. He smiled as the colour all but evaporated from the technologist's face. "Don't call me on this number again."

"You bastard." Andrej was almost speechless. "He's up there?"

"Best to wait for professional help, I'd say. If he were to try and wrestle himself free, well... I'd wager his football's the better swimmer."

"What do you want?" Andrej asked.

"Nothing much," Steinberg said. "For you to drive me to a lo-cation of my choice and submit to a few questions. That would be a good start. If you can do that, then I don't see any reason why Florian shouldn't be discovered safe and well."

"You'll call someone?"

"You have my word," Steinberg smirked. "Now let's get going." He ushered Andrej back towards the car. As he was leaving, he caught sight of a lone man surveying the scene as it played out before him, a pair of binoculars dangling around his neck. Probably just a tourist. But in truth it didn't matter. They wouldn't come after him until they had found the boy...

Half an hour later, they were outside what appeared to be an aban-doned warehouse. Steinberg had taken the precaution of blindfolding Andrej, just in case he tried to get a message to one of his colleagues – though how he intended to communicate, Steinberg wasn't sure. He had confiscated his phone back in Neuhausen. If he could relay information through his watch – a big digital number that Steinberg assumed was popular within the climbing community – then good luck to him.

Steinberg beeped the horn twice and the gate opened to receive the car. He drove through and parked it in the middle of a large room. It must have been a garage at one point. The right side of the room was taken up by a large reception counter, behind which a narrow iron staircase led upstairs to a viewing gallery and a small office. To the left, there were various parking spaces, divided into sections by the ceiling-high iron girders. One of the parking spaces was set on a lifting platform. In a far corner, Steinberg could make out a small glazed room that must have served as the lab. Beside the entrance to the lab were three black vans. It was dark apart from the car headlights, and the few lamps needed to inspect Andrej's vehicle. A small number of ventilation shafts in the ceiling provided the only air.

After Steinberg had exited the vehicle and led Andrej to the reception counter, a group of men in blue boiler suits approached the EV and pushed it onto the lifting platform. As well as the beefcakes, Steinberg noted the presence of three individuals whose proportions were much more in keeping with the norm. These, he assumed, were the technologists who would dismantle the vehicle and extract whatever information they needed from Andrej Pečjak along the way.

"Can we get our friend some coffee?" Steinberg said. "And take him upstairs to the office so we can get started."

"What about Florian?" Andrej said. It was the first time the technologist had spoken since leaving the waterfall.

"I told you, you have my word," Steinberg took out his cell phone, patted Andrej sympathetically on the shoulder, and moved to the far corner of the room, just out of hearing range. As long as Florian's whereabouts were still unknown to the others, the technologist would be a fool to try anything.

"Steinberg?"

"Dominik, listen, I have to keep my voice down. I'm in Singen, at our depot. The technologist's here along with the car. We're going to take it apart, do some tests."

"Andrej will cooperate?"

"At the moment he doesn't have a choice."

"Well, what can I say, I'm impressed," Dominik said. "But I should tell you that we've been to his offices in Slovenia. There's nothing there. At least on paper, that is."

"What are you saying?"

"He's got everything stored in the Cloud. However, all the files are in Chinese characters and our cryptologists are getting nowhere fast. They think there might even be a double encryption. Apparently it could take 1,000 years to crack, even with our systems."

"What does that mean for me?" Steinberg asked.

"It means it's imperative you extract as much information as you can from Andrej himself. I scarcely need to remind you of tonight's importance. For you, for me, and for the future of our organization."

CHAPTER TWENTY-EIGHT

Hendrik

Saturday late-afternoon – Zurich

Since separating from Martin and Magali earlier that afternoon, Hendrik had been in Zurich looking for Florian. Even though Steinberg claimed to have the boy, no-one was taking any chances.

There had been no confirmed sightings of him since his disappearance before the start of the parade. In the meantime, Hendrik had been joined in his search by Alain and Stephan Schwarz. After Steinberg's call, Magali  had asked Alain to lend a helping hand, while Stephan had been contacted by Nils.

Stephan Schwarz had been just as Nils had said he would be. Physically, he was average height with a round, friendly face and horn-rimmed spectacles. An architect by training, he was also discreet, reliable, and efficient. He had sworn to Hendrik that he wouldn't breathe a word of what they were doing to anybody, not even his colleagues from the Tesla club, if and when they were enlisted in the search. Hendrik wondered what Nils had told him exactly. They had agreed it was best if Stephan wasn't in possession of all the details. Nevertheless, he needed to know the facts. Namely, that a nine-year-old boy had been kidnapped and on no account were the police to be involved.

If Stephan Schwarz had conformed to Hendrik's expectations then so too, unfortunately, had Alain. It had been more than twenty-four hours now since the pair had last spoken. After Hendrik had confirmed that he had been hired to do surveillance work, Alain had done his best to give the blogger the cold shoulder. Hendrik was hurt, but he understood. Ultimately, however, it didn't particularly matter if Alain was frosty – as long as he was engaged wholeheartedly in the search.

After all, locating a nine-year-old boy in the midst of a city-wide party was no picnic. Since that afternoon, they had pursued a series of leads, but they had all turned out to be dead ends. No-one had seen an unaccompanied child that morning; and those who claimed they had looked as though visions of imaginary boys would be the least of their worries. The whole city was drunk, and there were crowds of people swaying in the streets.

Hendrik had spoken to an office worker with a gap between her two front teeth; an Englishman brandishing a six pack of beer; a rotund university lecturer muttering about medieval churches; the list went on... but the result had always been the same.

 Now, night had fallen and Hendrik was losing hope fast. He was grasping his cell phone tightly in order to make sure he could still hear it if there was any news. The music was so loud he wouldn't have had a chance if it remained in his pocket. With every hour that passed, he had become more and more depressed. The sight of all these people enjoying themselves was a stark reminder of what his life could've been like if he hadn't taken this damn job. Ever since Florian had gone missing, he couldn't shake the feeling that he was responsible. Was he cursed or something?

He had lost his parents and his kid sister; and he had almost added another young girl to the list in Deutschlandsberg. What if Florian sustained more than a broken leg? The thought was too horrific to countenance.

Suddenly, his cell phone sounded. Magali. After leaving Zurich, she and Martin had concentrated on searching the local hospitals before heading to Neuhausen via Duebendorf. All four – Hendrik, Magali, Martin, and Alain – had been forced to officially withdraw from the expedition.

"Have you got him?" Hendrik asked.

"No. Frank saw it all," she said. "Florian was never in the picture. We think he might still be in Neuhausen somewhere. Steinberg said something cryptic about him being in the thick of the action."

"What the hell does that mean?" Hendrik asked.

"We don't know either, but apparently there's a huge rock in the heart of the falls."

"And that's where you think he might be? Shit." Suddenly Hendrik was feeling the pressure. He rubbed his face with his hands several times, before continuing. "So what do we do?"

"We need you to stay in Zurich. Talk to Stephan – you're still with him, right? – and see if he can spare us a couple of bodies. Frank could use the extra help."

"Where are you going?" Hendrik wasn't sure he could do this alone. Right now, all he wanted to do was curl up into a little ball and cry.

"We're going after Steinberg. Finish the job we were hired to do. Andrej's car's been equipped with a radio module, so we'll be able to see where they hole up for the night. My guess is it'll be somewhere local. What's the news from Nils?"

"Nothing new," Hendrik said, just about managing to compose himself. "He's still working on Steinberg's route out of the city."

"OK, we'll be in touch."

Hendrik replaced his cell phone and motioned for Stephan to join him. The architect had been trying to extract information from

297

a group of students. He shrugged his shoulders as if to say it was hopeless.

"Can you send two cars to Neuhausen?" Hendrik asked urgently.

"Neuhausen? I thought we were basing our search here."

"We are," Hendrik took a deep breath. "But the sooner we can rule one location out, the quicker we can intensify our search. Zurich's too big an area to cover; Neuhausen on the other hand…"

"I understand. Just let me make a few calls." Before he went, Stephan paused for a moment. Hendrik knew what he was going to say and it killed him. But sooner or later, one of them had to address the elephant in the room. "How do we know he hasn't dumped him in the Rhine?"

"We don't," Hendrik said. The thought had terrified him from the start. "That's what we're trying to find out."

In the meantime, Hendrik and Alain continued the search. They agreed to remain on foot for the time being, and to reconvene every half hour so that they could update each other on their progress. Right now Hendrik needed to be occupied. Keeping busy was the only way to take his mind off everything that had happened. Florian was gone; and Nils had been forced to go back. While he searched, Hendrik's thoughts turned to Dominik.

How much did he know about it all? Granted, he was rotten to the core – but would he seriously sanction the kidnapping of a nine-year-old boy? For a piece of technology? Somehow Hendrik didn't think so. It was too wild for Dominik, too reckless. The only way it made sense was if Steinberg had acted under his own steam and was using Florian as a bargaining tool. First as a means of getting Andrej out into the open; then as leverage with Dominik. To climb the ladder, save his own skin. Whatever. In truth, the details weren't important. The main thing was if Steinberg had taken Andrej, then Florian had already served his purpose.

Hendrik stopped himself. Better to concentrate on the job in hand. That meant finding Florian. Only then could he worry about how everything else fell into place.

"Anything?" The voice was Alain's. Hendrik hoped that a rapprochement could be on the cards if they found Florian. "It's pointless doing this on foot. Any minute now it'll be pitch black and all we'll be able to see are crowds of people lurching from one bar to another. Good luck wading your way through them."

But before Hendrik had a chance to answer, his cell phone rang. "I need to take this," he said. "It's Magali. Maybe they've found something…"

"Hendrik," Magali said. "We've just heard from Frank. There's no sign of Florian anywhere. He's checked the whole site, as well as the car Steinberg used to drive there."

"How'd he know which one to check?"

"There was only one vehicle in the parking lot that had been reported stolen."

"OK. But what about what Steinberg said, about Florian being in the thick of the action?"

"Martin lent Frank the drone. There was no-one anywhere near the platform…"

"Which means there are two possibilities. First, he… tried to wrestle free," Hendrik was struggling to articulate his thoughts.

"But failed. Yes, I'm afraid we can't rule that out. Second?"

"He was never anywhere near the falls in the first place. Think about it. What else could 'the thick of the action' mean?" A light seemed to go on inside Hendrik's head. "That he's still here… in Zurich… somewhere in the middle of all *this*…" He gazed at the swathes of people slicing their way through the Swiss capital. "It has to be!"

"We want you to intensify your search. Anyone Stephan can spare. Make sure you get Nils involved. Frank's staying in Neuhausen for the time being. If Florian took matters into his own hands, then it won't be long before he's washed ashore."

There was a long pause. Neither Hendrik nor Magali knew quite how to continue. The possibility that all this could still prove in vain was too much to bear.

"What about you?" Hendrik said eventually.

"We're on our way to Singen. That's where Steinberg is. If we find Florian, we should still have time to get a message to Andrej."

"OK, good. Then, fingers crossed. We'll be in touch."

"What did she say?" Alain asked after Hendrik had returned his cell phone to his pocket.

"That it's time we broadened our search. There's a good chance Florian's still in Zurich somewhere."

"Let's think about it for a moment. Put ourselves in Steinberg's shoes." Alain began. His tone was decisive, lacking the edge it had previously contained. "He needs to get the technology to a safe place as quickly as possible. A nine-year-old boy complicates things. Maybe he did leave him somewhere in Zurich?"

"OK, but he still needs to buy himself some time. If we had found Florian before the exchange took place, then Steinberg wouldn't have been able to use him as leverage. He must have chosen somewhere that shuts down for the weekend."

"Or somewhere that's never open."

"Right, a warehouse or an abandoned building. Something like that."

"Neuhausen am Rheinfall is to the northeast of Zurich," Stephan said. He had re-joined the pair after arranging for two cars to be sent to Neuhausen. "The parade started on the east side of the city. So that's the way he leaves. East past the university, and on towards Winterthur."

"Only that's not what he did. Wait, I need to speak to Nils."

Hendrik called his friend. "Nils, just a quick one. You said Steinberg took a strange route out of Zurich. What do you mean? Can you be more precise?"

"Well, just that," Nils said. "OK, so maybe he doesn't know the city, but direction-wise it's a no-brainer. He should have gone east."

"And you're saying?"

"That he did the exact opposite. He was caught on camera near the main station."

"Which is west?"

"It's west of where he ought to have been. It could've added a good half hour to his journey."

"OK, thanks, Nils. Stay put. I might need to call on you again."

By the time Hendrik had finished his conversation, Alain had already produced a pocket map of the city.

"What have you got?"

Alain smiled. "What might just be the key to this little mystery. Have a look yourself."

Hendrik crouched over the map and followed the road west with his finger.

"The industrial quarter?"

"Precisely," Stephan said, wresting the initiative from Alain. As a local, he had more knowledge about Zurich than the pair of them. "And do you know what the best thing is? It's in flux. The quarter's changing. New offices, apartment blocks, arts venues. There's bound to be somewhere that's just been bought – or vacated. This Steinberg could take his pick. Especially this weekend. Everybody's here. To-night, it's all about downtown Zurich."

"OK, here's what we do. We focus on the west. Check every abandoned building. It's vital we leave no stone unturned. You go ahead. In the meantime, Stephan, can you send for some extra cars?" The latter nodded. After hours spent in the throes of a deep depression, Hendrik was just beginning to see the light.

Alain must have been feeling more hopeful too, for just as he was making to leave, he turned and started back in Hendrik's direction.

"Everything OK?" Hendrik asked.

But all Alain had wanted to do was shake the blogger by the hand.

Shortly afterwards, a group of Tesla club members arrived with flash-lights and coffee at the agreed meeting point near the Prime Tower. Although it was a warm evening, both Alain and Hendrik accepted the offerings gratefully. No-one knew how long the search would last, and Hendrik was already battling severe fatigue.

After a short meeting, during which Stephan helped divide the party into different groups, they continued their search. Alain and Hendrik meticulously inspected every open door or window they could find, looking for any hint of forced entry. It was a gruelling process and it took up a lot of time. After several hours had elapsed, the zeal with which the group had set about their task had given way to a general despondency. By now, the group had combed the area all the way from the main station out west along the river. Increasingly, however, it seemed as though Hendrik and Alain had been wide of the mark.

As tiredness crept in, tempers, naturally, started to fray. The situation wasn't helped by the fact that there was still no word from Neuhausen. It meant that as the night wore on, certain individuals expressed incredulity that they had spent so long searching in the industrial quarter. For all they knew, Florian might never have been here in the first place. The thought that they were wasting their time was too much for Hendrik to bear. What if Florian *had* been in Neuhausen all along? Hendrik couldn't shake the image of Florian struggling in vain against the coruscating force of the Rhine Falls.

Nevertheless, he remained determined that the search should continue as long into the night as possible. If necessary, they could work in shifts.

"Anyone who needs to rest for an hour is welcome to do so," he said to the group, who had reconvened for an emergency meeting. "We don't want our search to be compromised by fatigue. If you don't think you can stay alert, take a break, have a coffee, do whatever you need to. But make sure you come back stronger."

"Well said," Alain patted him on the shoulder. "But I can see why they're becoming restless."

The sound of his cell phone precluded Hendrik from replying.

"Sorry, Alain. It's Nils. I'd better answer. Let's hope it's good news."

Alain nodded and headed back towards the group.

"So, about an hour ago, I'm sitting here with all these surveillance tools, thinking it's about time they were used to help people, instead of scaring the shit out of them," Nils began.

"That's very interesting. But we're kind of in the middle of something here. Are you calling for a reason? Or is this just another one of your stories?" Hendrik said.

"OK, I understand; it's late, you're a little tetchy. I'll get to the issue at hand." Nils took a deep breath. "So, it seems there's a guy doing fire damage restoration along the river. Don't ask me why he's doing it so early. Maybe he's got a long day ahead of him. Who knows? It doesn't matter. The point is he's there; and about quarter of an hour ago, he calls his boss. Says he's found a child in a burnt-out apartment building. Doesn't think much of it at first, but when he looks closer he sees the child is tied-up and – get this – has enough food and water to last for *days*."

"How did you hear this?" Hendrik asked, elated by the news.

"So you're interested now? Well, you see, as I said, I've got a lot of tools at my disposal. They allow me to gather *any* data I want. The trick is to work out what's important. Anyway, one of these tools enables me to screen all calls within a certain area. So that's what I did: I chose a location and – hey presto. It's not like there are that many calls coming from the industrial quarter at this time in the morning. Actually, that's not entirely true – it seems there are a lot of prostitutes down there… But you've made me lose the thread. What was I saying? Oh yeah, so this guy calls his boss. As you'd expect, neither of them is quite sure what to do, but I realize that if they alert the police, then I need to intercept the call."

"What are you saying? You pretended to be a cop?" Hendrik had never heard of anything like it in his life.

"Sort of – in fact, I pretended *you* were a cop. I'll message you the address. They're expecting you in twenty minutes. Might be a good idea to bring a friend. I'm pretty sure cops work in pairs…"

"Alain," Hendrik shouted, the relief palpable in his voice. In the meantime, Nils had terminated the call. The flashing light on Hendrik's cell told him the address had come through. "We've got him." He glanced at the information Nils had just provided. "He's in a disused block of flats by the Europabruecke. Tell the others. You and I are heading out there now. I'll call Magali to tell her that we are onto something."

On the way, they decided that Alain should do the talking. Being older, they were less likely to query what he said. The question of ID, however, was more problematic. Was it better to flash a card and hope that would be enough? Or forget about it altogether and simply introduce themselves? It wasn't like the men they were meeting would be expecting anyone else.

In the end, they needn't have worried. Alain had explained that they were just coming off duty when they had taken the call. The fire restorers nodded. It was only natural that they were mainly interested in the boy.

"He was reported missing this morning," said Alain. "And, before you ask, we've got a good idea who's responsible."

In the meantime, Hendrik dashed over to Florian.

"Don't worry. We'll get you out of here in a minute, mate," he said, holding a finger to his lips.

Florian ran to Hendrik with open arms and hugged him. He was sobbing, and soon Hendrik was wiping the tears away too.

Prior to their arrival, Hendrik had been concerned that Florian might give the game away. But he soon realized there was no chance of that. He was sobbing so much he could barely say a word.

"Must have been quite an ordeal for the little fella," one of the fire restorers said.

"I don't doubt that," Alain replied, shaking his head. "I think it's best we return him to his family. You gentleman won't mind making your statements tomorrow?"

"No, not at all. We've got a lot of work to do here anyway."

The pair gave Hendrik their numbers, and with that the episode was over. Alain, Hendrik, and Florian returned to the car and began making their way east towards the city centre. Within minutes, no doubt overcome by exhaustion, Florian was sound asleep.

"What do you think?" Hendrik asked.

"He doesn't seem to be hurt."

"No, but he needs some rest. Why don't we see if Stephan or one of his team can put him up for a few hours."

Alain smiled. "That's a good idea. It'll give us a little time to think about whether we should take him to the Umweltarena for the last leg of the expedition."

"Not that much time," Hendrik said, looking at his watch. "I need to update Magali. Tell her we've found him. Then they can contact Andrej." Hendrik had almost forgotten that Andrej had been in danger all this time.

"If Andrej manages to get out, what are we going to do with Steinberg?"

"I need to talk to the others about that. My guess is that we'll hand him over to the police."

"After what happened in Arosa? Forgive me Hendrik, but we can't possibly take that chance again."

"Well then, what do you suggest?"

"Make him pay."

"C'mon, Alain. You know that's not going to happen. We'll have to find some other way of bringing him to justice. But right now, I need to speak to Magali."

"On you go then." Alain let Hendrik out of the car in front of a twenty-four hour shop. There was still a huge amount of noise coming from the centre. "I can look after Florian."

As he crossed the road and headed towards a more secluded spot, Hendrik felt his legs almost give way beneath him. A wave of fatigue passed over his body and for a moment he wasn't sure he'd have the strength to go on. He struggled over to the other side and leaned heavily on the wall behind. He looked across towards the car. Alain had moved to the back seat and had his arm around Florian. Hendrik retrieved his cell from his pocket and

305

selected re-dial. He was surprised to find his hands shaking. Slowly but surely exhaustion was taking over. He pressed the name on the display and waited for a response.

"Hi Magali. We've found him. He was in the industrial area."

He didn't need to see Magali's face to sense her relief. "OK. He's been found," the second sentence must have been addressed to Martin. "We'll get to work here then. Tell Andrej we're waiting for him."

"What about Steinberg? Alain seems to think we can no longer hand him over to the Swiss police. That they've been compromised by what happened in Arosa. What about the Germans? You're there already, after all."

"Wait a minute, Hendrik, Martin's trying to say something."

Hendrik waited, but he could already hear Martin loud and clear. He was saying that the German authorities were likely to be just as unreliable. That they hadn't exactly covered themselves in glory these last few months.

"I heard him, thanks. But if the German police aren't an option either, what the hell can we do? If we can't work within the confines of the law, then…"

"Then we'll just have to buy ourselves a little more time. We don't know what stage they're at inside, but I'd be willing to bet that if Andrej escapes, Steinberg will be only too happy to come after him."

"So, Andrej needs to tell him where he's going."

"Precisely."

"And where's that going to be?" Hendrik didn't think he could play this game much longer.

"We need to get him as far away from here as possible. Somewhere where there's no chance he'll be lent a helping hand."

Hendrik thought long and hard. He still wasn't quite sure what Magali was trying to say.

CHAPTER TWENTY-NINE

Steinberg

Sunday morning before dawn – Singen

Every so often, Steinberg would poke his head into the office to check how the interrogation was going. Night had fallen, and the heat of the day had been replaced by a cool darkness that required all those in the warehouse to stamp their feet periodically to stay warm.

Spurred on by the thought that Florian was still in danger, Andrej, it seemed, had been talking all evening. The expert responsible for the questioning was noting down what he had to say, before uploading it onto the system so that the two technologists could dismantle Andrej's creation in the lab. It was as if by stripping back the vehicle they were slowly but surely peeling away the layers standing between them and Andrej Pečjak's soul. Whatever lay beneath, Steinberg knew it was his ticket out of here – though whether Andrej would be so lucky remained to be seen.

Did he feel any sympathy towards him? Perhaps for the position in which he found himself. For here was a learned man with no choice but to compromise his greatest discovery, all for the safety of a boy he barely even knew.

"Time to get some rest," Steinberg said. "I've had the men set up a bed in the corner of the lower floor. You'll need your sleep."

Andrej followed him out. There was a sentry posted on each of the exits. The technologist had ceased to ask about Florian. Perhaps he realized that whatever happened, it had never really been in his power. No doubt he had concluded that it was best simply to cooperate in the hope that Steinberg would eventually do the right thing.

Steinberg sighed. It was useless trying to second guess what was going on in Andrej's mind.

After he had showed him to his bed, Steinberg decamped to the office. There he found the expert who had interrogated him. She couldn't have been much older than thirty. Pretty – but not smart enough to know, yet, who she was really working for.

"How was he?"

"Very cooperative," the woman said. "He knows his stuff."

"And it all adds up?"

"We're still to finish dismantling the car. But so far, yes," she replied.

"What's so special about it then?" Steinberg needed to pass the time somehow.

"It's not any one thing in particular. The whole concept is extremely interesting. Andrej has combined two types of batteries and managed to get the best out of both of them. On the one hand, he's equipped his EV with a lithium-polymer battery. They've been around for years: they're efficient and you can recharge them thousands of times. But he has used cells that were originally developed for a solar-powered airplane. They have a greater energy density than traditional cells. The revolution is that the whole system can work with currents in excess of seventy amperes, which is the maximum these cells can usually cope with."

"Go on."

"Well, normally, accelerating creates such a high current discharge that the cells can be damaged. The same thing applies if you want to re-charge the battery within a short space of time. But Andrej's car has been equipped with super-capacitors that buffer the surplus current. The second battery is a lithium-air battery, a new kind that's still being developed, and is known in certain circles as the holy grail of electric mobility. It has a special anode material—"

"Let's cut to the chase." Steinberg was beginning to lose patience.

"OK. The long and the short of it is that the battery can conserve ten times as much electricity thanks to its increased energy density. However, as I said, it's still being developed, and you can't charge it nearly as many times as the first battery. Right now, a lot of people are put off EVs by the limited range. They're afraid of being left stranded in the middle of nowhere. The thing about Andrej's EV is that this second battery only becomes operational once the first is already empty. But since most people don't drive more than one hundred kilometres in a day, it's rarely needed."

"Meaning it doesn't matter that you can't charge it so often. It's a kind of back-up?" Steinberg asked.

"Precisely. But that's not all. There's a six-phase synchronous-asynchronous motor with an efficiency of ninety-eight percent, the bodywork's more aerodynamic, and many of its components are made out of a light-weight combination of Kevlar/carbon fibres. Thin-film solar cells on the roof and transparent dye-sensitized cells on the side windows generate additional energy which is fed into the battery. On top of all that, you've got the intelligent software for the power management…"

"And how do you imagine our clients would react to its appearance on the market?"

"They'd think it was a joke at first. A curio. But if Andrej manages to find an investor and have, say, 10,000 produced in a series, then the automotive industry could be in real trouble!"

Just then there was a crash. Steinberg couldn't place the noise.

"What was that?" he said.

"Search me," said the woman. "It's not like there's anything to break in here."

Steinberg left the office to investigate. The two sentries were standing by the doors and the bed hadn't moved from the corner of the showroom floor. From the contours of the duvet, Steinberg thought he could just make out a body underneath.

"Did you see anything?" he asked.

"Nothing," came the response.

"Steinberg? You'd better come and take a look at this," the second man said. Suddenly the horn of Andrej's car sounded twice.

"What the hell?" Steinberg muttered under his breath, but before he could get to the sentry, a gust of wind came in through one of the ventilation shafts, blowing a tattered sheet of white paper into the air. It must have been on the camp bed. That could only mean...

"Shit," the first sentry said.

"How the fuck did he get out there?" Steinberg gazed up towards the open shaft. In his hand he held the sheet of paper. The writing was barely legible in the darkness. *See*, it said. *See you in Zurich.* Then there was a number. A car registration perhaps? No, it was too short for that. The only other thing it could be was a flight number. That made more sense. He was going to the airport...

"The stupid bastard," Steinberg muttered to himself. What the hell was he playing at? Jeopardizing the boy's safety like that? Perhaps the tension had got to him. Stress, lack of sleep, all of it could lead to moments of madness. But there was something about the note: something calculated.

"Shall we go after him?" the second sentry said.

"No, we still have the car. That's the main thing. Besides, I doubt we'll find him in the darkness. There's every chance he's headed for the volcano."

"Hohentwiel?"

"That's the one," Steinberg confirmed. "It's extinct – but there's woodland all around."

It didn't matter if the sentries didn't buy it. Whatever sympathy he might have felt for the technologist was gone. All Steinberg wanted now was the satisfaction of letting him know in person, preferably with the aid of a gun.

CHAPTER THIRTY

Nils

Sunday – Zurich

"Walter, I've decided to stay. I know it probably doesn't make much sense after all that's happened. But last night after the abduction, I just thought that if all this was in the hands of the right person…"

"When I didn't get your signal, I thought something must have been up," the director of intelligence said. He sounded weary. His voice was heavy and tinged with resignation. "If you're serious about staying, and God knows I've done my best to dissuade you, then you need two things. The first is a way in."

"And the second?"

"A way out." Walter paused. "Let's start with the latter. As long as I'm alive, you can leave at any time. I need only inform my escrow holder and Dominik will have no choice but to do as I say. Later this afternoon, I will make arrangements to ensure that, should anything happen to me, you will inherit access to the account. Stephan Schwarz has now dealt with both you and Hendrik, and has been most impressed by what he has seen. I have no doubt that he will be happy to assist you in the future."

"Walter, I don't know what to say."

"Then don't say anything. Far better for you to concentrate on how you are going to win Dominik's trust, on how you are going to become a part of the inner circle. Although this mission has largely been a failure, my understanding is that Dominik remains keen to secure your services. After a week of unmitigated disaster, your recruitment has offered a lone crumb of comfort. Perhaps you have already heard that the technologist has escaped; and that the technology turned out to be rather less than the sum of its parts. Good, Dominik still has access to a range of encrypted files, but we do not possess the means to crack them. They're protected by a 256-bit AES key, as well as an RSA encryption. In short, I hardly need say this is not the result Dominik desired."

"Which was?"

"To use the technology as a means of precipitating the CEO's downfall, by showing our most important clients that Adler had become arrogant and lost touch with the markets."

"So what can I do?"

"At the moment, you are tainted by the mission's failure," Walter said. "Whatever else Dominik might think about you personally, that much is still true. Nevertheless, there are still marginal gains to be made. In all likelihood, an unsanctioned operation has taken place. Worse, it has ended in failure. As you know, the operative responsible is still on the loose."

"What are you suggesting?"

"Only that Dominik has a problem. And with careful planning, you might just be able to provide the solution."

"I can rely on you to help?"

"I had hoped that was a question you no longer needed to ask. Call me when you are ready to get to work."

Nils replaced the receiver and began to think about how he might take care of the Steinberg problem. But he was tired after a night without sleep and soon after resting his head for a minute on the desk, he had fallen into a deep slumber.

He was awoken by the sound of someone crashing around the office. For a moment Nils was concerned. It was early Sunday morning and there was no need for anyone else to be at work. The cleaners, when they came, were usually a lot quieter. That could only mean... but no, he was being stupid. He dismissed the possibility almost as soon as he had entertained it. It couldn't be a break-in. At least not a random one. Whoever was here obviously knew their way around.

The mystery was soon solved. Dominik, looking tired and

aggravated, burst into the room and started shouting.

"Don't tell me you're sleeping here now? What? The hotel isn't good enough for you? The four-star hotel we have funded for the past *week* and which is located less than five minutes' walk from our offices?" Nils was somewhat taken aback by the outburst. Dominik didn't give a damn about money. That much had been made clear during the recruitment process. "And now you look at me like some sort of lost puppy dog. I don't believe it! I don't fucking believe it!"

With that, he returned whence he came, slamming the door long before Nils had the chance to respond. Nils replayed the scene in his mind. It was probably just a case of being in the wrong place at the wrong time. He had borne the brunt of Dominik's ire only because he was there.

Still, the question of money was interesting. Maybe things were tighter than Nils suspected. What, he wondered, would happen if the department's budget was cut? If they were forced to rely on fewer people? Then his own role would become more significant. All the more reason to do as Walter said; and make sure whatever mess had gone before was neatly packaged at the end.

Nils took a deep breath, rubbed the last bit of sleep from his eyes and made a beeline for the closed door of Dominik's office. A plan was slowly forming in his mind. The first step was to get everything out in the open.

He knocked on the door.

"Come in," a voice said from within, calmer now. The trajectory seemed to suggest its owner was sitting down. Upon seeing Nils, Dominik continued: "Please accept my apologies for what happened just now. As I'm sure you have gathered, it has been a rather tense forty-eight hours."

"Don't worry about it," Nils said. "Better out than in."

"You wanted something? Other than an apology?"

Nils stood there for a moment, unsure whether or not to proceed. If he started something now, there would be no going back.

"Look, Dominik, this may not be my place..." Nils hesitated.

"But in my position you hear things. Hendrik was pretty upset when he discovered a nine-year-old boy had gone missing. That's right, he told me about it. Didn't know what to make of it. So, I did a little digging. The boy was there at the start of the world-record parade, before his phone went offline. Obviously, I was a little concerned, so I checked Hendrik's footage from just before the parade. Also got my hands on some other material. There was nothing unusual there. Lots of WAVE participants and a few passers-by. But then the parade started and there was someone missing, someone who didn't crop up on the official films for the Guinness Book of Records anywhere. It was this guy William Steinberg, who joined in Grossglockner. I thought I was on to something, so I checked Hendrik's recordings from earlier in the expedition. It seems this guy Steinberg comes and goes. He was there in Arosa and La Punt but nowhere to be seen in Rorschach. *Rorschach.* The name set me thinking. All that business with the dead body that was found…" Nils shrugged his shoulders. "Well, it doesn't take a genius to work it out…"

Dominik held up his hand as if to say enough was enough.

"He's one of ours. Steinberg, that is. Look, I should have told you. When Hendrik went missing, I wanted to be absolutely sure. I thought he might have blown his cover. So I sent another man in. He was supposed to get things back on track. Provide a little back-up." Nils knew that Dominik was lying, but it didn't matter. He waited to see what would come out next. "It was top-secret. Not even the DI knew. But it was a mistake. He started taking matters into his own hands. Going behind my back. There's a right way of doing things. We have procedures here, channels you need to go through." Nils struggled to conceal a smile. He was willing to bet that Dominik broke with procedure as a matter of course. "The incident you refer to is just the latest in a long line…"

"What are you going to do?" Nils asked.

"I haven't decided yet. I have a meeting with the CEO this afternoon. In the meantime, it may interest you to know that the boy has been found."

Nils wondered how Dominik had found out. Had he got wind of what Nils had been doing overnight? How he had intercepted a police phone call? A shudder went down Nils' spine – but he couldn't show any signs of weakness.

"And the technology?" Had he gone too far?

"We're still not sure. If you had asked me this morning, I would have staked my life on it being Andrej Pečjak. But the test results don't look good. Or at least they're not good enough to bring about a revolution." Dominik hesitated before continuing. "Maybe we'll have more luck with the encrypted files we retrieved from his office. Either way, it's clear that Steinberg has been thoroughly outmanoeuvred. I need to find a way to deal with him."

Several more minutes passed before Nils took his leave. He had got what he came for: confirmation that Steinberg was a thorn in Dominik's side.

"You're serious about this? You'd be crossing a big line." The voice was Walter's. Nils had just spent the better part of ten minutes outlining his plan. Walter was right. Morally, it was a little dubious but if carried out properly, it would be highly effective.

"Why? Don't you think I can do it?" Nils asked.

"No, it's not that."

"Then what?"

"If I didn't know better, I'd say Dominik had come up with it himself," Walter concluded the call.

What sort of compliment was that? It was almost time to set everything in motion. Nils ducked out of the office and made another call.

"Hendrik, what can you tell me?"

"Andrej's safe," the blogger replied, "but no-one's sure what to do with Steinberg. We've tried to buy ourselves some more time. If everything goes to plan, he'll be at the airport in less than three hours."

"Leave Steinberg to me. I have a plan."

"What are you going to do?"

"You'll find out in due course," Nils said. "Right now, you have to go under. Get out of Zurich. Don't let anyone see you for a few days. Otherwise this will never work."

"Nils…?"

Nils took a deep breath and went back inside. Within an hour, he had everything he needed. A quick cigarette out front and then the games could begin…

"William Steinberg?" Nils said into his phone, after he had finished smoking.

"How did you get this number?"

"We don't know each other," Nils said, "but we have a mutual friend. I have important information for you concerning Andrej Pečjak's whereabouts. Forget about your rendezvous at the airport and meet me in downtown Zurich. Ganymede statue in one hour."

Nils sat back and thought things through for a final time. By now, Walter would have deleted Hendrik's file and created a new one for Steinberg.

When he had weighed up his options earlier that morning, the first thing Nils had thought about was Steinberg's police record. If he could just alter it, then perhaps… but no, he had decided it would take too long. Besides, there was no guarantee it would work. Nils needed a solution that allowed him to be in control, not one that relied too heavily on other people. Nevertheless, the answer had refused to come. Not that there was a shortage of ideas, or potential solutions. Quite the opposite. The problem was that none of them were quite right. Each one had a minor flaw, a chink that someone like Steinberg would all too easily expose.

In the end, he had gone back to the beginning. Perhaps he hadn't been so far off the mark the first time. It wasn't Steinberg's police record he needed to focus on, but his medical record. That afforded far greater possibilities. Particularly in the middle of a three-day-long party where there were ambulance crews stationed at every corner. One of the systems in the office had enabled Nils to track the movements of all visitors in the centre of Zurich that weekend. There were so many that the capital had been close to a mass panic, and it seemed the emergency services had responded accordingly.

Nils checked he had everything he needed. Steinberg's wallet was prepared and the package had arrived. Pre-rolled. Looked just like a cigarette. Amazing what you could get on the internet these days...

By the time Nils made it downtown, the party was still going strong. There would have to be one hell of a clean-up when tomorrow came. Beer cans, cigarettes, food wrappers, bottles: the city already resembled a land-fill site – and the final hours would only

make it worse. Despite the mess, Nils found himself feeling sorry for all those people who would have to return to work the next day. Then again, he reflected, an office desk could be a strangely comforting place, particularly after a weekend of excess. That much Nils knew from experience.

For all his bravado, Nils still wasn't sure if he was doing the right thing. Perhaps it would have been more prudent to leave it to Dominik after all. But no. He had taken it this far; there was no going back now. In the meantime, he realized his hands had started to shake. Something to calm his nerves would be no bad thing. He still had a little time. Besides, Steinberg had no idea what he looked like.

Work hard, play harder. He went into the bar on Buerkliterrasse and ordered a shot of vodka. The alcohol relaxed him, told him he was master of the situation. When all this was over, he was going to have one hell of a party...

After finishing his drink he surveyed what was going on below. The bar was on a raised platform and from his current position he had an excellent view of the crowds that had taken over the Swiss capital since Friday. No sign of Steinberg, however. Perhaps he wouldn't come. Perhaps he would take his chances at the airport, in the hope that the situation – whatever the latest was – could still be remedied.

Then Nils saw him, slicing his way through the crowd, before climbing the stairs to the viewing platform and the statue of Ganymede.

"William Steinberg?" Nils said, as he approached. "We spoke on the phone earlier."

"You have something for me?" came the curt response.

"Yes, but we can't talk here."

Nils fished a packet of cigarettes out from his shirt pocket, helped himself to one but paused before lighting it.

"Cigarette?" he asked.

There was only one left in the packet. According to his file, Steinberg was an occasional smoker. But he never resisted a certain brand. He leaned towards Nils and accepted his offer of a light, enjoying a long drag once the cigarette was aflame.

Nils was about to light his own, which was dangling from his lips, when somehow it slipped and fell onto the street.

"Don't worry, I always keep a spare behind my ear," he said. "It's a bad habit. Still, helps with the girls."

A nervous joke. He should have known Steinberg wouldn't be in the mood for pleasantries. Nils' palms were drenched in sweat, and he fumbled around with the lighter. Just stay calm, he told himself.

In the meantime, Nils studied Steinberg's face. He looked tired, despondent, as if the weight of the world was on his shoulders and he no longer had the strength to carry the load. Nils allowed himself a smile. He'd be resting soon enough.

The pair made their way towards a café that, despite the presence of a host of independently run stalls just outside the entrance, had chosen to remain open throughout the weekend.

Steinberg was fidgety, and seemed preoccupied with something. Nils wondered if it was too soon for the contents of the cigarette to take effect. For all his experience on the party scene, he was a total novice when it came to drugs. They had never interested him. Still, they weren't hard to come by. A simple internet search had enabled him to get his hands on a whole range of legal highs.

For what it was worth, Steinberg had just smoked a cigarette that had been cut with bath salts, designer drugs that had nothing to do with their more prosaic namesake. Side effects were impossible to predict but included dilated pupils, increased heart rate and, in the most extreme cases, psychosis.

In Steinberg, Nils could now see, it appeared to have induced a kind of drowsiness, coupled with a slight loss in coordination. As they sat down, Steinberg had begun to sweat.

"Are you OK?" Nils asked.

"I'll be back in a minute," Steinberg said. He rose from his chair and all but knocked the table over, before swaying to other side of the café and into the gents'. His jacket he had left hanging over the edge of his seat. Nils took the opportunity to rifle through it, removing anything that might enable Steinberg to be correctly identified.

When the latter emerged, his face and hair dripping wet with cold water, his condition seemed to have worsened. It was one thing, Nils supposed, to take drugs in full awareness of the side effects they might induce; quite another to find yourself suddenly and inexplicably disorientated. Walter was right. Nils had crossed a line. In other circumstances, what he had done would be unforgiveable. Here it had been the only means of ensuring everyone Nils cared about got out alive.

"What the fuck is wrong with you?" Nils said. He knew that a display of aggression was likely to confuse Steinberg even further.

"You bastard," Steinberg replied slowly, no doubt sensing that something was seriously wrong.

"Have you been drinking?" Nils persisted.

"Fuck you. Hell, you know I haven't touched a drop." The words, however, had come out as a slur. Steinberg attempted to deal him a blow but in the process knocked two glasses onto the floor. They smashed into tiny pieces and the incident drew angry glances from both customers and the proprietor. Sensing that all eyes were upon him, Steinberg rose to his feet – shakily, and with a little help from the table – and started to utter incomprehensible threats to anyone who would listen. Most of them were directed at Nils.

"I'm sorry, sir," the proprietor said to Nils. He seemed embarrassed that he had been forced into taking action. "I don't know what's going on here, but I'm afraid I'm going to have to ask your friend to remove himself from the premises."

Before Nils could respond, however, Steinberg had attempted and failed to grab him by the scruff of the neck, completely lost his balance, and ended up face down on the café floor. As Steinberg lay there mouthing obscenities, Nils saw that his hands had been badly cut by the glass that was glistening all around.

"And take him to the first aid station while you're at it," the proprietor remarked, not unsympathetically, as he and Nils helped Steinberg, now drowsy and disorientated, to his feet. "There's an ambulance just around the corner. It's probably nothing, but best get everything seen to in case it becomes infected."

"I'm sorry," Nils said, "I really don't know what the matter is."

Steinberg was now almost completely reliant on Nils' support.

"Who have we got here then?" the ambulance woman said as Nils and Steinberg hove into view.

"I found him by the river, shouting, swaying, and being a general nuisance to the public. At first I thought he was just drunk, but then I saw his hand, and realized he could barely walk. I thought it would be best for a professional to take a look. Wasn't easy getting him here, mind."

"We don't get many good Samaritans these days," the woman smiled. "Do you have any idea who he is? In case we need to contact his next of kin?"

"His wallet was on the ground beside him. If you look at the picture, it's definitely him."

"William Steinberg," the woman said. She produced a tablet

from inside the ambulance and typed in his details. Nils stood nervously waiting. Forget the cars, forget the surveillance. This was the real test. Would the file Walter had created be able to take in a medical professional? "Oh!" she said suddenly.

"Is something the matter?"

"Well, I probably shouldn't say... but it seems we've got a lucky break here. The man you've brought in is an escaped psychiatric patient, history of drug use, prone to outbursts of violence. We'd better take it from here. Reto!" she called to one of the other crew members.

Nils watched as Steinberg, who by now looked both completely lost and utterly harmless, was strapped to a gurney and wheeled inside the ambulance. Then the doors were shut, the sirens went on, and the ambulance began its journey out of the city centre.

Nils breathed a sigh of relief and headed in the direction of the nearest bar, knowing that tomorrow there were sterner challenges to come.

The next day, he arrived to find Dominik waiting there for him.

"Nils, I don't know what to say. I'm sorry."

It took Nils a moment to work out what Dominik was talking about.

"Thank you," he said eventually, avoiding Dominik's gaze.

"All of this is my fault. Hendrik had so much of his life ahead of him."

"No, it's me who should be taking the blame," Nils replied, wiping a tear away from his eye. "I'm the one who lured Steinberg to Zurich last night."

"But if I hadn't sent Steinberg to WAVE, maybe none of this would have happened. He was covering his tracks. Making sure there were no witnesses. It's exactly what I was hoping to prevent."

Dominik's duplicity was awe-inspiring. He had wanted rid of Hendrik for the best part of a week. Walter must have told him. It had been Walter's job to "identify" the body. Some poor kid who had lost his life in a car accident two days before. It had been mentioned in the paper, but only in passing. No next of kin, just like Hendrik. Walter had switched the records, changed the cause of death. Steinberg's involvement had been a little trickier to prove, as he had been nowhere near Hendrik at the time. Still, it was amazing what you could do when you had access to the entire country's CCTV footage. Now Steinberg was sure to be linked to Hendrik's death: a "murder" that had never even occurred in the first place.

"I know. That's why I had to act. In case he came for me next." Nils could play the game too. He paused to lend his next sentence emphasis. It was vital that Dominik thought it had been a calculated decision; that Nils hadn't simply ripped up the rule book to suit his own ends. "Or for you."

Dominik didn't react at first. Instead he looked at Nils long and hard. "That was you? I have to say I was wondering why an ambulance crew had picked him up. Then I read the file. I was about to put the police onto him in any case." Suddenly he seemed to realize he ought to say something else. "Walter told me about Hendrik. Again, I can't express how sorry I am. Needless to say, his funeral has all been taken care of."

Then, all of a sudden, his expression changed. Clearly it was Dominik, not Steinberg, who ought to have been taken away. The man wasn't human. It was as if he had *learned* the correct response for every situation.

"I underestimated you," Dominik continued.

"Surely you didn't hire me to drink champagne?"

"No, but perhaps it should have been you out in the field. Well, you'll get your chance." Dominik handed Nils a limited edition luxury phone, brand new. "We're going to have to ease off Andrej for the time being. At least until the cryptographers have deciphered his files. In the meantime, there's someone else we'd like you to keep an eye on. You leave tomorrow morning." Dominik shook Nils by the hand. "Welcome to BIRD."

After Dominik had gone, Nils sat down to take a look at the device in his hand. It was elegant, with titanium casing. Did he detect the sparkle of an expensive stone or two sparkling as well? Nils had to give Dominik one thing: he certainly had an eye for luxury goods. He opened the program on the start screen and scrolled through to find the project folder. A single click revealed a photo of a man wearing a fitted suit. A financier, perhaps, or a politician of some sort. It hardly mattered. Nils was only interested in the destination.

The Gold Coast, it said.

Located on Barbados' western shore...

CHAPTER THIRTY-ONE

Dominik

Two days later – New York

"Dominik, this is not the first time you have interrupted me in the middle of an important meeting."

Adler was in Lower Manhattan, attending the opening of the One World Trade Center, the centrepiece of the new World Trade Center complex and, standing at some 1,776 feet – a reference to the date of the United States Declaration of Independence – the tallest skyscraper anywhere in the western hemisphere. The symbolic reference was typical of the Yanks, Dominik thought to himself. Their sentimentality had always been their undoing. The Burj Khalifa in Dubai, built by the same architect, was almost 1,000 feet taller, and had been completed in a shorter space of time.

"I'm aware of that, sir. And I'm sorry," Dominik said. Calling at inopportune times was his way of undermining the CEO. "But I thought you would like to know that the mission has now been aborted, as per your instructions last week."

"Good. Anything else? Or may I return to my reception?"

"There was an incident, sir. It's serious. I'd like to see you in person, if I may. I'm in New York. Should we say the Press Lounge at seven this evening?"

"Make it half past. And I want a table outside. Or else there'll be hell to pay," Adler smirked.

"Very good, sir," Dominik said. The bar was in Hell's Kitchen.

The Press Lounge, overlooking the Hudson River, had become a real hit with New Yorkers since opening a few years before. Enormous glass walls, which could be opened in summer, led out to a glorious wrap-around roof terrace, according drinkers a sensational view of midtown Manhattan. With its well-stocked bar and extensive wine list, it was already a favourite of the New York establishment.

Given the news he was about to receive, it was important that Adler should be in comfortable surroundings. Dominik had no idea how he would react to the news of his protégé's death. And that, along with the strange pleasure Dominik felt at sharing the news, had combined to lend the evening an extra frisson of excitement.

Even so, Dominik knew better than to keep the old man waiting, and had arrived a good half hour ahead of schedule. Safely ensconced at their outside table, he had decided to order a bottle of expensive single malt from the bar. He couldn't stand whisky, but he knew that Adler would approve of the gesture.

"So, the party is over; the electric vehicles have returned from whence they came," the CEO said as he entered ten minutes early, his tone as usual carrying an undercurrent of sarcasm. "And what do we have to show for it?"

"A series of encrypted files. Once they've been deciphered, we might be able to make something of them." Dominik allowed his final sentence to hang in the air. Adler should know that the systems he had arranged for BIRD to have access to hadn't been good enough to crack the code. Dominik couldn't be blamed for that.

"And this?" Adler pointed around about him, trying to take in his new surroundings. "What is all *this* in aid of?"

Dominik poured the CEO a double measure of Scotch.

"I'm afraid I have some bad news. When you said you wanted things shut down, I put our best man onto it straightaway. Both the boy and Walter's guy," Dominik was referring to Hendrik and Peter, "have been taken care of. Neither of them will talk."

Adler nodded. He knew that Dominik meant neither of them *could* talk.

"And this *incident*? There's something you're not telling me."

"Jaeger, sir. We sent Jaeger in." Dominik had to make sure he phrased his next words very carefully. "He carried out his mission and then…" Dominik took a deep breath and continued. It was important that Adler saw how much Jaeger's death had affected him. "And then he was found the next morning – in Lake Constance. They tried to resuscitate him but – I'm sorry, sir – he's gone."

Adler took the news calmly at first, draining his whisky at a single gulp. Then he stood up and walked over to the edge of the roof terrace, where he proceeded to let fly a volley of invective. The outburst was so surprising, the language so shocking, that for a moment the bar staff seemed minded to intervene. Dominik waved them away with a look that said *it won't be worth your while.*

"No-one's quite sure how it happened, sir. We're in the process of launching an enquiry," Dominik said as he joined Adler by the rail, placing a hand on the old man's shoulder. The CEO batted it angrily away. Needless to say, the enquiry would conclude that Jaeger had taken his own life. It wasn't in anyone's interests – not in Walter's, and certainly not in Dominik's – for the real facts to emerge. "I know how fond you were of him."

"He was like a son to me," Adler said angrily. Dominik couldn't be sure if there was a tear in the CEO's eye. "Jaeger? You sent Jaeger?" Adler uttered disbelievingly. No doubt it would take a while for the shock to sink in fully.

"He was the best at what he did," Dominik added. Not an answer exactly, but a justification nonetheless. In the meantime he had refilled Adler's glass and poured one for himself. He had no intention of drinking it. "To tell you the truth, I'm not sure he can be replaced. Slàinte."

Dominik raised his glass, but Adler refused to clink with him. Both slowly returned to their seats.

"I would take a thousand Jaegers over you. His blood is on your hands," Adler said at last. Dominik feigned indifference. He had been expecting a certain amount of criticism. "He was loyal, he followed instructions, and he got the job done. You…" Adler was pointing now, "you do none of these things."

The CEO paused for a moment before continuing. "Nevertheless, Jaeger was never going to fill my position. That much I have always known. I need someone with ambition, with vision. Someone who isn't afraid to break the rules from time to time." Adler's gaze was now focused on Dominik. A wry smile appeared, betraying the CEO's ruthlessness. He might have lost a son, but it was business as usual. "We both know that mavericks only survive as long as they get results. Is there anything you can say to convince me you're not just some jumped-up office boy who happened to strike it lucky?"

Dominik was momentarily taken aback by Adler's tone, but he shouldn't have been. The CEO had been a calmly threatening presence for years. He might, just now, have allowed himself a moment to mourn the loss of his protégé, but he had since recovered and Dominik needed to reassure him he was still the right man for the job.

"Well, as I said, there is the presence of the encrypted files."

Adler scoffed, waved his number two aside.

"Beyond that there is Nils."

"Nils?"

"One of the probationers. He has proven a worthy addition to our unit."

That much was true. Dominik had always had Nils down as corruptible, but he had never envisaged a situation where he would use Hendrik Herder's death to fuel his own ambition.

"After Jaeger died, we ran into some difficulties. Nils ensured that they were handled with the utmost discretion. I'll spare you the details."

Dominik knew that Adler regarded discretion as an indispensable tool in any employee's armoury. The mere mention of the word was usually enough – unless it appeared in tandem with its ugly twin.

"Good. I'd hate to think you were being *indiscreet*. I understand one of our operatives had something of a turn in Zurich. I won't ask what he was doing there in the first place, as long as the matter has been dealt with accordingly."

"You have my word, sir."

"Does that count for anything these days, I wonder? Young people may not approve of the sentiment, but let me assure you that in my world an oral agreement still goes a long way. If you are serious about stepping into my shoes, then it's time you emerged from the shadows. Absence does not make the heart grow fonder; it only leads to missed opportunities. Now leave me alone, I would like a moment to mourn the passing of a friend."

As Dominik exited the bar, he was left to ponder the meaning of what Adler had said. It was true that he had been rather distracted of late. After all, the Board for Industrial Research and Development didn't only have links to the automobile industry. There were other markets that were enormously important for Adler Reilly, market segments that relied on BIRD's discreet support. Was Adler suggesting that they were starting to feel neglected? His closing remarks had been impenetrable – like the network of favours and counter-favours that had helped BIRD obtain such awesome power. A meeting here, a drinks reception there. Lunch in London followed by dinner in Madrid. Who could say where it would all lead? A small investment, a dropped charge, the sudden appearance of a lucrative contract. The point was you needed to be there. Technology was a wonderful thing, but you couldn't, yet, use a computer to shake someone by the hand.

As a younger man, Dominik had read that eighty percent of success was showing up. Only now, however, was he beginning to understand its meaning. With Adler gone, a lot of his contacts would simply disappear. Old networks would die; and favours would remain forever outstanding.

More than ever, someone needed to bridge the gap between the old world and the new. Dominik was the right age to do both – but he wouldn't achieve anything without being seen.

He would stay in New York for a few days, glad handing the great and good. Then he would move on. There were opportunities elsewhere: in India, in China, in Hong Kong.

Adler had spoken of his world. But Dominik knew that meant the West. The old man had treated the emerging markets like unwanted stepchildren.

It was time someone gave them the love they deserved.

CHAPTER THIRTY-TWO

Alain

Late August – London

As Alain surveyed the small group which had gathered that afternoon in London, he reflected on how differently things might have turned out. He had reserved a room at Babylon, a restaurant on the seventh floor of a former department store located on Kensington High Street, which was also home to the city's exclusive Roof Gardens. It would, Alain hoped, afford the group the privacy they required.

He was forced to admit that events at WAVE had got way out of control. What had originally seemed like a simple case of industrial espionage had gradually given way to sabotage, torture, and murder. Even the kidnap of a nine-year-old boy hadn't been off limits.

Alain cast his mind back to that final day. Not a single member of the group currently present had been there during the latter stages of the expedition, even if, almost two months later, none of them would ever forget its final weekend. When Steinberg had failed to turn up at the airport, everyone had feared the worst. Eventually, however, they had been reassured that everything was under control. It was a minor miracle that no-one had been seriously hurt. Nevertheless for some, things could never be the same again.

To Alain's immediate left sat Hendrik Herder, though he was no longer known by that name. Initially Alain had been disgusted by the blogger's confession that he had been hired to spy on the technology. But in truth, Alain was equally disappointed in himself. He had spent whole days travelling with the blogger and had never suspected a thing. In Alain's eyes it was only during the search for Florian that Hendrik had redeemed himself. He could see how much it hurt Hendrik to think that his actions had led, however indirectly, to both the injury of the girl in Deutschlandsberg and the kidnapping of an innocent child.

Hendrik himself had been obliged to go under and had spent the latter part of the summer working at an independent TV channel in London while studying Computer Forensics and IT Security. His change in appearance had confused Andrej and his wife, Jasna, though the technologist knew better than to ask questions about matters that didn't concern him. The pair had taken their places alongside the ex-blogger and were anxiously awaiting Alain's announcement. Martin and Magali from DISECUPRO seemed a good deal less concerned. Rumour had it that at some point in the aftermath of the expedition they had become lovers, a state of affairs that promised to give their superior Frank, who occupied the head of the table opposite Alain, a minor professional headache. Their colleague Vivien, who had been charged with guarding Andrej's EV at night, was also there: a silent but reliable presence in the background, as he had been for much of the expedition.

Finally there was Tom Schmidt, the man who had first brought Andrej to Alain's attention and who had been mercifully spared the ordeal of the ten-day long testing process.

That made eight in total, though there were far more expected later that evening for the reception. One person who had already sent his apologies was Nils Karrat. Although Hendrik was the only person who knew him personally, the others had all been keen to express their gratitude for the work he had done, and it was to Nils that Alain had first asked the group to charge their glasses as he commenced his short after-dinner speech.

"A toast to all those whose work behind the scenes goes unnoticed. May they one day be accorded the recognition they deserve."

The group raised their glasses.

"Ah, yes," Hendrik said. The change of scene appeared to have done him good. "The workaholic Nils, last seen at Tomorrowland after a month in Barbados."

The others smiled. Tomorrowland, they had learned that

afternoon, was one of Europe's largest electronic music festivals.

"And we, too, may soon be joining him – in the metaphorical sense of course. The land of tomorrow. How will it look?" Alain continued. "I dare say that we are a step closer to finding out. Andrej, Jasna; it is time I laid my cards on the table." What little chatter there had been ceased and all eyes were on Alain. "Some months ago, I had the good fortune of running into Tom Schmidt in Scotland. Tom, seated here to my right, is a man for whom I have always had the greatest admiration and respect. So when he informed me that he had been approached by a Slovenian technologist who had developed a concept that would help make electric vehicles available for the mass market, I was curious. Why did he choose me? Well, luck played its part for sure. But Tom also knows just how much the survival of our planet means to me. As a businessman, I am in the fortunate position of being able to invest in the causes closest to my heart. But that does not mean that I give out money to whoever comes calling. The product is important, as, of course, is its aim. But the person behind it is equally significant and it was for this reason – to get to know the man behind the technology – that I decided to take part in the expedition itself."

"You were spying on me?" Andrej asked incredulously. For a moment, Alain was worried that he was offended, but soon the technologist's face had broadened into a wide grin.

"I hardly need say that my mind was made up almost from the start. And over the course of the past ten days, I have been privileged to observe a true gentleman at work. Kind, calm, and dignified at all times, Andrej has passed every test I have devised for him and many others along the way. I know that the man to my left," Alain gestured toward Hendrik, "will never forget his kindness in Bled; and it is quite possible that his quick thinking and generosity of spirit – in conjunction with the help of those seated around this table and beyond – saved the life of a nine-year-old boy."

At this point, the table broke out in spontaneous applause.

"Don't forget about your own contribution," Frank interrupted. "You looked after Florian in Zurich and had him checked out by the

331

best doctors in the city. Then after you learned that his parents would not be returning from their holiday for another day, you took him to the Umweltarena in Spreitenbach and then cruising in a yacht on Lake Zurich. On the Monday, you were even generous enough to take him up to Stanser Horn."

"After all he had been through," Alain replied, "it was the least I could do for him. He loved the cabrio cable car that took us up to the mountain, and was even more impressed when he discovered that it was powered by a 919 kilowatt electric motor. That said, we almost missed his parents because my cell phone ran out of battery. Thankfully, having been inspired by Martin, I've taken the liberty of purchasing each one of us a solar bag, so that no-one around this table will ever be in that position again," Alain began to distribute the packages that lay on top of the chest of drawers by the wall. There were business versions for the men, and a sleeker model for the women. "Florian has one already of course. He's been keeping me up-to-date on how many kilowatt hours he collects every week. It's grown into a kind of competition. Through an online community we can use the solar energy we collect to support different projects around the world. Each week we count how much more energy we still need in order to plant a tree in the Amazon or send a child in India to school for a month. In the bags, you'll find a photo."

The group looked inside to find a beaming Florian posing for the camera with a sheet of paper showing the amount of kilowatt hours he had collected since the end of WAVE.

Next, Alain turned to face Andrej. He had a serious look in his eyes.

"Andrej, I have not always been honest with you, and for that I apologize. I can only say that I had my reasons. Nevertheless, I have gathered you together today, in advance of the celebrations this evening, in order to make it known – no secrets this time! – that following the successful completion of the testing process, I have decided to invest in this new and exciting technology."

For the second time, the eight bodies around the table broke out into spontaneous applause.

"And now, without any further ado," Alain continued, "I hand you over to the man of the hour."

Buoyed no doubt by the lunchtime wine, the other members of the party had begun to chant "speech", quietly at first, but with increasing vigour the longer Andrej held his tongue. It was, Alain thought, entirely in keeping with the man that he should affect embarrassment at his own stellar achievements.

"Thank you," he said finally. "First of all I would like to thank Martin, Magali, Vivien, and Frank for ensuring that Jasna and I were provided safe passage throughout the expedition. Without your help, the test would never have been a success. Thanks also to Alain, whose generous investment, we have just learned, has provided a platform for us to achieve a longstanding dream. But Alain's true identity is only the first surprise of the evening." At that moment, the technologist smiled at Tom Schmidt, who subsequently asked all those present to ensure their cell phones were switched off. Tom then requested that they place their phones in a special protective compartment of his suitcase, before taking the case out onto the balcony.

"Thank you, Tom. A small security measure. I hope you'll understand," Andrej winked. "I have been very careful, up until now, not to give too much away concerning the exact details of my invention. When I was questioned on its design two months ago in Singen, I told my interrogators that my EV was a fusion of different concepts that would take range anxiety out of the question and enable EVs to travel over 1,000 kilometres on a single charge. The combination of a highly-efficient electric motor and super-capacitors to buffer the surplus current for the battery cells, as well as an intelligent energy management for the whole power system, including fast charging possibilities, seemed revolutionary enough for them – certainly for a Slovenian. This is also the information which Tom would have divulged to you, Alain, in the hope of securing your investment. However, it is not, and never has been, the whole truth. *That*," Andrej continued, "has been secure in our Cloud since the turn of the year, double encrypted and safe from even the world's most powerful secret services."

Alain was smiling now, too. It was a day for revelations, and he sensed that Andrej's, when it came, might just surpass his own.

"Needless to say, the information about the batteries proved more than enough for my interrogators," Andrej went on. "In truth, I do not blame them. Although they had a good understanding of current developments, I suspect they are not blessed with the ability to think outside the box. They swallowed what I told them because it already appeared fantastical: a holy grail that, until now, had always been out of reach. Perhaps in their minds it even justified the lengths to which their organization had gone to secure my secrets. Little did they know. I ask that what I have to say to you, my most trusted group of friends, goes no further than these four walls, as I have filed a patent application. It has been accepted and should be granted any day now."

It was almost as if a hush had descended upon the whole restaurant in anticipation of what the technologist would say next. Even Martin and Magali, who had spent most the meal lost in their own little world, were suddenly all ears.

"Alain, I thank you again for your kind words just now; and I want to say that I believe you have invested wisely. It has been a bumpy road at times, but we have managed to reach our final destination," he rested his hand on Jasna's right shoulder. "The test results are in and a series is soon to been confirmed." He glanced across at Tom one last time and smiled. "I can hardly believe I am saying this…"

"You haven't said anything, Andrej. I think you're stalling for time," Alain joked.

"Truly, range anxiety is a thing of the past. I have succeeded in building an electric car with a unique power source…" In the meantime, he had produced a laptop, whose screen showed a blown-up image of a tiny metal object.

"What's that?" Hendrik asked.

"That, my friends, is a micro windmill made from a nickel-alloy. It's smaller than a grain of rice and yet extremely resistant. It was developed at the University of Texas in Arlington by a research associate and a professor in the Electrotechnical faculty; and costs almost nothing to make. The low cost of production is down to the design, which combines origami techniques with concepts from the semi-conductor industry. Through a special galvanizing process, simple two-dimensional metals turn into complex 3D structures by obtaining additional layers, which are also flexible. Thanks to the help of a company from Taiwan, which automatized the process, these micro windmills are now available on the mass market. You see, researchers soon realized that they could be used to charge cell phones. If you apply a significant number of these mini windmills to the casing of a cell phone and connect them to the battery, then all you have to do to charge your cell is wave it in the air for a few minutes at a time."

Andrej displayed another picture on his laptop. It showed an exploded view of a vehicle, with the emphasis placed on a component that was present in all traditional gasoline models. "The Americans always say "Think Big", and that is precisely what I have done."

The group gazed at the picture open-mouthed. Alain had heard of equipping vehicles with small turbines to help charge the battery, but he had never seen anything like this.

"What you see on the picture might look like a normal radiator. But in fact it's a mini power station. In place of the cooling fins of the radiator, there are a number of wires upon which we soldered the micro windmills. The situation in the rear spoiler is exactly the same. In fact, there are millions of mini windmills, which provide the vehicle with up to fifteen kilowatt hours of energy while driving. Still, that's only enough for your average vehicle in normal driving conditions, and that's why we need these here," Andrej gestured towards the batteries, "to provide additional support. To start the motor, the vehicle needs more energy than the windmills typically can provide when the vehicle is stationary. The same goes for driving uphill. This is where the power from the first battery, made out of lithium-polymer cells, comes in. Going downhill, the braking energy will combine with the energy from the windmills, and enable the battery to recuperate. If the latter is fully charged and in danger of overheating, the energy will be transferred to the second battery, made out of lithium-air. It has a far greater energy density."

"That means the second battery's current weakness – the fact it can only be charged a limited number of times – is less of an issue, because it will only be used in the event of an issue with the first battery?" Martin asked.

Andrej nodded.

"Electronically controlled flaps in front of the radiator constantly optimize the power to wind ratio. The flaps are used to reduce the air drag and thus increase the efficiency. The flaps can also limit or even stop the windmills from producing energy. In order to ensure everything runs smoothly, we also require intelligent software, which is housed here." Andrej pointed to another component.

"How come Steinberg and his colleagues didn't notice any of this in Singen?" Magali asked.

"For that, I have your colleagues," Andrej gestured towards Frank and Vivien, "as well as the good people of EMPA, to thank. I was intending to dismantle the radiator and second battery so that they could be tested at EMPA anyway. That meant replacing the second battery and using another kind of software for the energy management, which I had already prepared at home.

"After Florian was kidnapped, we had to change the plan. Thanks to the hard work of EMPA's employees, we were able to modify the car on the spot and install several solar modules based on thin-film and dye-sensitized cells. We left the second battery in the car, added an on-board charger, and flashed the electric control unit with a revised version of the software so that the technologists in Singen believed what I was saying."

Some hours later, Alain was still in a state of shock. When Andrej had revealed his secret, he had almost felt his jaw drop, and he was still walking around with his mouth wide open.

In the meantime, he had left the group and gone outside onto the small roof terrace to have a moment to himself. A group of birds began to chirrup in the sky.

From his vantage point, he could see four flamingos surrounded by ducks in the stream below.

Truly, it was a world away from the big city, seven floors below. His gaze alighted on the Gherkin, standing tall, far in the distance. He had only recently learned that the building, which dominated the London skyline, had been put into receivership. Apparently it had been defaulting on its debts for a number of years. The problem, Alain had read, was that its upkeep was funded by a loan denominated in both Swiss Francs and Sterling. In the wake of the financial crisis and the weakening of the pound, a currency liability had arisen. Alain supposed it wasn't always the billion-dollar investments that paid off. But he knew that what *Andrej* had just shown them was a revolutionary development. Everything he had used had existed previously – but the combination was what made it stand out. If these mini windmills could be used to charge smartphones, why shouldn't the same apply to EVs as well? Just then the lights adorning the tree below came on, as if to say "why not indeed?"

He made his way down a level to the party he had organized on the floor below. After everything that had happened during WAVE, a number of participants hadn't had the opportunity to say goodbye to one another. This was their chance. After surveying the club, Alain took his leave just as the wavy-haired DJ, Uwe, who had come recommended by Hendrik, was beginning his set.

Latin music... Apparently Hendrik had met Uwe in Zurich at the beginning of the summer, though both had since moved on from that period in their lives. Uwe, Alain suspected, didn't really belong in the corporate world – at least if his dance moves were anything to go by!

Next, Alain went outside into the Spanish garden. It was intriguing to see people mingling after WAVE had come to an end. Many of those here would barely have exchanged more than a few words over the course of the expedition, yet tonight they were acting like long-lost members of the same tribe.

Alain spied Jochen chatting with Manfred and Tamara, while Jean-Pierre and Monika stood alongside. To think that Alain had thought that either one of the couples were the agents from DISE-CUPRO. In another corner, Leora was recounting her hospital ordeal to a gaggle of admirers, which included Stephan Schwartzkopff and Olaf Feldmann, the unfortunate victims of the incident in Deutschlandsberg who had been unable to complete their race.

Stephan Schwarz was also there, along with a number of his friends from the Tesla club. Alain had invited them to say thank you for their contribution during the search for Florian. Gordon, meanwhile, a London resident, was attempting to persuade a number of onlookers to take a ride along the Thames in his e-boat, stationed near the Houses of Parliament: a proposal that had so far attracted a number of takers. Louis Palmer was also present, appearing calm and contented as he sat on a bench overlooking the action. Louis was happy, no doubt, that he was finally able to take a backseat and leave the organizing to someone else. Was that a glass of wine in his hand? Alain must have been seeing things…

He strolled further on through the Spanish garden, loca- ting a mini hideaway at the far end that looked like part of a hacien- da. There he found the blogger deep in conver- sation with Martin and Magali on the sofas.  The lovers gave no indication that three was a crowd.

"Did you have a name for your mission?" Martin was asking.

Alain was curious to hear the response.

"Of course we did. Nils wouldn't have had it any other way."

"So, what was it then?" Magali pressed.

"Black Hungarian."

"Because Louis is Hungarian and always dresses in black?" Martin ventured.

"No, although that's not a bad guess. As what we were doing wasn't supposed to be made public, Nils suggested "black" as in "black op". The Hungarian bit is pretty tenuous, even for Nils. It refers to the world's most famous poker player, Stu Ungar. I guess Nils just loves poker…"

Alain gazed blankly at the blogger.

"Ungar," Hendrik said, "is German for Hungarian."

Laughing, Alain moved past the Tudor garden with its marquee tents and on round into the English garden where he had seen the flamingos half an hour before. The technologist and his wife were enjoying a moment together on one of the benches near the stream. Despite the presence of the club behind them, they seemed to have found their own mini-sanctuary.

"A shame Florian couldn't be here," Andrej said, upon seeing

Alain. He invited him to join them for a drink. "He would have loved this. It's perfect for hide and seek."

"I meant to say. He sent me an email last week. Said none of his friends believed what had happened to him."

"So he's OK?" Jasna asked.

"Seems like it. He wrote about WAVE for his school magazine. I was thinking someone should do the same…" Alain's voice trailed away.

"Write a book? About an electric car expedition? Are you out of your mind?" Jasna said. The thought obviously so amused her that she couldn't stay in the pair's company any longer.

"You don't think there's a story to tell?" Alain protested.

Andrej smiled mischievously. "I think," he said slowly, emphasizing each individual word, "that you've had too much red wine."

Alain waited a moment before giving his response.

"You're probably right…" he said finally, as the pair made their way back towards the party, each with an arm around the other's shoulder, both grinning from ear to ear.

EPILOGUE

Dominik

Autumn – Singapore

As dusk fell, Dominik Brandt stepped out of the pool and gazed at the *Flyer* and the armada of vessels.

He had deci-ded against the fitness room, and taken the hundreds of steps up to the fifty-seventh floor in order to swim his lengths. Neverthel-ess, he was more than satisfied.

His recent trip to New York had been a real success. In the fast-paced world of finance, it was particularly important to be the first to recognize new trends and invest in them ahead of the competition. His contacts in the US had drawn his attention to several projects in Southeast Asia. Like Do-minik, a number of market speculators saw lucrative opportunities in countries such as Vietnam, Laos, Indonesia, and the Philippines – four of the ten membership states of the Association of Southeast Asian Nations, or ASEAN, for short. In places like Cambodia, Malaysia, and Myanmar, enormous infrastructure projects had seemingly been con-jured out of nothing. Who was better placed to offer a kindly word of advice and influence developments than Dominik Brandt?

The operation at WAVE might have failed, but all that was in the past now. Walter had agreed to keep an eye on the technologist

– discreetly, of course. The last thing anyone wanted was another fiasco, as Adler was unlikely to be so understanding the second time around. Alarm bells had sounded when a number of the participants journeyed en masse to London, but it turned out to be nothing more than a simple reunion. Otherwise, there had been little to report. Even the investor, Alain Blanc, appeared to have forgotten about the technologist, as there had been no contact between the pair since late summer. For his part, Andrej Pečjak seemed to have returned to his provincial Slovenian existence.

There had been one rather unsettling piece of news. It seemed that those upstarts at Tesla had released all their patents to the public domain. Initial conversations between BMW and Nissan had already taken place, and the three companies had decided to focus their energies on standardizing EV charging. At first, Dominik had been unsure whether or not to react. However, after discussing the matter with Walter, the pair had concluded that in their hysteria, EV fanatics had wildly overestimated the power of the Californian manufacturer.

Even if BMW and Nissan were working in conjunction with Tesla, the established car manufacturers had waited out a number of crises before, perfecting their delaying tactics over the course of many long years. More to the point, a standard couldn't be established per se: you could only say something was a standard when the majority had already adopted it. And BMW, Nissan and Tesla hardly represented a majority of the world's total car market. If more car companies became involved in the development process, decisions would only be delayed further. After all, too many cooks *always* spoiled the broth. So, they would wait. As much as Dominik hated to admit it, Adler was right: electric cars were a minor headache, nothing more. Whatever pain they were causing would soon abate.

Speaking of headaches, the appointment of Nils Karrat all those months ago had proved to be anything but. The young man was learning quickly. After a successful outing in Barbados, Nils had been assigned to another target, this time at a music festival in Belgium. Despite his occasional failure to observe protocol, Nils had again carried out his role to Dominik's satisfaction. The methods he had employed might have been unconventional at times but they were damn effective, and that was what mattered in the end.

If Dominik could keep Nils happy – a combination of gadgets and luxury would suffice – then in time he would become a cornerstone of BIRD's overseas operations. In truth, Dominik saw a lot of his younger self in the boy. That was important. If Dominik was to succeed Adler one day, then he would need a number two he could trust. Nils seemed to fit the bill.

That was one of the reasons Dominik had sent him to Beijing. China was an increasingly powerful country and its megacities provided just the right mix of novelty and adventure. Nils' remit was to strengthen Adler Reilly's client base in Beijing.

The consultancy firm was currently linked to a new project in the South China Sea. Officially, the project concerned the construction of artificial islands to create new land to help develop the country's fishing industry. In reality, however, it was all about oil. Apparently, there were vast reserves under the sea, the discovery of which would ensure the survival of a number of branches of industry for years to come.

Dominik himself had flown to Singapore after a number of meetings with financial consultants in Macau and Hong Kong. The tiger economy of Singapore was fast becoming the nerve centre of the whole of Asia, linking the old West with the emerging ASEAN economies.

Many of Adler Reilly's clients already had offices, as well as research and development centres, in the city-sovereign state, as life in Singapore was deemed to be safer than that in Kuala Lumpur or

Bangkok.

Dominik looked at his watch. It was time to meet his clients in the Raffles Hotel.

As he climbed into his taxi a few minutes later, a shiver went down his spine. The driver explained that his car was an *EVA*: an electric taxi that had been specially developed by universities in Munich and Singapore for use in tropical mega-cities.

***

INTERESTING GOODIES

WAVE 2013 travel report

The NSA scandal and other risks

Insights and tips from an IT security expert

Overview of current electric vehicles

EVs in a nutshell

Project partner

TRAVEL REPORT

WAVE 2013 unites pioneers and enthusiasts

The third World Advanced Vehicle Expedition, an electric vehicle event organised by Swiss solar pioneer Louis Palmer, took place in Europe from the 28th June to the 7th July 2013.

The international group of participants united respected pioneers and globetrotters with dyed-in-the wool enthusiasts, who have already achieved cult-hero status in their respective fields. The majority were taking part for the second or even third time in the hope of achieving their combined aim: to generate enthusiasm for electric vehicles and drive home the importance of protecting our increasingly embattled planet. A visit to the Pasterze glacier at Grossglockner, whose length decreases on a yearly basis, emphasised just how desperately a change of attitude is needed.

During the expedition, the teams driving cars from California-based company Tesla amply demonstrated their technical superiority over models manufactured by the traditional automobile industry; while an equally successful challenge was mounted by a winner of the 2013 Rallye Monte-Carlo des Energies Nouvelles. Along with a number of professionally converted vehicles, whose composition reflected their drivers' detailed knowledge, the rest of the field was made up by motorcycles and unusual vehicles, each one contributing to the lively atmosphere and sense of camaraderie.

The route took the battery-powered vehicles (any hybrids were obliged to seal their tanks) across the Alps from Vienna to Zurich. Following a punctual start in sunny Eichgraben, it was on through Vienna and Baden – via the casino and its venerable spa gardens – to the state-owned Palace Square in Eisenstadt. Next it was a day of sport. After a night bedevilled by charging difficulties, displays of driving prowess on the test circuit at Gleisdorf alternated with attempts to determine individual vehicles' load capacity, the latter played out against a backdrop of wildly enthusiastic school pupils at an event in Deutschlandsberg.

The following day saw a selection of vehicles attempting to prove their range in a special stage taking in the beautifully situated Slovenian town of Bled. Not even the extensive tasting of the local speciality, vanilla cream-cake, and the fluctuations in weight associated therewith, could prevent the intrepid vehicles from reaching their evening destination. After an impressive presentation on PlanetSolar, the first solar-powered catamaran to circumnavigate the globe, Weissensee was at its picturesque best the next morning, ensuring that filming of the start – punctual, as ever, to the minute – would take place in perfect weather.

Once the last drops of coffee had been served from the battery-powered espresso machine, participants emerged fully-charged (in every sense of the word) to undertake the expedition's greatest challenge thus far: overcoming the High Alpine Road, a task made even more difficult by the decision of many drivers to visit the glacier at *Kaiser Franz-Josefs-Höhe*. The route involved an ascent of some 1,400 metres and tested a number of vehicles to the limit.

In fact, it was only due to the brave intervention of a Think-driver, who risked his own vehicle in mounting a rescue operation, that all EVs were able to complete this adventure-filled leg of the journey. The longer charging breaks were met without comment by the on-looking marmots; and the charging status of the batteries themselves was shown to be of the utmost relevance, if only in the older EVs. It seems that recuperating energy during braking can prove to be hot work for an already fully-charged battery. Fortunately, keen minds were at hand to make use of the cooling effect provided by the Alpine snow.

The next stage was made easier by the effects of a mudslide on the Gerlos Alpine Road, which necessitated a change of route for some drivers. Thereafter, the drive through Innsbruck and Landeck was uneventful. The participants' attempts at recharging not only their vehicle's batteries were greatly aided by the extravagant evening buffet in La Punt, where teams were warmly received – as was the case throughout the expedition. The next morning, the field, by now reinvigorated, made their way to a further expedition highlight in the company of a regional TV channel. Their destination: Arosa, via the Albula Pass. Upon arrival, the participants were accorded the red carpet treatment and inspired by the hotel owner's ambitious plans to expand his already impressive solar energy plant.

The next few days were to prove just as exciting for participants. First, it was a question of stirring the next generation of EV drivers, as teams were asked to deliver one-minute pitches on design and innovation to groups of children in various regional schools. Before the participants themselves became temporary students of material science at EMPA in St. Gallen, an evening stopover by the Bodensee provided them with a warm summer night of leisure. Meanwhile, a presentation by the Chargelocator founder detailing his 80 day voyage around the world in a Tesla Roadster had a number of participants longing for the open road. But even after Baden, where teams were afforded the pleasure of a city tour on e-Bikes, there was still a great deal more to come.

The world-record parade, which was held during the Züri Fäscht on the 6th July, was an unforgettable experience for all those who took part: flanked by EVs of all shapes and sizes, the participants, along with some 388 vehicles in total, attempted to create what one wit described as the longest electric vehicle tailback in history. It is still not clear whether the final vehicle – a German e-Boat towed by a battery-powered bus – was counted or not. There was also some speculation as to whether there had ever been more Teslas in the same place at any given time.

After the world-record parade, a number of drivers joined the expedition teams in setting off through the Canton of Zurich for the Tour of Open Doors. In Neuhausen, participants were able to share their memories of the expedition over a glass of wine, as they gazed in wonder at the breath-taking Rhine Falls. Following a trip to the Umweltarena in Spreitenbach, the expedition finally came to an end on Sunday 7ᵗʰ July in Küsnacht. There was a touch of melancholy in the air, and it wasn't just the youngest participant, at nine years old, who was affected. Existing friendships had been deepened; and new friendships forged.

If this expedition proved one thing, it is that open competitions promote development. Charging breaks were an excellent opportunity for participants to make new contacts and exchange experiences. They were also used as a means of obtaining tips, some of which were then surreptitiously applied during later stages of the expedition. However, when push comes to shove, EV pioneers always place the welfare of the group before the success of the individual. The industry would do well to take a leaf out of their book!

Now and then, rumours began to surface about a revolutionary piece of technology being covertly tested at WAVE. There was talk of spies, working on behalf of a *Black Hungarian*, attempting to ferret out various secrets. The majority, however, were happy to write it off as pure fiction.

German version first published in the magazine keNEXT 10/2013

THE NSA SCANDAL AND OTHER RISKS

The parties involved and their tools

Since June 2013, the debate surrounding the effects of industrial espionage has taken on an extra dimension thanks to Edward Snowden's revelations about the work of the National Security Agency.

One of the largest US intelligence agencies, the NSA's official remit is to do anything within its power to help the American government and its allies gain an advantage when it comes to decision-making. In the main, the NSA obtains information from abroad by intercepting signals of all kinds – Signals Intelligence, or SIGINT, for short – before collecting the data and subjecting it to a risk analysis.

In addition, the NSA is also responsible for ensuring that sensitive US government information does not fall into the hands of foreign powers. To facilitate this, the agency has taken on the lead role in the field of encryption techniques and is charged not only with developing products and services for computer networks but also with monitoring their use by other agencies. The primary focus is on international terrorism, the narcotics trade and any other activities deemed hostile towards the United States.

In total, there are sixteen different agencies belonging to the US intelligence community, all of which come under the jurisdiction of the Director of National Intelligence, who is appointed by the President himself. The most powerful intelligence services are the CIA, the NSA, the DIA, the NRO and the NGA, also known as the "Big Five". Of these five, only the CIA is independent, while the rest report to the US Department of Defence. Not to be confused with the "Big Five" are the "Five Eyes" (FVEY), an Anglophonic alliance comprising Australia, New Zealand, Canada, the US and the United Kingdom, which is controlled by the NSA and the British intelligence and security organisation, Government Communication Headquarters (GCHQ). It has emerged that in the past three years, the latter has received funding to the tune of £100 million from its American counterpart.

But GCHQ is not the only European intelligence organisation to have been placed under scrutiny recently. The French newspaper *Le Monde*, for instance, has reported that the country's own Direction Générale de la Sécurité Extérieure (DGSE) has been collecting data from text messages, telephone conversations, emails and communications via Facebook and Twitter and storing it long-term for analysis. Meanwhile, both Norwegian and Swedish intelligence agencies (NIS and Forsvarets Radioanstalt respectively) enjoy a bilateral data exchange with the NSA, with a focus of their cooperation being activities taking place in Russia.

Despite numerous press reports detailing the alleged collection of millions of data records, the nature of Germany's relationship to foreign intelligence agencies such as the NSA remains unclear. The fact that cooperation between both domestic and foreign partner agencies has been strengthened is generally justified by pointing to the complexity of terrorist networks. One of the only public pronouncements has been the acknowledgement of a trial programme called "Projekt 6", which uses analysis software to evaluate any data collected. The software was adapted to the demands of the Federal Office for the Protection of the Constitution with the help of an anonymous partner agency.

Although the programme was discontinued in 2010, it has proved instrumental in the development of information systems that are still being used today. Further details have been declared classified, as their acknowledgement could both hinder the work of German intelligence agencies and jeopardise the relationship between Germany and its foreign partners. That said, the latest revelation that two employees of the German agency provided confidential documents to the CIA caused quite a stir as it came only months after the revelation that various cell phone conversations of Bundeskanzlerin Angela

Merkel were recorded. Merkel herself informed the American President in no uncertain terms that she disapproved of such practices. The CIA representative responsible was expelled from Germany and left the country in July 2014.

Details of individual programmes

With the programme **PRISM**, the NSA has combined different tools which enable data to be mined by accessing the servers of specific internet companies. Details from emails, documents, chats and video conferences (video and audio), as well as information from social networks and data sent to third parties, can be specifically selected and targeted to individual accounts. According to the information released, a number of major companies have been engaged as "sources" since 2007. In chronological order: Microsoft, Yahoo, Google, Facebook, YouTube, Skype, AOL and, most recently, Apple.

UPSTREAM is also a data collection and analysis programme. However, it is different from PRISM because it enables data to be collected through fibre-optic cables *as* it is being transferred. The NSA recommends that their analysts use PRISM and UPSTREAM parallel to each other.

Similarly, the British programme, **TEMPORA**, has enabled GCHQ to tap into and store data drawn from 200 fibre-optic cables. On the basis of the figures alone, it has been estimated that up to 21 petabytes (roughly equivalent to four billion MP3 files each measuring five megabytes) can be collected daily. In December 2013, it was revealed that British Telecom, Verizon, Vodafone, Global Crossing, Level 3, Viatel, and Interoute all agreed to cooperate with GCHQ in their use of the programme.

According to the information made public thus far, **X-KEY-SCORE** is the NSA's most comprehensive data analysis programme, encompassing some 700 servers spread across 150 different sites around the world, and capable of scaling linearly. On the one hand, it allows analysts to run queries on specific search terms such as individual email or Mac addresses; on the other hand, it also enables them to search for data using descriptive attributes such as country, language, file-type (document or spreadsheet) and file characteristics (encrypted, non-encrypted).

STATEROOM refers to a Five Eyes espionage programme, which involves the interception of radio and satellite signals, and is operated worldwide out of the diplomatic suites, embassies and consulates of signatories to the multilateral UKUSA Agreement. Alongside Berlin, programme headquarters were in Geneva, which led to the Swiss Prosecutor's office laying charges against persons unknown, and eventually launching their own investigation into the matter.

Other programmes include the whimsically titled **ROYAL CONCIERGE**, with the help of which diplomats' hotel reservations can be monitored. Meanwhile, over 200 million international text messages are served up to the NSA on a daily basis thanks to the programme **DISHFIRE.** One can only guess at the personality of the NSA employee who came up with the name **BULLRUN** for the agency's highly clandestine decryption programme. However, there is altogether less mystery surrounding **MUSUCULAR:** an initiative that has seen the communication links connecting Google and Yahoo data centres around the world brutally prized open.

Nor is there any **QUANTUM** of solace to be found in the NSA's method of installing specific radio-wave technology in computers (hidden in external USB connectors or installed directly via mini-circuit boards). With the help of an outstation no bigger than an attaché case, data can be intercepted up to distances of 13km away, even when a computer is not connected to a network. The programme's main goal was to monitor the Chinese Army.

The **TAO-TAILORED ACCESS OPERATIONS**, carried out by the agency's own hackers, require some serious leg-work. Servers, computers, external hard-drives and wireless routers are intercepted at the delivery stage so that hackers can add hardware backdoors or directly install surveillance programmes. The description of this process as **ANT-ADVANCED/ACCESS NETWORK TECHNOLOGY** borders on the sarcastic. Device manufacturers such as Cisco Systems,

Dell, Hewlett Packard, Huawei, Juniper Networks, Samsung Electronics, Seagate Technology/Maxtor and Western Digital are all affected. In the same context, it was also revealed that the IT security firm RSA was paid $10 million by the NSA to provide weak encryption systems.

Alongside all these surveillance programmes, it is worth remembering that the US government not only has access to all EU bank transaction data (thanks to the SWIFT-agreement), but also to biometric data such as iris-scans and fingerprints.

Hunger for Data

Through the **SAFE-HARBOR-AGREEMENT**, which more than 1,000 American companies have already entered into, major companies like IBM, Microsoft, Google and Facebook have access to EU citizens' data. Owing to their questionable data-protection practices, Facebook and Google, in particular, have recently been subject to intense scrutiny.

In the past few years, Google has gone from being an internet company to a global conglomerate, and is venturing into more and more industry branches. The latest coups are the formation of the Open Automotive Alliance (OAA) with vehicle manufacturers Audi, GM, Honda and Hyundai; and the acquisition of the thermostat making company Nest Labs. Alongside the mobile phone, the internet giant, it seems, is increasing their hold on consumers' lives with each passing day.

Industrial espionage in the free market economy

There is no technology on the market that can offer a 100% guarantee against espionage. Nevertheless, the Snowden case shows that one of the principal risks actually lies elsewhere. According to one former NSA employee, simple **HUMAN WEAKNESS** is often a factor: agents can be recruited through money, ideology, coercion or ego.

A recent corporate trust study suggests that industrial espionage led to $4.2 billion worth of damage to the German economy. The same study indicates that more than half of German companies have already fallen victim to industrial espionage; and that in more than 50% of cases, the process was set in motion by company employees themselves. The most sought-after data concerns prices and clients, closely followed by information about production and development strategies. Almost a quarter of recorded incidents take place in mid-size companies, with around a fifth occurring in major companies. Small businesses, where 15% of incidents are said to take place, appear to be the least affected.

In more than 20% of cases of industrial espionage, company employees fall victim to the increasingly widespread practice of **SOCIAL ENGINEERING**. Employees respond in good faith to questions (which can also be personal in nature) posed over the telephone or at trade fairs. Trojans are then smuggled onto employees' devices through their email addresses, usually with the help of an innocuous looking link. Once the Trojan has infiltrated the system, it can be used to search an employee's hard-drive, bug their webcam and microphone, or even monitor their keyboard.

Owing to current developments, the risks are increasing exponentially. One example is the automotive industry. More and more clients are being asked to install mobile-end devices or similar applications in their cars. In turn, a desire to keep pace with the ever-changing demands of the consumer industry has led car manufacturers to install radio access networks in their vehicles and thus provide consumers with software updates.

Given that employees of the American agency DARPA managed, in 2013, to control braking and accelerating functions remotely through the diagnostic port, it is surely only a matter of time before this is also possible via wireless technology. With the Internet of Things, meanwhile, the future could take on a genuinely terrifying appearance. From the remote regulation of electricity and water, to the potential to manipulate a diabetic's wireless insulin pump, the possibilities are seemingly endless.

German version first published in the magazine keNEXT 1-2/2014

INSIGHTS AND TIPS FROM
AN IT SECURITY EXPERT

Ralf-Martin Tauer works as a *Directeur de Projet* for leading French IT services and consulting company SQLI and is responsible for internationally acting customers. He currently advises companies in all aspects concerning IT security and strategy.

Every day and with increasing frequency, we hear about new data scandals, system vulnerabilities and targeted espionage by intelligence agencies, or phishing of valuable information by criminal individuals - both in business and private life. The recent accumulation of these incidents raises legitimate fears in people about the fragility of their respective *digital selves*. They ask themselves what conclusions third parties can draw by looking at their publically available digital footprint - which can be created by connecting all bits of information from a myriad of sources.

The frequency of data scandals and the number of abuse cases is increasing exponentially; both are caused by a growing number of decentralized IT systems that are nevertheless connected to one another. The fact that these connections are so poorly protected against security breaches is more than alarming.

Let's focus on ourselves and visualize a normal day in our lives:

Due to the increasing use of data-hungry gadgets, for example activity trackers or networked scales (clue: "Internet of things"), the provider of the device knows what time we usually get up in the morning. Online retailers have evaluated our historical click times and navigation paths through their portfolio of products based on cookies.

They have created their very own picture of us. They send us an e-mail with matching items that may be of interest to us, just as we are sitting at the breakfast table and turning on our smartphone. While reading the electronic newspaper on the iPad at breakfast, we continue to shape our digital self. The bits of information we provide by clicking on certain political articles, and the time we spend reading them, may even reveal our political point of view.

On the way to work we pass a gas station, a grocery store or a coffee shop where we pay, of course, by credit card. Needless to say, we want to collect points on our loyalty card to get a free DVD free at the end of the year. However, we produce important demographic data and motion profiles by doing this. These loyalty program providers evaluate, interpret and sell the information gathered - at a profit, naturally - to others, and we subsequently receive emails, which are even more perfectly tailored to our personal consumer behavior.

On the way to the office, we start the crowd-based navigation on our mobile phone, because it works a lot better in the early morning traffic jams than any traffic information on the radio. The provider of this free app is now aware of which route we usually take and how much time we need for it. The company makes their money by selling this data to traffic information services. Meanwhile, our car connects to our smartphone via Bluetooth and is now online thanks to our phone's mobile network. Who knows, perhaps our car is already talking to its manufacturer and telling him that we are four weeks late for the planned inspection.

Arriving at work, we open the gate to the parking lot with our smart card. Now our employer knows that we are finally there and he books the time (minus the minutes it usually takes us to walk from the parking lot to the entrance) into our personal time account. By the way, our colleagues in the human resources department had a brilliant idea last week. They are trying to convince the boss to divide this year's bonuses only among those who walk the 500 meters from the parking lot to the building 30 seconds faster than normal. According to the US consulting company which had all our data reviewed by a subcontractor in India, walking velocities below 3 km/h are evidence of a reluctance to work.

Then, there's lunch break. Like all our colleagues, we pay for lunch in the canteen with our badge. This allows the canteen operator to simplify planning and tracking of purchases. But in addition, everything we eat is recorded. If we develop diabetes or other diet-related diseases, the company doctor is already aware of our unhealthy eating habits. Naturally, this information is shared with our health insurance provider, which then aims to offer *special activity seminars* to people at risk - like us - before it's too late.

In the evening, the data logging system records something strange, namely that you're able to walk the distance from the office to the parking a lot quicker than in the morning. The system sets a value in a special field in the database which, in case a downsizing of the work force is necessary, will enable the human resource consultant to create a list of potential candidates much faster.

Up to this point - without really wanting to do so, we have already revealed much about our personal profile. Sleep times, consumer behavior, food habits, geo-localization, job satisfaction and even our political orientation. However, not all information is directly measurable. Some values are open to interpretation; it just depends on the combination of the underlying bits of information, and who is trying to draw what conclusion.

I don't want to paint a dark picture of the future like George Orwell did in his novel *1984* or Ridley Scott in the movie *Blade Runner*. In simple terms, possessing information in the 21st century means having power.

Power over ordinary citizens, because how and especially what conclusions are drawn generally remains the secret of consulting companies. Services are becoming more interconnected and the amount of information available is thus becoming increasingly dense. There is lots of room to interpret information in great detail, but also far more room for misinterpretation and errors. This is a clear and present danger to all of us.

We can address this danger by being more careful about accessing social networks; by paying attention to what traces we leave; and by limiting access to our information to small user groups whom we know personally. We should create a unique combination of user name and password for each service instead of using the automatic authentication mechanisms that Facebook or Google offer with their logins (clue: Single Sign On).

Everybody who ignores this simple, but golden, rule and uses the same username and password combination everywhere is prone to hacker attacks aimed at their complete digital self. Alarming proof of our technical vulnerability was provided by the recently published *Heartbleed Bug,* which affected nearly half of worldwide SSL-secured data connections in online banking portals, payment systems and shopping sites on the Internet.

Precautions I take in my personal life

I buy a lot of things offline at the shop around the corner. There, I pay mostly with cash. I avoid loyalty programs such as Payback, Igaal, webmiles or other discount or club portals. That said, the providers of these portals are mainly interested in aggregating activity data of people who work for big firms and buy or book for entire departments, as this data allows portals to draw conclusions about the travel behavior of their corporate clients.

When using Google, I strongly recommend turning off the geolocation function. In Facebook, it is important to check all the privacy settings on a regular basis. When using external WLANs, I make sure I connect to the individual portals via an encrypted browser page. If this is not possible, I do not use the WLAN. It pays to keep the antivirus program on my home PC up-to-date. Investing in tools like Bitdefender won't hurt you as much as a security breach can.

Precautions I take at work

Although it may seem obvious, one of the most important tips is to raise awareness among employees of the need for secrecy.

In addition to confidentiality agreements used for exchanging secret information, either on paper or digitally, between business partners, these simple rules are just as important:

1) When discussing particularly confidential information, do this in a face to face meeting and use a room without a computer and landline or mobile phones;

2) Resist having conversations with colleagues about clients, projects or products in public places. It might be that someone from your competition is on the same plane or train, just a row behind you;

3) Working on confidential documents on your computer in public places should be avoided. It is always interesting to see what new product developments a person is working on in the airport lounge. So-called privacy screens provide some protection against nosy people looking over your shoulder;

4) Ensure that no confidential documents are on the table or your computer screen when having a conversation with your business partner via a video conference system.

OVERVIEW OF CURRENT ELECTRIC CARS

as of summer 2014

Type	⌀ electr. range in km	⌀ kWh consumption per 100km	⌀ cost per 100km[1] (€)	Power kW	Battery capacity kWh	max. speed (electric)	Price €	Charging (household socket) in h	Charging (fast charge 80%) in h	Fast charging system
BMW i3	160	12.8	3.84	125	22	130	34,900	8	0.5	CCS
BMW i8 (Hybrid)	30	n/s	n/s	96	5.2	65	126,000	2	–	–
Chevrolet Volt (Hybrid)[3]	60	26.6	7.98	111	16	130	42,950	6	–	–
Citroen C-Zero[4]	150	12.6	3.78	49	16	130	29,393	6	0.5	CHAdeMo
Ford Focus Electric	130	14.4	4.32	107	23	137	39,990	10	–	–
Mercedes Benz B-Class ED	200	16.6	4.98	132	33 (estimated)	160	40,000	n/s	–	–
Mercedes Benz SLS AMG Coupe ED	250	24	7.2	552	60	250	416,500	24	2	–
Mitsubishi i-Miev[4]	150	12.6	3.78	49	16	130	23,790	6	0.5	CHAdeMo
Nissan Leaf	190	15	4.5	111	24	150	29,690	7	0.5	CHAdeMO
Opel Ampera (Hybrid)[3]	60	26.6	7.98	111	16	130	38,620	6	–	–
Peugeot iON[4]	150	12.6	3.78	49	16	130	29,393	6	0.5	CHAdeMo
Porsche Panamera S-E Hybrid	30	16.2	4.86	70	9.4	135	110,409	4	–	–
Renault Kangoo ZE	170	15.5	4.65	44	22	130	24,157[2]	7	–	–
Renault Twizy	80	9	2.7	13	6.1	80	6,999	3.5	–	–
Renault Zoe	190	14.6	4.38	92	22	140	21,700[2]	7.5	0.5	(43kW)
RIMAC Concept One	600	n/s	n/s	800	92	300	1,000,000	–	–	–
Smart Fortwo ED	120	15.1	4.53	55	17.6	125	24,000	6	2	(22kW)
Tesla Model S (60)	370	18.1	5.43	310	60	210	65,300	24	0.7	Supercharger
Tesla Model S (85)	480	18.1	5.43	310	85	210	74,900	29	0.7	Supercharger
Toyota Prius Hybrid	25	12.5	3.75	60	5.2	100	36,550	1.5	–	–
Volkswagen eGolf	190	12.7	3.81	85	24.2	140	34,900	13	–	–
Volkswagen eUp	150	12	3.6	60	18.7	130	26,900	6	0.5	CCS
Volkswagen XL1 (Hybrid)	50	n/s	n/s	20	5.5		111,000	2	–	–

1) based on EUR 0.3/kWh
2) additional monthly fee for battery rental
3) identically constructed
4) identically constructed

EVS IN A NUTSHELL

Short explanations by *eMobilitaetOnline.de*

Range

Modern electric cars have a range that is sufficient for most people's daily needs. According to studies, the majority of drivers don't travel more than 100km per day.

The range is calculated as the relation of the maximal battery capacity to the energy consumption of the vehicle per kilometer. The consumption is influenced by various factors such as the power of the electric motor and the weight of the car. On average, most of the car models available can cover ranges between 120 and 170 kilometer per charge. Manufacturers have started to offer several battery sizes for their vehicles, allowing customers to choose between different ranges and prices depending on their requirements. Currently Tesla's Model S offers the highest range, with over 400 kilometers driven purely electric with one charge. Some small companies, which specialize in converting conventional cars to electric cars, offer vehicles that provide a range of up to 700 km.

Safety

Electric vehicles are just as safe as conventional gasoline cars. In several cases, they even perform better: many manufacturers use the new design of the powertrain to equip their models with the latest technical developments and auxiliary systems.

The battery management system is an essential part of the car. It monitors the most important parameters such as charge current and cell temperature. In case of undesired operational conditions, the battery is immediately disconnected from the vehicle grid to avoid injury of passengers or surrounding people. Additionally, the body structure of electric vehicles is designed for the highest safety, as many components are no longer required: the battery is mounted into the bottom of the chassis, providing a lower center of gravity for the vehicle. The front of the car (the engine compartment in conventional cars) offers a larger space to absorb more energy during crashes. Crash tests showed outstanding results for the Tesla Model S. Nissan's Leaf, Renault's Zoe and Volkswagen's e-Up! were also awarded a five star rating.

Charging types and time needed to charge

BEVs, battery electric vehicles, need to be charged with electric current. The physical limitations of the battery and the power source, as well as the onboard charging technology provided by the manufacturer, influence the time needed to charge the vehicle. Currently, there are four ways to charge EVs:

1) Conventional charging (AC):
   a. One phase household socket (16A and 220V): 3kW charging capacity
   b. Three phase electric power (32A und 380V): 11kW
2) Fast charging (DC):
   a. Combined Charging System (CCS): max. 50kW (BMW, VW)
   b. CHAdeMO: max. 50kW (Nissan, Renault)
   c. Supercharger: max. 130kW (Tesla)
3) Battery swap: ca. 3 minutes (Tesla)
4) Inductive charging: not yet available in series production vehicles, could be done during driving in theory

The time needed to charge depends on the charging power, as well as the battery capacity. Charging a small to medium sized EV, like the Renault Zoe or Nissan Leaf, takes up to eight hours using a household socket and only 30 minutes using a CHAdeMO charging station.

The type of cable and adapter needed depends on the method of charging (i.e. CCS requires a Type 2 connector; CHAdeMO and Supercharger have proprietary connectors).

Additionally, there are other developments taking place to

provide power for the car via fuel cells or flow batteries which can be refilled. The refueling process typically takes place within a few minutes.

Costs

Currently, electric vehicles still cost more to buy than comparable models with combustion engines. According to the manufacturers, the main reason for this is the battery.

However, people often forget that the operational costs of electric cars are lower. A medium class vehicle consumes approximately 12-15 kilowatt hours per 100 kilometers, thus generating energy costs of around 3.60-4.50 Euros (based on an electricity rate of 0.30 Euro per kilowatt hour). Some public charging stations have even been made available free of charge. Californian manufacturer Tesla offer Model S customers free charging at their superchargers.

Insurance and tax costs can be much lower than for conventional vehicles. Many countries subsidize electric vehicles. If you factor in maintenance and operational costs, the total cost of owning an EV can be much lower over time. If the damage caused by CO_2 emissions were also taken into account, conventional vehicles would have ceased to be competitive long ago.

Maintenance and repair

Most of the components requiring high maintenance or exchange on a regular basis are not needed in electric vehicles. Service operations such as oil or filter exchange do not apply.

Additionally, several other components have longer operational lifetimes than they do in conventional cars: for example, the wear and tear of brakes is lower because in most cases the electric motor is used to slow down the vehicle in order to recuperate a part of the motion energy and charge the battery.

If an electric vehicle needs to be repaired, you will need to visit a specialized workshop as other repair centers are not allowed to work with high-voltage components.

PARTNER

A HEARTFELT THANK YOU TO OUR PARTNERS

THE AUTHORS

Niall MacRoslin

 Niall MacRoslin was born and raised in Edinburgh, Scotland. Upon finishing school, he swapped the grey skies of Scotland's capital to read modern languages at Trinity College, Dublin. Somewhere in the midst of his Irish soujourn, Niall developed a love of all things German and decamped to Lake Constance for a year.

Since his return from Baden Württemberg, Niall has worked as a teacher, book reviewer and proof-reader. He has also successfully completed an MSc in Translation Studies, supporting himself in the meantime by taking jobs as a waiter, barman and – briefly – charity shop manager. All of which he believes stands him in good stead for his new career as fiction writer.

He currently lives in London, where the grey skies remind him of home.

Alice N. York

Alice N. York was born and raised near Munich, Germany. Following her profound hunger for all things technical, she studied industrial and production engineering, and took on the challenge of playing the game.

Before starting her second career as a writer she travelled the world and worked in several sales and marketing positions in technological industries. Now she has remembered her roots and is following her heart. It still tells her: Nothing ventured, nothing gained.

Alice currently lives just outside of Munich near the Alps.

ABOUT CAPSCOVIL

We are a publisher who can't be pigeonholed. Our hearts beat for innovation and we are passionate about technology, viewed from a sustainability point of view.

Technology is what gives that extra dash to a literary cocktail or dish. It's the main spice in our kitchen where feature articles are formed, short stories shaken and novels like Project Black Hungarian cooked up.

Capscovil has been an owner-managed business since it was founded in December 2009. Our company name reflects our passion for word games and spicy food: It's a combination of Capsaicin - *the active component of a chili pepper that defines its heat level* - and Scoville - *the unit in which the heat level of a chili pepper is measured (naturally, an engineer always needs some kind of measuring means)*. The combination unknown to Google back then.

We considered this a good sign.

Find out more about us and meet the team or browse through reading samples of our fictional work or gather more facts from feature articles on http://capscovil.com

Project Black Hungarian is - just like all our books - available through book stores and online as printed edition or electronic version. For larger quantities or special editions please get in touch with us directly and we will be happy to assist you.

Aside from that we are always keen to receive feedback and learn about your opinion which can only help us to get better.

SAVE THE BEST FOR LAST

We are particularly grateful to the following people, each of whom, by dint of their outstanding contribution, has helped to make this project into something quite unique:

Louis Palmer and the many participants at WAVE 2013 for their trust, support and willingness to serve as models for the characters;

The test readers Heike Hinner, Helen Pope, Tony Garner and Marcel Gauch for their patience and detailed feedback;

Ralf-Martin Tauer for his article with valuable tipps and insights into the world of IT security;

Marc Kudling for his expert contribution to chapter three;

Special thanks go to Helen Veitch, Louisa Kronthaler, Sabine Haseitl and Gerhard Tikovsky, each of whom has, in their own way, helped to improve the book immeasurably;

Above all, we would like to thank those who have continued to support Capscovil and, in so doing, helped to make this project a reality, in particular you – our readers.